The WEIRD

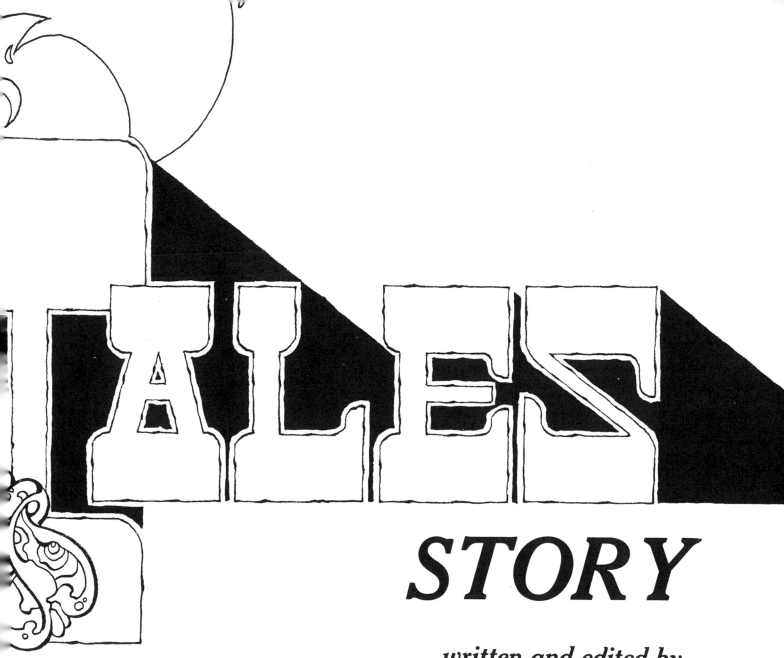

TALES
STORY

written and edited by

ROBERT WEINBERG

 **COLLECTOR'S EDITIONS**

To Margaret Brundage,
whose covers might not have reflected
the contents of Weird Tales *but surely*
sold a lot of copies.

CONTENTS

All chapters written by Robert Weinberg except
2 (by E. Hoffmann Price)
3 (editorial)
5 (by various authors)

Preface

With the publication of the first issue of *Weird Tales* in March 1923, a tradition was born that would last for more than thirty years and two hundred and seventy-nine issues. When the magazine folded in 1954, it was a legend in its own time. In its pages were published the best weird fiction of every major author of the bizarre and unusual of this century. While not discovered by *Weird Tales*, it was in that magazine that the great Howard Phillips Lovecraft saw the vast bulk of his professionally published material appear. Robert E. Howard, who in the last few years has gained a huge following, saw his first work published in *Weird Tales* and it was in its pages that Conan of Cimmeria trampled the jeweled thrones of the Earth under his sandaled feet. Edmond Hamilton was discovered by the editor of *Weird Tales* as were Arthur J. Burks, August Derleth, Frank Belknap Long, C.L. Moore, Henry Kuttner, Robert Spencer Carr, Donald Wandrei, and dozens of others, including even Tennessee Williams. Fantastic fantasy artist Virgil Finlay sold his first professional work to *Weird Tales* as did Hannes Bok. The magazine was a trailblazer, publishing stories that broke taboos and defied conventions. It was subtitled "The Unique Magazine" and no other publication ever more richly deserved that heading. Yet, with all of its historical importance to both the field of science fiction and fantasy, relatively nothing has ever been written about the history of *Weird Tales*.

The magazine has been mentioned in several works dealing with famous authors who saw print in its pages. Few, if any, of these books have contained more than a bare minimum of information about *Weird Tales*. Several have contained major errors, usually based on misinformation and half-truths gathered not from source material but secondary references.

The purpose of this book is to examine *Weird Tales* and the people who made it great. Every attempt has been made to keep strictly to the actual facts. Rumors and stories, no matter how interesting or revealing, have not been included unless they could be authenticated through research and examination. At the same time, all efforts have been made to make this work as complete as possible. Of course, not every fact could be printed, every story reviewed, every illustration described. To even attempt a small part of that task would take an encyclopedia, not a one-volume history.

An author without prejudices and preferences would be more than human and the author of this book makes no claim to that title. While I have tried to maintain as fair a balance as possible, I will confess in advance a liking of the works of Robert E. Howard, H.P. Lovecraft and Edmond Hamilton. In the field of art, I possess no credentials as a critic and make no pretentions to do so in chapters dealing with art in the pulp. In all cases, throughout the book, the opinions expressed are strictly those of the author, though I have tried to be as objective as possible.

To help make this work as complete as possible, a number of pieces by authors and artists who worked for *Weird Tales* have been included. For, in reality, this book is more their story than the author's. Except for rare cases when certain specific dates were wrong, no rewriting has been done on these pieces. They are the memories of the contributors as they recalled them.

The book begins with a brief history of the actual magazine. It is followed by a lengthy memoir of Farnsworth Wright by his close friend, E. Hoffmann Price.

Reprinted in its entirety is the editorial, "Why *Weird Tales?*", which is as timely today as when it was published over fifty years ago.

The chapter on the stories deals with both the fiction and poetry published in *Weird Tales* as well as the people who wrote them. All other chapters are self-explanatory.

It is hoped that this book will encourage others to further study in the field of fantastic literature in the American pulp magazines. For THE WEIRD TALES STORY is not the end of all possible research but just the beginning.

This book was made possible through the assistance of many people. Foremost among them was Leo Margulies, without whose aid this work could never have been written. Each contributor who shared his memories helped make this work a bit more complete. E. Hoffmann Price, and Margaret Brundage, both who answered innumerable questions about their association with *Weird Tales* as well as the actual magazine itself, have to be singled out for their invaluable assistance.

Many others contributed important information. They included Glenn Lord, Celia La Spina, Vincent Napoli, Tom Cockcroft, Sam Moskowitz and J. Grant Thiessen.

My wife, who shared me with my typewriter for these long months has to be commended for her patience and invaluable assistance in all phases of this volume.

Lastly, I must thank my publisher, FAX Collector's Editions and Ted Dikty in particular, both for his encouragement and his understanding of my ever-postponed deadline.

All of these people and more helped make this book a reality. I can only hope that my readers enjoy this volume as much as I enjoyed writing and editing it.

ROBERT WEINBERG

Alsip, Illinois
November 1976

Eerily yours,
Farnsworth Wright

1

A Brief History

The most famous writer of weird fiction in the English language was the literary grandfather of *Weird Tales*. J.C. Henneberger, the creator and thus father of the fantasy magazine, explained Poe's importance in the following:

> As a lad of 16, I attended a military academy in Virginia. The English department was headed by one Captain Stevens, a hunchback who was a rather chauvinistic chap in that he favored Southern writers. One entire semester was devoted to Poe! You can imagine how immersed I became in him.

Jacob Clark Henneberger always wanted to be a writer. When he attended college in Lancaster, Pennsylvania, he organized a press club. He was soon earning $5.00 a column for his articles on college happenings.

In 1913, Henneberger traveled to Portland where he lived with a brother and did newspaper work. In 1917, he joined the Navy. 1919 saw him in Indianapolis working for a weekly newspaper. The urge to write had now turned into an urge to edit and publish:

> Here I met a map and atlas publisher who employed college students to sell their products during the summer months. I sold them on the idea of a national magazine for the college undergraduate to be called *The Collegiate World.*

The Collegiate World was a smashing flop. As Henneberger explained it, the magazine featured articles on different colleges. The magazine sold well on the featured campuses but didn't sell well anywhere else.

However, Henneberger showed his genius by changing the title and contents of the magazine to *College Humor.* The new humor magazine sold out for twelve consecutive issues at the high price of 50¢ a copy. It was one of the great magazine success stories of the twenties. Henneberger started another magazine in the same vein, *The Magazine of Fun.* It also sold well.

In 1922, Henneberger started a new company. He and J.M. Lansinger formed Rural Publications, Inc. Two new magazines were started in early 1923. One was *Real Detective Tales and Mystery Stories.* The other magazine was *Weird Tales.* When asked why he started a magazine that

was such a radical departure from his earlier moneymakers, Henneberger stated:

> Before the advent of *Weird Tales*, I had talked with such nationally known writers as Hamlin Garland, Emerson Hough, and Ben Hecht then residing in Chicago. I discovered that all of them expressed a desire to submit for publication a story of the unconventional type but hesitated to do so for fear of rejection. Pressed for details they acknowledged that such a delving into the realms of fantasy, the bizarre, and the outre could possibly be frowned upon by publishers of the conventional. . . .
>
> When everything is properly weighed, I must confess that the main motive in establishing *Weird Tales* was to give the writer free rein to express his innermost feelings in a manner befitting great literature.

To edit the two magazines, Henneberger called on Edwin Baird, a well-known Chicago writer. Helping Baird was music critic, Farnsworth Wright and author, Otis Adelbert Kline.

Edwin Baird (1886-1957) was born in Chattanooga, Tennessee. He began writing in 1906 and appeared in numerous magazines and newspapers of the time. He later became a feature writer for *The Chicago Daily Journal* and *The Chicago Evening American.* After his association with *Weird Tales* and *Detective Tales* he founded the *Real American Magazine.* Baird died in Chicago.

Top rate for the new magazine was 1¢ a word. Most writers received much less, with ¼¢ to ½¢ a word the average. The magazine bought, when possible, all rights. Payment was not until publication, and in some cases, not until long after publication.

The first issue of *Weird Tales* was dated March 1923. It was 25¢ a copy, a high price for a pulp fiction magazine. It was 192 pages long, 6″ by 9″ in size, and subtitled "The Unique Magazine." It featured 24 stories. The first issue featured one serial, by Otis Adelbert Kline, and it carried serials in nearly every issue up to 1940. There were no interior illustrations.

The second issue was somewhat better. A new serial was begun, overlapping the Kline issue. This idea was standard practice in pulps during this period. While one serial ended, another began, hopefully catching the interest of the reader, hooking him from issue to issue. The second issue contained twenty stories.

May 1923 saw a major change in the size of the magazine. It went to bedsheet size (8½″ by 11″) and went down to 64 pages in length. The number of stories remained about the same. The May issue featured the first half of "The Moon Terror" by A.G. Birch. The serial was so popular that this issue was the only one of the first year to sell out on publication.

Baird was less than an inspired editor. Henneberger claimed that Baird did not like Lovecraft's work and printed it only because Henneberger made sure that all of HPL's submissions were bought. As editor, Baird also rejected Greye La Spina's "Invaders From the Dark" as too commonplace. The novel was bought by Wright in 1924 and proved to be one of the most popular stories published in the early years of the magazine.

When asked about Baird, E. Hoffmann Price remarked, "Baird was an idea man. Once the magazine was going, he swiftly lost interest in it."

Whatever the reason, the magazine just did not sell. Articles and stories by Houdini did not help circulation. The Henneberger magic could not make Weird Tales go. Drastic changes had to be made. Reorganization was the only answer.

Henneberger decided to stick with Weird Tales. He sold the rights to Detective Tales and College Humor to John Lansinger and obtained all rights to Weird Tales. Otis Adelbert Kline and Farnsworth Wright put together one gigantic issue, really three months of the magazine combined into one, which was published as the Anniversary issue, dated May-June-July 1924. The issue remained on the stand for three months. It was 192 pages and was a bargain at 50¢. During that time, Henneberger continued to reorganize.

There were two problems that had to be faced. First, the magazine owed approximately $40,000 in back debts. This money had to be paid or Weird Tales would go into bankruptcy. Henneberger did not have this money. Only one solution presented itself. Henneberger entered an agreement with B. Cornelius, the owner of the printing company and his major creditor. Cornelius became chief stockholder with an agreement that if the $40,000 owed him was ever repaid by profits from the magazine, Henneberger would be returned the stock. There were still other debts to be paid, but with Cornelius as the printer, the magazine could continue. The agreement was not a good one for Henneberger but he had hopes of getting money from another printer to help him regain complete control of the publication.

The second problem was the editor. When Lansinger assumed control of Detective Tales, part of the agreement was that Edwin Baird was to be editor. Henneberger needed a new editor for his magazine. His first choice was H.P. Lovecraft. According to Henneberger, he went to see Lovecraft in Brooklyn. The author had just married and his wife expressed no interest in moving to Chicago. Lovecraft, who could not stand cold weather, was not in favor of the move either. Henneberger made Lovecraft the fabulous offer of 10 weeks salary in advance and full editorship of Weird Tales. Lovecraft turned the offer down.

Henneberger then turned to his original staff. He asked first reader, Farnsworth Wright, to take control of the magazine. Wright accepted and became editor. William Sprenger, who had worked for Henneberger, was made business manager. Sprenger had no interest in weird fiction. He was a business man and the magazine was his business. He was in charge of finances. Wright had complete control of editorial policies and stories. Cornelius was treasurer and signed the checks.

Farnsworth Wright (1888-1940) was born in California. He was educated at the University of Nevada and University of Washington. When the United States entered World War I, he went to France as a private in the infantry. He served as a French interpreter in the A.E.F. for a year. In 1919, Wright had a mild case of sleeping sickness. Two years later, the disease returned in the form of Parkinson's Disease. The condition worsened throughout the rest of Wright's life. By the end of the twenties, the shaking caused by the disease was so bad that Wright could not sign his name.

Wright returned to Chicago after the war and was music critic for the Chicago Herald and Examiner for several years. Even after becoming editor of Weird Tales, he continued his music critic chores on a part-time basis.

In 1929, Wright married Marjorie Zenk, a girl he had known in college. His son, Robert, was born a year later. Parkinson's Disease continued to plague him. During the last few years working in Chicago, Sprenger had to help him to and from his office. Soon after his replacement as editor of Weird Tales in 1940, Wright was operated on to help alleviate the pain of the disease. He never recovered fully from the operation and died soon afterwards in June 1940. His passing was given a full-page obituary in Weird Tales.

In the past few years, a number of rumors and stories were circulated about Wright. One of these was that he was "erratic, inconsistent and idiosyncratic." These charges are dealt with in the chapter on the fiction in this book. However, this statement was answered best by E. Hoffmann Price:

> "They" appear to have taken the viewpoint of the artist. Each considered himself a literary person, rather than as a businessman. This may be an oversimplification but it is, I believe, fair enough. In any event, neither regarded fiction writing as a sole or even as a major source of income.
>
> Among those who regarded fiction as a business, a full-time business, as did I and others whose only income came from fiction sales, I do not recall one who regarded Wright as "idiosyncratic, arbitrary, erratic, etc." We did not become so attached to any story to feel in the least wrenched, financially or emotionally, by a rejection. A rejection was a rejection and that was that . . . Sell the story elsewhere— or rebuild it and sell to Wright. Or, scrap the script! That is business. To protest and debate and question ---leave that to the "sincere artist."
>
> Contrary to others, I found Wright open minded, very helpful, more than willing to give an author every possible break.

Also recently appearing in print was a ridiculous statement that Wright was an alcoholic. This remark hardly deserved an answer but one was stated just to keep the record straight. With his health problems, Wright could not indulge heavily in strong drink even if he wanted to. Moreover, numerous instances pointed out Wright's uninvolvement with strong drink. E. Hoffmann Price related how numerous times he, Wright and Otis Kline would have dinner together. While Kline and Price sat up to sunrise, drinking, Wright would leave early. Wright never took more than a few drinks at the many social events he attended with Price, often wild bashes celebrating a sale. To quote Price, "He was abstemious by temperament. He was conspicuously sober, conservative and abstemious in a crowd which had a taste for drink. His health, if nothing else, would make excessive or steady drinking dangerous."

Another rumor was easier to trace and refute. Fantasy fan John Vetter interviewed Hannes Bok shortly before the artist's death. In the course of conversation, Wright's name came up. Bok stated that Wright did not receive a salary for much of his editorial work for *Weird Tales*. This statement has appeared twice since that interview in hardcovers, thus adding credulity to the statement. While definite evidence does not exist, the truth of the remark seems to be based on very shaky evidence.

To quote E. Hoffmann Price again, one of Wright's best friends during the period in question:

> To state that Wright received *no* salary from WT during the early part of the depression is a ticklish one to answer *meaningfully* . . . I was his and Marjorie's guest in 1933 . . . All outer signs suggested that Wright was enjoying a far higher income than I was (I was superintendent of Union Carbide's New Orleans plant). Wright always had a level of "gracious living" far beyond my own . . . In 1926 Wright bought an Auburn, not a luxury car, but in those days a car was very non-essential, for a Chicago dweller.

> Wright bought a costly Spanish style buffet, a real bargain, only $600. The Spanish-style dining room suite was also way above my level.

> In 1927, Wright and I used to talk, speculatively, of my joining the staff [Price did serve for some time as a reader for the magazine] . He was drawing approximately $600 monthly from *Weird Tales* while I was drawing $260 monthly from Union Carbide.

Weird Tales did have some financial problems during the early 1930's according to Seabury Quinn, who wrote to Virgil Finlay that the bank where much of the magazine's money was deposited closed and never reopened. However, nowhere was there evidence that any salaries were cut. Price further wrote:

> Edmond Hamilton—who met Wright about the period I did, sustains me in this, with independent evidence of his own, He—like Robert Carr—saw Wright a few weeks before Wright's death. He found Wright living comfortably, though not luxuriously.

All evidence pointed to the notion that Hannes Bok drew logical but incorrect inferences from statements he did not have in their entirety.

Some mention should be given to William Sprenger, who served as business manager of *Weird Tales*. Sprenger was a quiet man, pleasant, of medium stature. He was a very matter-of-fact man, his feet always on the ground. He had a very quiet sparkle, according to Price, with good humor, keen eye, and was always cordial.

Both Price and Margaret Brundage remembered that Sprenger enjoyed playing the horse races. According to Price, Sprenger did well, methodically analyzing the history of the horse and the probabilities of the race. Both Price and Brundage remember him as being very strict in regards to the money matters involving *Weird Tales*. Mrs. Brundage also stated that "Sprenger helped Mr. Wright those last few years in Chicago when Wright's health was failing. I doubt if Farnsworth Wright could have managed in the late 1930's without Sprenger's help."

Under the steady hand of these two men, Wright and Sprenger, *Weird Tales* began to make progress. Slowly, as years passed, many of the debts incurred during Rural Publications days were paid. Popular Fiction Publishing Co., the new company that published the magazine was not overly successful, but it did reasonably well. Rates in 1924 and 1925 were ½¢ a word maximum, with some authors getting even less. By 1926, rates were up to 1¢ a word for their top authors. Later, a few writers were even paid at the high rate of 1½¢ a word. While the money might not sound like much, it was a better pay scale than some science fiction magazines pay in the 1970's!

Editorial offices during the middle 1920's were located in the Baldwin Building, in Indianapolis, Indiana. In late 1925, that building was torn down and offices were moved to the Holliday Building. In late 1926, editorial offices were moved to Chicago. First offices were at 3810 N. Broadway. Soon, offices were moved to 840 N. Michigan, where they remained until the magazine was sold in 1938.

Henneberger continued to hope to regain control of *Weird Tales*. The depression destroyed his last hopes. Robert Eastman, of the Hall Printing Company, found himself carrying a large number of magazines on credit due to the hard times. Eastman couldn't even pay his own staff. He was the man Henneberger had always hoped would bail him out of his situation. Eastman had problems of his own. He died in 1934, ending Henneberger's last hopes to regain control of his brain-child.

As far back as 1927, Popular Fiction Publishing Co. tried to expand its line. In that year, it brought out an attractive hardcover edition of the popular *Weird Tales* serial, "The Moon Terror." The book, which contained three other stories along with the lead novel, was a flop. It remained a stock item, often selling for 25¢ a copy, into the late 1940's. In 1930, Cornelius tried again with *Oriental Stories*. The magazine, which featured many *Weird Tales* regulars, had Wright as editor. It also was a financial failure.

Wright was a canny editor. Rarely did a good story get past him, even from an unknown author. *Weird Tales* featured more stories from authors who were only published with one tale than any other science fiction or fantasy magazine. Wright got stories from everywhere and everyone. Oscar Cook, who had four stories in "The Unique Magazine," was editor of the *Birmingham Gazette*. W.E. Hawkins, who appeared in the first issue of *Weird Tales*, was the editor of *Author and Journalist*, a writer's trade magazine. Wright once stated that of 100 manuscripts submitted, approximately two were bought. *Weird Tales* was also copyrighted in Great Britain and offered its material to British magazines. *Mystery Story Magazine* bought many reprint rights to stories from *Weird Tales* for British audiences.

Wright also placed advertisements in the early science fiction magazines. These small box ads always listed some tale of super-science much like those being published in *Amazing Stories*. Usually the author of the advertised story was Edmond Hamilton, a name well known to science fiction fans. Wright also stocked hardcover editions of several books written by popular *Weird Tales* authors such as Otis Adelbert Kline and sold them through the magazine.

The size of the magazine was 6½″ by 9½″, in November 1924 when the magazine returned to the stands after several months absence. It contained 144 pages. At first, the large number of stories remained but, as years passed, the number of stories per issue went down while quality went up. In 1930, the size changed slightly to approximately 6-3/4″ by 9-3/4″. With rare exception, the magazine contained 128 pages through 1938. In 1939, for a short period, the page count was increased to 160 pages. Up to this time, the price remained steady at 25¢. The price in 1939 was dropped to 15¢.

In the early 1930's, the magazine underwent another financial crisis. The bank where much of the firm's money was kept went under. The pulp went bi-monthly for a period in 1931. However, rates never went down and after a short period, the monthly schedule was resumed. Otis Adelbert Kline had an interesting anecdote which he told about those days:

> Along in 1931, I was taken to the hospital for a series of operations, while working on a serial for them. They were publishing the installments as I wrote them, and paying me for each installment as it was finished. I nearly died from the effect of one of the operations—my heart stopped for three minutes. When I told Sprenger about it the next day, he informed me that he had deposited $500 in my bank for me, although his firm owed me nothing and wouldn't owe me anything more until I finished the serial. I told him I might kick off. What would he do then? And he said he'd run a contest to have the readers finish it . . . I dictated the next installment to Bill Sprenger, who sat by my bed with a typewriter.

As Kline also stated, "I never knew anyone to shoot squarer with a person, than that."

In late 1938, Cornelius decided to retire from publishing. Henneberger sold his own interests to Delaney, a shoe manufacturer who had recently gotten into the publishing business. Cornelius turned over part of his stock to Wright and Sprenger as reward for their faithful service. The rest went to Sprenger. Henneberger was still connected with the magazine in a small percentage role. Part of Cornelius' agreement with Delaney was that Farnsworth Wright would be retained as editor of "The Unique Magazine." Offices were moved to New York. Wright made the move but Sprenger did not and severed all ties with the magazine.

New editorial offices were set up in Rockefeller Center. Delaney was more concerned than Henneberger or Cornelius in turning the pulp into a paying, profit-making proposition. His first idea was to increase the page count from 128 pages to 160 pages. He also used a cheaper quality of paper, making the issue look even thicker than before. The first of these thick issues appeared in February 1939. However, the idea did not catch on and sales dropped steadily. Another of Delaney's ideas was to cut rates, both to artists and authors. The policy showed as quality quickly dropped. In another effort to boost sales, the size was cut to 128 pages in September 1939 and the price was dropped to 15¢. The magazine still did not sell.

Delaney had previously bought *Short Stories* from Doubleday and Doran. The associate editor of the magazine had been Dorothy McIlwraith and Delaney retained her as editor for *Short Stories* and associate editor for *Weird Tales*. In a move to further cut costs, Delaney let go of Farnsworth Wright. March 1940 was the last issue to carry Wright's name as editor. From then on, Dorothy McIlwraith was editor for both *Weird Tales* and *Short Stories*. Assisting her was Lamont Buchanan, who served as associate editor and art editor for the two pulps.

Dorothy McIlwraith was a capable pulp editor who was not adverse to spending money to get quality material. The only trouble was that *Weird Tales* was the lesser of the two magazines she edited. *Short Stories* was the money-maker and the bigger name. Most of the budget went to its upkeep. Also, the war hit both pulps hard. Ms. McIlwraith did the best she could with *Weird Tales* but the best days of the magazine were past. In 1943, the page count dropped to 112 pages. In May 1944, another drop brought the page count down to 96 pages. In September 1947, the price was raised quietly from 15¢ to 20¢ an issue. In May 1949, the increase in price went to 25¢. All during this time, the quality of the magazine dropped. Dorothy McIlwraith got the best material she could. The one problem was that the authors who had made *Weird Tales* great were gone—either dead or moved up to better-paying pulps.

In September 1953, the magazine went to digest size in a last effort to keep alive. The hope was a short-lived one. Its last issue was dated September 1954. In all, it ran for 279 issues.

2 Farnsworth Wright
by E. HOFFMANN PRICE

Never having fancied myself as a graphologist, I had made no attempt to picture the appearance and personality of the man who for more than two years had been my only editorial friend; the man whose painfully shaped signature, with a tremor in every stroke, always came as a mild shock at the end of those cordial letters. A friend, seeing one of those notes of acceptance, remarked, "He must be awfully old, or else he's got one foot in the grave."

Shortly after *Weird Tales* moved from Indianapolis to Chicago, I called at Wright's office, and found that he was not "awfully old." That wavering and labored signature embarrassed him else he would hardly have hastened, so early in our first conversation, to blame it on writer's cramp. I've often wondered if, even then, he did not actually suspect the truth, though denying it, even to himself, as part of his long campaign against the mysterious ailment which indirectly caused his death in June, 1940.

Wright's office was not the necromancer's cavern I had so often pictured. The room was brightly lighted, overlooking the lake, large enough, though seemingly much too small for the man. He was tall, very tall, and somewhat stooped; a large-framed, long-legged man, conspiciously and prematurely bald. My first impression was that his face gave no suggestion of his wit and sparkle. Neither did his voice, which was on the subduded rather than on the hearty side, but his eyes had a twinkle, keen and blue, and friendly.

Even in 1926, the palsy which made him handle a pen with such difficulty had contributed to a certain general slowness of motion, which was so pronounced as to be a hesitance rather than natural deliberation. This suggestion of lack of muscular coordination was revealed also in his facial expression and in his speech. I remember my instant of discomfort, and how quickly Wright's cordiality dispelled it, and along with it, my awe at meeting the man who had bought eight stories in a row.

"Price? Not E. Hoffmann Price?"

The smile and the eyes coordinated. I felt at home, and ceased telling myself that I had a hell of a nerve to take up a busy man's time, just on the strength of eight sales, a good portion of which had been due to his kindness and patience in suggesting revisions. I assured him that this was indeed E. Hoffmann Price, in person. And what made me feel like one of the family was when he turned and called, "Oh, Bill! Come on out—"

He wanted Bill Sprenger, *Weird Tales'* business manager, to greet the visiting fireman. Bill was short, alert, intensely on his toes; pleasant, yet all business and a go-getter. He never read *Weird Tales*. Writers were pests who always howled for money. We all had a laugh on that. He and Wright were slowly but surely pulling *Weird Tales* through a financial reorganization, devoting most of the current profits to paying off the obligations of the original management. They were a contrasting pair: matter of fact Sprenger, and Wright, for all his level head, a poet and the soul of whimsy.

A year and a half previous, when it was doubtful whether *Weird Tales* could continue publication, much less be able to pay for what had been published, I wrote rather pointedly about an overdue check for "The Raja's Gift." Wright answered one inquiry. Bill Sprenger answered another. By then, feeling sour, I retorted, "I have heard of penniless and starving authors, and have fancied myself one. However, the novelty of a penniless publisher is appealing, even refreshing. Only one thing could be more refreshing—to wit, since I've heard from editor, and from business manager, I should now get a message from the third member of the Trinity, Mr. Cornelius, the Treasurer.

Finally, meeting Wright and Sprenger, approving of them and hoping that it was mutual, I learned that my sarcastic letter had packed a wallop. Sprenger admitted having said, "Why, the son of a bitch! Don't ever buy anything else from him!" Whereas Wright, whose sense of humor never failed, rather appreciated the balanced phrasing of the letter, and had himself written an answer that entirely appeased my momentary wrath, and brightened a somber and unpleasant winter.

I don't and never did blame Sprenger for his outburst, just as in the end, he did not blame me. But a comparison of their immediate reactions offers a clue to Farnsworth Wright's personality. In spite of being the editor of a rather shaky pioneer in a new field, he could chuckle when an enraged author commented on the novelty of a starving *publisher*. However, during the eighteen years in which I have been selling fiction, I have learned that my quip was ill timed. I have seen more penniless publishers than authors.

Wright had scarcely found me a chair when he repeated, in effect, what he had written me from Indianapolis, in May of that year. I quote from the letter which I still have on file: "Please permit me to thank you for the latest story, 'Peacock's Shadow.' It has all the exotic witchery in its imagery, that one would expect to find only in Gautier. I would be false to our readers were I to reject it, for it will give tone to *Weird Tales*—in fact, I think it would give tone to *Blackwood's* or to *Century* or *Harper's*."

This tribute, perhaps as florid as the story itself, was absolutely sincere. In all the years I knew Wright, I never knew him to tell a pleasant lie. He could be, and often was, uncomprimisingly blunt. He liked "The Peacock's Shadow," and he was generous enough to admit it, unlike many editors who fear praise will spoil a writer, or encourage him to yell for higher rates.

Wright loved the florid, exotic, the richly phrased, the high flight of fancy; he believed in his magazine, which I think is the reason why he successfully piloted his way into a field which thus far no one had penetrated. Today I believe that he overated "Peacock's Shadow," but it is easy to forgive a man for such error! He gave me confidence in myself.

As an example of his matter of fact bluntness: I quote from his letter of September 5, 1925, written from Indianapolis, about a year before we met in Chicago: "I was in Whiting a few days ago and had a notion of going to Hammond to look you up, but didn't."

This is the middle paragraph of a nine-line letter. Whiting, Indiana is perhaps six miles from Hammond. One might have expected that, since he hadn't looked me up, he'd not mention having thought of doing so; or, having mentioned it, that he'd elaborate on the lousy bus and street car service, and the uncertainty of locating a person who from 8:00 P.M. to 5:00 A.M. was assistant superintendent of an acetylene plant. Farnsworth, as I said, ranged easily from unembroidered bluntness to glowing fancy.

I left his office, that afternoon, with the original cover painting for "The Peacock's Shadow." He had made me feel that I had arrived. That my first novelette had hogged the cover of *Weird Tales* was a triumph.

From then on, I used to drop in at intervals of a month or so, for Chicago was only forty minutes from Hammond. Since I was night superintendent, I had every afternoon free, but in spite of the cordial welcome Farnsworth had given me, I rather hesitated to intrude the personal element into what had started as a business relationship. As I look back at it all, this was an error, certainly needless scruple, for when he was at his desk, he was not influenced by friendship.

It was in Farnsworth's office on West Ohio Street that I met Otis Adelbert Kline, fantasy author and *bon vivant* with whom I collaborated on several *Weird Tales* stories, and who in 1932 helped me get my stride as a full-time writer. In those days, Farnsworth lived in a hotel. His restaurant hospitality, lavish as it always was, never gave him the chance to show his real talents as a host. Our friendship ripened at Otis Kline's home, and later, in my own apartment in Hammond, where a discussion of exotic dishes led to the invention of the "Varnished Vulture"—a capon, stuffed with rice and Greek currents and pistachios, and basted with sherry, the cooking sherry which even those evil days permitted. We three—Farnsworth, Otis, and I—made a ritual of the entire process of "varnishing" a "vulture," and finally, as our group expanded, we called ourselves "The Varnished Vultures."

Early in 1927, Farnsworth brought a protege to one of these banquets in Hammond: a chubby, round-faced, owlish-looking kid, Robert S. Carr, whose stories had appeared in *Weird Tales* during the previous two years. Carr himself is the subject of a saga; suffice it to say that at the age of seventeen, he had left his home in Ashley, Ohio, with a bag of cookies, the maternal blessing, and a bale of penciled manuscript, his novel of the high school generation. He had come to Chicago to consult Farnsworth on marketing this non-weird story.

Carr, like many others, including the present writer, was one of Farnsworth's discoveries. Farnsworth spent many an hour helping the kid cut and revise the MS. At times, this youngest "vulture" was a trial, but the outcome justified Wright's faith. Months later, "Rampant Age" was published, serially, in *Smart Set*, and then in book form; it was banned in London, it was translated into German, and it got the precocious author a Hollywood contract.

An editor, they say, is a would-be writer whose frustration is expressed by grinning fiendishly as he stuffs a rejection slip into a return envelope. That's the popular tradition, and like most widespread theories, it's way off the beam, simply because a man so warped by resentment could not maintain the open mind needed for his duties. But if that thesis were only partially justified, Farnsworth would have been an outstanding exception. In helping Bob Carr make his first step from what was, and still is, a magazine of limited circulation, he was depriving himself of a contributor who had been a drawing card from the start. "Spiderbite," we called the kid, because of a yarn which had made the entire circulation list shudder and call for more. Since the publication of "Rampant Age," Carr has never had the time to contribute to *Weird Tales*; it was inevitable that he would not have. It was inevitable, of course, that he would eventually branch out, regardless of any one man offering or withholding his assistance, yet this does not detract from Farnsworth's generosity. He was even then ill and overworked, for in addition to his editorial duties, he was music critic for a Chicago paper.

Our opening definition of an editor may have an unfair implication: to wit, that Farnsworth nobly avoided the effects of frustration. This is not the case. I read one of his published slick paper stories, done years before he took charge of *Weird Tales*. There were others, though I remember only that one, which, incidentally, he did not give me time to finish. He showed it to me for only one reason: the yarn contained a pun in French, and he was proud of that! And he dismissed his writing by saying that he had soon realized that while he could sell fiction, he could not produce sufficient quantities to make a living.

As to the correctness of his self-appraisal, no one could say, not even he himself, for he did not, as far as we know, ever put the question to the ultimate test.

That pun? The locale of the story was France, where he had served during World War I, as in interpreter. Whether he wore the Sphinx insignia from the start, or later got it as recognition of his linguistic ability, I never learned. But the pun: *la plus sale d'Orleans*, that is what he wrote when the context of course called for *la pucelle, Jean d'Arc*. He took a boyish pride in that quip, for he did love puns.

He never passed up a chance; he never disputed the contention to the effect that puns were the lowest form of wit, and he never gave the impression of thinking them either clever or witty. They merely amused him. He loved words, their flavor, likeness of sound balanced against unlikeness in meaning. He rolled words in his mouth as he would an old wine; he savoured them, whether his own or someone else's. And one of the high spots in our friendship was when I explained that in Arabic, the pun was esteemed as the utmost in wit and mental agility.

I repeat, Farnsworth loved words: the relish with which he would recite George Sterling's "Wine of Wizardry" is the most certain clue to his lavish appreciation of my first novelette. Prose, to him, needed rhythm, sonorous phrases; it needed balance and imagery, for he had the heart of a poet. And I was not surprised, the other day, when Marjorie Wright mentioned a collection of his verses. He had never thought enough of them to have them published. More than that, he had always been opposed to publishing them.

Farnsworth's sense of humor covered the entire field, and with his knowledge of French, Spanish, German, and I think, Italian, as well as Latin, that field was wide. No matter from what you dredged a quip, you did not have to supply blueprints to get a hearty laugh from Farnsworth. There was nothing too subtle, nor anything too bawdy; in a flash, he would switch from a *jeux d'esprit*, as delicate as Hungarian Somlyoi, and to a barrackroom jest as rugged as Demerara rum. To say that the man was no prude is the ultimate in understatement.

Unhappily, selections from his repertoire might be misunderstood. I never knew a man whose mind was farther from the gutter; it was rather that, like Rabelais, a jest was a jest, no matter where you found it, and an unusual rhyme was music, regardless of the context. He reserved these flights of fancy for stag gatherings; in mixed crowds, he was scrupulously proper in his humor. He soared to the heights, he plumbed the depths of English and other languages, and kept his mind clean—nor was his a sheltered existence. Unlike many of his contributors, he had met and known many people and many types and many places. And each fed that agile fancy.

Here is a typical Wright quip. It is typical in that it has a certain oddity and twang which he especially relished and one which he could with especial effectiveness render. Those same pet quips of his, however carefully rendered by others, fell terribly flat. His success with them must have been in the delivery. The quip: "I hate spinach, and I am glad that I hate it, for if I did not hate it, I would eat it, and I loath the filthy stuff."

He forbade the publication of his serious verse, yet he recited, and with what gusto, the most outrageous of limericks. Whimsically mimicking the Persians, we used to sit in his office and, one giving the opening line of a limerick, the others present, each in turn, had to extemporize the succeeding ones. After several such experiments, we agreed that, in view of the ease with which Persian rhymes, and the difficulty of rhyming English, that Hafiz and Jami and the others were not, after all, prodigies!

Farnsworth's face, his low, even voice, tending at times towards a monotone, contrasted sharply with the sparkle and flash of his utterance, the twinkle of his eye. His gravity, his solemnity of expression, both heightened by a high forehead and premature baldness, were a perfect foil for his wit, and when, very rarely, he spoke in wrath, it was terrific.

I remember a dinner, a "Vulture Banquet" in my apartment in Hammond. Farnsworth, Bill Sprenger, Otis Kline, were there; also, several guests who did not write. Among these last was a girl who wanted to meet an editor—she later did have some stories published—and then a girl from Hammond's aristocracy, one who had just returned from a tour of Europe. Also, a girl who worked in an office; not one of the elite, an opinion which was exclusive with the one aristocrat present, and which this patrician made quite plain.

It was one the most obvious pieces of catiness I have ever witnessed, and all the more unwarranted, because the working girl was the girl of one of my guests, whereas the patrician creature was merely the guest of a guest and no friend of mine. I went poker-faced behind my cigar and prayed for a custom-built thunderbolt to annihilate the wench.

Farnsworth sat there, solemn faced, with that half-asleep expression he so often wore; apparently, he had drawn so fully into himself that he saw nothing and heard nothing. Meanwhile, having wearied of a personal and pointed ribbing, the Aristocrat began to swamp us with reminiscences of Europe. When she got to France, she paused for breath. She had to, finally.

Farnsworth straightened up. "Pardon me," he asked, for the first time addressing her, "How long were you in Paris?"

"Why—for three days," she answered.

"Ah . . . I thought so," Farnsworth said, languidly, and went back into the silence.

And after all these seventeen years, I still remember the empty, silent seconds which followed that utterance. My prayer had been answered. Farnsworth Wright had forged and hurled a thunderbolt. The devastation lay in the delivery, neither resonant nor full throated, words spoken only with the lips, in little more than a whisper, deliberately and in a monotone: it was the delivery, rather than the actual words which blitzed the target, and thrilled all the others. We heard no more that day of Europe, or of her.

She couldn't hit back. The man had not even bothered to inflect his voice, much less to raise it. He had made her aware, somehow, of how she had impressed everyone else in the room, and then he had gone back into his silence.

As always, Farnsworth was the friend and champion of the unknown and the obscure. The vengeance he exacted was on behalf of a girl he had never met before. And to this day, she gratefully remembers Farnsworth Wright and his insecticide which finished one of Hammond's codfish aristocrats.

It was in 1926, some months before I met Farnsworth,

that I first followed up my long-submerged interest in oriental rugs. In 1927, he bought my story, "Saladin's Throne Rug." That hobby became another of the many tastes we had in common. We used to prowl about, pawing our way through Sarkis Nahigian's magnificent stock, though rarely buying. Our interest rather than the size of our purchases assured us always of a hearty welcome. Then, when Farnsworth moved from his hotel, and took an apartment, late in 1927, he started what would have become quite a collection, had it not been for the ruinous sums he was spending in his fight against ill health.

As it was, his first purchase has always made a colorful spot in my memory: a Turkoman weave, distinctive in pattern and color, and odd in shape. Apparently, its upper corners had been clipped off, but after closer scrutiny, we decided that it had actually been woven to that shape. Some years later, his rug was the starting point—I hate the word "inspiration"—of my first professionally-written story, which Farnsworth bought after two or three revisions.

Later, he picked up other orientals, including an exquisite Shiraz. And in my last letter to him, that letter which was not mailed in time for his reading, I believe that there was an account of an auction, and of the "rare and costly" carpets I did not buy.

Farnsworth's apartment gave him means of expression which restaurant hospitality always lacked. Of all the many bootleg liquors Chicago offered, he selected Bacardi rum, whether genuine or doctored, I can not say, though the stuff was very kind to those who drank it. He specialized in a tall drink, as nearly as I remember, a planter's punch; his own recipe, and mixed with his own hands. In those days, I served Georgia corn, hauled a thousand miles in a suitcase, or else local corn moonshine; in either case, aged in charred kegs until it was a fair substitute for legitimate Bourbon. Otis Kline specialized in wines, brandy, liqueurs, and prescription whiskies. Thus, Farnsworth's bar was not only refreshing, but also, different.

I had, by then, made somewhat of a hobby of cooking. The Varnished Vulture was for solemn conclaves. On other occasions, grilled fowl was in order, on Indian curry, both of which Farnsworth fancied. Whenever I was invited to his dinners, he gave me the pleasant task of taking over the kitchenette, and preparing one of my specialties for his guests, while he mixed the rum punch. I remember one gathering in particular: the climax was an assortment of cheeses, limburger, liederkranz and other notorious stenches. Far from being content to offer intellectual refreshment, Farnsworth insisted on stimulating every sense and every faculty.

But to disparage his restaurant hospitality would be unjust. One of his friends, an exquisite and fascinating young lady, had at the last minute announced that due to the unexpected arrival of her sister, the proposed dinner and theatre party would have to be a threesome unless Farnsworth could locate a fourth. Of all the people he could have called, he nominated me. And, characteristically, wondered if I would oblige him, and hoped that the blind date would not prove uncongenial.

The details have escaped me, after all these years. I remember only that both ladies were charming, that the evening was pleasantly spent; but the outstanding recollection is Farnsworth's courtesy to his guests. I had expected,

of course, that he'd do things right; I'd never seen him do anything any other way. But his solicitude, his anticipation of trifles which first-class hospitality need not have anticipated: the fact sticks with me, long after I've forgotten the details. Indeed, I am now inclined to think it wasn't so much what he did as host, as it was the kindness and generosity behind his attentions.

But there is one detail! That sense of humor. The four of us had seats which were just right; we would have, of course. The show was "Night in Spain," or it may have been "The Kid From Spain," a colorful and gay bit of froth. I haven't the foggiest idea any more who was starred, though it was someone noteworthy. The show was well received, but one line, for some reason, missed fire.

A bit of slapstick; girl and a guy, the former nagging the latter, right from the start. Finally, after devastating speech and gesture, she turned and swivel-hipped toward the wings. The male comedian's next move was swift. He booted the gal, right where the booting was best, and he quipped, "Pardon me, but did I hurt *your* feelings?"

That line missed fire. There were just two responses in the whole house. Farnsworth doubled up and howled; my own laughter was on the Olympian side. Each had recognized the sally as the kind of jest which could have popped up spontaneously almost any afternoon in the editorial rooms of *Weird Tales*. Seconds passed before it dawned on us that ours were the only two laughs in that corner of Chicago. We eyed each other, and he said, "It seems that we are conspicuous."

Many a time, long thereafter, Farnsworth and I discussed that phenomenon; but we never could figure out why that obvious, and to us, perfectly marvelous play on words fell so totally flat. We did, however, quickly and gravely and very modestly concede that we two were, beyond any doubt, gifted with the most agile minds in Chicago.

For all I know, the present audience may be wondering at the laughter of the gods. Maybe one wasn't supposed to "larf right out." Maybe the playwright had not intended "feelings" to have *double entendre*.

Speaking of *double entendre*, Farnsworth and I mulled over the theory and practice of *triple entendre!* Not that we seriously expected to create a verbal play with three meanings, one of which would be perfectly proper; rather, it was an ideal toward which the agile mind could work.

Prudery and smugness and intolerance: these, as nothing else, aroused his intolerance. Once, shortly after he bought what I believe was his first car, an Auburn sedan, we drove to Zion City, the headquarters of a cult which insisted that the world was flat. Farnsworth was broadminded enough to admit that every man was entitled to write his own cosmography, and let it go at that. He had heard that they served a top flight luncheon, and as long as the chef knew how to fry a chicken, his astronomical errors were irrelevant.

The meal wasn't bad, but Farnsworth felt that it had been over-rated, even at half the price, which was stiff enough for a banquet. It wasn't the expense, it was the principle of the thing. But even so, he was tolerant. This, however, did arouse his fury, and his crusader spirit: he learned that smoking was prohibited within the corporate limits of Zion City.

Now, Farnsworth smoked little at any time, and smoked

less as his health became worse. But, "By God," he said, his voice trembling with indignation, "I am going to have a cigarette, no matter what these bastards say. I am going to smoke, purely as a matter of principle, and without paying the customary fine these———s impose on culprits."

A few yards short of the city limits, we fired up, puffed furiously, and triumphantly crossed the line. Then he threw his cigarette away, and brightened up. Having broken a lance against a windmill, he had partially avenged that sub-standard luncheon.

One of his prime grudges was against Lady Isabel Burton, who, surviving her husband, Sir Richard, destroyed the MS. of his translation of Kamashastra, on the grounds that despite its anthropological value, its obscene passages made it utterly unfit for publication. The public, Farnsworth felt, was a better judge of that colorful adventurer's works than any prim and meddling widow!

Inevitably, Farnsworth was thrilled by the works of Charles Fort, the rebel who spent a lifetime in trying to shatter the solemn pretenses of science, and in debunking the sacerdotal attitude of scientists. Whether he agreed or disagreed with Fort, I don't know, and it makes no difference; the essence of it was that he admired the iconoclastic approach, the startling phrases, the audacity of the wildman who juggled suns and stars and sciences.

And Farnsworth rebelled against the long list of tabus which circumscribe the average editor. As long as an author did not violate good taste and common decency of thought and expression, that author's work was published as written. The story itself was the only criterion. He had no place for arbitrary standards.

On the other hand, he did try to avoid any pointed offense against sincere religious conviction. My story, "Stranger From Kurdistan," was held for more than six months unpublished, in spite of his having had room in his schedule for it. While he was enthusiastic about the yarn, and while he saw clearly that the author's intent was just the opposite from blasphemous, he admitted that he had had his qualms. Quite as frankly, once he had risked publication, he wrote me, " 'The Stranger From Kurdistan' is one of the most popular stories we have ever run . . . " It was not until some years later that I fully realized what courage it must have taken for the editor of a not too well established magazine to publish a story which in 2400 words presented Christ and Satan, face to face, and in the last paragraph crucified the human race! Several devout friends condemned me; several acquaintances ostracized me. But Farnsworth reprinted the story, by popular request, five years after.

His intuition had been right. Despite qualms, he stuck to his guns, and he did not regret it. That story was what won me my *Weird Tales* following; that story, and Farnsworth Wright's courage in following up his convictions, gave me the boost needed for others.

Though not himself professing (to my knowledge) any orthodox creed, he was death on hypocrites and advocates of intolerance; and while "The Infidel's Daughter" doubtless had certain merits as a narrative, I have often thought that his prime motive in buying it was because it was a none too thinly veiled satire damning the Ku Klux Klan. Those masked apostles of intolerance had, of course, recently finished themselves; some of you may remember that juicy scandal, rape with trimmings, which took place in an Indiana hotel in 1926 or 1927.

A clansman in the South wrote a blistering letter and canceled a subscription. He would have nothing to do with a "vile publication which maligned an organization devoted to fostering Americanism." I felt that perhaps I had gone Voltairean with more enthusiasm than judgment, and I told Farnsworth how I regretted that he had lost a subscriber. He laughed and said, "Oh, hell! It's really a compliment having a ____ like that object to our policy. Moreover, a story that arouses controversy is good for circulation, we gain more than we lose, and anyway, it would be worth a reasonable loss to rap bigots of that caliber."

A third story, "Lord of the Fourth Axis," drew a long and incoherent blast from the deep South, the usual charges of sacrilege and blasphemy, and an exhortation to the author, before Satan took him completely in charge, to open his Bible and pray.

Pardon me if I seem to be hogging the show: that is not my intent. Really, I am sticking to my subject—Farnsworth Wright's independence to tabus.

In order to keep my afternoon visits from interfering with his duties, and on occasion, to enable him to leave an hour or two earlier, I used to take half of the day's heap of MSS. and read them: this at his suggestion, as I'd hardly have presumed to set any such valuation on my editorial judgment. This helped me a great deal more than it did him; it gave me a better idea of the requirements of the man behind the desk, a clearer idea of story values in general.

And there was one lesson more valuable than any of the others: one day, after a very long night shift, I was too groggy to do justice to anyone's MS., and I told him so. It would not be fair to the author. Farnsworth retorted, "You are wrong. You forget that while we have many quick witted and intelligent readers, we also have many whose intelligence is rudimentary. When you are 50% below par, you need a solid impact. A story that moves you, wakes you up, is bound to have sufficient to make the mill run reader sit up."

I took him at his word, though I had my doubts. I nodded my way through half a dozen MSS. some of them well written, well phrased. I said, "This is not working out. These yarns seem all right. I'm convinced I'm just too dopey to do them justice."

"Go ahead and read," he persisted. "I'll glance over them later, if you continue to feel that you're not fair to the author."

Another half dozen MSS., and I sat up with a whoop! Farnsworth had been right. The vitality, that indefinable something which makes a phrase live, makes a paragraph glow, makes an entire story sparkle, had put me on my feet. He chuckled, and he did not glance over the dead ones. He knew that I had learned a lesson: that a writer deserves exactly as much attention as his manuscripts compel, and not one bit more. And he went on to say, "It's really not necessary to read each dud to the horrible ending. If they don't come to life within the first two pages, they'll remain zombies to the finish."

After reading a hundred or two impossibles to the last line, I learned that he was right. But in those days, writing only two or three stories a year, a manuscript, even one in pencil—he received a few of that kind!—was a thing to be treated ceremoniously, even though my grim and stubborn reading was somewhat on par with the hearty breakfast the condemned gets.

You may think that Farnsworth was radical in his methods of reading MSS., and cynical in his disposal of authors and their work. This was not the case. He was merely honest and realistic, refusing to waste his time on causes which according to his experience and logic were lost from the start. In the time saved by this realism, he went to great trouble to analyze "living" stories whose mechanical details were wrong, and to suggest revisions to make them acceptable. This was, he confessed, a thankless task on the whole, one which often brought him a letter packed with indignation and fury; but once in a while, an author cooperated.

I should add that Farnsworth's attitude was more generous than the average editor's, rather than less so, that in the entire publishing business, no manuscript with dull opening pages is ever read to the end, simply because a dull or inept opener would certainly not do anything but make the cash customer yawn, if that story did get into print. As for his letting me judge the MSS. of fellow beginners, that also had a precedent. The ultimate consumer does not have editorial training; he is a person seeking entertainment. Willie the Office Boy is the best possible judge; Willie, and the girl at the switchboard. The editor's job—but wait a minute! We're still discussing Farnsworth Wright.

He liked to share his discoveries and his enthusiasm; he fairly glowed when he found a striking story in a mountain of trash. Every so often, he would cut greetings to the minimum, dig into his desk, and thrust a manuscript at me. The accompanying sales talk would have made the hypothetical Man from Mars mistake me for the prospective purchaser, and Farnsworth for the author's agent.

H. Warner Munn's horror story, "The Chain," took precedence over my bottle of "Napoleon Brandy," as he whimsically called the Georgia corn liquor which I used to tote to East Ohio on state occasions. Donald Wandrei's "Red Brain" was another which I had to read right then and there. But the highest peak was reached in 1933, when he handed me a MS. by one C.L. Moore.

And that did take my breath. "For Christ's sake, Plato, who is C.L. Moore; He, she, or it is colossal!" This, of all times, was when my enthusiasm equaled Farnsworth's. He quit work, and we declared a C.L. Moore Day. Some years later, when I met the young lady, and told her of the furor, she said that while she'd love to believe I wasn't a polite liar, she simply couldn't.

Now, the "Plato," meaning Farnsworth?

We Vultures were a whimsical lot, in spite of keeping our feet close enough to the ground to keep from starving. Farnsworth loved to recite a dripping and scandalous poem attributed to Eugene Field, dealing with doings of Socrates and other ancient Greeks; and there was a phrase which stuck: " . . . Pious Plato's pleasures . . . "

No one else could ever read or recite those many lines as Farnsworth could. So, we called him, "Pious Plato." When *Oriental Stories, Weird Tales'* companion magazine, made us Arabic minded, we even translated the name into that language. Those were playful days, zestful days. Without the least disloyalty to previous friendships, it seems to me

that in meeting Farnsworth and those who centered about his office I had met kindred spirits, stimulating persons who encouraged the development rather than the suppression of imagination.

Farnsworth, however, was no solemn mentor; scholarly, talented, with a musical background at least as full and rich as his literary and linguistic background, he was never on the lecturer's platform. We, the group, met as equals; each contributed a specialty, and expanded in the appreciation of the others. There was no one-sided hero worship, except, for a little while, on the part of Robert Carr, who outgrew that with his teens. He also contributed to the local legendry, and in ways that at the time seemed gruesome: but this is not the saga of Robert "Spiderbite" Carr.

It may seem odd that I know practically nothing of Wright's earlier years, of his family, or his background. I'm hazy as to his age, though he did once mention it. Yet this should not seem anything but natural: we accepted each other as stimulating companions, and our respective antecedents really didn't matter, for there was far too much of immediate moment to be praised, burned in effigy, appreciated, derided. After so many references to Farnsworth's failing health, I must reiterate, the man was intensely alive, savoring life with gusto, living zestfully.

In many respects, he was a total stranger; what I saw and remember is all that I can offer as a clue to what he had seen and been. And when Marjorie Wright, his widow, sent me some information about his earlier years, nearly every statement was a revelation. True, I did once meet Farnsworth's sister, and I had gathered that he had been devoted to his mother; that he had once worked, during a school vacation, somewhere in Oregon or Washington, as a labor foreman in charge of a gang of Hindus. At this stage, he would say, "An experience which makes me eminently fit to edit *Oriental Stories.* I learned enough Punjabi to ask for a drink of water."

Mrs. Wright's letter was to supply data to round out my sketch. I must quote, for certainly I could not amend anything, and it is equally certain that meddling would fail to improve the flavor. She says,

"I think there is more to Farnsworth's background than the editorial and literary side which you knew first hand. There is the musical side. Perhaps you were acquainted with that, too, as music was the breath of life to him, and I hardly think you could have known him without knowing something of that.

"He was brought up in an atmosphere of music, his mother being a singer. She was trained for grand opera, but never had a career, marrying, instead, Farnsworth's dad, George Francis Wright, who was a graduate of Annapolis, and finding her career in bringing up a family of four children. Farnsworth told me she had a wonderful voice, and the most glorious trill of any singer he ever heard, and as a music critic, he heard many.

"Farnsworth's father died when F. was four years old. About the only recollection he had of him was that he could take a sliver out of a little boy's finger without hurting him. His father was a civil engineer—had something to do with laying out the town of Santa Barbara, and the water works, but I would have to get such details from Paula, for I am not sure of my facts there.

"I do know that Mrs. Wright taught music and supported her family that way after Mr. Wright's death. Farnsworth's brother Fred was more than just a big brother to Farnsworth and to Raymond, who was two years younger than Farnsworth.

"Fred was the most wonderful fellow Farnsworth ever knew. He must have been. I know he wrote wonderful letters to me and Farnsworth. I felt that I knew him, although I never met him. He took his father's place in the family and helped with all his youthful might to eke out the family income. He was the most unselfish and kindest of brothers, and he had that same rare sense of humor that Farnsworth had. His letters were often in rhyme, and he was a good story teller too. Fred put himself through Stanford University and graduated in Herbert Hoover's class. He helped Farnsworth through college—I think he probably helped Raymond, although I don't know that. One of the first things Farnsworth did was to pay Fred back, after he got his first job as a reporter in Chicago in 1915.

"Farnsworth was devoted to his mother. They were very close to each other. I have a lovely poem he wrote to her for a birthday present when he was a student in the University of Washington, and she was out in Manila with Fred and Raymond. Fred was surveying there for the U.S. Army, and Raymond was attending the University of the Phillipines. Mrs. Wright died out there. The cablegram was a terrible blow to Farnsworth. He told me he was going home to the dormitory through the woods on the corner of our campus and that he felt his mother's presence so strongly that he called out to her, 'Mother!'

"When he got to the dorm there was the cablegram. It was Christmas vacation and the dormitory was practically deserted, and Farnsworth was awfully alone and grief stricken. I wish I could have known him that Christmas as I knew him so many years later, to have comforted him when he needed comforting so much.

"Farnsworth and I always wished we had fallen in love when we were in college, instead of fifteen years later, but we didn't know each other very well then. He was well known and very active on the campus, and I always knew who Farnsworth Wright was, but I was a campus nobody, and only had a nodding acquaintence with him. He went with a friend of mine, a *little* girl who could walk under his arm—so I *heard* lots about him!"

I am sure that all the friends of the Wrights have often echoed that wish of Farnsworth and his wife. Farnsworth's life, full and rich as it was, was not really rounded out until he had a home instead of a bachelor apartment. Unlike so many men who are noted for kindness toward friends, his thoughtfulness reached its peak in his home, and toward his family, Marjorie and their son, Robert. Nor was this a front put on for the benefit of a guest; the man was too straightforward and sincere to stage an act for anyone.

As an old friend and "visiting fireman," when I dropped in from New Orleans to see Farnsworth in Chicago, my welcome was certainly to be taken for granted, either as house guest or dinner guest. Yet Farnsworth would never think of inviting me without phoning Marjorie; not so much to inquire whether my presence was acceptable, or even to give her fair warning that a third plate was in order, but rather, as a courteous gesture to the mistress of the house.

And that consideration was mutual. No one ever tried to decide which of the two Marjorie mothered the most, young Bobbie, or Farnsworth, whose valiant efforts toward health had no chance of realization. A grim fight, but a gallant heart, and a smiling front. Wright must have known what his friends feared; he was too level-headed and realistic not to have been the first to know, yet he could not, would not admit the loss of ground. He kept on attacking. And I can not help but feel that his wife and son gave him added courage, for it was only spirit that kept him going, those last years of his life.

I was shocked, the last time I saw him, in the fall of 1933, after a two-year absence from Chicago. It took me some minutes to recover; and then, suddenly, the man's spirit took command, and I became unaware of the increasing palsy, the perceptible drag of one foot. He even convinced me he was recovering. Damn it, he always did! He wanted no sympathy. And I shall risk this statement: we were never *sorry* for Farnsworth Wright!

You can only be sorry for the weak, the beaten, the inferior; this man, *the man himself*, was strong, and when he could not sign a letter with one hand, I am sure he used both to do the job. His body was beaten, but *he* was not. Nor did he ever take those sour, temperamental turns that are so characteristic of chronic illness. His mind was generous and open as ever. Let me give an example:

More than a year previous, I had met H.P. Lovecraft in New Orleans, and we had, to celebrate the meeting, agreed to collaborate on a sequel to "The Silver Key," a Randolph Carter story. Lovecraft took my 6000 word draft and rewrote it, bodily, making a 14,000-worder which contained like two or three of my original lines. That is, it was really a Lovecraft story, and not a collaboration at all. This digression is relevant.

Farnsworth rejected it, and with sincere regret. He felt that it was too abstruse for popular consumption. Perhaps it was. I should say, rather, he had reason to hold that view. And when I saw him in the fall of 1933, some months after the rejection, I did not bring the matter up for discussion. After dinner, however, he or Marjorie did mention the "Gates of the Silver Key," and he asked me, "What do you think of the story? What do you think of its chances to appeal to our readers? There is no question as to its merits, as such, you understand. I like it, but I am afraid of it."

He had me on the spot. He expected me to be just and impartial and detached, simply because he himself had those qualities to such a great degree; doubtless he made his errors, and enough of them, but they were always honest errors. So I said, "You know the history of the yarn. You know while I am technically a collaborator, the work is actually Lovecraft's, I am really no more than the catalytic agent which set Lovecraft's fancy working and creating. On the other hand, I do have a stake in the sale, even though I had resolved to accept no more than 25% instead of a collaborator's usual 50%."

Marjorie quietly refereed the friendly duel. I sensed very quickly that she wanted him to gamble, and that she nevertheless hesitated to elbow into the management of his magazine. A nice example of consideration, for she was eminently qualified to offer an outright opinion. For my part, I hesitated to use my ally's influence against Farnsworth's qualms. The magazine was at an all-time low, and I did not wish him to publish something that he feared would not click.

He did his best to pin me down, in spite of my admitted interest in that 25% cut, and my interest in Lovecraft's affairs. I finally said, "Previous Lovecraft yarns have been, I believe, just as abstruse, and they were popular. The author is sensitive beyond the average. Unless you are very sure that this story will flop, unless the risk is really grave, why not publish it as *an investment in Lovecraft*? Such publication will stimulate him to further activity, whereas a rejection will put him on ice for perhaps a few years, perhaps forever. You say you like the story. Isn't that sufficient?

"If you were not sold on it, you'd not discuss it with me. Now that you've cornered me in spite of hell and high water, I can only say—publish it. At your own risk, for I'm not an editor, it is neither my skill nor my business to predict public reaction."

As I remember it, Marjorie edged the MS. into the accepted list. We changed the subject, but I felt that the yarn was in the bag. He had put me on the spot. As it turned out, the story was well received. Again, his first judgment had been correct, and only the savage twists of business, that and the previous year, had made him waver for a while.

Perhaps he never realized how thoroughly he had put me out on a limb, simply because he was, in matters of business, so uncompromisingly straightforward. In 1932, I came to Chicago, just a month after starting as a full-time writer. I showed him my first detective story. Otis Kline had arranged to have me meet Edwin Baird, editor of *Real Detective*. Farnsworth read the MS. then and there. He said, "I do not like this. It does not sound like you. Do as you please, but my advice is, do not show this to Edwin Baird, he simply can't buy such a story, and if he saw it, it might turn him against a better offering."

There was no hemming and hawing there! I may add that a board of "experts," who publish a writer's journal, and conduct a "training course," had a carbon copy of the story, and even while Farnsworth read the original, these splendid and learned chaps were dictating a "criticism"— they thought the story was pretty good.

Farnsworth was dead right. The yarn was a dud. He convinced me of that in just a few words, sharply directed at weak spots. As a recheck, I read it to a friend; the narrative literally put the poor girl to sleep! That confirmed Farnsworth's estimate. The only difference was that he resisted the soporific effect, and for once, read beyond page two of a dull MS.

He never soft-soaped his decisions. He wrote me once, long before I met him, "Sorry, but this isn't really a story, it's rather a fairy tale." And what he wrote to a stranger, he just as readily told an old friend, face to face. I accepted this as a compliment: he knew that I could take it.

Farnsworth had a peculiar skill in judging fiction. Some pieces he bought because they aroused his enthusiasm, thrilled him, made him whoop with glee; others he bought because of an intellectual conviction which told him that a substantial proportion of his readers would like such a story, whether he himself did or did not like it. This made for the diversity of *Weird Tales*.

Here is an extract from a letter which gives another man's view of Wright: "Your letter was the first word I had of Farnsworth's passing . . . having seen Farnsworth in New York as recently as October of last year, when he could no longer walk without assistance, I feel that I have a special right as well as a reason to repeat what is not often true: it must have come as a welcome relief to him. It solved an otherwise insoluble, unjust, and intolerable situation.

"Whoever writes our entrances and lines gave Farnsworth a more heroic exit than most of us will get these days. I, for one, would have blown my brains out years ago, had I been he; yet Farnsworth remained cheerful and even witty at the last gathering I attended in his home. But his was the only vivacity and laughter; the guests felt a saddened constraint. This is as close as I can come to conveying my feelings at this time."

I was in Denver, early in June 1940, and for the first time in years, I was alone and looking back, instead of being among friends and looking forward. Two novelettes, going toward completion concurrently, should have kept me too busy for backward looking, yet something—perhaps the mere fact of being alone in a strange city—made me sit down and address to Farnsworth a letter which I had for weeks been intending to write him. And among other things, I said, "I am thinking of those days, a long time ago, when you and I and others met in Chicago; and none of us will ever again be as young as we were then . . . "

Banal, of course; but it seems to me that that which stirs one's emotions usually is something trite as old friends, old times. There was much else, of course, which moved me to write then, instead of waiting for a lessening of fiction-writing pressure. For instance, a group of Farnsworth's friends, incensed at hearing that he had been relieved of command of the magazine he had virtually, if not actually, created, had started a campaign to boycott *Weird Tales*, as a gesture of indignation. I could not ignore the appeal, for it was sincere, and an expression of loyalty to a man who had helped and encouraged us all. Yet it struck me that, lacking details, we had hardly the right to make it difficult for Farnsworth's successor, who in all probability had not been in any way responsible for the change; and, moreover, it seemed to me that we could be more constructive if, instead of a boycott which could not help Farnsworth, we did what little we might to toward finding an opening for him, since writers inevitably pick up rumors, often accurate, of impending vacancies in editorial offices. Then, too, being sure that his talent would eventually find him a spot, I went on to suggest that we could help most by giving him first look at appropriate offerings, even though perhaps at a rate lower than our customary figure, thereby enabling him to prove to his employer or business associate that he did indeed have a following of specialists.

Having written in that vein to those who had asked me to join the boycott, I felt that regardless of pressure, I had to sit down and tell Farnsworth how I had replied; and I joined the boycott, I'd of course said nothing about it. It was an awkward topic, as you may well imagine, but, knowing how gossip spreads, I felt sure that Farnsworth would learn of the boycott, and would learn also that I had refused to take part—and so, it was important that he hear my motives directly, rather than by way of the grapevine telegraph.

But that letter became more than merely a matter of keeping the record straight; a curious and persistent nostalgia drove me on and on, and I was haunted by the none too striking idea that "none of us will ever be as young as we were then . . . "

Not having his address at hand, I sealed the envelope, to be mailed when I went back to my files at home. A few days later, three letters arrived, each telling me that Farnsworth Wright was dead. There was really not much impact in the second, and practically none in the third; the first had really rung the bell.

Worst of all, I knew that if I had mailed my message in time, he would have received it before he "achieved the fullness." And so, ever since that day, I have had an urge to tell of him, as I remember him, and before time blurs the image.

There is a peculiar fatality about these things I put off. Hurrying home from Mexico City to finish a book, I felt that I had not the time to detour to see Robert E. Howard, particularly as I had visited him en route to Mexico. Six months later, he died under tragic circumstances.

Then, H.P. Lovecraft: after a good many busy weeks, I finally got around to writing him, little suspecting that his failing health was the reason why his letters were ever further apart in their spacing. When I heard of his death, I sat there wondering if he had received and read the lines I might have written sooner.

And then, Farnsworth. So, one evening in the sandhills of New Mexico, in Jack Williamson's study, all these things came back with a rush, and I said, "Jack, this is getting me down. I never write these important things on time, the only deadlines I make are those that don't count! So, before I forget, before the memory of these men becomes blurred, I am going to tell about them, their sayings and their ways, and I am calling it "Book of the Dead."

Thank God, Marjorie Wright and Paul Cook kicked and prodded me into it, or Chapter I would still be unwritten!

For nearly nineteen years, I have sold fiction, and for nearly eleven, writing has been my profession; and while Farnsworth Wright was not, by fully a week, the first editor to buy my work, he was the first to encourage me. And I am only one of a large crop.

A man is known best by his work, and his life is best measured, not by his years, but by the fire he has kindled in the memories of those he had influenced; so that, for all these reports of his death in New York, he still lives. Those beginners he discovered nearly twenty years ago have, many of them, justified him as well as themselves. Wright's magazine never had more than a narrow circulation, and Wright himself had a correspondingly narrow fame, as numbers go; but his one-time beginners cover today's newsstands.

I remember how Robert Carr, suddenly rich from the sale of his first novel, leased a needlessly expensive apartment, and, realizing his error, sought to move out. But this was not to be accomplished so readily. Legal sharks may point out that a minor—Bob was around eighteen at the time—could not be held to a contract, though it is possible that in the case of subsistence or quarters, a minor's agreement is legally binding. Let's skip the details. The point was that Bob's boyish enthusiasm had led him into a deal from which he deserved a quick escape.

Farnsworth pondered for a moment. "Come with me, and say nothing, just stand there."

In those days, Bob was very young, and round-faced, and wide-eyed, and not as self-possessed as he is today. The manager of the apartment, loaded for bear, decided there would be no lease breaking that day, and nailed Bob with a stern look. But Farnsworth was not impressed.

Farnsworth, tall and solemn-faced and soft-voiced, waited for Bob to fidget and gape and gulp and look owlish. Then he said, in what was apparently yet not actually designed to elude Bob's ear, "Now, I realize your position. But you must not be disturbed. I am his. . .er. . .*guardian*. He really does not wish to break the lease. That was merely a whimsy . . . he is . . . ah . . . flighty, but really . . . harmless."

The manager's eyes lost their coldness and hostility, and he became uneasy. Bob, hearing all, and catching the full implication, began to squirm and fidget in earnest! It takes a lot of poise to stand unmoved and hear one's self described as "harmless."

The manager asked in a stage whisper, "You mean—you are *that* sort of guardian?"

"Now, you must not worry. I assure you he never causes trouble. All that you have to do is tactfully ignore his . . . peculiarities . . . he merely accosts strangers and asks them silly questions."

Bob in those days did have a habit of "gathering story material" by the simple process of cross-examining any person who looked like a good prospect. Farnsworth's solemn expression, and the implications of voice and gesture, made Bob's practice seem real dynamite. The manager said, "See here, Mr. Wright—you get him out at once, do you understand? We can not have morons wandering around the place, lease or no lease!"

Farnsworth sighed and sadly shook his head. He took Bob by the arm, and by now, Bob's embarassment had made him look as if Farnsworth had been guilty of understatement.

These things, to me, are more important than his editorial or literary influence; and I call my task complete only if I have made you see and know the Farnsworth Wright I knew.

There have been, and will be other fellowships: but none quite like that one which centered about Farnsworth Wright. This, of course, may be true because none of us will ever again be as young as we were then. Or it may be all the more true because, more seasoned, we could better appreciate him today than we did then.

3 Why Weird Tales?

This editorial was published in the Anniversary issue of 1924 and was reprinted in 1934. Unsigned, Otis Adelbert Kline later claimed authorship of the piece. No matter who the author was, the editorial was a firm statement of the policies followed by *Weird Tales* throughout its entire existence.

Up to the day the first issue of *Weird Tales* was placed on the stands, stories of the sort you read between these covers each month were taboo in the publishing world. Each magazine had its fixed policy. Some catered to mixed classes of readers, most specialized in certain types of stories, but all agreed in excluding the genuinely weird stories. The greatest weird story and one of the greatest short stories ever written, *The Murders in the Rue Morgue*, would not have stood the ghost of a show in any modern editorial office previous to the launching of *Weird Tales*. Had Edgar Allan Poe produced that masterpiece in this generation he would have searched in vain for a publisher before the advent of this magazine.

And so every issue of this magazine fulfills its mission, printing the kind of stories you like to read—stories which you have no opportunity of reading in other periodicals because of their orthodox editorial policies.

We make no pretension of publishing, or even trying to publish, a magazine that will please everybody. What we have done, and will continue to do, is to gather around us an ever-increasing body of readers who appreciate the weird, the bizarre, the unusual—who recognize true art in fiction.

The writing of the common run of stories today has, unfortunately for American literature, taken on the character of an exact science. Such stories are entirely mechanical, conforming to fixed rules. A good analogy might be found in the music of the electric piano. It is technically perfect, mechanically true, but lacking in expression. As is the case with any art when mechanics is permitted to dominate, the soul of the story is crushed—suffocated beneath a weight of technique. True art—the expression of the soul—is lacking.

The types of stories we have published, and will continue to publish, may be placed under two classifications. The first of these is the story of psychic phenomena or the occult story. These stories are written from three viewpoints: The viewpoint of the spiritualist who believes that such phenomena are produced by spirits of the departed; the scientist, who believes thay are either the result of fraud, or may be explained by known, little-known or perhaps unknown phases of natural law; and the neutral investigator, who simply records the facts, lets them speak for themselves, and holds no brief for either side.

The second classification might be termed "highly imaginative stories." These are stories of advancement in the sciences and the arts to which the generation of the writer who creates them has not attained. All writers of such stories are prophets, and in the years to come, many of these prophecies will come true.

There are a few people who sniff at such stories. They delude themselves with the statement that they are too practical to read such stuff. We can not please such readers, nor do we aim to do so. A man for whom this generation has found no equal in his particular field of investagation, none other than the illustrious Huxley, wrote a suitable answer for them long ago. He said: "Those who refuse to go beyond fact rarely get as far as fact."

Writers of highly imaginative fiction have, in times past, drawn back the veil of centuries, allowing their readers to look at the wonders of the present. True, these visions were often distorted, as by a mirror with a curved surface, but just as truly were they actual reflections of the present. It is the mission of *Weird Tales* to find present-day writers who have this faculty, so that our readers may glimpse the future—may be vouchsafed visions of the wonders that are to come.

Looking back over the vast sea of literature that has been produced since man began to record his thoughts, we find two types predominating—two types that have lived up to the present and will live on into the future: the weird story and the highly imaginative story. The greatest writers of history have been at their best when producing such stories: Homer, Shakespeare, Milton, Dante, Irving, Hawthorne, Poe, Verne, Dickens, Maeterlinck, Doyle, Wells, and scores of other lesser lights. Their weird and highly imaginative stories will live for ever.

Shakespeare gave forceful expression to the creed of writers of the weird and highly imaginative, when he wrote the oft-quoted saying: "There are more things in Heaven and Earth, Horatio, than are dreamt of in your philosophy."

The writer of the highly imaginative story intuitively knows of the existence of these things, and endeavors to search them out. He has an unquenchable thirst for knowledge. He is at once the scientist, the philosopher, and the poet. He evolves fancies from known facts, and new and startling facts are in turn evolved from the fancies. For him, in truth, as for no other less gifted, "Stone walls do not a prison make." His ship of imagination will carry him the four thousand miles to the center of the earth, *Twenty Thousand Leagues Under the Sea*, on a journey to another planet millions of miles distant, or on a trip through the universe, measured only in millions of light-years, with equal facility. Material obstacles can not stay his progress. He laughs at those two bogies which have plagued mankind from time immemorial, time and space: things without beginning and without end, which man is vainly trying to measure; things that have neither length, breadth nor thickness, yet to which men would ascribe definite limits.

To the imaginative writer, the upper reaches of the ether, the outer limits of the galactic ring, the great void that gapes beyond, and the infinity of universes that may, for all we know, lie still further on, are as accessible as his own garden. He flies to them in the ship of his imagination in less time than it takes a bee to flit from one flower to another on the same spike of a delphinium.

Some of the stories now being published in *Weird Tales* will live forever. Men, in the progressive ages to come, will wonder how it was possible that writers of the crude and uncivilized age known as the Twentieth Century could have had foreknowledge of the things that will have, by that time, come to pass. They will marvel, as they marvel even now at the writings of Poe and Verne.

It has always been the human desire to experience new emotions and sensations without actual danger. A tale of horror is told for its own sake, and becomes an end in itself. It is appreciated most by those who are secure from peril.

Using the term in a wide sense, horror stories probably began with the magnificent story of the *Writing on the Wall at Belshazzar's Feast*. Following this were the *Book of Job*, the legends of the *Deluge* and the *Tower of Babel*, and *Saul's Visit to the Woman of Endor*. Byron once said the latter was the best ghost story ever written.

The ancient Hebrews used the element of fear in their writings to spur their heroes to superhuman power or to instill a moral truth. The sun stands still in the heavens that Joshua may prevail over his enemies.

The beginning of the English novel during the middle of the Eighteenth Century brought to light Fielding, Smollett, Sterne and several others. Since this time terror has never ceased to be used as a motive in fiction. This period marked the end of the Gothic romance whose primary appeal was to women readers. Situations fraught with terror are frequent in *Jane Eyre*. The Brontes, however, never used the supernatural element to increase tension. Theirs are the terrors of actual life. Wilkie Collins wove elaborate plots of hair-raising events. Bram Stoker, Richard Marsh and Sax Rohmer do likewise. Conan Doyle realized that darkness and loneliness place us at the mercy of terror and he worked artfully on our fear of the unknown. The works of Rider Haggard combine strangeness, wonder, mystery and horror, as do those of Verne, Hichens, Blackwood, Conrad, and others.

Charles Brockden Brown was the first American novelist to introduce supernatural occurrences and then trace them to natural causes. Like Mrs. Radcliffe, he was at the mercy of a conscience which forbade him to introduce specters in which he himself did not believe. Brown was deeply interested in morbid psychology and he took delight in tracing the working of the brain in times of emotional stress. His best works are *Edgar Huntly*, *Wieland* and *Ormond*.

The group of "Strange Stories by a Nervous Gentleman" in *Tales of a Traveler* proves that Washington Irving was well versed in ghostly lore. He was wont to summon ghosts and spirits at will but could not refrain from receiving them in a jocose, irreverent mood. However, in the *Story of the German Student* he strikes a note of real horror.

Hawthorne was not a man of morose and gloomy temper. An irresistible impulse drove him toward the somber and gloomy. In his notebook he says: "I used to think that I could imagine all the passions, all the feelings and states of the heart and mind, but how little did I know! Indeed, we are but shadows, we are not endowed with real life, but all that seems most real about us is but the thinnest shadow of a dream--till the heart be touched."

The weird story of *The Hollow of the Three Hills*, the gloomy legend of *Ethan Brand* and the ghostly *White Old Maid* are typical of Hawthorne's mastery of the bizarre. His introduction of witches into *The Scarlet Letter* and of mesmerism into *The Blithedale Romance* shows that he was preoccupied with the terrors of magic and of the invisible world.

Hawthorne was concerned with mournful reflections, not frightful events. The mystery of death, not its terror, fascinated him. He never startled you with physical horror, save possibly in *The House of the Seven Gables*. With grim and bitter irony Hawthorne mocks and taunts the dead body of Judge Jaffery Pyncheon until the ghostly pageantry of the dead Pyncheons—including at last Judge Jaffery himself with the fatal crimson stain on his neckcloth—fades away with the coming of daylight.

Edgar Allan Poe was penetrating the trackless regions of

terror while Hawthorne was toying with spectral forms and "dark ideas." Where Hawthorne would have shrunk back, repelled and disgusted, Poe, wildly exhilarated by the anticipation of a new and excruciating thrill, forced his way onward. Both Poe and Hawthorne were fascinated by the thought of death. The hemlock and cypress overshadowed Poe night and day and he describes death accompanied by its direst physical and mental agonies. Hawthorne wrote with finished perfection, unerringly choosing the right word; Poe experimented with language, painfully acquiring a studied form of expression which was remarkably effective at times. In his *Mask of the Red Death* we are forcibly impressed with the skillful arrangement of words, the alternation of long and short sentences, the use of repetition, and the deliberate choice of epithets.

But enough of Poe. His works are immortal and stand today as the most widely read of any American author. The publishers of *Weird Tales* hope they will be instrumental in discovering or uncovering some American writer who will leave to posterity what Poe and Hawthorne have bequeathed to the present generation. Perhaps in the last year we have been instrumental in furnishing an outlet to writers whose works would not find a ready market in the usual channels. The reception accorded us has been cordial and we feel that we will survive. We dislike to predict the future of the horror story. We believe its powers are not yet exhausted. The advance of science proves this. It will lead us into unexplored labyrinths of terror, and the human desire to experience new emotions will always be with us.

Doctor Frank Crane says: "What I write is my tombstone." And again—"As for me, let my bones and flesh be burned, and the ashes dropped in the moving waters, and if my name shall live at all, let it be found among books, the only garden of forget-me-nots, the only human device for perpetuating this personality."

So *Weird Tales* has endeavored from its inception, and will endeavor in the future, to find and publish those stories that will make their writers immortal. It will play its humble but necessary part in perpetuating those personalities that are worthy to be crowned as immortals.

4
The Stories

1. The Baird Issues

Lunatics and compulsive writers filled the pages of the first thirteen issues of *Weird Tales*—those edited by Edwin Baird. That is not to say that the writers for the magazine fell into these two categories but that of the more than two hundred stories published during this period, a majority of the notable ones were told by inmates of asylums or transcribed in a diary.

Baird, as editor of "The Unique Magazine," evidenced several major faults which hindered the growth of the pulp under his rule. As *Weird Tales* was a new type of magazine, there was no basic pattern established as to its contents or format. Baird relied heavily on traditional type material of the ghost story variety. Very short stories were the rule. Even serial novels were quite short. Many of the stories published in the first year of *Weird Tales'* existence would have benefited from a strong blue pencil policy. Fortunately, with change of publisher and format, Farnsworth Wright assumed editorial control and the magazine began a swift ascent in quality. Wright, at first, was hesitant of major changes in story type, but as the readership made its wishes known, he acted in accordance to modernize his contents. The Baird issues, however, cannot be dismissed as not having quality material in them. It was just that the percentage of such stories was dismally small.

The cover story for the first issue of *Weird Tales* was "Ooze" by Anthony Rud, Jr (1893-1942). Born in Chicago, Rud was a Dartmouth graduate who turned to writing. He was a prolific adventure writer who contributed to numerous magazines. Later in life, he served as editor for *Adventure* and *Detective Story Magazine*.

"Ooze" was a combination of the lunatic and the diary motifs. The hero goes to the deep South to investigate the death of a close friend, the man's wife, and the man's father. We soon learn that the father was a famous scientist who disappeared soon after the son and daughter-in-law vanished. Through a series of clever clues, the hero learns how a practical joke backfired and all three were absorbed by a giant amoeba. The diary of the scientist father forms an integral part of the novelet (as well as spelling out all the unusual clues for those who could not follow the plot).

Less notable in the same issue was "The Dead Man's Tale" by W.E. Hawkins. Instead of a diary, the story was told by Automatic Writing. The tale was an overly sentimental muddle of how a dead man tried to kill his former sweetheart so that they could be together again in death. Just in time, he realized his mistake and managed to save the woman's marriage as well as her life.

Otis Adelbert Kline (1891 1946) was present in the first issue with his first professional sale, "The Thing of a Thousand Shapes," which was serialized in two parts. Kline did not start writing until almost thirty and his best work was not published until years later, mostly in *Argosy*. Kline was a robust character with a taste for exotic foods and wine. He enjoyed the outdoor life and was one of the few writers for the pulps who actually knew something about swordfighting. He later became a literary agent for a number of the *Weird Tales* circle.

His first story was less than exceptional. It did set the pattern for serials in the magazine's future. It was more science fiction than fantasy; it was quite short, not much more than a long novelet; and it was mediocre. *Weird Tales* was not noted for its fine serials.

The second issue of the pulp featured two exceptional stories. One was told by a lunatic, the other transcribed in a diary.

The lunatic story was "A Square of Canvas," again by Anthony Rud. The tale was told many times before and has been told many times since but never with as much intensity or credulity. A visitor to an asylum comes across an old man in a garden and he proceeds to tell her how he came to be in the place. Once a famous painter, the narrator describes how he was only able to paint when inspired by the death of something he loved. The horror of the story was accentuated by the matter-of-fact declarations of the madman. The final revelation of his "supreme masterpiece" was both unexpected and wholly logical.

Henry Hasse, a long-time *Weird Tales* fan, sent to The Eyrie in 1934 his list of the best stories for the first year of

Weird Tales. His pick for the best "madness" story was "A Square of Canvas." Many years later, Hasse used much the same formula with completely different setting for the very effective, "The Violin String," published in *Fantastic.*

Equally as good as the Rud story was "Beyond the Door" by Paul Suter. First anthologized in CREEPS BY NIGHT in 1931, the Suter story was reprinted many times in anthologies since. While it suffered from excess padding and an ending much too long, the story was a shuddery ghost story with a punch. The bulk of the story was in the form of a diary, read by the nephew of a man who died under strange circumstances. Again we had a tale of mounting horror as the writer of the diary tried to fight the inexorable urge that pulled him to the cellar of his house where he had buried a girl he had driven to suicide. Suter wrote a number of other stories for *Weird Tales* but he was never again able to equal the power of his first work.

More typical of the contents of the early issues was "Six Feet of Willow Green" by C. Michener, also in the second issue. This was a pointless short story of an American in Asia and his involvement with a Chinaman and his snake, the six feet of willow green referred to in the title.

With its third issue, *Weird Tales* changed to large bed-sheet size. Unfortunately, the change in size did not signal a change in quality. Lead story for the issue was "The Moon Terror" by A.G. Birch, the first part of a two-part serial. "The Moon Terror" was a typical Chinese menace adventure novel of the period. A group of mysterious Asian wizards threaten to destroy the Earth through use of gigantic earthquakes. A heroic scientist and his friend, with the aid of the United States Navy, defeat the menace. There was a great deal of exclamation points and wild action in every chapter. The novel was extremely popular and the third issue was one of the few that sold out soon after publication. Prompted by the success of "The Moon Terror," Popular Fiction brought the novel out in hardcover in 1927. Even at a low price, the book did not sell; it lingered on in stock until the late 1940's, often being offered free with any subscription to the magazine.

In the same number was "Jungle Beasts" by William Barron. The story was a diary of a lunatic describing his battle with a sacred cat from Tibet. Much better, though also in the form of a diary, was "The Floor Above" by M.L. Humphreys.

The writer received a note from an old friend not seen in ten years. The friend wrote, "I'm afraid I'm in a bad way." The hero goes to the friend and discovers that a bad way was the mildest form of description. His friend had not left his home in ten years and seemed to be in a drugged, almost comatose state. The story had a fine building of horror up to its conclusion with the narrator finding the rotted corpse of his friend, dead for ten years, bent over a table, with a note beginning, "I'm afraid I'm in a bad way." H.P. Lovecraft thought highly of the story, the only one by Humphreys ever to appear in "The Unique Magazine."

Also notable in the third issue was "Penelope," a short whimsical tale by Vincent Starrett. But for every good story in these early issues there were dozens of terrible ones like "Two Hours of Death," "The Man the Law Forgot," or "The Two Men Who Murdered Each Other."

"The Gray Death" by L.B. Sugarman made the June

20

Otis Adelbert Kline

Seabury Quinn

1923 issue readable. A tale of fungus that devoured everything alive that it touched, the mood was properly set early in the story when the main character stated, "The light makes it hard to talk—of unbelievable things. One needs the darkness to hear of hell."

Otis Adelbert Kline was present in the fourth, fifth and sixth issues of *Weird Tales* with three minor works, the best being "The Cup of Blood" in which the truth about a haunted castle was discovered by two American adventurers.

The October 1923 issue of *Weird Tales* was a historic one. It featured the first appearance of three authors all who were to become top names in the fantastic fiction field. Seabury Quinn, already a veteran pulp author, was present with a story and an article. "The Phantom Farmhouse" was a fine tale of werewolves which was reprinted several times since its original appearance. His article on Bluebeard was first of a series of articles published under the heading of "Weird Crimes."

Quinn (1889-1969) was born in Washington, D.C. His full name was Seabury Grandin Quinn. He was named after Archbishop Seabury, the first bishop of the Protestant Episcopal Church in the United States, and a direct ancestor of Quinn. His middle name served as the inspiration for his most famous creation, Jules de Grandin. Quinn graduated from the National University Law School and practiced law from 1911 through 1918. Later in his life he edited *Casket and Sunnyside*, a trade journal for morticians. However, for most of his life, Quinn earned his living as a pulp magazine writer. Without a doubt, he was the most popular writer ever to work for *Weird Tales*.

The second author to make his debut in the October issue was Howard Phillips Lovecraft (1890-1937). Lovecraft was born and raised in Providence, Rhode Island, where he spent most of his life except for a few years living in New York City. He was a protected child raised by two aunts, and was in poor health much of his life. A solitary person, he was an omniverous reader and great letter writer. Early in life, he became involved in amateur press work and it was this work that brought him to the attention of J.C. Henneberger, the owner of *Weird Tales*. His first story for "The Unique Magazine" was "Dagon."

Lovecraft, urged by Henneberger, submitted five stories to *Weird Tales*. All were handwritten and thus rejected by Baird. However, Baird did state that he liked the stories and that they should be resubmitted when typed. All were bought. Lovecraft mentioned in one of his letters that Baird actively solicited stories and was enthusiastic about his work. However, J.C. Henneberger stated that Baird did not care for Lovecraft's work but that he, Henneberger, made sure that all of Lovecraft's material was bought and published. Unfortunately, as both Baird and Henneberger are dead, the exact truth of this contradiction will never be known.

Frank Owen was the third popular author to make his debut in that memorable issue of *Weird Tales*. Owen was represented with a very minor story, "The Man Who Owned the World." Within a short time, Owen, who never visited the Orient, would achieve reader acclaim with his tales of China and the Far East.

"Lucifer" by John Swain was a powerful story in the November 1923 issue. Told in a matter-of-fact way, it was a

H.P. Lovecraft

tale of a man whose son was born with a club-foot. The man made a deal with a cult of devil worshippers to cure his son's affliction. A very ordinary seeming man came to the boy's house and leaves after being alone with the child for a short time. To the astonishment of all, the boy's club-foot has been cured. The only problem was that the boy was dead.

There was no December 1923 issue. The next issue was dated January 1924 but the magazine continued to be monthly. Top honors in the issue went to Lovecraft with "The Picture in the House," a story of cannibalism that possessed no actual fantastic element. The same issue saw publication of several pieces of poetry. In July 1923, two short poems by Clark Ashton Smith were published. However, they seemed more the exception than the rule. With 1924, poetry became a part of *Weird Tales*. For the rest of its history, the magazine would regularly feature poetry by all of the greats in fantastic fiction.

The dread NECRONOMICON was introduced the next month in Lovecraft's story, "The Hound," in which a pair of grave robbers get more than they bargained for when they rob the grave of a wizard, stealing a sacred amulet.

Harry Houdini, the famous magician and escape artist, had expressed interest in *Weird Tales* from the very start of the magazine. His first story for "The Unique Magazine" was a two-part serial, "The Spirit Fakers of Hermannstadt," which started in the March 1924 issue. However, Houdini could not compete with the Lovecraft story in the same issue. "The Rats in the Walls" was one of HPL's most powerful tales. Back again was the madman, telling his story from the confines of an asylum. A powerful story of degeneracy and cannibalism, the novelette reached an unbelievable climax of horror. It was Lovecraft at his best.

Lovecraft and Houdini were both back in the next issue of *Weird Tales*. Houdini had a department, "Ask Houdini," and Lovecraft was present with "The White Ape," later reprinted under the title, "Arthur Jermyn."

The last issue printed by the Rural Publications, Inc. was the first Anniversary issue, really three issues combined in one, dated May-June-July 1924. However, the issue was not under the editorial guidance of Edwin Baird. In a letter to Dr. I.M. Howard, Otis Adelbert Kline, a reader for *Weird Tales* along with Farnsworth Wright, claimed editorial responsibility for that issue. Baird was already gone in a shakeup of the magazine and its staff. While Kline probably did write the editorial published in that issue, "Why *Weird Tales*?," it was doubtful that he had complete editorial freedom. Stories were obviously from those already bought under Baird's reign and the assembling of the issue was not the same thing as actual editing.

The issue did feature several fine stories. Lovecraft was present with two pieces of fiction. One was the cover story, "Imprisoned With the Pharoahs," ghost written for Houdini, a rather silly story about Houdini's adventures in Egypt. However, the story behind the story was extremely interesting, as stated by J.C. Henneberger:

> Not long after I had inaugurated *Weird Tales*, I had a call by Houdini at my Chicago office; he expressed more than usual enthusiasm for the magazine and the meeting resulted in a friendship lasting until his untimely death a few years later. He often regaled me with experiences of his that rivaled anything I had ever read in books. Several of these I published but they were written in such a prosaic style that they evoked little comment.

> However, one day he unfolded one astounding story of a trip to Egypt that I knew only a Lovecraft . . . could do justice to. Lovecraft did a masterful job on the outline and details I sent him but asked not to have his name associated with publication.

Adding to the above story was the fact that Lovecraft wrote the story shortly before his marriage to Sonia Greene. In best slapstick fashion, HPL managed to lose the manuscript and to meet his deadline, the story was rewritten on his wedding night, with Sonia doing the typing.

In the same issue was "Hypnos," one of Lovecraft's more minor stories, revealing mainly his interest in ancient Greece and Greek mythology. Lovecraft also had a good deal to do with another story in that issue. C.M. Eddy, Jr. was a friend of Lovecraft who had contributed several stories to the early issues of *Weird Tales*. His tale, "The Loved Dead," received some rewrite help from Lovecraft.

C.M. Eddy, Jr. (1896-1967) and his wife Muriel Eddy were good friends with HPL from 1923 on. Eddy was primarily a songwriter but also did some writing in the detective and weird fields, as well as some ghost writing for Houdini. He was working with Lovecraft on "The Cancer of Superstition" for Houdini when the magician met his tragic end. Eddy also worked as a proofreader for Oxford Press and a theatrical agent. He served as the President of the Rhode Island Writer's Guild. All of his stories were overwritten and minor, but "The Loved Dead" did manage to create a furor.

"The Loved Dead" was a wild piece of purple prose which graphically described the feelings of a maniac who thrived on death. The story contained one mention of necophilia. Cannibalism was acceptable but unnatural sex was not. Eddy claimed that Citizen's Groups in several cities had the magazine removed from the stands (though a diligent search by the Editor has not been able to find any evidence of such removals). Eddy further claimed that the resulting publicity gave *Weird Tales* a necessary boost which kept the magazine alive. However, statements on the financial troubles of the magazine during this period by J.C. Henneberger and Otis Adelbert Kline, among others, belied this statement.

"The Loved Dead" ended with the narrator in a graveyard writing down (as always) his own story with a howling mob on his trail. It concluded with the immortal line of purple prose so often used since, "I can - write - no - more . . . "

Otis Adelbert Kline was present with a minor science fiction story, "The Malignant Entity," which was unique in one respect. When *Amazing Stories* began two years later, the Kline story was reprinted in the June 1926 issue.

"The Sunken Land" was the contribution of G.W. Bayly. It was an interesting adventure in a living forest in the wilds of Canada. Along with several other stories from the early issues of *Weird Tales*, it was reprinted in BEWARE AFTER DARK, edited by T.E. Harre, published in 1929.

A very minor story, "Tea Leaves" made little impression on readers of the Anniversary issue. However, its author, Henry H. Whitehead (1882-1932) soon became a favorite with *Weird Tales* readers.

Whitehead was born in Elizabeth, New Jersey. He attended Harvard where he was a classmate of Franklin D. Roosevelt. He later received his Doctorate degree. In 1912, he graduated the Berkley Divinity School and was ordained a deacon of the Episcopal Church. By this time, he had already begun writing, and he appeared with stories in numerous pulps until his premature death. He served as Acting Archdeacon in the Virgin Islands for much of his later life.

Henry S. Whitehead

This West Indies background served to make his weird fiction set in that part of the world eminently believable as well as extremely entertaining. His obituary in *Weird Tales* was written by his good friend, H.P. Lovecraft.

The Anniversary issue was the last gasp of a dying magazine. Four months later, *Weird Tales* was back. Except for the title, it could have been a new publication. The publisher was different, the size was different, and the first reader, Farnsworth Wright, was now editor. Changes in material within was slow in coming for several reasons, but come they did. The magazine was laboring under heavy debts as well as a backlog of stories from the Baird reign. But changes were in the making.

2. The Wright Issues

The first issue of *Weird Tales* printed by the Popular Fiction Publishing Company was dated November 1924. The editor was Farnsworth Wright. The main difference between this issue and those preceding it was the size of the magazine—it was back to the original size of 6x9—and the cover was by a new artist, Andrew Brosnatch. The contents, which listed twenty-one stories, were of the same low quality as published in the Baird issues. Two new names were present, though, each to become an important cog in the revival of *Weird Tales*. Frank Belknap Long (1903-   ) was a young friend of Lovecraft who was urged by HPL to submit work to "The Unique Magazine." His first tale was

Greye LaSpina

a minor one, but within a short time, Long would be one of the most able contributors to the publication.

The second writer new to *Weird Tales* was an authoress. Greye La Spina (1880-1969), soon to become one of the most popular writers for *Weird Tales*, made her debut with "The Tortoise Shell Cat," a story of voodoo.

Greye La Spina was born Fanny Greye Bragg in Wakefield, Massachusetts. She won several writing prizes and this work later encouraged her to try her hand at professional writing. In 1918, she submitted her first story, "Wolf of the Steppes," to *Popular Magazine*. The story was accepted but instead of appearing in *Popular* was the cover story for the first issue of the legendary publication, *The Thrill Book*. She continued to sell to that magazine until it folded. At the same time, she was probably the first woman newspaper photographer in New York and later was an office manager long before women's lib made itself known.

She was married twice. Ralph Geissler was her first husband and a daughter was born in 1900 from this marriage. Mr. Geissler died in 1901. In 1910, she remarried, to Robert La Spina, who left behind him in Italy his title, the Baron di Savuto.

Also present in the same issue with these two important contributors were stories by Whitehead, Kline and Quinn. And, another author made his debut, though no one realized it as such. E. Critchie was the name of the author of "Thus Spake the Prophetess." Hidden behind that pseudonym was Arthur J. Burks, an ex-Marine who was to become one of the giants of the pulp era.

Frank Belknap Long's next contribution to "The Unique Magazine" was the cover story of the next issue. "Death Waters" was a gruesome tale of revenge taking place in the Amazon. The issue featured the first half of a two-part serial, "The Valley of Teeheemen," by Arthur Thatcher, one of four novels he did for the magazine, all about lost tribes of Incas, all equally terrible.

1925 was the first full year of Wright-edited *Weird Tales*. During that span of time a few changes became apparent. For one thing, the number of stories per issue began to drop (though the actual number was not greatly reduced until a year later). Also, a group of regulars began to make itself known. Wright developed this cadre through encouragement and creative criticism, as well as cash bonuses. One of the major faults of the Baird issues was that many of the authors who contributed good stories, such as Humphreys and Sugarman, only had one story published in the magazine. Wright knew the value to his publication of establishing regular favorites.

"Invaders from Outside" by J. Schlossel was the lead story for the January 1925 issue. It was a science fiction story of little note, one of several that Schlossel did for the magazine. As this was still a year before the advent of *Amazing Stories* such stories of pseudo-science had a large following among the readers of the magazine. Schlossel later became a popular contributor to the early science fiction pulps.

E. Hoffmann Price (1899-   ) made his debut in this issue with a short short story, "The Rajah's Gift." Price, who was to later work for a short spell as a member of the editorial staff of *Weird Tales*, was a West Point graduate and ex-soldier. In the early 1920's, while living in Newark, New

E. Hoffmann Price

Frank Belknap Long

Jersey, he decided to try his hand at writing after learning that a girl he knew was selling regularly to the pulps. His first sale was to *Droll Stories*, his second was "The Rajah's Gift." However, after these first two sales, little else was bought. The advice of his landlady, while he was working in Atlanta, put him on the right track. She pointed out that he was successful in his work with Union Carbide because he knew his work. Perhaps he would be successful as a writer if he knew more about his work in that field as well. Price haunted the library, reading everything he could on writing technique. Within a short time, he was selling everything he wrote.

The same issue also contained Lovecraft's "The Festival" and Frank Belknap Long's third appearance in a row. Arthur J. Burks (1898-1974) finally made print with a story under his own name.

Burks received his commission in the Marines in 1921. He served in the Corps for 11 years and was aide-de-camp to General S.D. Butler. He traveled widely both during his stay in the Marines and afterwards, going to most South American and Central American countries. His own favorite nation was Santo Domingo, where many of his early stories were set. Burks became a prolific pulp writer after his first work was published in *Weird Tales* and sold in all fields during his pulp days.

With all of these major stories and writers, it was Henry Whitehead who had the best story in the issue with "The Fireplace." A traveler takes a room in a hotel with a large fireplace. In the room, the traveler meets a very gentlemanly ghost who relates how he was killed by four villains who then cremated his body in the fireplace. The traveler is asked by the ghost to pursue the four and bring them to justice. The man agrees to do so and leaves the next morning. Unfortunately, the traveler soon forgets the promise. Years later, he returns to the same hotel and is given the same room. The next morning, he is found strangled at the foot of the fireplace. The story was told in a lively manner and with the right dash of sardonic humor to make it a minor masterpiece.

Lovecraft was present again in the next issue with the brief but entertaining "The Statement of Randolph Carter." However, more important was "Whispering Tunnels" by Stephen Bagby, the cover story for that issue. A less-than-inspired ghost story, the tale was very popular with readers and for a number of years was ranked the second most popular story ever to be published by "The Unique Magazine." Bagby was an infrequent contributor to *Weird Tales*, with only three stories published. The main problem still with the magazine was the number of stories in each issue. With 22 stories in 144 pages, no development of plot or character could take place.

Thatcher returned with another Mayan serial the next month. The debut in that issue was a young author who had just moved to Chicago. He was Robert Spencer Carr who became famous a few years later for his novel, RAMPANT AGE.

April featured a cover story by an author with a strange name and even stranger manner of writing. Nictzin Dyalhis' first story in *Weird Tales* was "When the Green Star Waned." This was a combination of an interplanetary story (with a Martian expedition to Earth) combined with an occult telling of the collapse of civilization from the battle between good and evil. The story is extremely dated now but it was the most popular story published in *Weird Tales* up to that time. The story continued to be listed as the most popular ever printed in *Weird Tales* and in 1933, writing for a fan magazine, Wright listed it as the most popular story, beating out tales by Lovecraft, Howard, Whitehead, and many others much better remembered today.

Nictzin Dyalhis (18?-1942) was an unusual man as well as a popular pulp author. He was a world traveler and adventurer but did not fit the standard mold of such men. Dyalhis was a short, small man with an unconquerable spirit. Of himself, he wrote in 1924:

> By profession, I am a chemist. In years, nearly fifty—in heart, about sixteen—my wife's mother says I've never grown up! One way she's quite right, for I am one of these sawed-off hammered-down, weazened-up runts weighing—when I'm fat-and-sassy—from five to ten pounds over one hundred.
>
> A long time ago I went to the Southwest. My intentions were good—I was going to assay all the ore west of the Rockies!
>
> Sure, I've done lots of other things since but—I went one trip snapper-fishing in the Gulf when only a kid-of-a-boy . . . I've signed out on more than one "tall water" cruise, but I invariably turned up missing before the return trip. Because why? Prospectin' was good somewheres up-country! . . . Did I ever strike it rich? I'll say I did! I'm worth exactly $11,700,000—in experiences which otherwise I might never had had!

The same issue also carried the first part of a three-part serial by Greye La Spina, "Invaders from the Dark." A werewolf novel in the gothic tradition, it also received a great deal of acclaim, vaulting Mrs. La Spina into the front ranks of *Weird Tales* contributors. The novel had earlier been rejected by Baird as being "too commonplace." It was just one of the many mistakes made by the earlier editor.

By June, the letters praising "Invaders from the Dark" were a veritable flood. The story was the most popular serial since "The Moon Terror." Arthur J. Burks wrote to Wright telling the editor that serializing the novel was a terrible injustice—that he had missed his wife's call to dinner while trying to finish the novel, only to discover it was a serial. Seabury Quinn told how he missed his subway station because he was so engrossed in the serial. C.M. Eddy, Jr. declared that "it should be published in book form with a great deal of success." Other readers declared "greater than DRACULA" and "the most wonderful werewolf story ever written." In a letter dated June 26, 1925, Farnsworth Wright stated "Invaders from the Dark" is exceeded in popularity only by two stories, "When the Green Star Waned" and "Whispering Tunnels." In a letter a few weeks earlier, Wright also declared "you are among our ten most popular authors . . . The [others are] Bagby, Quinn, Dyalhis, Long, Burks, Lovecraft, Nichols, Scholossel, and Hammerstrom."

July 1925 was an extremely important issue in the history of *Weird Tales*. Lead story for the issue was "The Werewolf of Ponkert" by H. Warner Munn (1901-   ). Inspired by a letter printed in The Eyrie by H.P. Lovecraft, Munn wrote a powerful tale of werewolves as told by one

H. Warner Munn

of the damned suffering under the curse.

In the same issue was the first story of a young Texas author, Robert E. Howard (1906-1936). "Spear and Fang" was a mediocre story of primitive life but its sale encouraged Howard to continue writing.

Robert E. Howard was born in Peaster, Texas, a small town forty-five miles west of Fort Worth. His family soon moved to Cross Plains, Texas, where Howard spent most of his life. Not a strong child, he was tormented by other children. Because of this, Howard became involved in body-building and exercises, making himself into a husky westerner not to be annoyed. He attended Howard Payne College in Brownwood, and it was while he was there that he made his first sale. Other sales came slow but Howard was dedicated to becoming a writer. He finally achieved some measure of financial success but, at the height of his popularity, committed suicide, overcome with grief at the realization of the impending death of his mother.

In the same issue were stories by Whitehead and Lovecraft, helping make the issue one of the best published under the new editorial banner. July also saw "The Conqueror" by A. Fordelorrar, a poem. Not an especially important one, except that it was the beginning of continued publishing of poetry in the magazine in a string of issues that would not be broken until September 1931! Weird and unusual poetry had become an integral part of "The Unique Magazine." Much of the early poetry was reprinted and included such works as Blake's "Tiger, Tiger" and Poe's "Eldorado." Wright also published several of his own poems under the pen-name of Francis Hard. However, within a short time, many of the regulars for the magazine were contributing poetry on a steady basis.

The next issue featured a fine story of voodoo in the Carribean by Arthur J. Burks titled "Black Medicine." Howard was present with "In the Forest of Villifere," a werewolf story that was to provide an effective lead-in to his first popular success. Also present was Murray Leinster (1896-1975) with "The Oldest Story in the World." Leinster, already a popular writer of adventure and science fiction stories, was the pen-name for Will F. Jenkins. He was only educated through the eighth grade but succeeded in becoming one of the most popular of all pulp writers. "The Oldest Story in the World" was a tale of torture set in India. It pointed out a major policy change. The story did not contain any actual supernatural element. It was simply an unusual story. Wright, as editor, was following the heading of the contents page which stated "A magazine of the bizarre and the unusual." There was no mention of the supernatural in those words and stories without fantasy but with a strong bizarre element were as welcome as those with fantasy. It was this policy that made *Weird Tales* unique.

It was also during this time that Wright began a new department. From almost the beginning of the magazine's history, reprints of old weird fiction had been used. Now Wright created a department, The Weird Tales Reprint, which, in each issue, reprinted a classic of horror. In this section, many rare and obscure stories of the supernatural and bizarre were rescued from oblivion by Wright. Many of the stories were translations from foreign languages and saw their first English publication in *Weird Tales*.

The October 1925 issue was another historic one for *Weird Tales*. Seabury Quinn appeared with "The Horror on the Links." Taking place in New Jersey, this was a story of brain transplants and a giant ape. The hero of the story was a dapper Frenchman visiting the United States, named Jules de Grandin. His aide in the story was a somewhat thick-headed Watson, Dr. Trowbridge. De Grandin was an instant success and he was back shortly with an adventure taking place in France. A third adventure took place in the Pacific. Soon, the Frenchman was back in New Jersey, living with Trowbridge, encountering all sorts of wild menaces, fighting both natural and supernatural horrors. De Grandin was the most popular character ever to appear in weird fiction magazines, with a total of 93 adventures published in *Weird Tales*.

"The Wicked Flea" by J.U. Giesy, was equally as important a story in the same issue. Giesy, a frequent contributor to *All-Story* and *Argosy All-Story*, wrote a number of stories for *Weird Tales*. "The Wicked Flea" was typical of the silly humorous stories that the pulp had featured since its beginning. It was about a flea that grew to enormous size and chased dogs around the countryside. Reader protests about this abominable story were so strong that humorous stories disappeared from *Weird Tales* for the rest of Wright's reign as editor.

Wright followed the letters written to The Eyrie closely. He stated his policy quite clearly in that department in the August 1925 issue:

> Certain stories have been so outstanding that they have called for scores of enthusiastic letters from the readers and it is from . . . the readers' comment on them that we are enabled to find out what manner of stories you want. For this magazine belongs to you,

the readers, and it is only by your constant advice and comment that we can know whether you are pleased with the magazine or not . . .

> It was the popularity of Mr. Quinn's werewolf story that led us to feature "The Werewolf of Ponkert" by H. Warner Munn in last month's issue . . . We cannot be satisfied unless we grow steadily in quality and literary merit of our stories; and this we can do only with your helpful comment.

Wright continued with comments of this type in many issues of The Eyrie. He closely watched reader reaction to stories and authors and, as a great editor does, molded his policy on what sold.

"Lukundoo" was a classic first published in the November 1925 *Weird Tales*. A tale of African vengeance by Edward Lucas White, the story was reprinted scores of times since its original publication. Rarely was it ever mentioned that the classic horror story saw its first publication in a pulp magazine.

The contents page had been shrinking in each issue during the year. 1926 saw a continuation of this policy as Wright continued to print longer stories. The added length enabled authors to build both characterization and plot. The short-short story continued but more and more of these stories were relegated to the back of the magazine as fillers with longer stories as the prime features of the issue.

April of that year featured two notable stories, one to become a classic in the field. H.P. Lovecraft's "The Outsider" was one of his most popular tales. In 1933, Wright listed it as one of the half-dozen most popular stories to appear in *Weird Tales* up to that time. Wright highly praised the story in future Eyrie columns and it was warmly received by *Weird Tales* fans. The fame of the story was later boosted by being used as the title story of the first Arkham House book in 1939. Even with its predictable ending, the fine writing in the story made it a classic of the macabre.

Robert E. Howard scored with his first cover story, "Wolfshead." A sequel to "In the Forest of Villefere," the story was a fast-paced action adventure taking place on the coast of Africa. The hero was a man who was bitten by the werewolf in the earlier story and suffered thereafter from the curse of lycanthropy himself. He redeemed himself by an act of bravry resulting in his death. Howard was established as a reader favorite with this story and was on the way to becoming a *Weird Tales* regular.

"The Ghosts of Steamboat Coulee" was a fine ghost story by Arthur J. Burks featured as the cover story for the next issue. One of the best traditional ghost stories to appear in "The Unique Magazine," it was reprinted a number of times since its first appearance. However, unnoticed in the same issue was the debut of a much more important figure in the world of fantasy. "Bat's Belfry" was the first published story by August W. Derleth, who was to become the most prolific writer for *Weird Tales* as well as the founder of Arkham House.

August Derleth (1909-1973) was one of the most prolific writers of the Twentieth Century. Derleth was a young correspondent of H.P. Lovecraft and was strongly influenced by the master macabre writer. While Lovecraft experienced difficulty in selling much of his work, Derleth easily sold thousands of pieces of fiction and non-fiction to all types of markets. His weird fiction was probably his most minor

August W. Derleth

work, with his Wisconsin history books gaining him his greatest fame. In 1939, Derleth and Donald Wandrei began a small book publishing firm to print the works of H.P. Lovecraft. In its more than thirty years of existence, Arkham House has published major collections of fiction from *Weird Tales* by many of the best writers of the fantastic. It stands as Derleth's most important contribution to the weird fiction field.

"Spider Bite," a story definitely written to make any person afraid of spiders a bit more so, was the best story in the June 1926 issue. It was Rober Spencer Carr's finest contribution.

"Laocoon" was the first story by Bassett Morgan published in *Weird Tales*. It set the tone for nearly all of the rest of Morgan's work. Two scientists in the South Pacific discover huge saurian aquatic monsters that gave rise to the legend of sea serpents. When one of the scientists discovers he has leprosy, he has his comrade transfer his brain into the body of the giant monster. This is done and for a time, the beast has the mind of a man. In the end the reflexes of the beast come to rule with disastrous effects. Morgan was fascinated with the idea of human brains in beast's bodies, and his later stories were filled with talking gorillas, tigers with human minds, and such-like creations.

By now, *Weird Tales* had developed into a quality magazine. In late 1926, Wright was able to tell E. Hoffmann Price, "Thank God, we've just about used up the last of the stuff Baird bought while he was editor." The magazine was Wright's now, and the changes continued as quality went up.

Every issue showed improvement over the last. However, the August 1926 issue would prove a hard one to match for some time afterwards.

One of the two or three most popular of all stories ever published in the history of *Weird Tales* was "The Woman of the Wood," by A. Merritt, the cover story for August.

Merritt, a fantasy writer whose popularity at the time was rivaled only by Edgar Rice Burroughs, was a reader of *Weird Tales* from its earliest days. When "The Woman of the Wood" was rejected by *Argosy*, Merritt submitted it to Wright who immediately grabbed it. The editor of *Argosy* later admitted that the rejection was probably his worst mistake in his entire tenure of editor of the pulp magazine. A gripping, haunting tale, it was the story of a man who fought a brutish family trying to destroy a forest, and the help the hero received from the mystical "Woman of the Wood."

Lovecraft was present with a minor tale, "The Terrible Old Man."

Two authors new to *Weird Tales* were also in that memorable issue. G.G. Pendarves presented "The Devil's Graveyard." Pendarves was in reality an English authoress, Gladys Graves Trenery, who, while never listed as one of the top contributors to *Weird Tales*, was always one of the best in sheer quality of her work until her death in 1939.

An invisible temple that housed an invisible god made "The Monster God of Mamurth" a stirring debut for Edmond Hamilton. The story had been submitted by Hamilton a year earlier. It was rejected but Wright wrote Hamilton a long letter telling the young man the story's faults. Hamilton rewrote the tale and it was accepted and published in the same issue with the Merritt tale. A fitting tribute as Merritt was Hamilton's favorite author.

Edmond Hamilton (1904-1977) quickly became one of the most popular writers of science fiction for *Weird Tales*, and shortly after, for the new science fiction magazines. Born in Youngstown, Ohio, Hamilton had graduated high school at 14 and began college soon after. He attended Westminster College but was expelled for cutting chapel at the Presbyterian school. Hamilton worked at odd jobs until he began writing. He was so successful at writing that he never again worked at a salaried job.

Hamilton was back in the next issue with the first part of a three-part novel, "Across Space." A wild adventure as Martians tried to destroy all life on Earth by pulling the planet out of its orbit, it was extremely popular. While Hamilton's first story was a fine weird effort, his name was soon to become associated with stories of super science like "Across Space."

Two shorter works shared the spotlight with the Hamilton story in the same issue. "Jumbee" by Henry Whitehead was a powerful story of voodoo in the West Indies, and it set the stage for a series of future stories in the same area.

Farnsworth Wright used his short-short stories, usually without an illustration, to fill up spaces in the rear of his magazine. From time to time, a story would make a strong impression with the readers. Wright was the first to admit that he completely underestimated the power of H.F. Arnold's "The Night Wire."

The story concerned men working for the news wire services during the twenties. The main character was John Morgan, an expert at typing out a story as it came over the telegraph wire.

The narrator related how one night a strange tale came over Wire #2, which Morgan typed out piece by piece as it came in. In a town named Xebico, a strange mist came slowly sweeping out of the town graveyard. The mist grew thicker. Reports came in at irregular intervals as people are reported vanishing into the mist. More and more people disappear. Horrible screams are heard. Finally, the last report comes in. The entire town was being destroyed by the unholy fog. The operator in Xebico has no idea what the fog is but describes it over the wire in horrifying detail.

The narrator, almost overcome by horror, contacted Chicago and discovered that Wire #2 was not operating the whole evening. No message could have come in. There was no town of Xebico listed. When the narrator tries to tell Morgan that the messages were a hoax, he discovers that the man is dead—and has been dead for hours, long before the Xebico story began!

"The Night Wire" was a gripping short story that does not loose its impact after many readings. It was one of the most popular short stories to appear in *Weird Tales* and was reprinted several times in hardcover.

The rest of the year saw publication of several other fine stories, most notable being "The Supreme Witch" by G.A. Terrill, a fine witchcraft story with a deeply religious slant, and R. Anthony's "The Parasitic Hand," a grisly story of unnatural growth. However, it was not until January 1927 that the magazine was to score again with another exceptional issue.

Lead story in the issue was the first part of "Drome" by John Martin Leahy. The serial was a fast-paced action story in an underground world that was later published in hardcover. Lovecraft was present with a tale of devil worship in New York, "The Horror at Red Hook." Robert E. Howard contributed "The Lost Race," and Frank Owen had "The Dream Peddler."

"Leonora" was an eerie ghost story by Everill Worrell which harked back to the Baird days as it was told by a madwoman writing in a diary. Still, it developed a fine sense of impending horror as a young girl was offered a ride by a mysterious stranger in a huge black automobile—a long ride that leads to the cemetery.

The most important event, though, was the publication of "The Last Horror" by Eli Colter. Elizabeth Colter, who was later to become a well-known writer for the "slicks," had been a regular for several years for *Weird Tales*, but "The Last Horror" was her one truly memorable contribution to the magazine and to weird fiction in general.

The tale was over-melodramatic and the last horror was no great surprise, but the topic of the story and its resolution was something unique for the time. The story was printed in the 1920's when racial stereotypes were still the accepted norm. Lynchings were still common and most people considered blacks, orientals and Jews as members of inferior races. In science fiction such stories as, "The Menace" by David H. Keller featured stupid blacks attempting to destroy the white race. "The Last Horror" was unique in recognizing the stereotype and destroying it.

A brilliant black scientist was held back from true greatness by the color of his skin. While able to make great scientific discoveries and amass great wealth, he was not accepted by white society. Angrily, he vowed to become white. He captured white men and had their skin exchanged with his by a mad doctor. Finally he needed only the skin of his face changed. He captured a group of hunters and the last exchange was made.

The genius bragged: "I tell you the skin doesn't matter one little bit. It's what's inside a man . . . And yet the world judges by the veneer. Well, I changed my veneer! . . . *I'm white!*"

With sarcasm and venom one of the hunters replied:

"You, who could have been one of the glorious vanguard! You, who could have been one in a million! You, who could have carried your race a step farther! You, who lost sight of something truly great in the lure of a treacherous mirage!

"Once you were an honest black and at least you could have been a man, an example of high incentive to all your race. Why didn't you go on and *prove* to the world that the color of the skin doesn't matter? . . . A black man, honest and clean of heart could shake hands with a white brother. But you've got to bow your head and sink into oblivion. Pervert, fiend, fool, sham! White? *Where?*"

A lecture, perhaps not shocking in 1976, but 40 years ahead of its time. While heavy-handed and melodramatic, "The Last Horror" was probably the most unique story ever to appear in "The Unique Magazine."

March of that year presented an exceptional story translated from the Russian, written by Leonid Adreyeff. "Lazarus" was a powerfully told story of what happened to Lazarus after he had been raised from the dead by Jesus, and the effect he had on the people he encountered. The story, a classic of the macabre, recently experienced a flurry of reprinting, with several anthologists claiming that it had been lost and forgotten. In reality, the story appeared in a number of times since its discovery by Farnsworth Wright.

Edmond Hamilton was present with one of numerous stories in the super-scientific vein he wrote during the period. "Evolution Island" was an entertaining adventure of a scientific experiment to speed up evolution on an island in the West Indies. Life goes through several changes until a dominant form of intelligent plant life came into being. The plant creatures prove to be almost too intelligent as they plan to wipe out mankind. They were stopped just in the nick of time by one of the experimenters. It was a fast-paced story and typical of the work Hamilton was doing not only for *Weird Tales* but *Amazing Stories* as well.

April 1927 featured the first appearance of the popular science fiction writer Ray Cummings. "Explorers Into Infinity" was another tale based on the concept of our solar system being an atom in a giant super-universe. Cummings had his explorers grow to titanic size and enter this "giant world." Based on a notion that had already been proven false the story and a later sequel still made for entertaining reading.

Ray Cummings (1897-1957) was one of the most popular writers of "scientific romances" ever to pen a story for the Munsey magazines. Cummings attended Princeton, worked in oil fields, and served for five years as personal assistant to Thomas Edison. His most famous story, "The Girl in the Golden Atom," was inspired by a Quaker Oats sign he saw on a subway train. A majority of his stories were based on the concept of atoms being in the form of solar systems, which had been proven false by the time he began writing.

Ensuing issues featured a number of entertaining stories, among them H. Warner Munn's sequel to "The Werewolf of

Ponkert" titled "The Return of the Master"; several Jules de Grandin stories by Quinn, and "The Left Eye" by Whitehead. However, the August 1927 issue was the next one to feature a major work of weird fiction.

The cover illustrated an Otis Adelbert Kline fantastic adventure, "The Bride of Osiris," most notable for the fact that it caught the attention of a young Robert Bloch and hooked him on *Weird Tales*. The premier story of the issue was by Frank Belknap Long. "The Man With A Thousand Legs" was one of Long's best stories and a masterpiece of strangeness.

"The Man With a Thousand Legs" was told by a series of people, beginning with a doctor who admitted a young man in an agitated state into his office late one night. The young man, it turned out, was a famous genius whose theories were recently termed nonsense and had fallen on bad times. Arthur St. Amand, in a frenzy of excitement, swore to the doctor that he would make the whole scientific world realize his genius.

Next, a short story writer told of a horrible monster that devoured children and men on a beach, though being wounded several times by people fighting it.

Then a druggist related the frightening visit by a young man with the same wounds as the monster. A woman rents a room to the same young man but makes him leave after certain frightening occurrences. Slowly, the pattern emerges. Arthur St. Amand discovered a way to change the protoplasm of a normal human cell into a writhing mass of protoplasmic life—a thing with a thousand legs. At first, the scientist's will was strong enough to control the change from one form to another, but after a while the change became uncontrollable. Finally he changed to a giant monster and died a strange death. The story was well told by a series of narrators and ended on an upbeat turn with a tramp saving the world from any future horrors.

October 1927 was another one of those issues that made *Weird Tales* the best magazine of its type ever published. Among the many fine stories featured in the issue was the occult novelette, "The Dark Lore" by Nictzin Dyalhis. E. Hoffmann Price was present with "Saladin's Throne Rug," where Price's own interest in Oriental rugs helped add an extra dash of authenticity to the story. Wallace West, a science fiction writer as well as a *Weird Tales* contributor, made his debut in the issue with "Loup-Garou." Quinn and de Grandin were also present.

The serial was "The Time Raider," a unique adventure novel by Edmond Hamilton. The theme was one that Hamilton used several times in the future and always made a fascinating topic. Men from various ages were scooped up from their time period and taken to the far future, by the mysterious "Time Raider." The main characters in the story were a group of men from different periods of history who banded together to solve the mystery of the Raider and its mysterious intentions. Not only a fast-paced story, it was also an entertaining idea well presented.

Lovecraft presented one of his most famous stories, "Pickman's Model." It was a powerful narrative of a painter who chose strange scenes and gruesome topics for his art. One such painting described in the story served as the basis for another fine work a dozen years later in "Far Below."

Donald Wandrei was one of the many authors whose first submission to *Weird Tales* made Farnsworth Wright's lot a little easier. E. Hoffmann Price told of how Wright thrust Wandrei's first story at him with the command "God damn it, read that!" The story, "The Red Brain," was one to excite even the enthusiasm of Editor Wright.

Wandrei (1908-   ) was only sixteen when he submitted the story to *Weird Tales* under the title, "The Twilight of Time." The young author later graduated from the University of Minnesota with a B.A. and worked for Dutton Publishing Co. and later as a public relations executive. With August Derleth, he was instrumental in forming Arkham House to help publish the works of his close friend, H.P. Lovecraft.

"The Red Brain" was a different type of science fiction story, one that was far beyond the imaginings of the writers for *Amazing Stories*. It took place in the far far future when the entire universe had been engulfed by cosmic dust and only one planet still possessed life—inhabited by giant brains who were struggling desperately to remain sentient. The Red Brain, a rebel, discovered the secret of stopping the dust. However, the Red Brain's secret was not what the readers suspected and the ending of the story was a true shocker, with a classic last line.

"The Infidel's Daughter" by E. Hoffmann Price made the December 1927 issue of *Weird Tales* notable. The story, at first glance, seemed to be one of Price's eastern adventure fantasies. However, the astute reader soon realized that the Price story was an attack on the Ku Klux Klan. When a southern subscriber canceled his subscription in protest, Price felt he had done the magazine a disservice by losing it readers, but Wright disagreed.

'Oh, hell! . . . a story that arouses controversy is good for circulation, we gain more than we lose, and anyway, it would be worth a reasonable loss to rap bigots of that caliber."

Farnsworth Wright, the man as well as the editor, speaking.

1928 started off well with the first three issues each featuring a story that was to become a classic in the weird fiction field.

January's contribution was "In Amundsen's Tent" by John Martin Leahy. Here was a fascinating tale of Antarctica which begins with a party finding a deserted tent containing a human head, and the inevitable diary. The notebook told of an early party of explorers who stumbled across a monstrosity from outer space so terrible that even the sight of it drove men mad. Horror builds up as, one by one, the members of the group are tracked down by the creature and killed. Even with the fate of the narrator known from the beginning, the story still managed to develop an atmosphere of dread expectancy.

Even though H.P. Lovecraft was one of the most popular writers ever to write for *Weird Tales*, the only cover story he had was for "Imprisoned With the Pharoahs," which was not even published under his own name. His story in the February 1928 issue surely deserved a cover as it was one of the most important tales ever to be printed in "The Unique Magazine."

"The Call of Cthulhu" had been rejected by Farnsworth Wright some years earlier as the editor felt it was too unusual and radical a story for his readership. No doubt this rejection and others like it helped anger Lovecraft against Wright. Recently, one or two writers complained of Wright's "rejection of Lovecraft's stories without rhyme or reason." The facts of the matter just did not support this view. Wright often wrote to Lovecraft detailing why he was rejecting a certain story. While Lovecraft fans *now* might complain about Wright's actions *then*, a close study proved that in most cases, Wright knew what he was doing.

In 1925, *Weird Tales'* audience was just not ready for the new and unusual concepts of "The Call of Cthulhu." Readers who praised the old-fashioned ideas of "Under the N-Ray" and "Whispering Tunnels" were not ready for Cthulhu and his minions. However, after several years of slowly maturing ideas and increased quality work, Wright was able to purchase the Lovecraft story and run it in the 1928 issue.

"The Call of Cthulhu" was an important story in that it helped revolutionize the horror story. Lovecraft's major contribution to the genre with the Cthulhu Mythology was the emphasis on the scientific approach and use of scientific analysis in the story. Many people have complained that the surprise endings of Lovecraft's stories contain little or no surprise. It was doubtful that they were meant to. As Robert A.W. Lowndes pointed out, the endings of the stories were the end result of a carefully constructed chain of logic. Step by step, Lovecraft brought the reader forward to one inescapable conclusion. Evidence was reinforced by more evidence until only one answer was possible. Lovecraft's stories were as well constructed as any scientific paper. First, the statement by the narrator of a terrible horror to be revealed (the goal); next the facts as related through first-hand evidence, newspaper clippings, or diaries (evidence); third, the confrontation between the narrator or another with the horror (the experiment); and finally, the realization of the horror as predicted and stated at the beginning (the conclusion). Lovecraft popularized the concept of a scientific approach as the method for building horror. He was by no means a science fiction writer, but a writer who used scientific means to create his stories.

A completely different type of story was the highlight of the March 1928 issue. G.G. Pendarves became a reader favorite with her story of occult horror, "The Eighth Green Man." As with all of Pendarves' better stories, nothing definite was ever spelled out. The occult, more than materialistic horrors or monsters, played a large part in the story. Unlike most horror stories of the period, Pendarves featured heroes who were not without powers of their own:

> But the Seven Green Men ringed us in, stretching out stiff arms in a wide circle, machinelike, obedient to the hissing commands of their superior.
>
> I leapt forward and with a cutting slash of my knife got free and strode up to the devil who smiled and smiled and smiled!
>
> "Power is mine!" I said, steadying my voice with hideous effort. "I know you . . . I name you . . . Gaffarel!"

"The Eighth Green Man" was a well-constructed horror story that was one of the five stories reprinted twice afterwards in *Weird Tales*.

By now, Wright had developed a stable of regulars who

forged a solid chain of readers for his magazine. If one did not buy the April issue for "The Jewel of the Seven Stones," the latest of Quinn's Jules de Grandin stories, there was always Robert Spencer Carr's tale, or H. Warner Munn's torture story, "The Chain." And, the Coming Next Month page promised a new Robert E. Howard story as well as Burks, Pendarves and Bassett Morgan.

Poetry also began to become featured more and more with work by Lovecraft, Long, Howard and Wandrei all appearing with frequency. 1928 saw first publication of a series of poems by Wandrei titled "Sonnets for the Midnight Hours," first of a number of sequences of poems that would be printed in *Weird Tales* over the next few years.

August 1928 featured an attractive Senf cover picturing a man in Renaissance garb bending over a dying girl. The story was "Red Shadows" destined to vault Robert E. Howard into the front ranks of authors for "The Unique Magazine."

"Red Shadows" introduced Solomon Kane, the first of Howard's series characters and probably the most interesting of the bunch. Kane was "a tall gaunt man . . . his dark pallid face and deep brooding eyes made more somber by the drab Puritanical garb he affected." The Puritan was a righter of wrongs and pursued villains to the ends of the Earth for revenge. In "Red Shadows" he chased the evil Le Loup from France to Italy to the jungles of Africa. Even the rogue was astonished by Kane's single-minded pursuit and asked him outright why he did it.

> "Because you are a rogue whom it is my destiny to kill," answered Kane coldly. He did not understand. All his life he had roamed about the world, aiding the weak and fighting oppression; he neither knew nor questioned why. That was his obsession, his driving force in life

Except for a brief encounter with African black magic, "Red Shadows" could have been a straight adventure story. However, reader reaction was overwhelming and Howard continued the Kane series with the supernatural element continually stronger.

By no means a classic story, another tale in the same issue was important to an even larger audience than Howard collectors. "The Vengeance of Nitocris" was a minor story of revenge in old Egypt. However, the young author, Thomas Lanier Williams, was so encouraged by his first professional sale that he continued writing. Thus, *Weird Tales* was the first magazine to ever publish a story by Tennessee Williams.

September 1928 was the first issue to feature a story by a poet who had been appearing in *Weird Tales* since July 1923. A friend of H.P. Lovecraft, Clark Ashton Smith (1893-1961) needed money to help support his elderly parents. The very minor story was no indication of the work that was to come from Smith's pen in a few years.

Clark Ashton Smith considered himself a poet and artist, never really a short story writer. Born in the mining country around Auburn, California, Smith spent most of his life living in Auburn, where he maintained a small cottage. Smith never was one to worry overmuch about money and most of his professional writing was done to support his elderly parents. Primarily, he considered himself a poet and had seven collections of poetry published in his life, several

*Clark Ashton Smith, with
visiting fans (circa 1942-45)*

CAS self-portrait

before the advent of *Weird Tales*. Smith's work was always noted for its unusual imagery as well as the author's exotic vocabulary.

One of the things that made Wright an exceptional editor was the vast variety of material he used in *Weird Tales*. Wright bought material not only because he liked it but because he felt that the *readers* would like it. He once admitted to E. Hoffmann Price that he bought stories that he did not like because he felt that they would appeal to his readers. He featured stories many times that were not up to the quality of the other fiction in the magazine but which he knew would sell copies. From time to time, he rejected stories that he should have bought, such as Lovecraft's "The Color Out of Space." Sometimes he turned down stories as being too fantastic or had endings rewritten that he felt were too gruesome. However, on the whole, he was an exceptional editor. That last word was the one that was most important. Wright was the editor of *Weird Tales* and it was to the magazine that he owed his loyalty. Writers often complained about his rejections or rewrite demands. E. Hoffmann Price pointed out, though, that among *professional* writers, those people who made their living totally from pulp writing and did well at it, there was no complaint. Wright did what he had to to sell his magazine. While some of his judgments may have seemed unfair in their day, on the whole, he exhibited a keen sense of fair play and good judgment. Anyone who could keep a pulp magazine going and slowly make it into a success at 25¢ an issue when most magazines were selling for a dime had to be a great editor—and Wright was exactly that.

Weird Tales was "The Unique Magazine." Not only did Wright publish ordinary supernatural stories, science fiction, and ghost stories, he also bought outre stories that fit into no other magazines. Much of the material he printed was of so unusual a nature that it is doubtful that it could be placed in a magazine today. Typical of such tales was "The Copper Bowl" by Major George Fielding Eliot.

Stories involving Chinese torture using rats were not new to the pulps. In the third Fu Manchu novel, Nayland Smith was threatened by just such a death. At least five other stories published in the pulps during the same period featured rat tortures. However, none of these stories ever achieved the fame of "The Copper Bowl." It was reprinted numerous times since its original appearance and was probably the best-known torture story ever written.

Again, it was a story that could only have found a home in *Weird Tales*. Even today, it is doubtful that the gruesome tale of torture and death could find a home other than in underground comic publications.

"The Chapel of Mystic Horror" was the lead story in the same issue, December 1928. It was the 23rd story in the series and probably the best of all the ninety-three de Grandin adventures.

While Seabury Quinn was by no means a great writer, he did add a great deal to the pulp. The de Grandin stories were unjustifiably attacked by many critics and fans as being mere hackwork. While no great masterpieces of literature, the stories were entertaining and different. For one thing, Quinn brought in a new element to the supernatural detective story. De Grandin used holy relics, charms and other magical inventions and discoveries as well. In "The Chapel of Mystic Horror," de Grandin fought several evil ghosts with a holy relic. To destroy the most powerful of the spirits, he resorted to a piece of radium—reasoning that the resurrected ghosts were beings of ethereal vibrations and thus could be destroyed by the much more powerful vibrations given off by the radium. Nonsense, perhaps, but a new and entertaining kind of nonsense. In a later story, de Grandin used a giant vacuum cleaner to catch a ghost by sucking in the being's ectoplasm! Quinn's stories helped destroy the stereotype that the only way to defeat a supernatural foe was by use of old tried and true religious methods used in hundreds of earlier ghost stories.

1929 started off well with a January issue that included Quinn, Bassett Morgan, Lovecraft ("The Silver Key"), and Howard's second Solomon Kane story ("Skulls in the

Stars"). A major policy change also shared top billing in the issue.

The Weird Tales Reprint had been a regular feature since the early days of the magazine. While the department featured many classic tales as well as translations from foreign languages, one source was forbidden. No stories from early issues were reprinted. Readers had long been after Wright to change this policy and in January 1929 he finally did so. At first, he used a story from the early issues of *Weird Tales* only once every three or four issues. As time went on, he used more and more reprints from his own magazine and only occasionally used something from other sources.

The first story reprinted was Dyalhis' "When the Green Star Waned." It was soon followed by "The Phantom Farmhouse" by Seabury Quinn, "The Hound" by Lovecraft, and "The Stranger From Kurdistan" by E. Hoffmann Price.

"Crashing Suns" by Edmond Hamilton had been the featured serial in the August and September 1928 issues. Hamilton followed up the novel with "The Star-Stealers" in 1929. These stories were unique in science fiction up to that time. The heroes were not only humans but included alien beings as well. All were banded together in a Confederation of Suns, a governing body of all space. Hamilton was the first to use this type of interstellar organization that was later popularized by E.E. Smith. However, while Smith's aliens were truly alien, Hamilton's were little more than carbon copies of the Earthmen.

"The Hounds of Tindalos" by Frank Belknap Long was a fine tale in the Lovecraft tradition which headlined the March 1929 issue. The master himself appeared in the next number with "The Dunwich Horror," the second of his Cthulhu Mythos stories. The strange occurrences in Dunwich formed a masterful web of horror culminating in the bizarre encounter with Wilbur Whateley's twin brother in one of Lovecraft's best-written climaxes.

"The Shadow Kingdom" introduced a new hero to the pages of *Weird Tales*, Robert E. Howard's personal favorite among all his stories was the first of three stories to feature King Kull, a barbarian king of ancient Atlantis and an ancestor of sorts of Conan. "The Shadow Kingdom" was an exciting novelette of swords-and-sorcery with Kull battling the machinations of the evil serpent men of Valusia.

The same issue also featured "The Inn of Terror" by Gaston Leroux. While not a memorable story, it was noteworthy as Leroux was the author of the famous novel, THE PHANTOM OF THE OPERA, and that fact was notably proclaimed on the cover of the issue.

Leroux was a French author and several translations of stories by him appeared in *Weird Tales*, along with one serial, "The Haunted Chair." His first three stories were printed in 1929 and all were cover stories with his name prominently displayed.

Leroux received the cover for the October 1929 issue but it was not his story that was best in the magazine. Howard again had the honor with one of the best Fu Manchu imitations ever written, "Skull-face." Kathulos was an exceptional villain in the Rohmer tradition, an ancient Atlantean sorceror who returned from the dead to lead an abortive rebellion against the white race. Racial war was a popular topic in the pulps and Howard used it as the basis of his menace. A sequel to the novel was started by Howard but never completed.

David H. Keller (1880-1966), a popular science fiction author of the period, was also present with the first of a series of pleasant fantasy adventures taking place in Cornwall, "The Battle of the Toads." Quinn and de Grandin were also present.

H.P. Lovecraft's name was not on the contents page of the November 1929 number, but his presence was there. "The Curse of Yig" by Zealia Bishop Reed was extensively rewritten by Lovecraft. The story was a well-done horror story based on a fear of snakes and was based on factual happenings. In recent years, some people have tried to tie the story in with the Cthulhu Mythos stories but the only tie that exists is the name, Yig, which was later used in a few Mythos stories. Careful reading of the Reed story shows it has no relation to the Lovecraft series.

The Depression was hitting hard by the end of the year and the magazine ended on a down note with another Leroux cover. The serial was a terrible story, "Behind the Moon" by W.E. Backus. Francis Flagg had the best story in the issue with "The Dancer In the Crystal." The dancer was not a human but a strange flickering light in a crystal and the story was about the unimaginable destruction caused by the damaging of the crystal home of the "dancer."

January 1930 started the new year on a better note, with a Quinn story, Hamilton, Whitehead, Frank Belknap Long, and Otis Kline also being present.

The next few months brought forth interesting stories but nothing exceptional. Clark Ashton Smith had "The End of the Story." Howard was present with several minor works. Hamilton and the Interstellar Patrol appeared as did Quinn and de Grandin. "The Black Monarch" was a five-part serial by Paul Ernst about an evil superman who ruled the Earth from a secret underground headquarters and the trials of the two men who sought to overthrow him. It was a notch below the usual poor *Weird Tales* serial level.

"The Moon of Skulls" by Robert E. Howard signaled better things in the June 1930 issue. A two-part serial, it was another Solomon Kane adventure. This time, Kane was in Africa hunting a kidnapped girl. He stumbled on a lost Atlantean kingdom and the action started. Clark Ashton Smith returned with another story, signaling that he was going to be a frequent contributor. Lovecraft was present in the reprint department with the classic, "The Rats in the Walls."

Unfortunately, this issue was the only break in a dismal year for the magazine. All of the regulars were present, with the exception of Lovecraft, but rarely were the stories first rate. The magic of 1928 and 1929 was dimmed by the harshness of the time. The depression hit hard and the bank where *Weird Tales* had its assets closed in the bad days, never to reopen. The hard work of getting the magazine into good financial shape had to be started anew.

"Another Dracula" was the terrible serial of the year. Ralph Milne Farley (1887-1963) was the author and it was the first appearance of this famous science fiction author. In reality, Farley was Roger Sherman Hoar. Named after Roger Sherman, a descendant, Hoar invented a method of sighting big guns used in World War I and was responsible for much of the theory of modern ballistics. He later served as a state senator and was a very wealthy businessman. Hoar was known primarily for his series of stories about "The Radio Man" in *Argosy All-Story*.

November 1930 brought back some of the old glory to the magazine. "A Million Years After" by K.M. Roof was a mediocre story of a resurrected dinosaur which made the cover. H. Warner Munn was back with The Werewolf Master, in the first story of a series entitled "Tales of the Werewolf Clan." The series, of which only three out of five planned saw print, detailed what happened to the cursed descendants of the first Werewolf of Ponkert.

Clark Ashton Smith proved that he was fast becoming one of the more popular authors for "The Unique Magazine." From his stories appearing in the rear of the magazine, he moved forward steadily to the front. "The Uncharted Isle" was one of the featured stories of the issue. A haunting, nightmarish tale of a man shipwrecked on an island and the hideous sacrifice he witnessed, it was a powerful weird story. Many years later, Smith chose "The Uncharted Isle" as his favorite story.

"Kings of the Night" introduced a new Robert E. Howard hero. Bran Mak Morn was the last King of the Picts, an ancient race who ruled England before recorded history. King Kull made his last appearance in *Weird Tales* as the King of Valusia was brought forward in time to fight with Bran in a battle against the Roman conquerors of Britain.

Edmond Hamilton was present with another interplanetary adventure. Lovecraft was in the issue with poetry, part of his "Fungi From Yuggoth" cycle.

January 1931 started off the new year on a good note. Whitehead was back with "The Passing of a God," a strange story of an unusual operation and Haitian voodoo beliefs. The story was one of the few reprinted twice in later issues of *Weird Tales*.

Munn had the third werewolf story, "The Master Has a Narrow Escape" in which the werewolf master became involved in the first witchcraft trial in America. Clark Ashton Smith returned with "The Necromantic Tale." Lovecraft was present with more poetry.

Lovecraft often had unusual dreams and he related one, "The Very Old Folk" to his friend, Frank Belknap Long. Long asked for and got permission to use the dream in toto as part of his novel, "The Horror From the Hills." This two-part serial was a combination of the cosmic horror of the Cthulhu Mythos and the fast action of a super-science adventure. It had a ludicrous scene of the heroes chasing the monster of the title in an automobile, trying to hit it with their special aging ray.

The next issue of *Weird Tales* brought new worries to fans of the magazine. Since 1924, *Weird Tales* had been published regularly every month. Now, it started a bi-monthly schedule. The Depression and the bank closing had been hard blows to the high-priced magazine. Nor was the issue a spectacular one. Quinn was present with one of the poorest de Grandin adventures, "The Ghost Helper," whose title gave away the entire plot. Whitehead was back with "The Tree Man" and Hamilton had an adventure story on Earth instead of far out in interstellar space.

The next issue was somewhat better. Clark Ashton Smith led off with the first of his series of a medieval kingdom of France, "A Rendezvous in Averoigne." The tale was a fascinating look at vampirism and also said a good deal about the character of man. It was a small masterpiece.

Howard also was present with "The Children of the Night." A tale of racial memory, it was of note primarily as it introduced Howard's own legendary book, NAMELESS CULTS by von Juntz.

June-July 1931 was the beginning of a new revival. It was the last of the bi-monthly issues and signaled a return to the high quality of the late twenties. Only, instead of sporadic issues with exceptional work, every issue was on the same superior level.

Otis Adelbert Kline vaulted into the front line of *Weird Tales* regulars with his long, six-part serial, "Tam, Son of the Tiger." The novel was reprinted several years ago but was severely cut, so it was never reprinted complete.

The novel was a good one of high adventure and wild fantasy. It was in the Burroughs tradition but with a life all its own. Tam, son of a white hunter, Major Charles Evans, was carried off by a white tiger and raised as a tiger along with the tigress' own cub. Years later, Tam and the tigers are found by the Lama, Lozong, who once cared for the tiger. Tam was quickly taught of his humanity by the Lama, who also taught him varied fighting skills.

Enter, Nina, Princess of Arya, from the underground kingdom of Iramatri. There, the ancient Gods of India were alive and plotting soon to emerge and conquer the Earth. Marvel topped marvel as Tam fought to prevent the evil Siva from his plans of destruction. Tam's true father and Lozon both enter the fray. All sorts of evil monsters and giant creatures were encountered. The standard Burroughs formula of capture, escape, capture, escape was followed. At the end, Good battled Evil as Tam fought Siva in a duel to the death. All ended well. The novel was episodic, jumping from one set of characters to another but was filled with plenty of fast action. Kline was big name in the pulps at the time, having scored well in *Argosy* with his novels of Venus and Mars. "Tam" received four cover pictures, the most given any serial up to that time.

Backing up the first installment of the novel was David H. Keller's unusual story, "The Seeds of Death." Keller wrote bizarre stories that often caught the readers by surprise. In "Seeds of Death," an evil young woman hated men and killed them by feeding them diabolical seeds which root in their body and grow into plants, killing them horribly. The young hero seemingly outwits the woman—or so he thought. At the end, evil triumphed. Again, the story pointed out Wright's virtues as editor. Few other magazines would have permitted the horrifying story where the villain won. Wright pointed out in reply to a reader in The Eyrie complaining about too many happy endings that in a survey of previous issues, good only won in approximately half the stories. Discard the de Grandin stories where the outcome was inevitable, the percentage would have even been less. The one thing readers knew with *Weird Tales* was that the unexpected was always possible. In that way, Wright was able to publish stories of true horror. For if the reader knew in advance that the ending would always be a happy one, then all threats and occurrences in the tale could not dispel the knowledge that all would be well in the end. That was the case with such magazines as *Horror Stories* and *Terror Tales*. Only in *Weird Tales*, with the outcome uncertain, was there ever a feeling of tension—because the reader was not sure if the hero would overcome the odds. It was that extra dimension that gave *Weird Tales* the monopoly on real horror stories during the era.

Lovecraft also added his talents in the Reprint with his most famous story, "The Outsider." Clark Ashton Smith and Henry Whitehead helped round out a most satisfying issue.

Just as good was the next number. Lovecraft returned with his first new story of the 1930's and his longest one ever in *Weird Tales*. "The Whisperer in Darkness" had a predictable ending made even more predictable by an illustration which gave away the surprise on the second page of the story. Still, as mentioned, the ending was not what made the tale what it was. The detailed buildup by Lovecraft, starting with newspaper clippings, leading to reference books, then to the correspondence, and the final actual confrontation, were what created the superb mood that needed no surprise to make it a classic of fantastic horror.

Also of note was Wallace West's "Moon Madness." This was a fine combination of science fiction and rationalized horror. Three people took off on an experimental rocket ship to the Moon. Once in outer space, they discovered that they were paralyzed from the lack of gravitational force. All three are safe in their acceleration couches but they cannot move or change position. They were facing the viewports. The Moon loomed larger and larger, dominating their vision. The constant staring at the Moon, made bright by the reflected light of the sun slowly drove the three mad. While now scientifically out-of-date, the story was well written and still makes interesting reading.

Edmond Hamilton returned with an unusual entry. Hamilton had long been a fan of Charles Fort and in "The Earth Owners" he wrote an interesting short based on the statement, "I think we're property."

Smith presented "A Voyage to Sfanomoe," another of his exquisite fantasies, completely unclassifiable but extremely popular with all *Weird Tales* fans.

The Reprint took on a new dimension with the first installment of a serial. The story reprinted was "The Wolf Leader" by Dumas, never before published in English. Unfortunately, the werewolf novel was not a very good one and reader approval of the serialization was mixed.

September 1931 kept the string of great issues intact. The feature story was the Solomon Kane adventure, "The Footfalls Within," where Kane battled both slave traders and a demon imprisoned by King Solomon. As was often the case, the story was ridiculously illustrated.

"Satan's Stepson" was a Seabury Quinn de Grandin adventure. For the first time, the story was a short novel in length. Otherwise, it was a typical vampire adventure of the French ghost breaker.

Smith appeared again with a science fiction horror story. "The Immeasurable Horror" was a fine adventure of the first expedition to Venus. Smith was soon to break into the science fiction magazines with stories similar to this one. After that, his contributions to *Weird Tales* were mainly fantasy tales, as his new market took the science fiction material, enabling him to place more stories quickly.

George Fielding Eliot was back with a short-short of torture, "His Brother's Keeper." A three-page tale of the Iron Maiden, it was not up to "The Copper Bowl," but it was still quite horrifying. Eliot was the master of torture tales and no one else in *Weird Tales* (or any other magazine for that matter) could equal the sheer horror he could get into a short story.

October 1931 was yet another good issue. The feature story was another Howard adventure, "The Gods of Bal-Sagoth." Of most interest was the fact that the story was an obvious sequel to "The Dark Man," but was published two months before that story. Lovecraft, Hamilton, Smith and Whitehead were also present.

The cover story for the November issue was "Placide's Wife" by Kirk Mashburn (1900-1966). Mashburn, who lived in New Orleans, did a good job of catching the atmosphere of the poor whites in the area, giving the story an air of authenticity.

Smith returned with the first of his Hyperborean stories, "The Tale of Satampra Zeiros."

Howard was back with probably the best of the non-Lovecraft Cthulhu stories, "The Black Stone." The story opened well describing the death of von Junzt, the author of NAMELESS CULTS. Howard told how the German worked in secret on a second book, locked in a room so as not to be disturbed. In the middle of the night, terrible screams came from within. When the door was broken in, von Junzt was found, clawed to bits, with the blood-stained marks of giant claws everywhere. The book was ripped to shreds. One solitary friend of von Junzt spent the rest of the night piecing the book back together. Then, the man read the book. In horror, he burned the book and then cut his own throat! A fitting beginning to a tale of horror and devil worship.

W. Elwyn Backus, who had contributed to *Weird Tales* as far back as 1924 was back with the last of his contributions, "Subterranea." The short novel was about a lost world inside the Earth and was on the level with such earlier-mentioned stories as "Behind the Moon."

"The Haunted Chair" by Gaston Leroux began in December 1931. While the French author did not rate a cover illustration, his name was still prominently displayed on the cover with the heading, "Author of THE PHANTOM OF THE OPERA."

The cover went to "The Dark Man" by Howard. The story had just a hint of fantasy as Turlough O'Brien, an Irish outcast, became involved with the statue of Bran Mak Morn.

Any year that began with Clark Ashton Smith on the cover and ended with the first Conan story had to be special. 1932 was just such a year.

"The Monster of the Prophecy" was one of Smith's best stories. It was a humorous tale but a different sort of humor than what had appeared years before. In a thinly veiled satire of humankind, Smith told of a far-off planet and the prophecy of the coming of "a mighty wizard accompanied by a most unique and unheard of monster with two arms, two legs, two eyes and a white skin."

Also worthy of note was a short story in the rear of the magazine titled "Mive." It was a prize-winning short from a college magazine by a young author, Carl Jacobi.

Jacobi (1909-   ) went to school at the University of Minnesota. He worked for some time on *The Minneapolis Star* as a reporter and rewrite man. He then turned to writ-

Carl Jacobi

Hugh B. Cave

ing as a full-time profession. Like many other pulp writers he contributed to many different pulps other than *Weird Tales.*

February presented one of the best issues ever. Jules de Grandin was back in his one and only serial adventure— "The Devil's Bride." A long, episodic novel, the story dealt with the attempts of a combine of devil worshippers, Communists, and other radicals to overthrow the major established governments. De Grandin and several associates fought the evildoers through six installments of the very popular novel.

"Night and Silence" by Maurice Level was a short short of classic stature. It was an eerie accounting of an accident that caused the death of two cripples, one a mute, the other a blind man.

"The Thing on the Roof" was a minor Howard story in the Cthulhu vein. Wallace West, Frank Belknap Long, Otis Adelbert Kline, and Edmond Hamilton were all present. Donald Wandrei told one of the more gruesome stories in "The Tree Men of M'Bwa." Usually Wandrei spent weeks composing a story. "Tree Men" came to him in a flash and he wrote the story in one day and mailed it off to *Weird Tales* where it was immediately accepted. A horrible death, turning into a living tree, awaited those men foolish enough to venture into a forbidden section of Africa.

David Keller was the reason for buying the March 1932 issue. His short-short, "The Thing in the Cellar," was a minor classic and has been called "the most frightening story ever written in the English language." It was a short masterpiece of psychological horror of a young boy who was afraid to go down in the cellar and how his parents decided to cure him of this fear. The story was copied many times since its first publication but few attempts ever duplicated the chilling ending of the Keller yarn.

Hugh Cave, later to become a contributor to the "slicks," made his first appearance in *Weird Tales* in May 1932. "The Brotherhood of Blood" was an interesting vampire story with the hero as the vampire. Clark Ashton Smith was back with one of his future horror stories, as two Earthmen on Mars discover the secret of "The Vaults of Yoh-Vombis."

The Weird Tales Reprint department began serialization of "Frankenstein" in the same issue. Wright announced plans for the serialization of "Dracula," but reader sentiment was so against this move, as well as the "Frankenstein" serialization, that after that Wright kept to a policy of reprinting material from early issues of his own magazine. Most people felt that the novels could be found in most libraries whereas early issues of *Weird Tales* were not so easily found.

Greye La Spina returned to *Weird Tales* after a long absence with the cover story for June 1932. "The Devil's Pool" was a good werewolf story further enhanced by the St. John cover that went along with it. Frank Belknap Long had a Lovecraftian tale, "The Brain Eaters." Arlton Eadie, a British contributor, presented "The Siren of the Snakes," an adventure in India and of a strange woman a British soldier encountered there.

"Wings in the Night" was one of Robert E. Howard's best. It was a Solomon Kane story in July 1932. In this saga, Kane battled a race of winged men who gave rise to the legends of Harpies.

"The Dark Angel" was a de Grandin adventure which also had a fine moral against religious intolerance. Even without any actual supernatural beings in the story, Quinn could pen an effective scene:

> I tried to cry aloud, to warn de Grandin of the visitant's approach but only a dull, croaking sound, scarce louder than a sigh escaped my palsied lips.

Low as the utterance was, it seemed to carry to the creeping horror. With a wild, demoniac laugh, it launched itself upon the bed where my friend lay sleeping and in an instant I heard the sickening impact of a blow—another blow—and then a high cackling voice crying "Accursed of God, go now and tell your master who keeps watch and ward upon the Earth."

A second marrow-freezing cry went up and then a flash of blinding light—bright as a summer's storm forked lightning on a dark night—flared in my eyes, and I choked and gasped as strangling fumes of burning sulphur filled my mouth and nostrils.

De Grandin, of course, was not dead, but he did solve the mystery of men who died with their skulls crushed and the mark of a gigantic goat's hoof on their brow.

Another series character to appear in the same issue was Pierre d'Artois, a soldier of fortune who battled the evil Abdul Malaak and his band of satanists in E. Hoffmann Price's "The Bride of the Peacock."

Jack Williamson's first story in *Weird Tales* was a memorable one. "The Wand of Doom" was a science fiction horror story. A scientist invented a machine that could make thoughts into reality. His first creation was a beautiful girl, the girl of his dreams. He, of course, immediately fell in love with the girl. Then, later, he dreamt of a giant spider . . .

Williamson (1908-   ) was born in a mining camp in Arizona Territory. Apaches and the Mexican revolution convinced the Williamson family to move to New Mexico where the young John Stewart Williamson was raised. Encouraged by sales of stories to *Amazing Stories*, Williamson left college to become a full-time writer. His early stories showed a marked influence by A. Merritt and he was dubbed "A poor man's Merritt." Williamson later returned to college and recently taught courses in science fiction at Eastern New Mexico University where he holds an associate professorship.

Clark Ashton Smith was present with another strange story in the humorous vein. "The Testament of Athammaus" related how an unkillable criminal rendered a city uninhabitable and was a perfect example of Smith's bizarre humor.

Otis Adelbert Kline was back with another serial beginning in November. This one also rated four covers, all by St. John. The novel was "Buccaneers of Venus," originally written for *Argosy* but rejected and sent afterwards to *Weird Tales*. It was a six-part adventure bringing together two Kline heroes, Zinlo of Olba and Grandon of Terra. Written in the Burroughs tradition, the story was very well received.

Backing up the story was one of Robert E. Howard's best works. "Worms of the Earth" was the last Bran Mak Morn tale to be printed in the pulp. In an effort to defeat the legions of Rome, Bran enlisted the aid of strange beings known only as "the worms of the earth." Only at the very end of the story did the Pict King learn just how strange his allies were. The tale was an effective blend of horror and adventure.

Not as good but more important to Howard's career was his story in the final 1932 issue. "The Phoenix on the Sword" was the first published adventure of Conan of Cimmeria. In it, Conan was king and battled both plotters against the throne and a monstrous demon sent by the Stygian wizard, Thoth-Amon. The story was not top-flight Howard. Much of it was rewritten or taken verbatim from an unpublished Kull story, "By This Axe I Rule." The dream sequence was poorly handled. Only in the fight with the conspirators did Conan take on any character. However, Howard liked this character better than any of his earlier creations, and Conan would be the only one to appear in *Weird Tales* from that time on.

The entire December 1932 issue was a good one. Discounting the two serials, only five stories appeared. In "The Man Who Conquered Age," Edmond Hamilton discarded spacial menaces and told of a mad scientist who invented a machine that sped-up the aging process. In a climactic battle, the hero and villain fought in front of the machine with each man growing older by the second. The story was well plotted and had several other novel twists.

"The Lives of Alfred Kramer" by Donald Wandrei was the most popular story in the issue. It was a tale of a man who discovered the secret of ancestral regression. The ending was predictable but still chilling. Vincent Starrett and Seabury Quinn rounded out the issue's contents.

January 1933 was another excellent issue. Quinn had another of the endless de Grandin adventures. Hamilton was back with "Snake-Man," a horror story under his Hugh Davidson pen-name. Murray Leinster made one of his infrequent appearances with "The Monsters," a science fiction adventure of gigantic insects attacking New York. The Reprint was "The Night Wire." Best in the issue, though, was the second Conan story, "The Scarlet Citadel."

The novelette was Howard at his best. In it, Conan was captured by sorcery used by his enemies. Conan was left a prisoner in an underground dungeon complex while his enemies go to conquer his kingdom. Conan escapes several traps but cannot get free of the underground prison. Finally, he chanced upon another captive, a wizard held by a plant that drains his mind of all thought. Freeing the wizard, Conan and the man make for the entrance of the prison. Suddenly a giant snake blocked their path:

> Conan tensed himself for one mad berserker onslaught —to thrust the glowing fagot into that fiendish countenance and throw his life into the ripping swordstroke. But the snake was not looking at him. It was glaring at the man called Pelias, who stood with his arms folded, smiling. And in the great cold eyes slowly hate died out in a glitter of pure fear—the only time Conan ever saw such an expression in a reptile's eyes. With a swirling rush like the sweep of a strong wind, the great snake was gone.
>
> "What did he see to frighten him?" asked Conan eyeing his companion uneasily.
>
> "The scaled people see what escapes the mortal eye," answered Pelias cryptically. "You see my fleshly guise; he saw my naked soul."

Compare this Pelias to the sorceror in the imitation Conan stories by de Camp, Carter and Nyberg. Others might imitate but they could never duplicate the Texan's skill at swords-and-sorcery.

Conan returned in March 1933 with a story placed much earlier in his career, "The Tower of the Elephant." The best story of the issue, though, was Clark Ashton Smith's, "The Isle of the Torturers." The story was one of his tales of

Zothique, the world of the far-distant future. The short told of a plague and the only survivor who was captured and held prisoner on an island where torture had been refined to a fine art. It had an especially effective ending. The prisoner succeeded by trickery to release the plague, dooming himself and all others on the island to instant death. As Smith put it, "And oblivion claimed the Isle of Uccastrog; and the Torturers were one with the tortured."

April 1933 featured one of the best covers in the magazine's history, again by St. John, for the serial, "Golden Blood," by Jack Williamson. This was the New Mexico author's best Merritt type story. A lost race novel set in the forgotten regions of the Arabian desert, "Golden Blood," was a fast-action serial that scored high with the readers. In contrast with the short serials of the twenties, Wright went in heavily for long novels during the next decade.

Williamson was ably supported in that issue with stories by Price, Hamilton, Smith, Bassett Morgan, August Derleth and W.C. Morrow. Best remembered from the contents was "Revelations in Black," one of the most reprinted of all vampire stories ever written. Carl Jacobi submitted the story to *Weird Tales* and had it rejected. Shortly afterwards, Wright contacted Jacobi. "That strange story about the twenty-six blue jays on the stone wall haunted me. Please resubmit it."

Hugh Cave's "Dead Man's Belt" astonishingly has never been reprinted since its original appearance in May 1933. The story was an important one for Cave:

> I recalled how I wrote it [Dead Man's Belt] originally as a straight short story, not a horror story; how I used it for a couple of years as a door-opener to various slickpaper magazines (because wherever I sent it I got back a letter from the editor instead of the usual rejection slip, even though it could never have been used in any of those magazines); and I recall, how, eventually, I rewrote it as a fantasy kind of thing and sold it to Farnsworth Wright.

The same issue contained one of Smith's best works, "The Beast of Averoigne." Also in the magazine was H. Warner Munn's famous torture story, "The Wheel."

"The Wheel" contained no trace of fantasy or science fiction. In it, a man sought revenge against a descendant of a Spanish Inquisitor. The descendant was trapped and placed on a huge rotating wheel, much like a ferris wheel in an amusement park. However, there was a burning pit of pitch beneath the wheel. The descendant must keep on top of the wheel or fall into the pitch. The story built up to a climactic scene of death and retribution.

July 1933 might have been subtitled "Cthulhu Month." Three stories appeared in that issue, all part of the loose framework of the mythology Lovecraft had created.

Best of the group was Lovecraft's own "The Dreams in the Witch-House." One of HPL's best, the story presented a fascinating mixture of fourth-dimensional travel, mathematics and ancient witchcraft to create a novelet of both engrossing fantasy and grim horror. Of all of Lovecraft's creations, Brown Jenkin ranked as one of his most memorable monsters.

Lovecraft was also present in rewrite form in Hazel Heald's story "The Horror in the Museum." An interesting Mythos story, "The Horror" suffered from a long overdrawn climax and conclusion.

Rounding out the trio was Clark Ashton Smith's "Ubbo-Sathla," which presented a unique concept of the beginning of life on Earth—one that was at odds with known facts but made for enjoyable reading.

If July was Mythos month, then October had to be "gruesome month." Mearle Prout, an Oklahoma author, made his debut in *Weird Tales* with a tale of corruption and decay appropriately titled "The House of the Worm." In later issues, Wright indicated that he felt that "Worm" received too little notice from his readers, as he thought it was one of the best stories of the year. Considering that competition in that same issue included Lovecraft and Howard, this was high praise indeed.

Clark Ashton Smith managed to match Prout horror for horror with his own tale of grue, "The Seed of the Sepulcher." A modern-day horror story, it dealt with the same idea used in "The Seeds of Death," but in much greater detail. It was not a story to start the reader talking to his plants!

E. Hoffmann Price related in a fanzine article the following incident:

> Wright's enthusiasm upon getting a new name from the "slush" pile" was beautiful to see ... And the time, I think in the early thirties, when I bounced into Chicago he was fairly babbling and stuttering; he had no time to greet me. He handed me C.L. Moore's first ms. and paced the floor and muttered as I read; and then he closed shop and declared it "C.L. Moore day."

The story in question was "Shambleau" and it stood as an extraordinary tale, particularly as it was the first one ever written by fledgling authoress, Catherine Moore.

Catherine Moore (1911-   ) was born in Indianapolis, Indiana. As a child, she suffered periods of ill health and was forced to turn to books as her only pleasure. Later, her health improved and she entered Indiana University. However, the depression forced her to quit school and she became a secretary. In 1931 she bought a copy of *Amazing Stories* and was immediately hooked on science fiction. After the success of "Shambleau," she became a regular on the *Weird Tales* roster. In 1938, she met Henry Kuttner whom she later married. The two worked together as a writing pair from their marriage in 1940 to Kuttner's death in 1958. Remarried, most of C.L. Moore's work was devoted to television scripting. In recent years, she made appearances at several west coast science fiction conventions.

"Shambleau" was an astonishing mixture of science fiction and fantasy. Its hero was Northwest Smith, a hardened adventurer and outlaw. Smith saved a girl from a mob on Mars. Within a short time, the spaceman discovered that the girl was not human but a strange female monster, a "Shambleau." Only the intervention of a friend saved Smith from an ecstatic end under the coils of the monster's hair. The tale was a masterpiece, blending ancient mythology and modern science fantasy into a perfect mixture of fine writing. It quickly became one of the most popular stories published in *Weird Tales*.

That same issue, November 1933, contained another story by a female writer. Mary Elizabeth Counselman, was

Mary Elizabeth Counselman

not as popular as Moore, but held her own against most competition. "The Accursed Isle" was a horror story with no supernatural element. A group of men were marooned on a desert island. One was a homicidal maniac. But which one?

One of the most popular novels ever to appear in *Weird Tales* was "The Solitary Hunters," a three-part serial by David H. Keller. The novel was ranked first in reader voting in all three issues it appeared, placing ahead of works by Williamson, Howard, Smith, Price and Hamilton. "The Solitary Hunters" was an adventure story where an investigator tried to learn the fate of criminals who disappeared. He learned by personal experience that the crooks were taken to a hidden valley where they were used as food for giant wasps.

February featured Nictzin Dyalhis' "The Sapphire Goddess." An entertaining story of swords-and-sorcery, the novelet suffered from too much action in too short a story. The events could have filled an entire issue instead of the few pages it did. Explanations rarely made much sense and the plot line was lost in a maze of fast action.

In the same vein but better was Howard's "The Valley of the Worm." A story of racial memory, it was also swords-and-sorcery but better plotted and with a good monster, a giant "worm" from the depths of hell.

April 1934 was a typical issue of the period. Now a line-up as presented would be good enough for many anthologies. Featured were stories by E. Hoffmann Price (a serial installment), C.L. Moore, Edmond Hamilton, Robert E.

Howard, Carl Jacobi, and a reprint of Arthur J. Burks' "Bells of Oceana."

The Moore story was best with Northwest Smith on Venus, to learn the true meaning of beauty, in an adventure that suffered only in comparison to his first adventure. Worst in the issue was Dale Clark's (a pen-name of Ronal Kayser) "Behind the Screen." The story was based on the oft-used plot of "Don't tell me I'm dead," in which the main character discovered just that.

Moore and Howard made the May 1934 issue memorable. Howard was back with Conan as a buccaneer, in "Queen of the Black Coast." Northwest Smith of Earth entered a lost world by the use of a scarlet cloth in "Scarlet Dream."

July of the same year had as its cover story the first installment of one of the longest serials ever to appear in "The Unique Magazine." The length of the novel was matched only by its mediocrity. Arlton Eadie, the author, was capable of entertaining work but the novel was a typical "thriller," with little to recommend it. The novel was padded in the extreme, and featured wooden characters and a silly plot.

Fortunately, in the same issue Wright also printed "Through the Gates of the Silver Key," a collaboration between E. Hoffmann Price and H.P. Lovecraft. The short novel was run complete in the one issue. It was a sequel of sorts to the earlier Lovecraft story, "The Silver Key," and contained both elements of fantasy and science fiction.

As mentioned earlier, Wright printed short story fillers in the rear of his magazine to complete an issue. From time to time, as in the case of "The Night Wire," a story would receive a great deal of reader acclaim. Another story in this vein was "Three Marked Pennies" by Mary Elizabeth Counselman.

In the short short, people of a small town awaken to find notices pasted all over town. Three pennies are to be found, each one marked with a symbol:

To the first, $100,000 in cash
To the second, a trip around the world.
To the third, Death.

The events of the strange contest made up the rest of the story. No hint was given as to the sender or why the contest took place. Yet, the story managed to generate a good deal of suspense in only a few pages. It was a reader favorite and mentioned in letters to follow for the next few years.

September 1934 presented an unusual happening. Conan returned in a three-part serial which ran concurrently with the longer "Trail of the Cloven Hoof." The Conan story was "The People of the Black Circle" in which Conan fought a group of evil magicians.

The Jules de Grandin adventure in the same issue was worthy of note. "The Jest of Warburg Tantavul" was cited in *Author and Journalist* for October 1934:

> Incest is, to all intents and purposes, an impossible theme, . . . yet the September 1934 issue of *Weird Tales*, a pulp magazine for popular consumption, nonchalantly carried a story of out-and-out incest by Seabury Quinn. Moreover, the author justifies it . . . And So What: Merely that tabus, like rules are apparently made to be broken.

"The Black God's Kiss" by C.L. Moore introduced a heroine to match Northwest Smith in the October 1934 *Weird Tales*. Jirel of Joiry was a female warrior in medieval France. In search for revenge against the conqueror of her castle, she entered a strange world of magic in search of the statue of a terrible black God.

The story was well received and two months later Jirel returned in a sequel, "Black God's Shadow." In the same issue, Conan matched the female warrior with perhaps his most famous adventure. "A Witch Shall Be Born" was a minor Conan adventure with one exceptional scene. Conan was crucified by his enemies and left to die in the desert. As he tired, vultures circled him waiting for him to die. One landed on the barbarian's chest. With a lunge, Conan caught the bird's neck with his teeth. With a wrench of his jaw, he killed the vulture.

Robert Bloch made his debut in the January 1935 issue with a short little shocker, "The Feast in the Abbey." While the ending of the story was no surprise, the handling of the tale made it a worthy start for an author who was to become one of the magazine's all-time favorites.

Born in Chicago in 1917, Robert Bloch (1917-   ) was always a fan of comedy and the cinema. In 1927, an aunt offered to buy him any magazine on the newsstand at the train station. Bloch selected the August *Weird Tales* with the first installment of "The Bride of Osiris." Bloch became a correspondent of H.P. Lovecraft and many of his early stories were influenced by HPL. Within a short time after his appearance with "The Feast in the Abbey," Bloch was a *Weird Tales* regular. Fame came late to the popular writer but with "Psycho" he became a Hollywood regular with many of his stories adapted to the screen.

April 1935 started off with a major disaster—"The Man Who Was Two Men" was a terrible science fiction comedy by A.W. Bernal, a story that ranked among the worst stories ever published in *Weird Tales*. However, the rest of the issue's contents made up for the dreadful lead story.

Howard Wandrei was present with "The Hand of the O'Mecca," an unusual werewolf story that was probably the only horror story to end in a pun. Howard Wandrei was the brother of Donald Wandrei who wrote several odd stories for *Weird Tales*. Otto (1911-1974) Binder and his brother, Earl, were present, writing under the name Eando Binder, with "Shadows of Blood." Otto, by this time, was doing most of the writing for the team and "Shadows" was a grisly story of death in ancient Rome which twisted historical fact to fit the unusual plot.

Clark Ashton Smith was back after a short absence with "The Last Hieroglyphic," one of his typical entertaining fantasies of Zothique. Hazel Heald presented another Lovecraft rewrite, "Out of the Eons." The story was worth of the master, dealing with the finding of an ancient mummy and the horror it revealed. As usual, the ending was no surprise but the climactic scene was as well handled as any of Lovecraft's.

Competition from the Popular Publications horror magazines made itself felt in 1935. Wright began running weird detective stories in an attempt to capture away readers from *Horror Stories* and *Terror Tales*. Arthur B. Reeve brought in Craig Kennedy in May 1935. Soon after, Wright commissioned Paul Ernst to write a series of novelettes in the weird-detective vein. Dr. Satan was the resulting character.

A full-column blurb accompanied the first story of the series, "Dr. Satan," published in August 1935. The Satan stories were good fun but did not catch on with the readers. Eight stories were published in the series and then it was killed.

September's highlight had H.P. Lovecraft neatly gobbled up by an invisible "Shambler From the Stars" from the pen of Robert Bloch.

October had a varied bag of characters. Edmond Hamilton used his earlier idea of "The Time Raider" in "The Six Sleepers." Six soldiers from various historical eras band together in the far future to save a beautiful young girl from a horde of rat men.

Northwest Smith battled one of his strangest foes in "The Cold Gray God." Jules de Grandin fought "The Dead-Alive Mummy" in a typical adventure. Another mummy was also present in Arlton Eadie's thriller, "The Carnival of Death."

Conan and Dr. Satan both headlined the November issue. However, the most popular story was a short by P.F. Stern, an anagram for author Paul Ernst. "The Way Home" was typical of the worst published in *Weird Tales* during the period. A man who cannot remember his name wandered through a city looking for "the way home." He finally came to the graveyard in the midst of a storm and found his own tombstone. He realized now that he was dead. Readers continued to praise this hokey tale for months.

Robert E. Howard's most ambitious story, "The Hour of the Dragon," a five-part Conan novel started in the December 1935 issue. Conan was king but was soon deposed by a combination of enemies and the fiendish wizard, Xaltotun. The evil magician was one of Howard's finest creations, a long-dead sorceror from the forgotten empire of Acheron. He was a marvelously evil villain.

"The Hour of the Dragon" was a fast-paced entertainment. As a novel, it did not stand up very well with little complexity. The characters were not very well developed. However, the plotting of the conspirators was believable and the action was fast and furious. All of Howard's faults as well as all of his virtues were on exhibit in the popular novel.

The new year continued the tradition of starting off in grand fashion. Seabury Quinn was back as de Grandin fought "A Rival from the Grave." Dr. Satan offered very expensive premiums in an insurance business that protected one from violent death, also offered by Satan, in "Horror Insured." Jirel of Joiry returned after six months in an unusual story, "The Dark Land," where she encountered Death himself.

Two short stories were also of note. Robert Barbour Johnson used three short pages to tell of an old man who guarded campers from a valley where "They" lived. J. Wesley Rosenquest would have made Ambrose Bierce chuckle with "Return to Death."

Lovecraft finished off the issue in grand style with "Dagon," the Weird Tales Reprint.

A long-time reader and fan of *Weird Tales* made his debut in the March 1936 issue. Henry Kuttner had a chilling tale of horror in "The Graveyard Rats." A stupid graveyard keeper battled with the rats in the graveyard for a newly buried corpse. The story was a masterpiece of underground horror that built to a gruesome climax.

Edmond Hamilton and Henry Kuttner

Kuttner (1915-1958) was born in Los Angeles, but spent most of his early life in San Francisco. He worked after graduation from high school in a literary agency. After his *Weird Tales* debut, he soon became a full-time writer. In 1940, he married C.L. Moore and from that time on, nearly all work appearing under the two bylines were written by the pair. The Kuttners also used numerous pen-names and were among the most popular writing teams ever in the science fiction and fantasy circles.

Edmond Hamilton was back with something different in the same issue. In "In the World's Dusk," Hamilton told of the last man in the world and his efforts to repopulate the Earth.

"The Room of Shadows" by Arthur J. Burks was easily the best story in the May number. A well-told story of an ancient Tibetan wizard who kept alive for ages by transferring his personality from body to body. The story managed to catch the reader by surprise in the last few paragraphs with a chilling conclusion. It was a short masterpiece of unsuspected horror.

Robert Bloch told of Nyarlathotep, "The Faceless God," in the same issue. While the story was well presented, most notable was the superb Virgil Finlay illustration that accompanied it, an illustration that inspired Lovecraft to a famous poem about it.

The last Conan story was a three-part serial, "Red Nails" which began in the July 1936 *Weird Tales*. Howard committed suicide approximately at the time when the story first appeared and "Nails," a lost race adventure taking place during Conan's pirate days, brought down the curtain on the series.

"Isle of the Undead" was the lead story for October

1936. Written by Lloyd Eshbach, the novelet was a typical gory horror adventure of an island of vampires and their attack on a cruise ship. It was filled with exclamation points and furious action but was not the type of material normally featured in *Weird Tales*. Readers' complaints were long and loud. After that one mistake, Wright didn't run any future horror tales of that type.

Much better in the same issue was "The Tree of Life," a Northwest Smith adventure. In the novelette, Smith entered another dimension where he encountered a demon that actually *was* the world. One fault became clear with the Smith stories now. The theme of each adventure was the same. Smith encountered some form of ancient sorcery, almost succumbed, and then, by strength of will, defeated the menace. However, the stories were so well written that over a period of time the sameness of plot did not become apparent.

Earl Pierce, Jr., a friend of Robert Bloch, contributed several stories to "The Unique Magazine" at the urging of Bloch. In "The Doom of the House of Duryea" he told of a curse of vampirism that haunted a family for all history and of the end of the Duryeas in a totally logical but unexpected manner.

Lovecraft returned to end the year in fine fashion. In "The Shambler from the Stars" Robert Bloch finished off H.P.L. in gruesome fashion. Now, following a suggestion made in The Eyrie, Lovecraft did the honors to Bloch in "The Haunter of the Dark." Robert Blake was the hero of the top-notch horror story. To add insult to injury, Nyarlathotep, the Mythos god used by Bloch in several of his stories was the instrument of vengeance that brought the author to his horrible end.

Howard was present in the same issue with a posthumous tale, "The Fire of Asshurbahipal." A fast-paced action story set in Afghanistan it was similar to the stories Howard had sold to straight adventure pulps like *Top-Notch*. The Fire was a giant jewel guarded by a Cthulhuian monster in a lost city.

Jules de Grandin started off the new year with his latest adventure. "Children of the Bat" was one of the worst novelettes featuring the Frenchman as he fought a secret society in Central America.

While not one of his best stories, "The Thing on the Doorstep" brought back Lovecraft for the second month in a row. Strange goings on at Miskatonic University and a moody young writer's unfortunate marriage formed the background for this typical tale of the Cthulhu Mythos.

G. Garnet was the pen-name used by Irvin Ashkenazy for his one story in *Weird Tales*. "The Headless Miller of Kobald's Keep" was an entertaining horror story that was later revised and published under the author's real name in *Fantastic* in 1965.

Even Seabury Quinn must have been getting tired of Jules de Grandin, for "The Globe of Memories," lead story for the February 1937 issue, did not feature the French detective. Instead, Quinn wrote of reincarnation and of adventure in medieval France. While not a bad story it was burdened with overbearing sentimentality and an ending which was of no surprise and little interest.

March 1937 was a good issue and displayed editor Wright's talents. Of the big names of the period,—Lovecraft, C.L. Moore, Quinn, Robert E. Howard, and Clark Ashton Smith, none appeared with a new story. Still, the issue was a good one with several fine stories by writers not as well known but equally talented.

G.G. Pendarves told of "The Dark Star," in which the hero of the story entered a tapestry to battle with the diabolical villain. Henry Hasse, a long-time fan, wrote about "The Guardian of the Book," a tale in the Cthulhu Mythos, though not related to any story or god. "Brood of Bubastis" was a minor Robert Bloch tale. Earl Pierce, Jr., Bloch's Milwaukee friend, was present with an unusual novelette, "The Last Archer," about a man who fought *himself* over the centuries.

"The Seeds from Outside" by Edmond Hamilton was a departure from Hamilton's action line. In the very short short, a man found a strange pair of seeds from outer space. He planted them and they grew into an alien woman and man. The hero fell in love with the woman and the plant man killed her in anger. At the end, both plants were dead and the hero desolate. It was a strange and unusual story, showing Hamilton quite capable of more than the usual adventure fare he ground out on demand.

April 1937 continued the trend of lesser authors with top stories with contributions by Hamilton, Derleth, and Pierce. Best in the issue was Bloch's "The Mannikin." Twins joined at birth formed the basis of a gruesome bit of the Cthulhu Mythos. It was accompanied by one of Finlay's best illustrations—which unfortunately gave away the climax of the story on the second page of the work.

"Mark of the Monster" by Jack Williamson was the cover story for May 1937. Williamson had been writing for *Thrilling Mystery* during the period and the piece read like

Robert Bloch

a reject from that magazine.

A man returned home after years away. He wanted to marry his childhood sweetheart but his relatives beg him not to do so. He was told that his mother mated with a monster from outer space and saw a hideous creature supposedly his twin brother. So far, a credible takeoff on "The Dunwich Horror." Unfortunately, the story swiftly went downhill, with the entire occurence a hoax perpetrated to swindle the hero out of his inheritance.

In the same issue, a long serial of Egyptian adventure began. "The Last Pharoah" told of an immortal ruler from Egypt who planned to wipe out all of the people in the world other than those under his rule and how a young American thwarted his plans.

Author of the novel was Thomas Kelley. Kelley was one of the few Canadian authors ever to write for *Weird Tales*. Son of the last of the medicine men in Canada he often dressed up as a little girl in his father's show while on the road. Later, he became a professional boxer. "The Last Pharoah" was Kelley's first story. One day he had the idea for a story involving heads living without a body to support them. He expanded the idea into a novel. Not knowing how to type, he dictated the entire story to his wife, who did his typing. The entire novel was written in 11 days and submitted to *Weird Tales*. It was bought for $700. Kelley managed to sell two other long novels to "The Unique Magazine" until it discontinued serials in 1941. However, in early 1942, Canada placed an embargo on American magazines. Kelley soon was writing stories for all types of Canadian pulps. Often he wrote two or three short stories a day. In later years, Kelley has written a series of semi-historical novels about a family, "The Black Donnellys."

"The Ocean Ogre" by Dana Carroll must have given some readers pause to wonder in the July 1937 issue. The story was a paragraph by paragraph paraphrase of "The Sea Thing" by Frank Belknap Long!

In June 1937, Farnsworth Wright published the news of H.P. Lovecraft's death. Beginning with August of that year, a string of Lovecraft's poems and stories started appearing in an unbroken line for more than a year. Some of the work was rejected material, others were early fanzine stories. It was ironic that after his death, HPL's work sold better than during his lifetime.

September 1937 was a throw-back to the very best days of *Weird Tales*. Edmond Hamilton led off the issue with the first part of a three-part serial, "The Lake of Life." The novel was an action-packed A. Merritt imitation. A band of diverse adventurers went looking for a lost valley where was rumored to exist a lake which gave eternal life to the user of its waters. There were two lost races, of course, one human, the other not. As was usual in such stories, the secret was not all that it was supposed to be.

Jules de Grandin had the cover with "Satan's Palimpest." Manly Wade Wellman updated an old-style ghost story in "School For the Unspeakable." Clark Ashton Smith horrified in a grisly tale of love and sadism with "The Death of Ilalotha." Poetry scored heavily with Lovecraft's narrative, "Psychopompos," Howard's "The Dream and the Shadow," and Kuttner's tribute to the master in "HPL."

Howard and Lovecraft were both back in the next issue. "The Shunned House" was one of Lovecraft's best short novels and it was published complete in the October issue. Howard was back with one of his best poems, "Which Will Scarcely Be Understood."

"Tiger Cat" by David H. Keller led off the issue. It was not fantasy at all but instead an unusual tale of torture and sadism and revenge that could only be placed in "The Unique Magazine."

Henry Kuttner and C.L. Moore collaborated for the first time in "Quest of the Starstone" in November 1937. The story brought together Moore's two characters, Jirel of Joiry and Northwest Smith. As more than a thousand years separated the pair, their meeting was somewhat contrived. A fantastic quest for a magic jewel, the tale was not up to the other stories in the series and was never reprinted.

January 1938 started the year as usual with Seabury Quinn. However, Jules de Grandin was not present. Instead, in "Roads," Quinn had a long romance of a mercenary soldier who by helping Christ evolved through the centuries into Santa Claus. The story quickly became one of the all-time favorites on readers' list. Conrad Ruppert, the famous fanzine printer, published the novel in hardcover. Later, the story was reprinted in an edition illustrated by Virgil Finlay and published by Arkham House.

"The Diary of Alonzo Typer" by William Lumley was highly praised by many readers as being worthy of the pen of H.P. Lovecraft. Not surprising as Lovecraft had revised the tale for Lumley long before its publication in February 1938.

Kuttner began his own series of barbarian adventures in the May 1938. In an effort to capitalize on the void left by Conan, Kuttner had four stories of a comparable hero, Elak of Atlantis. In "Thunder in the Dawn," Elak and

Lycon, his friend and companion, fought monsters and wizards by the score. The main trouble with the Elak story was just that. Each chapter contained some new menace or new monster. The plots tended to run away with the story. There was little chance for characterization or complexity. Instead, the plot dashed along with Elak and Lycon killing everything that got in their way. The Kuttner stories were entertaining but lacked the true savagery that made the Conan stories memorable.

November 1938 saw *Weird Tales* under a new publisher. The cover story was a new serial by Thomas Kelley. "I Found Cleopatra" was a much better story than Kelley's first novel. It contained enough fantastic elements for five novels. Kelley was another writer who believed in throwing in some new element with each chapter. There was a wolf-man, Cleopatra alive after two thousand years, the original Tree of Life from the Garden of Eden, Arab marauders, an underwater kingdom, huge reptilian monsters, and much much more. The novel was episodic with the standard capture and escape, capture and escape. The plot had little complexity and the novel was padded with bizarre twists. But, in spite of all its faults, the serial moved well and caught up the reader in its fast pace.

Each part of the serial was quite long and the novel squeezed out many short stories. December 1938 only saw five other stories, the best of these being G.G. Pendarves' occult adventure, "The Sin Eater."

February 1939 saw the first major change in format of the pulp since 1924. Page count went from 128 to 160 pages. The increased size made it possible to run many more stories per issue. It was the last gasp of a magazine trying to recapture the glory of other days.

Manly Wade Wellman (1903-   ) had been writing for "The Unique Magazine" for years. His serial, "Fearful Rock," was the lead story for the February issue. Other contents included stories by Clark Ashton Smith, August Derleth, Seabury Quinn and Donald Wandrei, as well as poetry by Lovecraft and Howard.

March had August Derleth with the first and best of his Cthulhu imitations—"The Return of Hastur." De Grandin was off-stage much of the time in "The House Where Time Stood Still." Instead, it was Dr. Trowbridge who was kept prisoner by a mad surgeon who created monstrosities as abominable as any Lovecraftian horror and much more real. The adventure was one of the most gruesome stories ever to appear in the magazine.

Using the same basic idea of "The Six Sleepers," Edmond Hamilton told of Ethan Drew who was drawn with several other soldiers into the far future to battle an evil dictator in "Comrades of Time." Drew and company returned the next month, complete with entire armies in "Armies From the Past."

"Hellsgarde" was the last of the Jirel of Joiry stories. It was a masterful tale. From its beginning, with Jirel coming upon the citadel Hellsgarde at dusk, to its eerie exorcism scene, to its sardonic conclusion, the story was a powerful one of dark forces and even darker hungers. It was a fitting conclusion to the series.

"Almuric" was a novel in the Edgar Rice Burroughs tradition that began in the May 1939 *Weird Tales*. The story, by Robert E. Howard, had been completed by the

Texan before his death but was only a first draft. The serial revealed the lack of rewriting. It suffered from hasty construction and a less-than-inspired plot.

"Far Below" by Robert Barbour Johnson was a tribute to H.P. Lovecraft that appeared in story form in the June-July 1939 issue. The story was based on a line from "Pickman's Model" and caused more than one New Yorker to have second thoughts about the subway system. Thirty-five years after its publication in "The Unique Magazine," the story still proved popular as the lead story in FAR BELOW AND OTHER HORRORS, as published by FAX in 1974.

August 1939 was one of the last great issues of *Weird Tales*. "The Valley Was Still" was one of Manly Wade Wellman's finest tales of the Civil War. A magic man offered help to help win the war against the North to a Southern soldier, for certain considerations made to an unnamed third party. Deciding that honor was more important than victory, the soldier turned down the deal with the devil.

E. Hoffmann Price was back with a humorous story which explained why black magic spells were always written in extinct languages. Robert Bloch told of the horror of "The Totem-Pole," and Jules de Grandin visited yet another strange house in "The House of the Three Corpses."

Most unusual in the issue was P. Schuyler Miller's "Spawn." Based on the discredited Arrhenius theory that life travels from planet to planet in spores, it was a powerful story of resurrected life. Three spores landed on Earth— one on a mountain range, a second in the ocean, and the third on the body of a dead dictator lying in state. Each came to life. The story was an accounting of how all three were destroyed.

"Spawn" was written in the style of the late Charles Fort, with snatches of story intermingled with bits of fact and stream-of-consciousness thought. It was a minor masterpiece by author P. Schuyler Miller which received little attention because of its unusual style and outdated science.

H. Warner Munn returned late in the year with his most ambitious story ever. "King of World's Edge" told of a group of Roman legionnaires, who along with Merlin the magician, traveled to North America in search of a kingdom for King Arthur to rule. On the unexplored continent, they battled diabolical fish men and treacherous Indians in a fight for freedom. It was an exciting novel though burdened in spots with military strategy. Two sequels to the novel were published in paperback in the last few years.

G. G. Pendarves appeared for the last time with a new story in November 1939. "The Withered Heart" was published posthumously and in a way seemed to signal the end of an era. The long decline was beginning. December 1939 saw C.L. Moore for the last time with a short story reprinted from a 1935 fanzine. Lovecraft, Howard, Whitehead, Pendarves, and others were dead. Clark Ashton Smith had stopped writing. E. Hoffmann Price, C.L. Moore, and Henry Kuttner had moved on to better-paying markets. New regulars would fill the places in the contents page but could never fill the places in the Hall of Fame of pulp fiction. While a few new discoveries would be made, they were few and far between. For Farnsworth Wright, there would be no more discoveries. The last issue edited by Wright was March 1940, though obviously, a number of issues afterward included stories picked by Wright. Dorothy McIlwraith, who had served as assistant editor for *Weird Tales* since its move to New York, took over as editor. A new era had begun for "The Unique Magazine."

3. The McIlwraith Issues

May 1940 listed a new editor for *Weird Tales* for the first time since 1924. Farnsworth Wright, due to both economic reasons and health problems, was dismissed by the publisher. Taking his place was Dorothy McIlwraith, already assistant editor of *Weird Tales* and *Short Stories*. Assisting her was Lamont Buchanan, who also served as art director. Ms. McIlwraith remained editor of *Weird Tales* until its final issue in 1954.

An an editor, Ms. McIlwraith was a competent craftsman but was not on the same level as Farnsworth Wright. She was a veteran pulp editor and handled the magazine as best she could. Her biggest trouble was that she was not as familiar with weird fiction as her predecessor. Another problem was that her ideas on what *Weird Tales* should be were somewhat narrower in scope than the beliefs Wright worked by. A publisher who did not let her run the magazine with as free a hand was no help. She did the best she could.

The forties was a bad time for *Weird Tales*. Most of the great authors from earlier days were either dead or writing for better-paying markets. There was real competition, from both science fiction magazines and top-quality pulp fantasy magazines such as *Strange Stories* and *Unknown Worlds*. And, the impending war bode ill for all pulp magazines.

At first, the McIlwraith issues showed little difference than those edited by Wright, primarily as much of the material had been bought by Wright. The change in policy was slow but sure in coming.

May 1940 was the first issue with Dorothy McIlwraith as editor. The issue was a good one. Cover was by Hannes Bok. The long lead story was "The City From the Sea" by Edmond Hamilton. It was a fantastic adventure of an island that rose out of the sea, with remnants of a lost race still present. It was an exciting adventure fantasy in the Merritt tradition.

Fritz Leiber, Jr. (1910-   ) had been submitting heroic fantasy stories to *Weird Tales* since 1939. The tales were of an odd pair of heroes, Fafhred and the Gray Mouser. The stories were all rejected and instead bought by John W. Campbell, Jr. for *Unknown*, always with the remark that "These would be better in *Weird Tales*." For some unknown reason, Farnsworth Wright and later, Dorothy McIlwraith did not like the stories. However, Leiber's first weird story taking place in modern day was printed in the May issue. "The Automatic Pistol" was first of a series of studies of ghost stories with modern backgrounds, including such classics as "Conjure Wife" and "Smoke Ghost," both published in *Unknown Worlds*.

E. Hoffmann Price and Robert Bloch also were present. But the Weird Tales Reprint was gone. In its place was a dreadful "fact" feature, "It Happened to Me," supposed true supernatural experiences from the readers.

July 1940 was the end of one era. "A Million Years in the Future" by Thomas Kelley, a long novel by Thomas Kelley that combined wild elements of both fantasy and science fiction, came to a conclusion after four long installments. Only one other serial was ever printed, and that under special circumstances. There was no room for continued stories in a bimonthly magazine. "All Stories Complete" was a popular slogan of the time. Another was "All Stories New—No Reprints." Both became part of the new credo of *Weird Tales*. Unfortunately, the two restrictions also narrowed the uniqueness of *Weird Tales'* contents. No longer were there wild adventure stories in the best fantastic vein. Nor were there reprints of classics often mentioned but rarely found. Both changes were major policy decisions, based mainly on the style of the time, not the reality of the situation. The editor and the publisher were just not familiar enough with *Weird Tales* and its followers. They tried to make it into another science fiction magazine featuring weird stories instead of science fiction. The problem was that *Weird Tales* was unique and copying the contents of others made it into a copy instead of an originator.

H. Bedford-Jones, one of the most prolific of all pulpsters, began a series of four stories in the July issue. Jones, who had rarely been published in *Weird Tales*, was a regular for *Short Stories*, the other pulp owned by *Weird Tales'* publisher. "The Adventures of a Professional Corpse" were four connected stories of a man who could feign death. None of the stories were fantasy and were rarely unusual. They were among the most minor stories written by Bedford-Jones.

Also in the same issue was Frank Gruber with "The Golden Chalice." Gruber was another pulp regular who had not contributed before to "The Unique Magazine." But, he had written for *Short Stories*. McIlwraith was using her regulars from one magazine to boost the other. She gambled on the big names from the non-fantasy pulps to boost circulation. The gamble didn't work. Worse, the stories were not particularly good ones.

September 1940 brought yet another *Short Stories* regular, Robert Leitfred, to the magazine. Leitfred sold one science fiction story to *Weird Tales* back in 1935. He later became a regular for *Short Stories*. With the sale of *Weird Tales* in 1940, he returned with several more science fiction stories featuring the same hero as his first story. Very possibly, they were rejections from the thirties which he was able to resubmit and sell to an editor more familiar with his work.

Humor had returned to the fantasy field with the advent of *Unknown* in 1939. John W. Campbell, Jr. stressed a logical approach to the supernatural and he showed a marked preference towards fantasy with a strong humorous slant. *Unknown's* rates were better than *Weird Tales* and it was a steadier market. *Weird Tales* found itself deluged with rejects from the Street and Smith magazine. It was an unequal competition. The best humorous stories went to Campbell. The rejects went to McIlwraith. The same authors appeared in both magazines, with only the quality of the stories separating their work between the two pulps.

"The Unusual Romance of Ferdinand Pratt" had a typewriter fall in love with a writer. It was by Nelson Bond, a pulpster who managed to sell space opera to *Planet Stories*, action to *Amazing*, and slick humor to *Blue Book*. His lesser humorous stories were published in *Weird Tales* during the early 1940's.

"Dragon Moon" by Henry Kuttner lead off January

1941. It was obviously a story bought some time earlier by Wright, the last of the Elak of Atlantis adventures. It was the best of the series. Elak was summoned to his homeland to fight a near indestructible creature known only as Karkora, the Pallid One. Kuttner showed unusual restraint and did not let the story run away from him. The villain was a truly menacing one and the plot was not too complex to follow with ease. "Dragon Moon" was Elak's finest adventure but also his last. There was no room in the McIlwraith *Weird Tales* for swords-and-sorcery.

The same issue contained a Seabury Quinn novelette, a David H. Keller short, "House of the Hatchet" by Bloch and contributions by Robet Barbour Johnson and Mary Elizabeth Counselman. It was one of the last golden age issues of *Weird Tales*. However, the Finlay poetry page was gone and instead an ineptly sketched page of "Superstitions and Taboos" took its place.

May 1941 brought "The Last of Lovecraft's." The novel was "The Case of Charles Dexter Ward" which was run as a two-part serial. The story, thought lost, was a treat for readers who had not seen a Lovecraft story in years. The buildup was superbly handled and while the ending was telegraphed early, the novel still possessed a fine confrontation between Dr. Armitage and Curwen.

September 1941 was a good issue with a Derleth Cthulhu Mythos story as the lead. "Birthmark" was a fairly decent Quinn novelette. Bloch had "A Sorceror Runs for Sheriff," a modern-day horror story with more than a trace of humor. Nelson Bond was present also with a Lancelot Biggs story. The Biggs tales were space opera of a bungler who always turned out to be anything but. They appeared in several science fiction magazines of the era. How they fit it into *Werid Tales* was a mystery.

January 1942 capitalized again on Lovecraft's name with first magazine publication of "The Shadow Over Innsmouth." The well-written story with a double-twist ending, it was published complete in the one issue.

Mary Elizabeth Counselman was also present with "Parasite Mansion" adapted for television years later. It was a vivid tale of poltergeists and ESP power.

Robert Bloch had the lead in March 1942 with "Hell on Earth." The devil was captured by a group of scientists but once they had him, the problem arose, what to do with him?

Lovecraft was back again—it seemed that lost or unpublished stories by him went on forever—with probably the most minor of all his stories. "Herbert West: Reanimator" was an early set of six stories which had been printed in the early 1920's in semi-professional magazines.

Jules de Grandin returned in May 1942. He had been fighting with the Free French but returned after wounded in battle to the United States. In "Stoneman's Memorial," de Grandin's opponent was a living statue. The story was weak and lacked some of the Quinn flair. Length, for one thing, was lacking. The new *Weird Tales* had no room for the long epics of years gone by. Now, pieces were short and snappy. Quinn's style was not suited for the quick-paced, continual-action approach and his pieces in the last decade lacked the vitality of his earlier work.

One of the best stories to appear during the period was Henry Kuttner's "Masquerade." This story, also, was adapted for television. It answered the question what happened to vampires in modern times. Did they adapt to change or remain the monsters of long ago? Tom Posten played the TV hero and managed to capture all of the wise-craking and sardonic wit of the story's main character without sacrificing any of the believability. It was one of the best humorous stories ever to appear in *Weird Tales*.

November 1942 saw the first of two stories by Bloch dealing with a man hired to be the zookeeper for a very peculiar group of animals. The protagonist was literally a "Nursemaid to Nightmares" as he encountered a satyr, mermaid, gorgon and other mythological creatures in a breezy novelette.

The same issue saw the first publication of a short story by a young fan who was to become one of the last great *Weird Tales* writers. "The Candle" was a very minor story that did not indicate the true talent of Ray Bradbury.

Bradbury (1920-   ) was born in Waukegan, Illinois. However, by the time he was fourteen, his family had moved to Los Angeles. There the young Bradbury came into contact with the large science fiction group there and was quickly converted into a rabid fan of the genre. From his earliest days in fandom, the cheerful Bradbury showed an interest in getting into professional print. He finally sold a short story to *Super Science* and his career had started. He received $25 for "The Candle," which was written with the help of his friend, Henry Kuttner. Within a short time, Bradbury was selling stories to a majority of the science fiction magazines as well as *Weird Tales*. His shorts in "The Unique Magazine" were well received but it was through his science fiction work that Bradbury would strike it rich. Bradbury began selling to "the slicks" in the late 1940's and ever since has been the one science fiction writer to make the transition from the SF field to the "literary" one.

Bradbury returned with "The Wind" in January 1943. Written in a conscious effort to imitate the style of Ernest Hemingway, the story was much better than "The Candle." In "The Wind," a man strived desperately to convince a doubting friend that the Wind was alive and was after him for knowing its secret. It was a stirring piece of fantasy fiction.

Edgar Allan Poe was Bradbury's model in May 1943. "The Crowd" was a strong effort which owed much of its idea to "The Man In the Crowd," by Poe. Both stories dealt with the phenomena of crowds that gathered immediately at the scene of an accident or disaster.

July 1943 contained a story that surprised its author, Robert Bloch. "Yours Truly, Jack the Ripper" advanced the theory that Jack the Ripper was alive and well in the United States. Using killings every few years as a means to satiate certain demon gods, the Ripper lived in eternal youth. Weaving a diabolical spell of fact and fantasy, the story built up to a tension-packed surprise conclusion. It was soon adapted to radio when Bloch began scripting such shows. It was dramatized many times since then, on both radio and television. It stands as a classic of horror fiction and one of Bloch's all-time best stories.

Edmond Hamilton returned after a long absence with the first of a loosely connected series of novelettes based on ancient myths and legends. "The Valley of Assassins" had the Old Man of the Mountain as an ageless fiend who ruled over a modern-day cult of Assassins. The action was fast and the writing smooth. Hamilton was the master of such pulp fiction and while they were no classics, each story fulfilled its primary duty—to entertain. Later stories dealt with Irish, Mayan, and Norse Mythology.

A big man—both physically and morally—made his debut in the same November 1943 issue. A creation of Manly Wade Wellman, the hero was John Thunstone and he battled evil with a deep rooted knowledge of both white and black magic. In "Third Cry From Legba," Thunstone fought the return of a voodoo god as well as the evil magician, Rowley Thorne. Thorne, who was loosely based on Alaistar Crowley, was the villain in a number of the Thunstone stories and always provided an entertaining contrast to the wholesome hero, as Thorne was the absolute in complete and total evil. The Thunstone stories were to the 1940's what de Grandin was to the 1930's.

August Derleth began a new Mythos novel with the first of a series of novelettes that were to be collectively called "The Trail of Cthulhu." The first appeared in 1944, and the final story in the series, in 1951. Dr. Laban Shrewsbury and friends delved into forbidden books to fight the minions of Cthulhu with both ancient sorcery and modern weapons. All of the novelettes were undistinguished and read like parodies of Lovecraft's work.

Much better was "The Peeper" by Frank Belknap Long, the story of a man who gave up his talent in the search of wealth and the strange death that came to him. Long was capable of doing all sorts of work—from dreadful space opera and mediocre horror tales to outstanding classics in both fields. His quality was uneven and so some of his work surprised the casual reader. He was one of the few writers to steadily contribute to *Weird Tales* for almost its entire run and his notable stories far outweighed his poor ones. "The Peeper" was one of his least-remembered and best stories.

Allison V. Harding contributed a long list of stories to *Weird Tales* in the 1940's, most of them undistinguished works that filled up space and were quickly forgotten. "The Guard In The Dark" in July 1944 was one of his few memorable tales. It paralleled much of the action in "The Thing in the Cellar." A young boy, quite intelligent, was brought to the attention of a doctor by his parents. The child used toy soldiers by the hundreds. Each night he positioned lead soldiers around his bed. The next day, he throws dozens of broken ones away. The boy claimed that the soldiers protected him. The doctor advised the parents not to buy him any more soldiers. Slowly the supply of soldiers goes down as there are no replacements. Finally there was but one soldier left. The next morning, the boy was found—a raving idiot. As the boy's tutor left the house of the family, he found the one toy soldier in his pocket.

> He brought the soldier closer, much closer to his face. Wilburt's fingers trembled. It was all quite impossible.
>
> The tiny lead face should be a blob of expressionless putty and paint. But it wasn't. Instead the toy soldier's countenance was frozen in a grimace of unspeakable horror—rivaled only by the face of the man so near his own!

One of the most interesting creations of the 1940's *Weird Tales* was The Shonokins. The legend was created by Manly Wade Wellman for his John Thunstone series but within a few months, readers were writing in to The Eyrie

Joseph Payne Brennan

about their knowledge of The Shonokins. Perhaps later, the same people wrote to *Amazing Stories* about deros. The Shonokins were a race of prehistoric beings who lived in North America before the coming of the Indians. A few of them stlll survived and they menaced Thunstone in several adventures. Wellman often quoted from real sources for facts in his tales, but the Shonokins were complete fabrications. But he couldn't convince some readers of that fact.

The troubles of the magazine were becoming apparent. Dorothy McIlwraith was not to be blamed for the decline of *Weird Tales*. Ms. McIlwraith did the best she could with what was available. The main problem was that there wasn't much around. The big names were gone, and costs were up.

July 1945 was the best issue of that year. Feature story was "The Watcher From the Sky," one of "The Trail of Cthulhu" series. Fortunately, the issue contained a number of better stories. Robert Bloch was present with "One Way to Mars." Wellman and Thunstone encountered a sword that could not be drawn without tasting blood in "The Dai Sword." Bradbury told of "The Dead Man" and Carl Jacobi wrote about "Carnaby's Fish." Top honors went to Edmond Hamilton with "The Inn Outside the World." It was one of Hamilton's best and probably the best story to appear in the last years of *Weird Tales*.

The story told of an Inn located in a spot outside of the normal universe where members could meet and talk about their different ages. For the Inn was outside of both time and space and people from all eras of history could enter. How one man proposed that the members interfere with the course of history and why his idea was defeated formed the basis of the story. The mysterious Su Suum was pivotal in the story and he spoke with Hamilton's voice as he gave the ultimate reason for non-interference. Hamilton chose the tale as his best work in MY BEST SCIENCE FICTION STORY, a 1949 hardcover anthology, and few would argue

with his decision.

Things went from bad to worse in 1946. De Grandin was back in "Three in Chains," "Catspaw," "Kurban" and "The Man in the Crescent Terrace," all minor adventures.

Wellman and his creation, Thunstone, continued to entertain but as with any series, the stories began to wear thin. The Thunstone adventures were fun but month after month escaping perils that began to have a wearying sameness started to take its toll.

Bradbury was in good form with several horror stories that would advance his reputation as the most popular of *Weird Tales'* regulars. "The Smiling People" was not fantasy but straight horror of a man driven insane by his relatives. "The Night" was a much better story and straight fantasy. "Let's Play Poison" returned to Bradbury's favorite topic, childhood and the fears of childhood, and it was an effective horror story.

Bloch had stories in five out of the six issues. Best of the group which included "Frozen Fear," "The Bogey Man Will Get You" and others was "Enoch." A strange tale of the strange creature that lived in a man's skull and whispered horrible things to him, "Enoch" was one of Bloch's favorite stories and has been reprinted numerous times since its first appearance.

November 1946 brought forth the "Spawn of the Green Abyss" by C. Hall Thompson. A direct pastiche of Lovecraft in both style and content, the story was similar to "The Shadow Over Innsmouth." However, "Spawn" was well written and entertainingly told. Thompson did several other Lovecraft pastiches until Derleth made *Weird Tales* stop from publishing them. Derleth maintained a stranglehold on all Lovecraftian ideas, though it was doubtful that he had any legal right to do so.

January 1947 started that year off somewhat better than past performances. "The Hog," an unpublished Carnacki story by William Hope Hodgson, was the cover story. "The King of Shadows" was typical Hamilton. Theodore Sturgeon (1918-   ) made his *Weird Tales* debut with "Cellmate," originally rejected years before by *Unknown*. Sturgeon would sell a number of stories not suited for the Street and Smith magazine to *Weird Tales* during the next few years and become one of the more popular authors for "The Unique Magazine" in its last years. Bradbury added to the issue with "The Handler," a chilling little horror gem that was later adapted into an even more effective comic strip by EC Comics.

Unfortunately, the rest of the year did not match the first issue. Clark Ashton Smith returned with an old story published in a private press edition in the 1930's, "The Quest of the Gazolba" as the highlight of the year. Bloch's "Sweets to the Sweet," with its memorable last scene was one of the few above-average stories in the dismal year.

March 1948 was the twenty-fifth anniversary of *Weird Tales*. An extra effort was made to make the issue a memorable one. It was a good try but again pointed out the difference between the thirties and the forties. Best in the 1948 number was Bradbury's "The October Game," with its famous last line. Other regulars in the issue included Edmond Hamilton, Clark Ashton Smith (with another old fanzine story), Manly Wade Wellman, Carl Jacobi, Robert Bloch, and Theodore Sturgeon. Lovecraft was present with a poem. Two authors who had never been associated with "The Unique Magazine" but who were excellent ghost writers, Algernon Blackwood and H.R. Wakefield, also were represented. It was a good issue but could not compare with the best of the thirties. The days of glory were gone.

Robert Heinlein's only story in *Weird Tales*, "Our Fair City" was the lead for January 1949. "Our Fair City" was an *Unknown* style story but with that magazine gone, it went to *Weird Tales*. The Heinlein contribution was a light-hearted adventure of how corruption in a big city was combated by a group of concerned citizens aided by a friendly whirlwind.

July 1949 featured "Come and Go Mad" by pulpster Fredric Brown. This novelette was an effective tale of a man driven to insanity by the knowledge that man was not the true master of the world. In the same issue appeared "The Masher" by Ewen Whyte, one of the most gruesome stories ever to appear in *Weird Tales*, with its frightening but appropriate last line.

May 1951 marked the end of a policy began in 1940. Reprints returned to help fill up the spaces left by more and more authors moving onto better-paying markets. The magazine was in hard times and the reprints offered big-name authors at no cost. Unfortunately, Arkham House had published much of the better stories from early issues in hardcover and *Weird Tales* was forced to use stories not as

well known. Nor did the publisher make any effort to capitalize on the reprint bonanza. The only way to tell that the story used was a reprint was by the small original copyright notice. The reprint policy escaped many—as one or two letter writers wrote in to express hope that there would be more stories from the new author, H.P. Lovecraft!

The last discovery of *Weird Tales* was Joseph Payne Brennan, a fine writer of entertaining horror stories. Brennan broke into *Weird Tales* at the very end of the magazine's existence. His novelette, "Slime," in which a creature from the sea attacked mankind, was a diverting entertainment from the mediocrity that had overtaken the magazine. Brennan contributed several other quality pieces before the magazine finally collapsed.

Death came in September 1954. Dorothy McIlwraith had done her best to keep *Weird Tales* going under a limited budget and under policies not always in the best interest of the magazine. But a general lack of interest in weird fiction and too much competition finally did *Weird Tales* in.

The magazine was finished but not so the fiction. Hundreds of stories from *Weird Tales* have been reprinted from it, beginning with anthologies edited in the 1920's through books being assembled today. It still remains the single most important source of modern weird fiction ever published. As long as a single story is reprinted, the fiction of *Weird Tales* will live on.

5
Recollections
of Weird Tales

FRANK BELKNAP LONG

In the heyday of the pulp magazines, it was not too remarkable a feat for an all-fiction publication with a distinctly limited audience appeal to avoid disaster for a great many years. But what *is* remarkable about *Weird Tales* is the "living legend" aspect which it has taken on today, when it has ceased to appear on the stands and close to half a century has gone by since the first issue made H.P. Lovecraft decide that he had perhaps found an audience for his genius-inspired macabre tales.

Only two other pulp magazines have acquired this legendary aura today: John Campbell's *Unknown Worlds* and the early *Astounding Science Fiction*. But they were of later vintage and the shining quality which makes them treasured collector's items survived for a much shorter length of time as a newstand phenomenon.

I've often found myself wondering just what it was that enveloped all three publications in an extended burst of glory, so to speak, and believe I may have come up with the answer. Very few of the contributors whose work is remembered today thought of themselves as popular magazine writers. Not a few of them went so far as to believe that they were what used to be known as "literary men," or "Men of Letters." That is considered a very old-fashioned, snobbish term today and writers in general shy away from applying it to themselves or to others. I'm quite sure that even Norman Mailer prefers to think of himself as a tough-fibered, hard-bitten "regular guy," and would flee from such a label with a backward glance of derision, branding it a Victorian hang-up.

But the term did have great validity at one time—when HPL was in his thirties and I was knee-high to a cricket—and it possessed such validity for Clark Ashton Smith, August Derleth and Tennessee Williams (whose first published story appeared in *Weird Tales*), Ray Bradbury, Robert Bloch, Henry Kuttner, C.L. Moore, Ted Sturgeon, Donald and Howard Wandrei, and a half-dozen other writers I could mention. I even suspect that when L. Sprague de Camp became an early contributor to *Astounding* and *Unknown*

Worlds he would have worn that designation with pride and no trace of self-consciousness. Of course, I cannot speak for him but his many-splendored, scholarly, deliciously humorous contributions to both publications bear the unmistakable stamp of literary genius. I don't know whether or not Asimov would have shunned the label, but I've always thought of him as a scholar and imaginative fiction writer of exceptional brilliance and I'm quite sure he would have been considered a wellrounded literary man before that term fell into disrepute and was widely abandoned.

Anyway, what I'm trying to say is that the early *Weird Tales* contributors whose work has survived were in all respects the exact opposite of pulp magazine writers. But they were, for the most part, very young and there was absolutely no other market in America for the kind of stories they prefered to write. And Farnsworth Wright was, despite his several editorial blind spots, an extremely discerning editor.

Some of the early contributors have since abandoned fantasy, supernatural horror story and science fiction writing and carved distinguishable careers for themselves in other fields. A few like Chesterton, died at an early age, "perishing in their pride." Others have turned to mainstream fiction, or have managed somehow to become successful physists, engineers, musicians and even abstract painters. But August Derleth has continued to write weird fiction despite his great fame as a regional novelist, and Robert Bloch now has not only PSYCHO but another major movie to his credit and has become America's Number One Horror Expert.

As for HPL—the literary recognition that has accrued since his death has already placed him on a higher pedestal than the one occupied by Bierce, and it can be predicted, with a fair measure of confidence, that in a few more years he will stand at Poe's side on the highest supernatural story pedestal of all. Ray Bradbury has written at least twenty stories on the imperishable, literary-heritage level and he currently enjoys both a popular and literary reputation far exceeding that of any other writer in the field.

So it is perhaps not too surprising that—as has been

rumored—there is a wealthy collector in California who keeps the early issues of Weird Tales in an enormous safe and could not be induced to part with them for all the gold in the rapidly rising gold market.

As a postscript, I should perhaps add that my own early contributions to *Weird Tales* seem to me, in the main, to be overwritten and altogether too wildly melodramatic. But although I've turned out twenty times as many stories in the intervening years—twelve paperback novels just in the past six years, and many short stories dating back to about 1950, when the so-called "new" science fiction first came into vogue—people still seem to keep hearking back to my early *Weird Tales* stories.

Memories that go back many years seldom have a date limitation attached to them when they are repeated after an interval of not more than five or six years. I suppose that is some kind of cliche or platitude, but it is not an often-stressed one, and so perhaps I can be forgiven in mentioning it in relation to the foregoing article, which I wrote for the July 1968 issue of *Deeper Than You Think*.

In substance, it would read the same way if I had written it yesterday, and I concur with Mr. Weinberg's suggestion that it would serve as an excellent introduction to some additional material of about the same length. In letting it stand in its entirety, two important amendments must be made, however. August Derleth was referred to in the present tense, and the great and tragic loss which the entire fantasy and supernatural horror story field has suffered with his passing was still in the future. And H.P. Lovecraft's fame, on both a popular and a serious literary level, has increased threefold.

Two huge HPL biographies are now in progress which will bear the imprint of major publishers, and the Cthulhu Mythos was recently referred to, on the cover of a Ballantine paperback volume as "The Myth that has captured a generation." Not only does this seem beyond dispute. It has left me just a little stunned and incredulous, for the kind of major recognition that I've never doubted would be accorded HLP eventually, I would have put much further into the future—perhaps twenty years from now, great as his renown was in certain circles in 1968, and even as far back as 1950.

The early contributors to virtually all magazines which continue to be published year after year are very likely to get to know one another quite well. Sometimes this results in the brief exchange of a few letters, or a chance meeting or two. More often, a dozen or more contributors will form a closely-knit circle which becomes identified with the magazine in a rather special way. This was particularly true of *Weird Tales*, because HPL, from its very inception, helped to bring it about through his wide correspondence with other writers in the genre.

I first met HPL through the United Amateur Press Association, when he saw my first published story in *The United Amateur* and wrote me a flattering letter in praise of it. This was about three years before the founding of *Weird Tales* and before the first issue of the magazine appeared he was also in continuous correspondence with Clark Ashton Smith.

In *Weird Tales*' heyday, the so-called "Golden Years," HPL made sure that at least a dozen of the early contrib-

utors remained in either close or fairly close touch, urging that we exchange letters or meet in person whenever that was feasible. The list included Bob Howard, Clark Ashton Smith, E. Hoffmann Price, Henry S. Whitehead, Donald and Howard Wandrei, August Derleth, Robert Bloch, Manly Wade Wellman, Henry Kuttner, and the present writer.

Though the Lovecraft Circle included several writers who were not *Weird Tales* contributors, so many of the members had one or more stories in the magazine that the WT group and the Lovecraft circle became, at one time, close to synonymous. Not entirely, of course, for there were about a dozen WT contributors—four or five of them writers of exceptional brilliance—who never corresponded with HPL and for whom the term "Lovecraft Circle" was no more than a hearsay appelation. But all of them, I'm quite sure, were impressed by HPL's contributions.

I should not wish to imply that the Lovecraft Circle actually "took over the magazine," for that would have been far from the truth. Farnsworth Wright was a powerful germinal influence from the very beginning. As I mentioned in the foregoing article, he was an editor of exceptional discernment, despite certain limitations which stemmed more from editorial necessity than otherwise.

Two incidents come to mind that seem, in some strange way, too prophetic to be coincidental. On my first visit to Providence some ten years after HPL's earliest stories had appeared in *Weird Tales*, we were walking along an elm shaded street on the Ancient Hill when he showed me an early letter from Robert Bloch which he had just received, enclosing a macabre drawing.

"This is from a sixteen-year-old correspondent," he told me. "He saw one of my *Weird Tales* stories and he has written me at length several times. He both draws and writes, and I can't decide whether his stories or his drawings show the greater promise. But I can tell you this. The kid is brilliant. He'll go very far—perhaps as far as Clark Ashton Smith. Just look at this—it's really quite tremendous."

That is one of those predictions which have about them an aura of the uncanny, and I've never forgotten it.

And George Houtain, who published "The Lurking Fear" in *Home Brew* when Howard was totally unknown—I had two early prose poems in the magazine at the time!—once told me, "Howard will have a permanent place in American letters. He doesn't realize it, it sounds insane, but it will happen—perhaps forty years from now."

Good old George! He was not what one would have called a literary man, but that remark was both inspired and Jungian. Just as HPL was prophetic about Bloch, a few others—not many—recognized Lovecraft's literary genius when they encountered it in the remote past.

GREYE LA SPINA

I was born July 10, 1889, in Wakefield, Mass. (Papa was a retired Methodist clergyman from a Texan Conference where he'd ridden circuit before the Civil War.) When naughty, I was reproved by the grave reminder that I was a Child of Prayer . . . I was never able to live up to that.

At the age of ten, I put out a small weekly publication containing items interesting only to contemporaries. It sold to neighbors for 15 common pins but died a natural death in the course of a few months.

When 19, attending Bridgeport, Conn. High School, I won first (and only) prize in a factual write-up contest on Major General Israel Putnam. This was published in *Connecticut Magazine*, lavishly illustrated. My ego was boosted higher when the publication withdrew all other prizes, with the statement that my manuscript has been unanimously chosen and all the rest were poor stuff. One of my intimate girl friends was a competitor and we just didn't like each other as well, after that contest!

I married Ralph Geissler in 1889. My next years were devoted to what I still consider my best production, a daughter who is still the light of my eyes. I did have interludes of designing embroidery and fine laces for women's magazines. Also painted in watercolor (at 9, I was doing oil painting and still have some of my masterpieces) and pastel and on china. Just having fun. . .

In 1918 I decided that it was time to start a new profession, writing. So one evening I typed out a rough draft of "Wolf of the Steppes," scaring myself to such an extent that I turned on all the lights when I finished it and retired at 2:00 A.M.

I selected Street and Smith's *Popular Magazine* as beneficiary and the editor, Eugene Clancy, immediately accepted the yarn as he was collecting material for a new magazine they were planning to publish, *The Thrill Book*. He encouraged me in my new project and I wrote voluminously for the new magazine and Clancy accepted practically all I sent him.

When the first issue of *The Thrill Book* appeared, my first piece of fiction was the cover feature, and the editor, Harold Hersey, wrote an encomium inside the front cover and continued accepting so much of my material that I had to use more than one pseudonym. Unhappily, we had a disagreement, and for some months my name did not appear on *The Thrill Book* pages until a new editor, Ronal Oliphant, contacted me and requested I resubmit the rejected stories. I did so and they were all accepted and I continued to contribute to *The Thrill Book* until its demise.

In 1921, *Photoplay Magazine* sponsored a short-story contest, buying 24 yarns during the year and awarding four prizes to the top four choices by their judges. I won 2nd prize of $2500.00. Octavus Roy Cohen got 1st prize but the editor (James Quirk) told me that in his opinion, I should have had the prize and had the judging points been counted differently, would have had it. Nice for morale but not particularly helpful to the purse.

By that time, I was in my stride and selling to various magazines of different types. I liked the occult and supernatural best and *Weird Tales* bought much of my material.

One of the finest editors I ever met was *Weird Tales'* Farnsworth Wright. His letters to me were enthusiastic and inspiring. His suggestions for my work went beyond the *Weird Tales* boundaries but he bought practically all the weird or occult material I submitted. I had great fun writing all kinds of fiction and selling it easily; it never occurred to me that writers could have trouble selling their yarns!

(*Editor's Note:* Greye La Spina died on September 17, 1969. The material published here, for the first time, was written some years before her passing.)

H. WARNER MUNN

What was it like to write for *Weird Tales?*

On the surface that seems like an easy question to answer. However, if it is true that during a period of seven years every cell in a human body is replaced, I am not the same person who once wrote for it.

This is the Fiftieth Anniversary of *Weird Tales?* Then I must be seven times removed from the person who marveled at its promise. I shared in its success and grieved in its decline.

Weird Tales existed in the exciting years of the lavish quantity of the Pulps. A lot of good writing was in those magazines, but there had been nothing earlier, comparable to *Weird Tales*, except *The Thrill Book*, published by Street and Smith, and this did not last through many issues. *Weird Tales* surprised a lot of people by its long run and its fairly consistent good quality.

To enjoy such a magazine calls for a suspension of belief in the reader. It helps if he has a good imagination and can cultivate his sense of wonder. All this occasionally drives some readers to try doing as well as his favorite authors in creating the effects he himself receives, in the minds of other people.

So it was with me. An only child, with books as companions, I had become something of an introvert. In itself, this can be good. Introverts often live in a private world of fantasy and imagination.

Here is day-dreaming, romance, great deeds of derring-do —all in the mind of the loner. Looking backward, there were probably many such in those who wrote for *Weird Tales*.

Robert E. Howard, most notably influenced by his environment, was certainly the most prolific. H.P. Lovecraft, now so highly regarded, but then so cruelly handicapped by semi-poverty and lack of recognition, was another.

My only contact with Howard was the exchanging of a couple of letters, but I met Lovecraft through the medium of a mutual acquaintance—W. Paul Cook, a printer in my home town of Athol, Massachusetts.

Cook was extremely active in the Amateur Press Association, a countrywide group interested in publishing and contributing to little privately printed magazines. Fan magazines we might call them now, but they were more than that. Although they formed an outlet for the publisher's sometimes biased views, much good fiction and poetry got into these irregularly appearing periodicals.

Most of Lovecraft's early work came out in this manner, without compensation. When *Weird Tales* came into being, it became a natural receptacle for Lovecraft's stories and that is where I read first, his most notable one I believe—"The Rats in the Walls," although "The Outsider" seems to be favored more by others.

"Dagon" was another that I liked in *Weird Tales*. About then, he wrote a letter to Farnsworth Wright, the editor, which intrigued my fancy. It was erudite and critical, as was usual with Lovecraft.

"Why," he asked, "has no one ever written a werewolf story, as told from the viewpoint of the werewolf?"

Why, indeed! I began to think about it. At work, at a factory desk, with some spare time, I set down my thoughts. I entered the mind of my protagonist. I lived and suffered with him. I existed with him in complete empathy. I almost died with him.

It was easy to describe his adventures. I had not the slightest doubt that *Weird Tales* would accept the story. It did. I was not even surprised. I was only pleased to accept the check for $65.00 and overjoyed to receive a letter of congratulations from HPL.

I showed it to Cook. He showed me some of the stories in his large collection of amateur printings and said: "Would you like to meet Howard?"

I was amazed. "You actually know Lovecraft? Oh, boy! Would I!" So we went to Providence, Rhode Island. My first live author! Wow! But that is another story, as Kipling would say.

Some people have a crawly feeling with snakes. Some with mice. I have it with spiders, so—in "The City of Spiders," my second acceptance—I tried to make my readers feel it also. Most did, I think—I know, one wrote me, I hope not seriously, that he would never eat another spider without thinking of me.

My euphoria and self-confidence got a nasty jolt. I had entitled it "City Arachnida." Wright changed the name. My baby! How could he?

It seemed to him that this title might make somebody believe that it was a thesis on Urban Insect Life. In *Weird Tales*? Not likely, but he was firm.

Also—"Why did I say that one of the giant spiders nodded its head—when the head is one with the thorax and has no intermediate jointing?" Good question. Simple answer. Ignorance!

But that wasn't all. I had mentioned that, after 10,000 years Vega was no longer the Pole Star. Wright agreed. It never been. I learned a lesson from that that no writer can learn too soon. Be Accurate.

Since then, I have been painfully so. Accuracy comes through research. Don't trust to memory. Check, re-check, and if there is still doubt eliminate the dubious point, or the story will be ruined for someone. He will remind you of it, too.

Fortunately, I enjoy research—but it does slow up production.

Later, I had another reminder not to be careless. It came during a series of short stories, using the descendants of my werewolf character—Wladislaw Brenryk—to carry on the curse which he had suffered under, each a generation apart.

Each dealt with some catastrophe, for which my evil daemon, The Master, was responsible. Saint Bartholomew's Massacre; the Thirty Years War; the Great Plague—and Fire —of London; the first witch executed in New England— these were some of the themes, of Tales of the Werewolf Clan.

The Wreck of the Santa Ysabel and *The Bug-Wolves of Castle Manglana* dealt with the wrecking of the Spanish Armada on the Irish coast. I was surprised to receive a letter from one of the descendants of a Spanish soldier who stayed in Ireland and married an Irish girl.

He took bitter offense at practically the whole story, raising many points. My facts, for background, were mainly drawn from a personal account of one of the survivors, as reported by the historian, Froude. Rather angry at this attack, I did more research and was able to refute all but one of his arguments.

I *had* misplaced the territory of an Irish clan by a good many miles, not by intent, but by lack of better knowledge. Today, I discover frequent errors in the work of other writers. I never comment on them. Doubtless, they are as sensitive as I am—or should be.

So many good writers developed in *Weird Tales*. Edmond Hamilton destroyed the world—worlds—universes— galaxies—about once a month, for years. Ray Cummings brought his magic to its pages, in similar plots, but different locales and gadgets. Miles Breuer, Murray Leinster, Nictzin Dyalhis—so many, many more.

I had nice letters from Seabury Quinn. He sent my first-born son a mother-of-pearl teething ring "to the little Werewolf!" and invited me to come to New York and share a bottle with him and Jules de Grandin. Times were hard. The Depression was on. I was not able to do any traveling. "The Werewolf's Daughter"—a long novelette—paid for the little Werewolf's birthing fee.

I heard from Clark Ashton Smith, Whitehead, Otis Adelbert Kline, E. Hoffmann Price—and others. All fine writers. I felt outclassed and honored by their notice. Still an introvert.

One day I was playing with a cat, lowering a long string, trying to hold my hand steady so that the string would settle down in a small pile. My fancy saw it as a chain, lowered into a deep pit, at first cold, then red-hot. Under it, I saw a man held prisoner, trying vainly to avoid it. I wrote the story, "The Chain."

This received much favorable comment. It was anthologized twice and appeared as a radio play. Too bad there was no T.V. then. Television could find much material in *Weird Tales* that has not yet been used.

I planned to write two more horror stories, before giving up that type. One, "The Wheel," was suggested by watching a fly fall into pitch and becoming hopelessly embedded.

If the pitch was hot, I thought, beneath a man—a whole lake of it surrounding an upright wheel on which he must try to keep his balance, or fall to his death? There was such a wheel in a lake of water, where I was lifeguard at that time, and I knew how hard it was to stay on it.

I made the victim's task more difficult by allowing his implacable enemy control the speed of the wheel and an ability to stop it, let it revolve freely, or even reverse its direction.

"The Wheel" was liked, well enough at least, to be plagiarized a few years later by a writer who flattered me by imitation and changed the story just barely enough so he sold his story to *Weird Tales* also.

My third horror story, "The Well," has not been written yet, but may be soon—using notes which I made long ago.

It is interesting sometimes to see what seed develops into a story. "The King of the World's Edge" (my first book-length serial in *Weird Tales*) later to be re-published in paperback, stemmed from one of the Welsh Triads. 'The Great Losses of Britain—How Myrddin, the Sage of Arthur, went to sea with his Nine Bards, in the House of Glass, and never was heard of more.'

An intriguing mystery! So Merlin Ambrosius, Ventidius Varro (the one who tells the story) a Roman Centurion—and some others, went to Alata—America—in the period of the Mound-Builders and became the Gods of the Aztecs, the Mayans and the Iroquois.

Indirectly, their adventures bought lumber for the house I was building at that time. Other stories, such as "The Cat Organ," "A Sprig of Rosemary" and "The Wheel"—in *Weird Tales;* "Dreams May Come," in *Unknown;* helped finish it.

Donald Wandrei came to visit Cook and myself. We called upon George Allan England at his summer camp—"San Souci" at Lake Sunapee, N.H., that weird district which still remembers the mile or so of ice which lay upon it during the last ice age, and groaned in distress while we were there, rattling the cups in Mrs. England's china closet.

Lovecraft stayed at my house several times, making much of my cats. We both liked these furry, aloof people. We had been together, earlier of course, before I married.

I was deckhand on the old *Sirius,* one of the paddle-wheel steamer fleet that plied the Hudson River, only to be cut up for iron—the name was The Iron Steamboat Company—before World War II.

When I had time off, I met with a small group which gathered mostly at the home of Frank Belknap Long. We talked, plotted stories and thrashed out difficult problems there. Some good stories came out of that workshop.—Frank being far the more prolific, after Lovecraft, than any of the rest of us.

I wrote "The Stairway in the Sea," at that time. It didn't sell and later I rewrote it twice and sent the final version to an amateur magazine which has now suspended publication, and whose editor has so far refused to answer any of several letters concerning it, or be courteous enough to return it. I must assume that it is now one of the lost classics of literature.

Poor, sad world! Little you realize what you have missed!

Mrs. Long—a most gracious lady—made us all welcome, effaced herself from our chatter, and afterward fed us Welsh Rarebit. She entered deep into my affections one horrible night of embarrassment when I unfortunately set the leg of my chair on the button which summoned the maid from the kitchen. That poor girl came in several times to no purpose, as I shifted my weight to and fro.

With sublime tact, she forebore mentioning this to me, until after lunch,—and then in private—merely signaling the maid to return to the kitchen each time and ignore the bell. Being shy, I appreciated her compassion.

Some writers began in *Weird Tales* and went on to considerable fame. While they learned the ropes, they sometimes made mistakes. Seabury Quinn thought Meinhold's Amber Witch was a true account of an actual happening and wrote it up that way.

Some of Arthur Conan Doyle's tales were plagiarized and re-told by other writers. From broad reading, I recognize these sources. It made me very careful in my own work. I prefer to find some obscure fact, legend, or idea and work on those—rather than re-work old material.

Probably that is one reason why I was not so prolific as many *Weird Tales* contributors. There were others.

A famous author was once asked by a gushy admirer, "How did you *ever* write such a remarkable book?"

After some thought, he gave the most honest answer any

writer can give. He said, "At the time, I couldn't think of anything else that I would rather do."

Unfortunately, I could think of a lot of things. So I got married, built a house, sheltered and fed some noisy little ones in it and quit writing for a long while—although dreams went on and on—until, at last, I began writing again, I hope, as long as I shall now live.

So—What was it like to write for *Weird Tales?* All of the foregoing is only preface. The answer can be given in one word.

FUN!

ROBERT E. HOWARD

I was eighteen when I wrote "Spear and Fang," "The Lost Race," "The Hyena"; nineteen when I wrote "In the Forest of Villefere," and "Wolfshead." And after that it was two solid years before I sold another line of fiction. I don't like to think about those two years. I wrote my first professional story when I was fifteen and sent it—to *Adventure,* I believe. Three years later, I managed to break into *Weird Tales.* Three years of writing without selling a blasted line. (I never have been able to sell to *Adventure;* guess my first attempt cooked me with them forever!) I haven't been any kind of a success, financially, though I have managed to get by. I could have studied law, or gone into some other occupation, but none offered me the freedom writing did—and my passion for freedom is almost an obsession. I honestly have paid the price of freedom by living with Spartan simplicity, and doing without things I really wanted. Of course, I've always hoped to some day make more than a bare living out of the game, and I was beginning to do that, when the markets started cracking up.

EDMOND HAMILTON

Two or three years ago, I went to a newstand and suddenly got one of those "remembrance of things past" shocks. There, on the rack, after all these years of absence, with its name exactly the same style of type, was *Weird Tales!*

It only lasted for a moment, and then I realized that this was a paperback anthology of stories from the old magazine, edited by Leo Margulies. But it did take me sharply back, and made me realize how big the magazine bulked in my memories.

Not just because I sold my first story to it, forty-two years ago this week. To a lot of us, who wrote for it and read it, *Weird Tales* was not just a magazine. It was a Club.

I didn't realize that I had joined a Club until I had been writing for the magazine for five years. Then, in 1931, I traveled to Minneapolis to meet Jack Williamson—we had gotten into correspondence and had lightheartedly decided to make a trip down the Mississippi River in a skiff. That was to be quite a trip but I was rather timid and naive, and never supposed that the editor of a magazine would be interested in meeting a writer. On the last day I was in Chicago, though, I hesitantly telephoned the office of *Weird Tales* to say hello. Bill Sprenger, the business manager of WT, was alone in the office and insisted I must come right over. When I did, he told me that another of their writers,

E. Hoffmann Price, was in town from his then-home in New Orleans and we must go to Farnsworth Wright's apartment, where Otis Adelbert Kline would also be. I did, and had a wonderful time.

On my return from the Mississippi, I found awaiting me a letter from Julius Schwartz, who had read my *Weird Tales* stories and other work. And that was the beginning of another friendship.

Last fall, almost thirty-seven years later, Leigh and I started on a trip around the world. The night we left New York, Julie Schwartz and his wife gave us a magnificent send-off. When we arrived in San Francisco, just before Christmas, there to meet us was E. Hoffmann Price. And that night, as his home, Ed and I sat up into the night, summoning up the ashes of all those in the Club.

So that you can understand, perhaps, why when I think of *Weird Tales*, I don't think of a magazine, or of stories, but of people. People like Wright, earnest, grave, utterly devoted to literature and trying to get as good a quality of it as he could into the magazine.

I think of sitting, with Price and Jack Williamson, with Clark Ashton Smith on his hilltop near Auburn, for all one long summer afternoon in 1940, drinking beer and watching the sunset while we talked of anything and everything.

And the night later, that same year, when I went with Julie Schwartz and Mort Weisinger to meet for the first time C.L. Moore, who had recently married Henry Kuttner. I told Henry that I had been looking in my old files of WT and that when he had been in high school, he had written the Eyrie that I was his favorite author, and that only a few years later, he had changed and written that C.L. Moore was WT's best author, and why had he done this?

And a year later, when Schwartz and I spent a summer in Los Angeles, renting a cottage-court bungalow and using it as a sort of welcome-center for all fantasy and s-f writers in the area, Leigh Brackett used to come by occasionally in the afternoons, and we always gave her cake, not thinking it would be quite the thing to offer her booze. When stocking up for an evening's gathering, Julie would always include a few bottles of Coca Cola for Ray Bradbury, who was very young and didn't drink anything, but who was earnestly hoping to sell a story—maybe even to *Weird Tales*!

I could go on with this, but nostalgia is starting to rise above the typewriter, and I'd better stop. But you can see why I always think of *Weird Tales* as a club of wonderful people.

As to the magazine itself, I think its strength was the catholicity of Wright's taste. He never type-cast his writers. You could write a certain type of story for years and then suddenly send him a completely different sort of yarn, and far from being upset, he would applaud you, if the story was good.

After Wright left *Weird Tales* (banished into outer space, is the way he wrote me about it), I happened to be in New York. I found out that he was living out at Jackson Heights, so I went out to see him, and was always glad I did, for he died only a few weeks later.

I recall that on that last occasion, Wright, though busy with a new project, did talk for a while about all the years of *Weird Tales*. He expressed a hope that some of the stories he had published in it, which he thought were good,

would someday be reprinted. And how that had come true! I wish he could have been here to see it.

WALLACE WEST

I sold my first story to *Weird Tales* in 1926, three years after it started publication and it was published the next year under the name, "Loup Garou." I was 26 years old when I submitted the yarn, my second effort. Street and Smith's *Sea Stories* published my first s.f. in 1926. I was a press telegrapher at that time and the story dealt with the invention of a bull horn by a radio operator whose tramp streamer was beset by natives while on a trip up the Congo . . . Have I ever sailed the Congo? Not on your life.

I really was not well acquainted with Farnsworth Wright, the editor of *Weird Tales*. I met him in '29 when I came to Chicago to work for United Press. He had his office on or near Michigan Avenue overlooking the old water tower. Even then he was suffering from some nervous disease . . . Parkinson's, I think . . . which made him look and act like a character in one of his magazine's stories. He couldn't have weighed more than a hundred pounds, shook like a leaf and was unable to sign his own name except by doing so on the typewriter. Wright was a tall, charming man and as thin as a ghost. I still have some of his letters. He was charming, an excellent conversationalist and he gave me much good advice about how to write fiction of any kind. I didn't take as much of it as I should have. Only for a few days at a time was I ever able to write his prescribed 5,000 words every 24 hours.

Wright was one of the few editors I have known who could write a letter of rejection that bore no sting. In his October 1927 issue he published "Loup Garou" and between then and February 1932, he published five others, the last being "The Laughing Duke." I later turned this into a radio script which was broadcast by CBS and CBC.

I have some charming letters from Wright in my files. Only one of them is a rejection. I had submitted a story entitled "Dust" which told how air pollution forced humans to retreat into the sea. Wright said that thesis was too fantastic, even for *Weird Tales*. In the late sixties, I dug "Dust" out of my trunk and submitted it to Bob Lowndes. By that time the idea wasn't fantastic at all but he published it in *The Magazine of Horror*.

Inadvertently I did Wright one dirty trick for which he forgave me. Wright couldn't pay much—between ½¢ and 1¢ a word, as I recall. So, when I wrote my first long story, "The Last Man," I decided that it should be published in a "Big New York Magazine." I sent it off to Hugo Gernsback's new *Amazing Stories*, on the theory that big magazines should pay more.

After six weeks, with no reply, I wrote to Gernsback. No reply. No return. Then I sent Hugo a stinging registered letter with return receipt requested, saying I presumed the manuscript had been lost in the mails . . . as McClurg Publishing Company actually did lose the original manuscript of my first novel, "Lord of Atlantis." I also told Gernsback that I was submitting "The Last Man" to *Weird Tales*. Not a word ever came back from New York but I got my receipt back so I knew Gernsback had received my letter.

After retyping the story, I sent it to Wright from Indianapolis, where I had just been made United Press Bureau Manager. Then I got married. And on my wedding night I received a frantic long distance call from Wright. What had I done! He had given "The Last Man" two advance notices and the cover of the February 1929 issue. Now he had found the story in the February issue of *Amazing*. What was I up to?

I explained as best as I could. "If you had only told me about sending it to Gernsback," Wright said, "I could have made Hugo behave. As it is, I'm out about $300 for the cost of the cover painting and that of revamping my February issue. Thank heaven the issue hadn't been run off, or I would have been in real financial trouble." Further, "Hugo is like that with his authors. Well, *Weird Tales* is still on the presses. I'll just have to tear it apart."

I assured him that I would sue Gernsback and did so immediately. Gernsback immediately went into bankruptcy, whether on account of my suit or not, I never found out. The New York attorney I had employed seemed to be in a quandry.

My suit dragged on. In the fall of 1929, on the verge of the Great Depression, I was transferred from the Indianapolis Bureau to New York by United Press. I looked up the lawyer I had hired for the case.

"Can't do a thing," he said. "*Amazing* has gone bankrupt."

"Then I have a first claim on its assets under the workman's compensation law," I told him, remembering my own days as a lawyer in Indianapolis.

"So you do." He actually blushed.

At my urging, he filed the lien and we collected $300. I paid the stupid lawyer $100 under protest; sent Wright $100 for his ruined cover, and kept $100 for myself. I later learned that when Gernsback could bring himself to pay an author anything, it was at the rate of 1/3¢ per word. I would have received a little more than $33 for the 10,000 word story.

But the story of "The Last Man" doesn't end there. In 1945, I learned that the story had been anthologized in THE POCKET BOOK OF SCIENCE FICTION. I complained to Pocket Books, Inc. Don Wollheim was then editor. He had bought the rights from the revitalized *Amazing* now edited by Ray Palmer.

Boiling mad, I wrote Palmer a registered letter with return receipt requested. Back came an answer by return mail. Palmer said he understood I was dead. This mainly because "you never submitted any more stories to *Amazing*. He would be glad to split any royalties. And would I please, please submit a story. I wrapped up two . . . "Outlaw Queen of Venus" and "The Tanner of Kiev." Palmer bought both, paying me 2¢ a word. He also gave me my first cover, on "*Fantastic Adventures*," making up for the one I lost on *Weird Tales* for "Outlaw Queen."

And there's one last sequel. I'm negotiating with DAW Books for an anthology of my stories. If it goes through, you can be sure that "The Last Man" and this amplification will be there.

MANLY WADE WELLMAN

Fifty years of *Weird Tales*? I didn't get in those pages quite that far back, I was only reading. A student at a midwestern country college, I started trying to string stories together. Farnsworth Wright, the finest and kindest and sternest of editors, made me revise and revise again, and began to buy.

"Convincing" was his big word, you had to be convincing, even if your characters were turning into werewolves. It was rough but it was great training. I've been writing ever since, more than forty years, and I've made that word my gospel, and have tried to preach it to creative writing classes here at the University of North Carolina. Apparently it worked with me. So many stories got into old WT, from short-shorts up to three-part serials. Now there's an anthology of some of my best, and putting it together, I dare think that some of them are still good, still convincing.

It was eating money during the depression years. We met and got to be friends, we who wrote for WT. Seabury Quinn, Malcolm Jameson, Augy Derleth—gone now where the woodbine twineth, where the most wonderful matters convince. And some are still here, still friends. Otto Binder, Belknap Long, Bob Bloch, Ed Hamilton, all those. We would meet in a German restaurant in Times Square, talk up all our fights, swap gimmicks, rejoice for each other's successes, explain away each other's disappointment. What's happened to writers like that? What happened to the Indians when the buffalo vanished? They went into the reservation. They don't hunt the buffalo anymore.

You'd write enormous impossibilities into what seemed probable for the moments of reading. You got almost believing yourself. Sometimes readers believed. They wrote to me about the Shonokins, that I thought I'd invented—apparently I hadn't. People insisted they had known about them from way back, were scared they might meet one on a dark night. Things like that made it a good life. I wouldn't choose any other. I still won't.

And meanwhile, *Weird Tales* is going again, riding the night wind and convincing its readers with what seemed to be 'Taint So Stories. Will the Old Brigade contribute as it used to? I hope so. I'm willing. Good luck, Sam Moskowitz. Farnsworth Wright is a hard editor to follow, but you know that. Give it the best asparagus you've got in the store.

CARL JACOBI

I was born in 1908. I attended the University of Minnesota. In Junior High, I earned pocket money by writing a series of what I called "Dime Novels" and selling them to fellow students for ten cents each. I fear I was greatly overpaid. In High School, I saw my first stories come into print in the school literary magazine, *The Quest*. All through high school I was interested in this publication, finally serving as editor. Years later, when I was at the University, the magazine asked me to contribute a story (from one of their alumni). I did so and later sold the story, "Moss Island," to *Amazing Stories.*

My first introduction to *Weird Tales* was the issue which featured the story, "The Stolen Body" by H.G. Wells. I remember it because a fellow student was reprimanded for reading such trash. The teacher proceeded to read in derision the titles of the stories, just to demonstrate what trash the magazine contained. But when he came to the name, H.G. Wells, he paused in some embarrassment. So I had been a reader of WT long before I submitted "Mive." The magazine fascinated me from the very beginning.

My very first sale was a short story named "Rumbling Cannon." It sold to a magazine which specialized in tales of international intrigue, *Secret Service*. I was a student at the University of Minnesota at the time and I guess that I "walked on air" for three or four days after I got the letter of acceptance. I was also an underclassman when my first story to *Weird Tales* sold. It was "Mive" and had actually appeared some time earlier in the university literary magazine, *The Minnesota Quarterly*.

"Revelations in Black" had its inception during a car ride from Minneapolis down the Rockford Road. There was an old farm house set back from the road but clearly visible were a number of life-size stone carvings in the grounds and on the house porch. The owner was apparently a stone carver by trade. But the effect in the moonlight was one that stayed with me.

Farnsworth Wright originally rejected "Revelations in Black," Later he wrote to me saying "that strange story about the twenty-six blue jays on the stone wall haunted me." He asked me to resubmit it. In all due modesty, I might say that its popularity is due to its difference in setting from other vampire stories and perhaps the mood which I tried to catch of this statue-lined garden in the moonlight.

Weird Tales was a great magazine. It published during its long career many things which were hack work and of no value as did many periodicals. At times it was lurid and cheap. Yet more fantasies have been reprinted from its pages and more writers who appeared in its contents pages have become accepted masters of their craft than any other similar publication.

ROBERT BLOCH

In the summer of 1927, at the age of ten, I opened my first copy of *Weird Tales*. In the summer of 1934, seven years later almost to the day, I sold my first story to the magazine.

Elsewhere, and at length, I have written about my progression from reader to contributor, acknowledging the help of H.P. Lovecraft who served as inspiration and literary mentor. It occurs to me that I've never really discussed what happened after "The Feast in the Abbey" made its appearance in November 1934, in the issue of January 1935.

What happened, briefly, is that in the not-so-brief period of the next seventeen years, I made seventy appearances in the magazine.

Yes, I know that certain bibliographies now extant and others now extinct list a lesser number. But a glance at my own biblio (recently compiled and published by Randall Larson) assures me that the enumeration is correct. It includes a collaboration with my friend Henry Kuttner ("The Black Kiss")—two semi-collaborative efforts which are basically my stories in terms of both plot and actual writ-

ing, although I preferred to see them run under the byline of my insistent colleague, Nathan Hindin ("Fangs of Vengeance" and "Death Is An Elephant")—and a story I rewrote for Jim Kjelgaard, and ran under his name to satisfy his longtime ambition ("The Man Who Told the Truth"). So from the aforementioned "Feast" to "Lucy Comes to Stay" in the January 1952 issue my total output for this particular magazine was seventy titles.

If certain well-meaning friends and relatives had their way my output would have been zero. Over a period of years I became inured to all the familiar arguments—why did I want to write for such a trashy magazine, how could I ever hope to get any recognition, for stories buried between the lurid covers of a cheap pulp, what made me bother to turn out material for 1¢ a word on publication when I could make 3¢ to 5¢ writing for *Love Stories* and *True Confessions* and why didn't I forget all this nonsense and aim for the Big Money markets such as *Collier's* and *The Saturday Evening Post*?

Dead issues, now. Dead as the issues of *Weird Tales*, itself, to say nothing of *Love Stories, True Confessions, Collier's* and *The Saturday Evening Post*. Sadly enough, a number of those well-meaning friends and relatives are dead, too.

But I—and my bibliography—can attest that quite a number of those stories presumably buried in *Weird Tales* are still alive. A cursory count reveals no less than 210 reprintings in magazines, newspapers, anthologies and collections here and abroad over the years for yarns which made their debut in that cheap pulp.

And when the fickle finger of fate prodded me in the direction of Hollywood, quite a number of my *Weird Tales* contributions surfaced on the television tube and the motion picture screen. As far back as 1944, my story, "Yours Truly, Jack the Ripper," began its career on radio and in 1945, it was one of the thirty-nine stories I adapted for my own radio series, "Stay Tuned for Terror." Well over half of the scripts were adaptions of my *Weird Tales* stories. The process continued in Hollywood where I did teleplays of "Waxworks," "The Devil's Ticket," "The Sorceror's Apprentice," "The Weird Tailor" and "The Indian Spirit Guide." Screen commitments prevented me from doing my own scripts for "The Cheaters," "Yours Truly, Jack the Ripper" and "Return to the Sabbath"—the latter, under the title of "The Sign of Satan," served as the American TV debut of Christopher Lee. Conversely, television commitments kept me from doing my own screenplay for "The Skull" which was adapted from my story, "The Skull of the Marquis de Sade." But I did the motion-picture adaptions of "Waxworks" and "The Weird Tailor" (both of which differ materially from my teleplays) as well as "Mannikins of Horror," "Enoch," "Sweets to the Sweet," "Lucy Comes to Stay," and "Frozen Fear." All these titles appeared as parts of omnibus films I wrote and all are from *Weird Tales*.

For the record, I believe I've had more of my material adapted to television and films and more reprinted in various media than any of my colleagues—which is probably attributable to luck and longevity rather than literary luster.

So it was that my *Weird Tales* appearances paid off, for me. Paid off financially; for in the end, I bettered that 1¢

a word publication-rate to a considerable extent. Paid off, also, in more important ways; in terms of training and apprenticeship for future work, and in enduring human relationships.

There's no time at the moment to elaborate upon these statements in detail, but I'll mention an example of each benefit.

Regarding apprenticeship—anyone reading my last *Weird Tales* story, "Lucy Comes to Stay," will have little difficulty recognizing the seminal source of "Psycho," written seven years later.

Regarding human relationships—it was through *Weird Tales* that I enjoyed the great good fortune of friendship or acquaintance with H.P. Lovecraft, August Derleth, Clark Ashton Smith, E. Hoffmann Price, Henry Kuttner, C.L. Moore, Fritz Leiber, Jr., J. Vernon Shea and a dozen other longtime contributors or readers of the publication.

Again, there's no opportunity for me to detail the many fringe-benefits which came my way—meeting and working with Farnsworth Wright and Bill Sprenger, later confrontations with Dorothy McIllwraith and Margaret Brundage, and correspondence with countless fans and pros over the years. *Weird Tales*—"The Unique Magazine," as it was described in its subheading—was indeed just that, for it inspired a unique allegiance on the part of both readers and writers.

It has been suggested by the editor that I mention my personal favorites from amongst my *Weird Tales* contributions. In so doing, I'll try my best to be objective. Certainly there will always be a special place in my affections for the early yarns written in the Lovecraftian style—the Egyptian cycle which gradually evolved from them—the humorous pieces such as "The Eager Dragon," "A Bottle of Gin," "Nursemaid to Nightmares," "Black Barter," and "The Strange Island of Doctor Nork," which allowed me to diversify a somewhat set and stilted style.

But if I adhere to objectivity, I must confess that my preferences as of 1973 would be "Slave of the Flames," "One Way to Mars," "Enoch," "Sweets to the Sweet," "The Cheaters," "Catnip" and "The Sorceror's Apprentice" —seven out of seventy.

Writing all of the seventy for *Weird Tales*, however, was richly rewarding. I'm proud and grateful to have had the opportunity to join the small and select circle of people who don't mispell the name as *Wierd Tales*. That, in itself, is pretty weird.

ROBERT BARBOUR JOHNSON

My association with *Weird Tales* began a long time back. It started in Louisville, Ky., when I was a boy of fourteen, having moved there from my natal, Hopkinsville, in the same state. There was a fire station near my home, still horse-drawn in 1923, with a newsstand adjoining. I strolled past one day, to look at the horses, and there was the first copy of *Weird Tales* ever published, on the newsstand. I bought it, for twenty-five cents, and I still think it was the best purchase I ever made. Somehow, it seems significant that it was near that "horse-drawn" station. Nothing so perfectly illustrates the extraordinary antiquity of a magazine that is still beloved, remembered and collected more than

fifty years later, in our present completely mechanized era! Incidentally, if I still had that copy (which, alas, I don't) I could get at least a hundred dollars for it, today. Quite a profit on a two-bit investment!

Its value, however, most certainlly was not due to its appearance. It was, in fact, just about the worst-looking pulp magazine I've ever seen in my life—and I was an inveterate reader of pulps, at that age. But this one really amazed me. There was a famous cartoon in *Esquire* during the Depression that showed a big executive exhibiting the graph chart of his firm, with a large blank space in it. He was explaining, "At this period, we couldn't even afford ink!" Evidently the publishers of *Weird Tales* couldn't either as the first cover was colorless! It was, to say the least, not impressive.

But its contents! Ye Gods, its contents! Never before had I seen a magazine devoted entirely to eerie fiction. Other magazines of the period, pulp and slick, had an almost universal taboo on such. But here was one, where every single story was of the ilk. It kept me awake several nights, just reading it. The feature tale was "Ooze" by Anthony Rud, a yarn about a giant amoeba that devoured people, still a classic. And there were plenty of other stories by authors long forgotten. But they certainly fascinated me! In fact, they considerably influenced my whole life; they and their magazine. I read religiously every copy of the publication, from then on. Quarters, for a teen-age boy, in those days, were not always easy to come by, but it was the only place I could find the stories I liked best to read. It was well worth any trouble. It was in those early issues I first came across the work of Howard Phillips Lovecraft, surely the greatest weird-fiction writer produced in our nation, with the possible exception of Poe.

Shortly after my discovery, I moved to New Orleans, a much larger city. Its fire department was completely motorized; there were no horse-drawn stations. And though there were newsstands, there did not appear to be any *Weird Tales*, either! I missed two issues before I discovered what happened. The magazine had changed its format completely; I was walking past it, and not recognizing it. It was now almost as large as the *Saturday Evening Post*, though still on pulp paper. The name was in script at the top, there was a crude drawing in the center of the cover, and it was surrounded by blurbs. While the issues looked terrible, they contained some great stories, including Lovecraft's "The Rats in the Walls" and "The White Ape."

I read every issue, with increasing enthusiasm and admiration. I finally decided to try writing for it, myself. I was planning to become a professional writer, among other things, but though weird tales were my favorite reading, my earliest writings were along quite different lines. However, I did manage to do a couple of very short tales, submitted them. Edwin Baird, the magazine's first editor, didn't publish them (for which I'm thankful). But he was most cordial, wrote me personal letters and encouraged me to keep on trying. Had he known I was merely a precocious high school boy, he might not have been so enthusiastic! But that was my specialty in those days; I looked, talked and acted at least five years more than my age, and was able to pass as an adult without question.

Nor did I follow Mr. Baird's advice. My earlier ambitions

were directed more towards journalsim than magazine writing. I had already wrangled a summer job with the *New Orleans Item*. I was writing stories for them which appeared with regularity, and being paid a salary, at the same time; albeit a small one. It struck me as a much more satisfactory arrangement. So I continued it and took a Journalism course at Tulane University.

Then fate deflected me again. I received an offer to be an assistant press agent with a traveling circus. I joined the show in Canada but soon found press work boring and gravitated to the Ring. I discovered a new talent, that of animal training. I was soon handling dogs, ponies, goats, horses, and even camels. I'm quite certain I was the only student in the U.S. who put himself through college by working summers as a circus performer! I toured almost the entire United States, all of Canada, and even parts of Mexico, riding circus trains. I also obtained enough material for scores of published circus and animal fiction stories in later years.

Weird Tales was my constant companion, on all those wanderings. I bought every issue and was always able to find them, even in the smallest towns. Apparently their circulation was better than generally believed. I also found, to my surprise, that circus "troupers" read and appreciated the magazine. I found it hard to hang onto my copies, people were always borrowing them. And I heard some very erudite discussions of it, sitting on the open vestibules of moving circus sleepers, by night. Living their lives among actual freaks, monstrosities and strange animals, the stories seemed far more plausible to them than to the general public. Most of them had experiences closely bordering on weird tales. One, for instance, left the show in Canada to try and capture a "Sasquatch," for exhibition. He had photos of the beast, even. He never caught one, or even saw one. But he was hunting them—thirty years before the first stories of "Bigfoot" began to circulate in the USA.

I dropped off one circus in New York State and decided to try living in the Big City. But I couldn't stand the climate —the first winter almost killed me. So I returned to New Orleans to recuperate and then decided to try San Francisco as a residence. It was then the only other city famous as a literary, artistic and cultural center. I had never seen it but it attracted me. So I set out for California in 1931. Oddly enough, two *Weird Tales* writers, H.P. Lovecraft and E. Hoffmann Price, arrived in New Orleans shortly after I departed! And it seems that HPL had been living in New York at the same time I was there. But fate decreed he and I should never meet in this life, though I would have given much to. We knew of each other, even corresponded briefly, and he complimented my work; but we never met. Mr. Price, on the other hand, I met frequently during my San Francisco years; we became friends, and he told me much of the gentleman.

In San Francisco, I wrote my first "Weird Tale" officially. I was living on Telegraph Hill, in one of the last of the "Artists' Shacks" and very much a member of the artistic and literary group centering around the historic Montgomery Block (now long torn down, replaced by a hideous skyscraper). My admission to the group, which included John Steinbeck, William Saroyan, Herb Caen, and virtually every other literary celebrity in Northern California, was oddly, as an artist. I'd begun painting circus scenes, in a gouache proc-

ess of my own; and was exhibiting in leading galleries, and even museums. My published writings, on the other hand, were only a few detective stories, mostly under pseudonyms.

Conversations in the "art bars" mostly concerned literary matters; and it was surprising how often *Weird Tales* came up. The magazine, by the early 1930's, had emerged as a really important publication. Every celebrated author in town was trying to get a story into it; and most of them had failed. Since I had read every issue and briefly corresponded with the editor, I was considered an authority. While flattering, it only emphasized to me that I never appeared in its pages. So I decided I must do something about that.

A couple of years before, I had written a very short tale, inspired by a peculiar glen I had discovered down the Peninsula, with a strangely unpleasant atmosphere. I'd titled it "They." I had neither characters, action or plot; but it was definitely weird. So I hauled it out, polished it, and sent it to Mr. Farnsworth Wright, who had long succeeded Baird as editor. To my surprise, he accepted it, and published it, and other purchases soon followed. A happy ending, you'd say. I thought so, at first. But it soon was apparent that there was a catch to it.

Mr. Wright, it appeared, did not like me!

I never knew why. But there was little doubt about it. I can quote you, word for word, the first letter of acceptance I had from him. It stated:

Dear Sir:
Your story "They" is acceptable,
though it will have to be carefully edited. I can offer you
$17.50 for it, on publication.
yours truly,
Farnsworth Wright.

The reason I can quote it exactly, even after so many years, is that it was absolutely identical with every other letter I ever received from him! He never wrote me a letter of more than a single paragraph, never added a personal word, never complimented a story, or offered the slightest encouragement over a period of more than eight years. And he always added that every story would have to be carefully edited. Though, of course, I compared each published tale with my carbons, and he never altered one by so much as a comma!

And Mr. Wright had other eccentricities. He was perpetually complaining that I had left a page out of my manuscripts, and demanding that I supply a duplicate. On one occasion, he did this twice with one story. Nor was the demand ever made immediately; he'd often wait several months before making the demand. It could hardly have been true; no other editor has ever complained of missing pages and I always checked carefully pages and numbers before I sent out one. Moreover, some of the early stories were so short that, if a page really had been omitted, he couldn't have made any sense out of them, or purchased them in the first place! On one or two occasions, toward the last, I had friends count the pages, just to make certain they were all there. But nevertheless, the same demand would inevitably occur.

But, if Mr. Wright did not like me, his readers did. It was astonishing the amount of attention "They" received. I'd been satisfied with one or two mentions but there was a deluge of mail for months about the story. (In fact, it seems to still be going on: Editor Weinberg, in his letter, mentioned "They" was one of *his* favorites.) And all the Eyrie writers that mentioned it, praised it; there was not one adverse comment.

So I was emboldened to try again. My second venture was not much longer; but it definitely had a theme, plot and characters. Indeed, Benito Mussolini was a character; very thinly disguised. He was on the verge of invading Ethiopia, at the time; the whole world was trembling with fear that it would cause another World War. So "Lead Soldiers" was quite topical; in fact the only topical story I ever wrote. Mr. Wright bought it with equal lack of enthusiasm; but it was received with even greater reader praise. Some even wrote me personal letters; among them, the great HPL himself! It wasn't a very long letter, just congratulating me, praising the story and the style, and saying that we seemed to have identical views on dictators. I replied immediately, of course, and I think he wrote again. But it didn't develop into a correspondence; and he died a short time later.

I decided to write a longer story. I'd run across a curious old French legend, about a French noblemen who was devoured by a horde of mice as the result of a family curse. I transferred it to Louisiana, a more familiar locale, making it a modern descendant of the Count, and patterning him on a college friend of mine, the detective writer, Roman McDougald. I must have portrayed him fairly accurately, since immediately after the story appeared I received a letter from him saying, "Hey! What the hell?"

"Mice" was one of my most successful stories. Mr. Wright accepted it as per usual and paid a fairly large sum this time. But apparently, he decided that he would have to do something drastic about me. The next two stories sent were rejected by standard rejection slip. Nothing was wrong with either. One actually was sold to *Weird Tales* but the magazine folded before it could be published. It seemed obvious to me that Mr. Wright wanted no more to do with me, so I ceased to submit for the next few years. That was the simple explanation of the "Gap" between my first *Weird Tales* appearances and my later ones.

So I turned to other activities, which proved considerably more profitable. I wrote a book on San Francisco's Golden Gate Park. I contributed extensively to local Art publications. And my circus paintings were selling well and being exhibited in San Francisco Museum and the Golden Gate Exposition.

I was in San Diego before the war. The atmosphere there was a bit weird and my tastes turned back in that direction. I produced a couple of eerie tales while there; and curious to see whether Mr. Wright's taboo still held, I sent one of them off to him. To my surprise, he bought it. So I sent him the other and he bought that too. Apparently, I was "in" again. The two were "The Silver Coffin" and "Lupa."

"Lupa" was loaded. I wanted to celebrate my return by making the cover. There was only one way to do that. For years, the amazing female pastel artist, Margaret Brundage, had been doing the *Weird Tales'* covers; probably the most

beautiful ever to appear on pulp magazines. But they were always nudes. So I deliberately "planted" a nude scene in "Lupa," hoping that it would be used. Unfortunately, by the time the story appeared Mrs. Brundage was no longer with the magazine. The story was not used for the cover. The interior illo, ironically, did illustrate that scene. But it wasn't what I'd been aiming at.

Curiously, I did make the cover with my next sale, which appeared before "Lupa!" Virgil Finlay did a very abstract painting based on a line of my tale that was so "far out" that I didn't realize it was from the story till friends pointed it out to me. My name, however, didn't appear on the cover. I never once had my name on a *Weird Tales* cover. I was always the Outsider.

"Far Below" was my greatest success and my "swansong," for the magazine. It was my least original story; written as a tribute to the deceased Lovecraft. I even used him as a minor character in the story, to make my intention clear. It was based on the ghouls of one of his best stories, "Pickman's Model." His artist had painted a "Subway Scene" in which the creatures were depicted wrecking an underground train and attacking its passengers. My tale assumed the monsters were real, the accidents as happening, and a police "Subway Patrol" organized to prevent them. I made no attempt to imitate the Master's style and avoided all references to the Cthulhu Mythos. My treatment was strictly realistic. My inspiration for it came, not from the New York Subway, but from the old "Forest Hill Tunnel" in San Francisco, which curiously resembled it. I happened to be sitting in it late one night when workmen were repairing the tracks; and the strange lights, barking inhuman voices and weird silhouetted shapes virtually acted out the whole story before my eyes. All I had to do was to set it down. It must have been convincing. Several readers have assured me that it made them nervous about night subway riding for years afterward!

By the time the story appeared, my check was from Dorothy McIlwraith, who was assistant editor. Mr. Wright, I learned, soon after, left the editorial seat. It didn't matter. The urge to write for *Weird Tales* no longer existed. I was writing circus and animal stories and making ten times as much as I ever made from my "weird" writing. I had a contract for a long time with *Blue Book* for six circus stories and novellas a year. It kept me busy and I had little time for anything else.

Years later, Miss McIlwraith picked "Far Below" as the best story ever from *Weird Tales*. While most complimentary, it wasn't and I've never claimed that nor shall I ever. Geniuses many times more talented than I wrote for the magazine. However, I did accept another title she bestowed on me, in that preface. She referred to me as "one of the younger writers!" I harassed all my writer friends with this for months afterward; pointing out that they might call themselves youthful, but I was the only one with written proof of it.

In the years since the magazine's passing I met quite a few of the writers for it and learned much more about the inner workings of the publication. Clark Ashton Smith and his wife became good friends. Others I met included E. Hoffmann Price, Fritz Leiber, Jr., Ray Bradbury and several others.

As for *Weird Tales*, there'll never be another. There are not enough good writers left to supply stories for it; and public reading tastes have declined too far for it to be appreciated. Alleged "weird tales" abound on all sides these days; in books, magazines, motion pictures, and television. There's never been a greater period of popularity. But it's mostly crude and second-rate; no research, no buildup; just rubber masks, gore and violence, for an audience composed of teen-agers. *Weird Tales* was not written for children, it was meant for adults, and literate adults at that. Alas, there aren't enough of them around anymore to support even one magazine!

My generation was uniquely favored, over almost our entire lifetime, a publication of such quality. In a very real sense, it influenced our lives. There was never anything like it before and there'll never be anything like it again. It will always live in history and the memories of literate men, and I'm proud and happy to have been associated with it. Even as an Outsider.

LEE BROWN COYE

Weird Tales was a large part of my creative life and I'm happy to be associated with this tribute to the magazine.

My introduction to *Weird Tales* was one of those fortunate combinations of circumstances that sometimes occur. In 1944, I had a commission to do *Sleep No More*, an anthology edited by August Derleth. Most of the stories in the book were reprinted from *Weird Tales*. Farrar and Rinehart didn't have the manuscripts for the stories, so it was necessary for me to go to the *Weird Tales* office and read them there. I spent three days in the *Weird Tales* library reading the stories and making thumbnail sketches of ideas. The art editor of *Weird Tales*, Lamont Buchanan, came in while I was doing this work. We talked and he asked me if I would like to try a story for *Weird Tales*.

I said I would and he gave me a galley proof of a story. That afternoon, I went to an art store and bought India ink and scratchboard, took them to my hotel and delivered the drawing the next morning. That was my introduction to *Weird Tales*.

Lamont and I became very close personal friends and I made scores of drawings for them including the feature "Weirdisms." I can't remember when "Weirdisms" started. The Wizard drawing was my favorite of the group.

I would get twelve or fifteen manuscripts at one time and have a deadline of two weeks and work like hell. I'd take a train at night, deliver the stuff and take a train back to Syracuse. Never missed a deadline that I remember in all those years.

Many artists called work for the pulps "pot boilers." There was a stigma attached to "pot boilers." They were something you did to make a fast buck. But even artists who aspired to have their work exhibited in the Metropolitan Museum or to become the great American artist found it necessary to do these pot boilers in order to exist.

In my philosophy, a chance to make a drawing was important, especially with the freedom allowed by such a magazine as *Weird Tales*. Although the rates were not high, they did afford a living after a fashion (along with other work) and gave me a great pleasure since I was making a drawing for a purpose.

Lamont told me that I should see the way some drawings were delivered. He would find them under his door in the morning, the day of the deadline, scribbled on wrapping paper or anything that was available. It was always my belief that a good drawing was a good drawing, whether it was in the archives of the Metropolitan Museum or in a pulp magazine and I still believe this.

Weird Tales and *Short Stories*, another pulp, were published from the same office. I believe the editor's name was Miss MacIlraith, a good editor and a very fine person. I eventually did some work for *Short Stories*. My field was in the macabre and *Short Stories* used illustrations of a more realistic nature. I did few for them outside a few covers.

There were several good artists in *Weird Tales*, but there are two who stand out in my mind—Virgil Finlay and Hannes Bok. Both of these men were excellent draftsmen but my favorite for the genre was Bok. Besides fine composition and draftsmanship, he branched off into the fantasy aspects which were delightful and in the spirit of *Weird Tales*.

On the other hand, Finlay, in spite of his marvelous craftsmanship, was a little too factual for my personal fancies. However, I enjoyed them both very much and learned a lot from them. Bok and I met occasionally in the *Weird Tales* office.

Ghost stories have always been my favorite reading, even long before I had any notions of illustrating them. The good writers in *Weird Tales* were myriad. I illustrated stories for many of them. However, Robert Bloch, August Derleth, Manly Wade Wellman, Ray Bradbury and Theodore Sturgeon stand out in my memory. It would be hard to pick a favorite out of this distinguished group.

One of the stories I enjoyed illustrating very much was Derleth's "Whippoorwills in the Hills." Another was Wellman's "Home to Mother," a story appearing in a 1950 *Weird Tales* about rats taking over the world.

My favorite horror story of all time was "The October Game" by Ray Bradbury, which I illustrated. It was perfectly horrible.

I think it is a fine thing that you are publishing a tribute to *Weird Tales*. It did give a great deal of work to authors, many of whom have become very prominent, and it kept many artists in business. I wish you success on your venture.

JOSEPH PAYNE BRENNAN

As I write, the original *Weird Tales* has been gone for nearly twenty years, yet the name of this magazine never fails to evoke, for me, a kind of ineffable magic—something that no other publication has ever done.

When *Weird Tales* was started, way back in 1923, I was only four years old. I can't name the exact year in which I "discovered" "the unique magazine." My writing career—if such it can be called—began, I believe, when as a freshman in high school I first fell under the all-powerful spell of Poe. Prior to that time, I had associated him merely with the tedious task of memorizing "The Raven" for classroom recitals.

From Poe, I went on to anything I could find in the

supernatural horror fantasy field. I ran across *Weird Tales* sometime during my subsequent high school days—probably 1934 or '35.

Quite naturally I was intrigued and fascinated by the magazine. I read issues from cover to cover, over and over. I think my life's goal at that time, was to become a *Weird Tales* contributor.

I quickly became aware that in spite of the fact that the magazine was a "pulp," that it might be looked on with condescension and even contempt by various uninformed academic asses, it was, nevertheless, a "prestige" magazine in its own right. Established writers tried to "crash" its pages and were happy to do so.

I was impatient. Without writing experience of any kind —unless you include high school "themes"—I began concocting stories for *Weird Tales*. I didn't even own a typewriter; the depression was scraping bottom. A typewriter was an expensive luxury.

Somewhere, buried in trunks or at the bottom of crammed cartons, a few of those first stories still exist. I recall one in particular which I entitled "The White Wolf." I thought it was a minor masterpiece. The editor of *Weird Tales*—Farnsworth Wright, I presume—thought otherwise. Actually, I doubt that he even read it—my handwriting at that time was fair, judged by present-day standards, but it was by no means what it should have been.

Some years ago I unearthed the manuscript of "The White Wolf" and reread it. I found the plot diffuse but the writing itself of average caliber. The story had convincing touches of atmosphere.

I entered college in the fall of 1936 and within a few months became editor of the freshman news sheet. The job, combined with a full schedule of courses, left me little time for freelance writing. I won the Freshman Scholarship Award and went on to my sophomore year. Early in 1938, after a relatively short illness, my father died of cancer. The family had no reserve funds. I was forced to quit college and take the first job available. There weren't many available. The Great Depression was still grinding faces— and feet—into the dust.

I got a job as a sort of office-boy runner for $11 a week. I worked six days a week; sometimes I didn't get home till 9 or 10 p.m. And there was no overtime pay.

In spite of scant time and depleted energy, I resumed writing. I tried both poetry and short stories. My first sale came in 1940. I sold a verse, "When Snow is Hung," to the *Christian Science Monitor* for $3.50.

I finally acquired a portable typewriter, but I still had no luck with *Weird Tales*. I believe I became discouraged and stopped submitting for a while.

During the next year or two, I concentrated primarily on poetry. I published a few poems but I was paid for only one. Winfield Townley Scott's "New Verse" column in *The Providence Sunday Journal* sent me exactly $1.50 for a poem entitled "To the Bacteria." It was not a very impressive sales record.

Late in 1942 the U.S. Army informed me in unequivocal terms that my services would be required immediately if the Republic was to survive.

I wrote and published almost nothing during the three years I was in the army. Eventually, of course, I ended up

as editor of the unit news sheet. One of my editorials was reprinted in the Division (26th) newspaper and I had a brief moment of local fame.

Discharged early in 1946, I returned to the Yale Library where I had been working when the Army crooked its khaki finger at me. I tried to resume writing. 1946, however, was not a successful year; apparently, I found it hard to readjust. I published only a verse or two and a few negligible "fillers." If I remember correctly, I again fired a story at *Weird Tales* but missed the target.

I made out somewhat better in 1947, selling poems to *The New York Times*, *The New York Herald Tribune*, etc., but it wasn't until 1948 that I sold my first story—a western—to *Masked Rider Western*. The story, entitled "Endurance," wasn't actually published till 1950.

I went on selling westerns (mostly to *Western Short Stories*), poetry, fillers to *True Detective* and book reviews to the local paper. I took occasional aim at *Weird Tales* but without success.

It was not until May of 1952 that I finally crashed the unique magazine. Dorothy McIlwraith, the editor, accepted a brief story, "The Green Parrot."

I suppose there is nothing *quite* so exciting as the sale of one's very first professional story; although I had placed seventeen western stories before selling "The Green Parrot" to *Weird Tales*, however, I think I found this sale—if I may be corny for a moment—the most "thrilling" of all. I had crashed *Weird Tales*! A few of my friends were mystified by my excitement. They knew I was selling stories with fair regularity. Why this sudden excitement? To them, *Weird Tales* was "just another pulp." Poor ignorant, misguided souls!

In September 1952 my cup spilled over. *Weird Tales* accepted another, longer story called "Slime." Imagine my delight when it appeared in the March 1953 issue with both a featured cover drawing and an inside illustration by Virgil Finlay!

I felt at last my existence was beginning to justify itself!

In 1953, I sold two more stories to *Weird Tales*: "On the Elevator" and "The Calamander Chest." I was way beyond the proverbial seventh heaven. The fact that during this same year I sold a short-short to *Esquire* somehow seemed of lesser importance.

About this time, *Weird Tales* changed its format from the former pulp size to a much smaller "pocket size." (At least it was considered pocket-sized at that time.) I was disturbed at the change but not unduly so. Little did I realize that disaster was close at hand.

My story, "The Calamander Chest," appeared in the January 1954 issue of *Weird Tales* ("On the Elevator" had appeared earlier.). Before the year ended, the magazine ceased publication.

I felt as if my world had come apart. I was depressed for months. With the disappearance of *Weird Tales*, there remained only the skimpiest market for supernatural stories. The science fiction magazines published a few with obvious reluctance. New magazines in the field appeared and vanished after an issue or two.

I had no real abiding interest in western stories. I wrote them because I had found I *could* write them and because I desperately needed the cash they brought in. I wrote supernatural and horror stories with a sense of excitement and dedication.

I might add that the entire pulp market, including westerns, disappeared, or was in the process of disappearing, at about the same time that *Weird Tales* vanished from the stands.

In 1957, in a mood of desperation, I launched a "little" magazine named *Macabre*. I stated in that now scarce first issue: "Macabre, with its non-existent physical resources and cash, cannot replace *Weird Tales*. But it can do two things. It can work for the revival of that unique magazine, and it can, meanwhile, serve as a rallying place for all those devoted to horror and the supernatural."

Macabre has survived twenty-one issues, and as I write this, the twenty-second is at the printer's; yet the little magazine has nearly gone under half a dozen times. It began as a semi-annual but is now published only irregularly, at long intervals. I intend to continue it, even if *Weird Tales* reappears, but it remains little more than a meager footnote compared to "the Unique Magazine."

The only magazine which can ever replace *Weird Tales* is a new *Weird Tales*—committed to the same themes and striving for the same goals! There can never be a substitute!

6
Cover Art

In the 1920's and 1930's, there were literally hundreds of different pulp magazines offered to the public, with oftentimes five score and more being crowded onto a small newstand. With the intense competition and pressure for space, cover art was one of the most important ingredients of a successful magazine. Only pulps with established titles such as *Argosy*, *Adventure*, and *Blue Book* did not have the problem that affected hundreds of other lesser-known magazines. With a title like *Weird Tales*, eye appeal to the casual browser was of prime importance. As *Weird Tales* could not count on well-known pulp authors such as Edgar Rice Burroughs or Talbot Mundy to attract readers, covers had the job of convincing the new buyer to purchase the issue. Only then could the writers catch the unwary and convert them into regular readers.

The cover of the first issue of *Weird Tales* was by R.R. Epperly. The story illustrated was "Ooze" and the painting was a fairly faithful rendition of one of the more exciting scenes in the story. However, the color used was poor, with the words *Weird Tales* in black letter and the border of the cover in washed out white. The entire color scheme was less than inspired and the picture was not one to attract any great interest (Fig. 1).

The next cover was a great improvement with a symbolic interpretation of "The Whispering Thing." The border was bright red with *Weird Tales* in white letters. The picture had a man being struck down by a mysterious ray while a pair of huge eyes watched. "Thrills! Mystery! Terror!" the cover blurb proclaimed in a much more effective manner.

However, with the third issue, the magazine changed size and the covers plunged into a pit of mediocrity which probably had a great deal to do with the failure of the pulp under Rural Publications. *Weird Tales* went large size and the cover illustrations were often no more than sketches done in small size with a huge border. If not that, they were pale two-color drawings with little hint of weirdness. R.M. Mally was responsible for a majority of these terrible covers. Mally showed little style or imagination and his

covers were never weird or fantastic, much less attractive. His best cover was for the 1924 Anniversary issue. It was a full-color, full-cover scene of Egypt with a group of men standing by the Sphinx, illustrating "Imprisoned With the Pharoahs."

With the resurrection of "The Unique Magazine" in November 1924, a new cover artist made his debut. This was Andrew Brosnatch, not a great artist but a tremendous improvement over the incompetents who had worked earlier. Covers were often done in full color (though some still were done in only two colors) and Brosnatch was capable of picking a weird scene and illustrating it adequately. The magazine was small sized again and at first, the title had no border. Soon, though, the red border returned, giving the covers a framed look. Brosnatch's first cover for *Weird Tales* was "Teoquiltla the Golden" (Fig. 2) and demonstrated that he could handle human figures with some skill, a talent lacking in many pulp artists. His second cover, for "Death Waters," was a good weird picture and was a favorite of the author of the story, Frank Belknap Long. While Brosnatch was not particularly bad, he was also not spectacularly good. Typical of the majority of his work was his cover for August 1925, "Black Medicine" (Fig. 3).

However, by the end of 1925, *Weird Tales* began to broaden its corps of cover artists. Several New York artists did work for the pulp, the first being Joseph Doolin, whose first cover was for the December 1925 issue. Nothing spectacular, the cover was for the Jules de Grandin tale "The Tenants of Broussac." Of major interest was that the picture featured a nude girl only partially covered by a giant snake. It was popular in the last few years to state that Margaret Brundage first brought nudity to the covers of *Weird Tales*. Nothing could be further from the truth. Nudity appeared on the cover of "The Unique Magazine" long before Mrs. Brundage began her work.

The philosophy behind nude covers was one that received a good deal of adverse criticism in commentaries on *Weird*

Fig. 1

Fig. 2

Fig. 3

Tales. All of this criticism always ignored one basic fact. Wright was editor for the entire period when the nudes appeared on the covers. William Sprenger was business manager. Neither man was a fool. A cover was picked after the artist submitted several sketches based on different scenes in the story. There was no necessity for a nude on the cover. It was stated many times that Wright preferred nudes because he *felt* that they helped circulation. It is quite obvious that if circulation was not helped by the use of nudes then Wright would not have used them for almost fifteen years! Yet, time and again, one reads how Wright used poor editorial judgment in using nudes on the covers because they did not accurately reflect the interior content of the magazine. Considering the less than spectacular success of science fiction magazines during the depression with covers that *did* mirror the contents, Wright's policy does not seem so foolish. Only his critics, who based their beliefs on their own opinions and not on any factual evidence, are the ones who fall into that category.

E.M. Stevenson was another New York artist who appeared on *Weird Tales* covers during 1926. Stevenson did five reasonably good covers. His first assignment was to paint the cover for Robert E. Howard's story, "Wolfshead." Stevenson did a good job but in the process, lost the first two pages of the manuscript. Wright had sent him the story instead of the printer's proofs of the tale. The latter was normal procedure but because of the time lag sending material back and forth from New York, the editor had been forced to send the manuscript. Wright was forced to contact Howard and ask for a carbon of the story. The young author had not made one! Instead, Howard took his notes and completely rewrote the story.

"Through the Vortex" was a typical Stevenson cover and one of the better fantasy covers of the period (Fig. 4).

C. Barker Petrie, Jr. was another new artist who did several fine covers for *Weird Tales* during this period. A

Fig. 4

Fig. 5

Fig. 6

Fig. 7

Fig. 8

Fig. 9

nude was the central figure illustrating A. Merritt's famous tale "The Woman of the Wood" (Fig. 5). Petrie was not adverse to drawing some unusual monster as part of his painting and did quite well with "Drome" for the January 1927 issue (Fig. 6). Petrie also did a nice cover for G. Appleby Terrill's "The Supreme Witch," in a style much like that of the next artist to dominate the covers of "The Unique Magazine" (Fig. 7).

With the move to Chicago in 1927, *Weird Tales* found a Chicago artist who was to dominate the cover art for the next few years. Curtis C. Senf (1879-1948) did his first cover for the March 1927 issue of the magazine and was to draw 45 covers through 1932. Senf's cover for that March issue was one of his best with a weird monster menacing explorers of "The City of Glass." The man was a reasonably good cover artist, though rarely did he do a weird scene. He was much more at home with normal humans than unearthly monsters. At least his covers were better

than his often dreadful interiors. Sprenger was notoriously thrifty when it came to spending money on art. Remarking on Senf's work, E. Hoffmann Price stated, "I have a feeling that Senf was one of Sprenger's bargains." A bargain, according to Price, was an artist who would work for the lowest rates and deliver art as fast as needed.

Senf was a capable artist and a good craftsman but he had little skill at drawing the outre inhabitants of the magazine he worked for. It is doubtful if the man ever read any of the work he illustrated. If the Brundage nudes did little to mirror the contents of *Weird Tales*, Senf's prosaic covers featuring 18th-century people in full and fancy dress did no better.

As stated, Senf was at home with detailed period piece illustrations of people in medieval dress and most of his best work was done in this style. These included "The Devil's Martyr" (Fig. 8), "Red Shadows" (Fig. 9), "The Werewolf's Daughter" (Fig. 10) and "The Witch's Sabbath"

Fig. 10

Fig. 11

Fig. 12

(Fig. 11). From time to time, Senf could do a truly weird cover, one of his best being for "The Bride of Dewer" (Fig 12).

Senf also used nude women in a number of his illustratons, especially those illustrating the Jules de Grandin stories by Seabury Quinn. First to realize that Wright and Sprenger favored nude women on the cover and often picked the cover story by taking that story which featured such a scene, Quinn made sure that each of his de Grandin stories featured at least one scene in which a beautiful nude girl made an appearance. In this manner, Quinn succeeded in having a disproportionate number of covers for his de Grandin stories. Some of these included "The People of Pan," "The Jewel of the Seven Stones" and "The Corpse-Master."

In late 1927, another artist made his cover debut. While he was primarily to be remembered for his interior art, Hugh Rankin did a number of fine covers for the magazine as well. Rankin was born in 1879 and thus did not begin to work for *Weird Tales* until he was in his late forties. One of the reasons was that up until this time, rates for the interior art were as low as possible. Sprenger kept magazine costs down by finding those artists who would work for the lowest rates he could offer. With the beginning of prosperity for the magazine, rates went up and interior art improved. Rankin did cover work for *Weird Tales* until 1931 and interiors until the middle 1930's. He died in retirement in 1957.

Rankin did his cover work in charcoal and water color and his best paintings often had the same indistinct, shadowy quality of the best of his interior illos. His use of colors was excellent and he was not afraid to draw a weird scene when necessary. And, Rankin was another artist who used nudes in both his covers and his interior art. Among his best work were his covers for "The Chapel of Mystic Horror" (Fig. 13), "The Devil's Rosary" (Fig. 14) and "The House of Golden Masks" (Fig. 15).

Senf and Rankin continued to alternate on covers until 1931 when Rankin left the exterior art to Senf alone. It was during this last period that Senf did his best work.

Among his finer paintings were a series of covers for "Tam, Son of the Tiger" (Figs. 16, 17, 18). Other good covers were done for "The Devil's Bride" (Fig. 19) and "The Monster of the Prophecy" by Clark Ashton Smith (Fig. 20). The Smith cover drew praise from readers for several years afterwards as being both attractive and at the same time, properly weird.

However, Senf's reign as cover artist was coming to an end. Though he was to remain friends with Farnsworth Wright for years afterwards, Senf's last cover for *Weird Tales* was for the July 1932 issue.

June 1932 featured the first cover by another Chicago artist, J. Allen St. John. At the time, the famous Burroughs artist was a professor at the Art Institute of Chicago and was at the height of his popularity. His work for *Weird Tales* was among the best color work done by St. John but the artist never liked it. This was because St. John did not have the artistic freedom working for *Weird Tales* that he did in illustrating for the Tarzan stories. St. John had to submit sketches of proposed covers and then paint the scene picked by Wright and Sprenger.

The first St. John cover was for "The Devil's Pool" by Greye La Spina and featured the usual nude girl (Fig. 21).

September of that year saw the debut of the most famous of all *Weird Tales* cover artists. Earlier in the year, a young fashion artist came to the offices of *Weird Tales* at 840 N. Michigan. Margaret Brundage had been having trouble finding assignments in the height of the depression. Deciding that perhaps there might be a market for her paintings in the pulps, she had gone to the phone directory to look for publishers located in Chicago. The only magazine she had been able to find with offices in the city was *Weird Tales*. Mrs. Brundage had no previous contact with fantastic fiction and had no idea what the magazine printed. However, both Wright and Sprenger were impressed by one picture of an oriental woman done in pastel chalk. Mrs. Brundage was commissioned to do a cover for the short-lived companion to *Weird Tales*, *Oriental Stories*. The cover appeared for the Spring 1932 issue, illustrating the story "Scented Gardens." It was a stunning painting of

Fig. 13

Fig. 14

Fig. 15

Fig. 16

Fig. 17

Fig. 18

an Oriental dancing girl. For several months, Mrs. Brundage heard nothing more from Wright. Then, he called and told her that the cover had been very enthusiastically received. Wright asked if Mrs. Brundage would be interested in going some more work, this time for *Weird Tales*.

Margaret Brundage was born in Chicago in 1903 and was the youngest student ever to attend the Art Institute. She later completed her art education at the Chicago Academy of Fine Arts. At the onslaught of the depression, she was a fashion artist with no fashions to illustrate. The *Weird Tales* money helped support a crippled mother and a young son. She was paid $90 a cover.

Her contact with the magazine and its staff was strictly on a business basis though she did get to know Wright and Sprenger fairly well. She would stop by the offices and pick up the story that was to be the lead for the issue being prepared. After reading the story, Mrs. Brundage would pick those scenes that stood out as the most dramatic occur-

ences in the story. She would sketch these incidents and show them to Wright and Sprenger. "They would always pick the one that showed a girl with the least amount of clothing," remarked Mrs. Brundage in a recent interview. "They felt that those pictures were best for the covers."

After a scene was decided upon, Mrs. Brundage would then draw it on canvas using pastel chalks. She was forbidden by Wright to use any foreshortening in her illustrations because Wright feared that the pictures would reproduce badly and give grotesque results. Thus Mrs. Brundage was forced to do all of her pictures flat, thus resulting in somewhat misproportioned women.

When a picture was finished, she would tack it up on a wood frame, using 2"-thick broad beams. She then delivered it personally to the *Weird Tales* offices. Wright, in The Eyrie, once commented that while the pictures were in his office, everyone was afraid to sneeze because the chalk pictures were so delicate that they were afraid any sudden

Fig. 19

Fig. 20

Fig. 21

Fig. 22   Fig. 23   Fig. 24

motion would destroy them. However, a number of the originals have survived to this day. When asked about this seeming contradiction, Mrs. Brundage replied, "Once the pictures were framed under glass, they could last forever without any real damage or fading."

Brundage did two covers for *Weird Tales* in 1932, both somewhat oriental in flavor and both showing her fashion design background. "The Altar of Melek Taos" and "The Heart of Siva" were both extremely popular pieces of work and were fairly weird in execution and design along with featuring exquisitely done near-nude women (Figs. 22 and 23).

St. John was back for the next four covers, all illustrating scenes from "Buccaneers of Venus" by Otis Adelbert Kline. St. John's style which made him such a popular Burroughs artist served him well. The novel was a fine ERB imitation and the artwork for it matched the best of St. John's Burroughs work. All four covers featured a good

deal of action and three of them had superb monsters threatening the hero. The first two paintings were exceptional (Figs. 24 and 25).

Seabury Quinn copped another cover with the March 1933 issue of *Weird Tales*. Brundage let out all stops with her painting for "The Thing in the Fog" (Fig. 26), a de Grandin adventure where the good Doctor battled werewolves. The cover showed a completely nude girl running alongside a devilish pack of wolves. One wolf was snarling at the reader. It was an extremely effective cover. The nude, now, was the center of attraction. On earlier covers, by other artists, the nude women rarely conveyed the deep sensuality as well as the stunning beauty of the Brundage nudes. The March 1933 cover was the true beginning of the Brundage domination of *Weird Tales* cover art.

St. John returned for two more covers, illustrating the first two installments of "Golden Blood" by Jack Williamson. The first cover (Fig. 27) was one of St. John's best.

Fig. 25   Fig. 26   Fig. 27

Again, it was properly weird and extremely attractive. The second cover (Fig. 28) was by no means as good with its prosaic adventure scene. However, St. John did the lettering of *Weird Tales*, using a new style of type. Wright was so impressed by the lettering that it became the standard logo for the magazine for the rest of its life.

Margaret Brundage was paid at the flat rate of $90 a painting, the standard fee for the time, with the magazine buying complete rights to the art (this was common practice during the thirties—it was later changed when such magazine material was declared taxable. Then the magazines only bought first rights to the art and returned it to the artist. Thus Mrs. Brundage never had any of her art returned). For the next 39 months in a row, that $90 fee served as a regular pay check as Mrs. Brundage was the sole mistress of *Weird Tales* cover art.

The Brundage string began in fine fashion with one of her best covers. "They were so impressed by the cover," stated Mrs. Brundage, "that they brought it to the best engraver in Chicago. Wright later told me that it generated the most mail ever for a cover for *Weird Tales*." The painting was for Robert E. Howard's "Black Colossus" and featured a totally nude girl crawling up to a huge stone statue of an ancient god. Some time later, Howard was to write to the pulp that the cover was one of his all-time favorites of all those illustrating his stories (Fig. 29).

"Howard was my favorite author," Mrs. Brundage declared during a recent conversation. "I always liked his stories the best."

When asked about Seabury Quinn, who we felt she must have liked since she illustrated so many of his stories on the covers, Mrs. Brundage affirmed Wright's policy.

"Quinn's work was alright but I liked Howard's much better. Quinn was smart though. He realized immediately that Wright was having me do a nude for every cover. So, he made sure that each de Grandin story had at least one sequence where the heroine shed all her clothes. Wright invariably picked the Quinn stories to be the cover story."

Did Mrs. Brundage know either Howard or Quinn?

"I had just about no contact with any of the authors of the stories that I illustrated. Quinn did write several letters to me but they were more personal letters than anything else. He sounded like a very charming man, who was having personal problems during that period. I never heard from any other authors other than an occasional letter from one that Wright showed me. When I learned of Robert Howard's death I was very upset. I came into the offices one day and Wright informed me of Howard's suicide. We both just sat around and cried for most of the day. He was always my personal favorite."

Quinn did know how to get the cover and the next Brundage cover was for a Quinn story, "The Hand of Glory." It again featured a nude girl, though artfully concealed by crossed limbs and whiffs of smoke (Fig. 30).

When asked about the nudes, Mrs. Brundage replied, "Wright told me that the nude covers did better than those that did not feature nudes. He said my covers sold the magazine better than the covers by the Burroughs' artist . . . [St. John we asked] . . . Yes, St. John, the Art Institute teacher. I would submit several sketches to Wright and Sprenger and they always wanted the ones with the scantiest clad girls. I drew what they wanted."

What they wanted were nude or semi-nude girls on the covers. To say that Wright made a mistake by using the Brundage nudes on the covers is to say that Wright and Sprenger did not know their business. Perhaps the covers did not accurately mirror the contents of the magazine but there is no evidence to indicate that covers that did indicate the contents would sell the issues. In fact, the only period that *Weird Tales* did feature such covers was during the late 1940's, in the days when the magazine was steadily declining in sales and circulation.

Moreover, the nudes were necessary to fight the competition. In 1933, Popular Publications retitled one of its mystery magazines, *Dime Mystery Novels* to *Dime Mystery*. The story line was changed from detective tales to fantastic horror stories with rational explanations. While the magazine rarely featured out-and-out supernatural stories, it did

Fig. 28

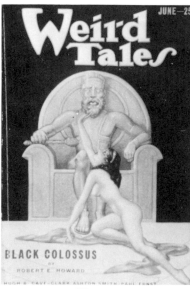

Fig. 29

Fig. 30

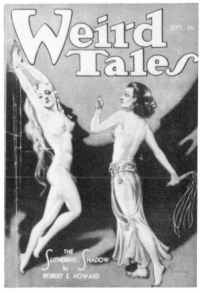

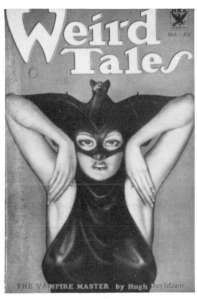

Fig. 31   Fig. 32   Fig. 33

offer direct competition to *Weird Tales*. And, from time to time, *Dime Mystery* did feature straight fantasy or science fiction stories. Many of the *Weird Tales* stable of writers including Hugh Cave, Mindret Lord and Ray Cummings wrote for the magazine. The horror pulp was so successful that within a short time, two more similar titles were brought out by Popular Publications. These were *Horror Stories* and *Terror Tales*. The magazines played up sex and sadism and were soon selling very well. Standard Magazines came out with *Thrilling Mystery* which featured the same type of story by such notables as Jack Williamson, Edmond Hamilton, and Robert E. Howard. Competition from the science fiction magazines had never been very severe. However, the horror-detective magazines were another story. The covers of these magazines usually featured nude or near nude girls being threatened with all sorts of grisly torture and death. The Brundage covers were the only competition that *Weird Tales* could offer against these new publications.

Torture showed up for the first time on a Brundage cover with her pastel rendering for Howard's "The Slithering Shadow." Two women were featured in a whipping scene, a cover that drew a storm of protest from irate readers. Wright knew that the steady buyer would not stop purchasing the magazine because of the covers as long as he continued to feature the best weird fiction writers available. And the Brundage covers attracted new customers (Fig. 31).

Brundage's next cover was a properly weird one illustrating one of the characters in "The Vampire Master" (Fig. 32). Many people consider it one of her best with a vampire woman staring out at the readers.

For two months, an experiment was tried with Brundage drawing straight weird pictures illustrating no actual scene from any story in the magazine. One cover featured a girl holding a skull in a loving embrace while the other crouched at the feet of a mysterious Oriental figure. While reader reaction was good, in January Mrs. Brundage returned to her usual style and the covers once again illustrated stories in the issue.

The next two years saw Brundage at her best . . . and her

worst. Mrs. Brundage's major faults as an illustrator was that she was not able to draw a realistic-looking monster. She could handle wolves to an extent but her other animals were lifeless. Her snakes had too large eyes. When it came to do a truly *weird* scene, Mrs. Brundage was usually less than effective. Only rarely did she produce a cover with any true strangeness to it.

On the plus side, nearly all of the Brundage covers were attractive. She possessed a fine color sense and many of the covers stand out primarily because of the bright backgrounds. Her women, while based on the same basic figure, were always alluring and she did manage to capture some expression in their faces. Unfortunately, the men in most of her paintings were emasculated beings who rarely met the qualifications of the red-blooded heroes of the stories she illustrated. Her Conan was a far cry from the Conan of Frank Frazetta and various comic book artists.

March 1934 (Fig. 33) was one of Brundage's worst. The face staring through the window was a mask and not a real creature, but even that fact did not make it any better. It was doubtful that the mask as envisioned would frighten anyone, as was the case in the story. It was more likely to evoke laughter than fear.

April 1934 brought back the best of Brundage. The story illustrated was E. Hoffmann Price's serial, "Satan's Garden" and Mrs. Brundage had a good whipping scene (Fig. 34). The girl in the picture was one of Brundage's finest and the villain's face watching from the sky gave the cover a reasonably weird effect.

"Queen of the Black Coast," the cover story for the May 1934 issue, had Brundage illustrating the final confrontation between Conan and the ancient winged man. It was the most powerful scene in the story and an obvious choice for the cover. Strangely enough, Rankin also illustrated the same scene as the story's interior art, a policy that Wright always cautioned his interior artists from doing. The cover had its faults; for one thing, the winged man's wings are in an impossible position, but they are there to make it clear that he *was* the winged man. Belit was attractive but

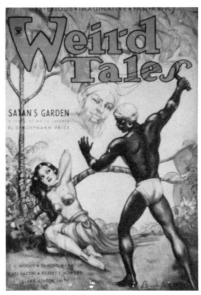

Fig. 34

Fig. 35

Fig. 36

looked little like the wild she-devil she was (Fig. 35).

A Conan story was again the cover illustration for the September 1934 issue of *Weird Tales*. Wisely, Mrs. Brundage chose a scene without Conan. The cover was one of the best of the entire Brundage period. "The People of the Black Circle" was the novel and Mrs. Brundage pictured the heroine in the grasp of the Master of the usual flimsy oriental style garb. The villain, however, was anything but ordinary. With skull-like face and burning eyes, he was a proper weird figure of menace and horror. His throne was a strangely carved structure, not too ornamental to make it unrealistic but with just enough features to make it look like the chair of a powerful wizard (Fig. 36). The contrasts of the light blue background of the picture with the beautiful girl and mummy-like wizard made the cover one of Mrs. Brundage's finest.

The next month featured the first Jirel of Joiry story by C.L. Moore and it rated a cover illustration. Mrs. Brundage

came forth with her second exceptional cover in a row. This time the background was bright orange with a black stone statue—"The Black God" of the story's title. The statue is properly weird without being grotesque and the picture is not overly cluttered, keeping the focus on Jirel and the statue. A perfect balance between beauty and horror is perfectly maintained (Fig. 37).

December 1934 had another whipping scene as the cover illustration (Fig. 38). In this fine cover, we are treated to two sisters from the story, "A Witch Shall Be Born." The cover was sure to draw protests but it was also designed to snare unwary readers. For that second purpose it was perfectly executed, with the cover being one of Mrs. Brundage's most effectively done pastels.

Whipping must have been popular with the editorial staff at *Weird Tales* for it made the cover again with the February 1935. One of Mrs. Brundage's most exotic covers, the scene was a typical occurence in the Seabury Quinn novel-

Fig. 37

Fig. 38

Fig. 39

et, "The Web of Living Death." The expressions on the faces of the girls was not the required terror but with three Brundage nudes on one cover, probably no one noticed (Fig. 39).

The nude and partially nude women on the covers were the source of continuous complaints but the loudest howls about the covers came during the next two months, neither featuring a nude. Mrs. Brundage first illustrated a science fiction story, "The Man Who Was Two Men" (Fig. 40) and then the weird detective story, "The Death Cry" (Fig. 41). Neither of the covers even featured a girl, much less a nude. The cries of outrage were overwhelming. The first cover was a dreadful mistake as Mrs. Brundage was totally incapable of illustrating that type of scene. The second cover, with Craig Kennedy staring at a tombstone was not badly executed—except that it was totally and completely bland, the type of cover to attract little or no attention on the newsstand. After those two covers, comments and complaints on the nudes slacked off for a few months.

The August issue again featured no nudes as we were

obvious attempt to lure newstand browsers, it was used for that one issue and never again. The cover had a too-cluttered look and the lettering detracted from the picture. Fortunately, the vampire from the title story was well done by Brundage and the cover was appropriately weird without being gruesome (Fig. 45).

The Brundage string of covers was broken by J. Allen St. John with the cover for the October 1936 issue of "The Unique Magazine." As per usual, there was a nude girl, though viewed from the rear, and much less attractive than the Brundage nudes. However, the girl was not the main focus of the painting. Instead, a horde of devilish looking fiends were featured and done in fine style by St. John. It was a truly weird and horrifying cover and set the readers clamoring for more the the same (Fig. 46).

Brundage returned with another completely nude woman on the November cover, for the de Grandin adventure, "Witch House" (Fig. 47). Then, St. John was back for his last cover ever for *Weird Tales* with "The Fire of Asshurbanipal" by Robert E. Howard. The cover, while not featur-

Fig. 40

Fig. 41

Fig. 42

treated to the sinister Dr. Satan in his laboratory. Since Wright was promoting the Satan series, he used everything he could to get the stories going. The sinister figure was well done but no one could do very much with the ridiculous costume the villain wore (Fig. 42).

Nudity returned the next month, startlingly so, as the heroine was not even partially clad. "The Blue Woman" featured a totally nude heroine being surprised by a somewhat surprised watchman (Fig. 43). Nudity was blatant also in the November 1935 cover which featured a nude girl surrounded by snakes, and in the January 1936 cover which had two totally nude women fighting against a background entirely of black.

1936 was a year of experimentation. May 1936 had the cover with a large red border, going back to the style of the 1920's covers. It was a very minor piece for one of the Dr. Satan stories (Fig. 44). June 1936 was another experiment. It left one side of the painting bare and listed the featured stories, along with a brief description of each. Another

ing any weird monster, was done in the usual St. John style and was one of his best, with two men staring in astonishment at an ancient skeleton holding a huge jewel. The cover painting was a perfect lead-in to the posthumous Howard novelet and made one wish that St. John had been allowed to illustrate more of Howard's stories (Fig. 48).

By 1937, a change was starting to take place in the cover department of *Weird Tales*. "I wasn't as smart as I should have been," admitted Mrs. Brundage. "With the regular cover assignment over a long stretch, I let the quality slip on several pastels. I experimented a little and one picture did not come out anywhere near the way I expected. So, in a way it was my own fault that they began to use other artists on the cover." It was not Mrs. Brundage's fault entirely though. Virgil Finlay had already become the rage of the interior art of the magazine. Reader demand for a Finlay cover was overwhelming. What most did not realize was that Finlay's unique style was much more suited to black and white detailed art than to cover paintings. His

Fig. 43

Fig. 44

Fig. 45

covers never reached the high peaks that his interior art did.

Brundage was paid at $90 a cover for several years. Wright paid Finlay $100 for his first cover. The reasons for this are complex. First and foremost, Finlay knew he was popular and the interest in Brundage's work was beginning to wane. Wright obviously knew of Finlay's popularity and the extra money was probably designed to help keep Finlay working only for *Weird Tales*. However, another factor has been ignored by most historians. Mrs. Brundage lived in Chicago and was able to deliver her paintings in person. She was able to show her sketches to Wright and begin work immediately. This was not the case with Finlay, who, during this period, lived in Rochester, New York. In all letters in the possession of the Editor, there was never any mention to any artist of postage money being forwarded to help pay costs. Even with the low postage rates, Finlay was forced to pay the shipping himself. When one takes into consideration the time and effort to ship covers to arrive

undamaged, the work that might ensue for any repainting in case something was wrong, and other problems, the extra $10 does not seem that much.

Finlay's first cover was one of the best he ever did. It was for the February 1937 *Weird Tales* and illustrated "The Globe of Memories." The cover was nicely weird with several horrifying figures threatening a young couple. As was to often occur, Finlay took a non-weird scene and made in into one with some imagination and more than a little dramatic license. In the Finlay painting, the lepers in the story looked more like the undead than victims of a disease. Still, the cover was very popular and readers demanded more (Fig. 49).

Another fact that must be considered in the $100 a cover argument was that Finlay did not receive any bonus for his interior artwork. Finlay was paid $8 an interior, the same rate as other artists. If Finlay deserved a higher rate, it was for his interiors much more than his cover work.

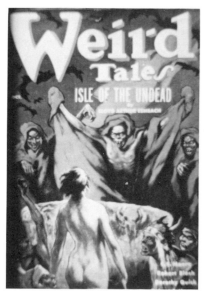

Fig. 46

Fig. 47

Fig. 48

Fig. 49

Fig. 50

Fig. 51

Brundage was back the next month with a typical cover. The next month again featured Finlay with his cover for "Symphony of the Damned" (Fig. 50). This cover showed that while Finlay could paint much more realistic people than Brundage, his monsters were often no better than those of the female artist. His satanic face in the Symphony painting spoiled an otherwise fine picture.

Brundage was by no means replaced by Finlay as the cover artist during this period as some people have claimed. Mrs. Brundage continued to dominate the front of the magazine until its sale in late 1938. Of the twenty-one covers used from February 1937, featuring the first Finlay cover, to the sale of the magazine and its move to New York in November 1938, Mrs. Brundage did 14 of the covers. Two out of three covers were done by Mrs. Brundage. Other factors than Finlay's popularity brought to an end her reign as the cover artist for "The Unique Magazine."

June 1937 featured a rare gold cover, with the novelet

"The Carnal God," illustrated in the best Brundage style. While the cover almost *exuded* sex, reading the story illustrated did little to convince one that babies were not found under trees. The Brundage art was well suited to lure the unwary with promises of lurid sex which were never fulfilled (Fig. 51).

Finlay was back with a much better cover than his last attempt for "The Thief of Forte" (Fig. 52). A sword-and-sorcery cover, it enabled Finlay to paint a beautiful picture with no monster. Instead, an attractive barbarian hero and beautiful heroine made the picture one of Finlay's best early attempts.

Brundage and Finlay shared the covers for the next year, with the female artist doing a majority of the paintings. Typical of her work during the period was her whipping scene for "Tiger Cat" (Fig. 53) and the stunning nude of "Incense of Abomination" (Fig. 54). Finlay's cover art improved but strangely, his work began to resemble Margaret

Fig. 52

Fig. 53

Fig. 54

Brundage's! Wright wanted the nudes, no matter who the artist was. At first look, the unwary reader could easily mistake the covers for February 1938 (Fig. 55) and April 1938 (Fig. 56) as being by Brundage instead of Finlay.

However, an abrupt change brought an end to the Brundage era and in most instances, an end to the Brundage style of art used by *Weird Tales*. In late 1938, the magazine was sold to a New York publisher and offices were moved to the East Coast. Farnsworth Wright was still the editor but major editorial changes were in the works.

The first cover for the New York-based magazine was by A.R. Tilburne. Tilburne was an old, professional artist who had been doing covers for *Short Stories* for a number of years. As the publisher of *Weird Tales* also owned the other pulp, it was no surprise to see the new artist (Fig. 57).

However, new artists were not the only change. Nudity was no longer used on the covers. While Wright obviously had not changed his mind after using the nudes for his entire editorial reign, the new publisher did not agree with his editor's opinion. Nudes were gone. Also, art rates were down. Covers were now paid for at a flat fee of $50. Art suffered immediately.

Why exactly the nudes were banished is a question that probably will never be answered. The publisher seemed to want a much toned-down magazine, without the sensationalism of the nudes. *Short Stories* had never been a flashy pulp and *Weird Tales* was to follow its lead. Also, in 1939, in New York, a crackdown was taking place on the newsstands. The mayor was out to banish sex from the pulps. Popular Publications was forced to tone down its magazines and several other companies just dropped their horror magazines. It is very possible that the new publisher did not want to risk a confrontation with city authorities about the covers for *Weird Tales*. Whatever the reasons, the nudes were gone. As to the drop in rates, that is easily explained. The publisher was trying to make *Weird Tales* pay. To show a profit, expenses were cut.

Mrs. Brundage did manage to do a few covers for the pulp but only rarely. She was still able to produce an attractive scene even with the toned-down policy on nudes, but an obvious problem kept her from doing much work. Margaret Brundage lived in Chicago—the offices of the magazine were now in New York. Covers were done with a minimum of advance preparation. Little was different with the new publisher. Mrs. Brundage encountered the same problem that had earlier bothered Finlay. It was almost impossible to submit sketches for a painting based on a story, have the editor pick out the one he though best, return the sketch to the artist, and have the picture done on schedule. Especially now with rates much lower than before. And there was another problem.

"Pastels are delicate," stated Mrs. Brundage recently. "The only way to make sure that they survive any sort of trip is to put them under glass. I could never find a company to ship them for me to New York. They were always afraid of breakage. No one would insure them. It was just physically impossible to get work to the magazine."

So, Mrs. Brundage was finished as an artist for *Weird Tales*. She did do an occasional cover for the magazine as well as several cover paintings for a short-lived Chicago pulp, *Golden Fleece*. After that, it was a long hard road

working at non-pulp painting. The artist still lives in Chicago and talks willingly and knowledgably about her days with *Weird Tales*.

Finlay was now the king of *Weird Tales* covers. However, the lower rates did not inspire Finlay to his best work. With the opening of other markets, he did less and less work for "The Unique Magazine." And, when the opportunity arose to work again for *The American Weekly*, Finlay left *Weird Tales*, not to return to the magazine till its last days. Of his 1939 covers, probably his best were for "Apprentice Magician" (Fig. 58) and "Towers of Death (Fig. 59).

However, with the departure of Finlay, another artist gave the covers a needed boost. A young artist from the west coast had had some of his work showed to Wright by Ray Bradbury. Hannes Bok soon was the bright new star for *Weird Tales*. In fact, several covers that were first given to Finlay to attempt were given to Bok after Finlay could not come up with a suitable sketch. Bok's style was completely different than any earlier artist for "The Unique Magazine" and evidently his weirder, more unusual style was more in line with what the publisher desired. Bok's work was nicely weird and yet at the same time, hauntingly attractive. His first cover was for December 1939 (Fig. 60). Bok used much of the technique of Maxfield Parrish, who he considered his teacher, and combined that method with an angularity all of his own.

Within a short time, the change in cover policy made itself felt. With many of its big-name writers gone, cover art was more important than ever to sell the magazine. Now there were science fiction magazines as well as several other fantasy magazines competing for the buying public. The covers had to sell. In a revealing letter from Farnsworth Wright to Virgil Finlay, published in BOK, a privately printed booklet by Gerry de la Ree, Wright mentioned that sales in 1940 were down drastically. In the same letter, Wright rejected a Finlay painting and mentioned he was going to give Bok the story to see what he could do with it. Bok did do the cover.

Wright was gone within a few months and Dorothy McIlwraith took over as editor. The low cover rates continued and cover art reflected that policy. Only Bok was consistently good and he finally revolted against the pay scale.

Bok was best when drawing unusual people and strange beings. He was not so good when attempting machinery. His cover for the July 1941 *Weird Tales* was indicative of his talents. His hero and heroine for the story, "The Robot God," were quite well done as well was the background. However, the feature figure of the robot was poorly done and hurt the total picture (Fig. 61). Much better was his famous cover for "The Book of the Dead" for November 1941 (Fig. 62).

March 1942 saw the last Bok cover. With the loss of this artist, *Weird Tales* covers sank into a bottomless pit of mediocrity. A number of new artists were tried but with the exception of a rare good cover by an older, more established master, the art was poorly done and did little to help the pulp. It was stated elsewhere that "for the first time in its history *Weird Tales* had truly weird covers." What that author failed to note though was that while the covers might have been weird, they were also terrible. There was and is no evidence that weird or fantastic covers sell a maga-

Fig. 55

Fig. 56

Fig. 57

Fig. 58

Fig. 59

Fig. 60

Fig. 61

Fig. 62

Fig. 63

Fig. 64

Fig. 65

Fig. 66

zine. On the contrary, magazines with the best weird artwork possible have never been successful. Perhaps the Brundage covers did not accurately portray the interior contents of *Weird Tales* but the magazine sold. The weirdest cover without interest or beauty could never do that for the later issues.

Ray Quigley, who had done some fairly competent covers for *Weird Tales* earlier contributed one of the worst covers ever for the pulp for "Vengeance in Her Bones," the May 1942 issue (Fig.63).

Brundage was back with one of her rare covers the next month. Tilburne returned the next month with a reasonably nice cover for a werewolf western, "Satan's Bondage" (Fig.64).

Tilburne was a quite capable artist and while not really a specialist in the weird art field, he could occasionally paint a nice weird cover with an air of terrible menace. His cover for "Death's Bookeeper" was one of his best (Fig. 65). More typical of Tilburne's work was his cover for "The Valley of the Assassins" (Fig. 66). It was not a bad cover but it was not a good one. The color scheme was especially bad, with a dull blue background and few bright colors.

Probably the best cover to appear during the 1940's was by Harold DeLay, an artist who had been doing interiors for the magazine since the late thirties. DeLay only did three covers for *Weird Tales* but all were quite good. His symbolic interpetation for "Dragon Moon," January 1941 (Fig.67) was a fine painting with a superb dragon. Even better was his outstanding cover for the January 1944 issue, the best of the era (Fig. 68). His werewolf master was a picture of sheer malevolence and horror. At the same time, the whole cover was a stunning painting that captured the browser's eyes and held them with an almost hypnotic grip.

Matt Fox made his debut with the November 1944 issue of "The Unique Magazine." Fox was a reasonably good craftsman and was not the least bit afraid to paint a monster or devilish creature for his central cover figure. Perhaps this was his greatest fault as well as his greatest asset. Fox was a cartoonist and much of his work betrayed

his background. His monsters were a little too bizarre to attract a new reader. Lovecraftian monsters were not proper beings for a cover illustration. They were too strange, too unbelievable to make a good picture.

Pete Kuhlhoff did some interesting work for the few covers he painted. His best was for the September 1945 issue illustrating no particular scene (Fig. 69).

Lee Brown Coye began his cover work for *Weird Tales* with a colored-in version of his black and white illustration for "Count Magnus," published in a hardcover anthology. Coye was an exceptional interior artist but like Virgil Finlay, his cover artwork was not up to his other work. Unlike Finlay, Coye's problem was more with his very style of art. Coye's covers were pictures much the same as his interiors. One style was not suitable for the other. In black and white, Coye's sketches had the shape of nightmares. With the addition of color, Coye's work suffered. Typical of his work during this period was his cover for "The Cranberry Goblet" (Fig. 70).

The end of 1946 saw another interior artist make the covers with the first painting of Boris Dolgov. Dolgov was a friend of Hannes Bok and his work bore a strong resemblance to Bok's style. However, Dolgov had his own brand of art and he contributed several of the better covers to the last years of *Weird Tales*.

Dolgov's first cover illustrated "Spawn of the Green Abyss" and was an excellent rendering done entirely in different shades of green (Fig. 71). It had the same magical quality of much of Bok's work and a special beauty that had been missing from *Weird Tales* since the days of that artist's departure.

Dolgov was back shortly after with his best cover, for the September 1947 issue, featuring Clark Ashton Smith's "Quest of the Gazolba" (Fig. 72). This fine cover featured some well-drawn people as well as an attractive background, all done in a light pastel setting. It was another fine piece of art.

Fox began to slowly dominate the cover art. His covers were usually cluttered with detail and could range from

Fig. 67

Fig. 68

Fig. 69

Fig. 70

Fig. 71

Fig. 72

Fig. 73

Fig. 74

Fig. 75

Fig. 76

Fig. 77

Fig. 78

Fig. 79

very good to unbelievably terrible. Fox did not draw humans very well and tended to keep away from them. Instead, he painted demons and witches and all sorts of monsters. His cover for "Shonokin Town" (Fig. 73) was a good one. More typical of his work was July 1949 (Fig. 74). This was one of a series of covers done using the devil in a variety of situations—operating a puppet theater, on a clock, etc. The covers were weird but the magazine did not sell. In 1949, Fox had four covers. Bookstores throughout the New York-New Jersey area for years later had huge stacks of returns of issues from this year, all with Fox covers. Demons were not the answer to *Weird Tales'* cover woes.

Coye contributed several covers above the level of his earlier work. His cover for the 25th Anniversary issue, not based on any particular story, was a much better painting than his average (Fig. 75). His painting for "Four From Jehlam" was not a bad piece of art but it suffered in com-

parison with the much better interiors Coye drew for the same story (Fig. 76).

The fifties saw a number of artists doing covers for *Weird Tales.* Even Virgil Finlay, needing work with the demise of the Popular Publications line of reprint magazines, returned to the fold. A few of the covers were of moderate high quality but most reflected the sorry state to which the magazine had fallen. The best of the covers of the period were November 1950 (Fig. 77) by the then just-beginning artist, Frank Kelly Freas, Finlay's "Hallowe'en in a Suburb" (Fig. 78) based on a Lovecraft poem, and "Slime" (Fig. 79), again by Finlay.

With its last few issues, *Weird Tales* resorted to reprinting earlier covers to save costs. Not surprisingly, two of the three reprinted were by Margaret Brundage and Virgil Finlay, the two cover artists best remembered for their work for *Weird Tales.*

7
Interior Art

One of the things that made *Weird Tales* "The Unique Magazine" was the high level of artwork used during much of the magazine's history. Graphics were rarely considered by the publishers of pulp magazines other than cover art. A lurid, exotic cover was a must to compete on the newsstand against the scores of other pulps vying for the attention of the potential customers. However, most editors rarely worried about the interior artwork in the magazine. There were a few pulps which featured any notable art. *Blue Book* specialized in colorful illustrations, with art on nearly every page. Even major magazines such as *Argosy All-Story* and *Adventure* featured little more than line sketches. Many magazines did not even have any illustrations at all. *Weird Tales* was a trend-setter in its use of superior artwork in the pulps.

The first year of *Weird Tales* as published by Rural Publications gave no hint of the fine art to follow. The first issue featured no illustrations at all. Artwork used in the next year was poor. All were small pictures with little attempt at the weird or unusual. Artwork was mainly done by Heitman, an artist notable mainly for his complete lack of imagination. Heitman's specialty was taking the *one*

scene in a frightening story that featured nothing at all frightening or weird and illustrating that. It was Heitman who illustrated nearly all of H.P. Lovecraft's early stories in *Weird Tales* and he succeeded in capturing none of Lovecraft's mood of brooding, building horror. Fortunately, Heitman's work disappeared when *Weird Tales* changed publishers in 1924.

November 1924 brought a major change in style for the interiors of the magazine. Now, each major story in the magazine received an illustration. These pictures were always the top third or fourth of the title page and the artist handlettered the title of the story and the author's name, as well as doing the illustration for the story. This style was kept well into the 1930's, and it was used often through the history of the magazine. A few years later, the pulp began featuring spot illustrations in the middle of the story as well. However, this practice did not seem to catch on and was dropped in the late 1920's.

Andrew Brosnatch, the artist who had taken command of the covers for "The Unique Magazine," also was the master of interior artwork. Brosnatch maintained his stranglehold on the art, doing virtually all of the art in the

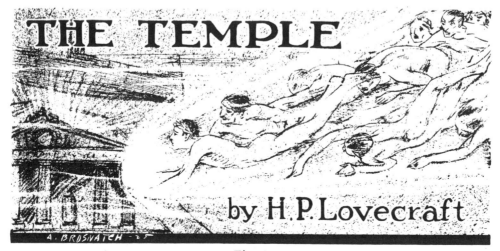

Fig. 1

Fig. 2

magazine until 1926 when a horde of new artists made their debut.

Brosnatch was neither a good nor bad interior artist. Some of his work showed a vigorous imaginative effect which produced an illustration complementing the story it accompanied, while other pieces were crude sketches that detracted from the tale. For example, Brosnatch drew the common heading used for the fact series, "Servants of Satan." The picture was a laughable cartoon featuring a witch with a pointed hat and huge, misshapen hands. In an opposite vein, Brosnatch produced a splendid fantasy illustration for Lovecraft's "The Temple" (Fig. 1). Wright evidently liked Brosnatch's heading for the Eyrie as he used it for many years on the department, though the picture had little artistic merit (Fig. 2). Brosnatch's artwork was mainly notable because he was the first of a long line of artists each who was to dominate the interior art of the magazine.

December 1925 saw the first new artist. Joseph Doolin (who signed his pictures JD) made his debut with an illustration for "The Tenants of Broussac," for which he also did the cover painting. Doolin was a good artist but unfortunately lived in New York. Wright did not like mailing stories or proofs to artists and thus continued to use hacks instead of running the risk of losing stories.

In early 1926, Robert E. Howard received a letter from Wright asking the author for a carbon copy of the story, "Wolfshead." It seems that Wright had sent the tale to a New York artist for illustrating. The artist had lost the first two pages of the story and would Howard send a carbon immediately. Unfortunately, Howard was just beginning to write and did not make carbons of his stories. Instead, Howard took his notes and rewrote the entire story from scratch! Wright's fear of mailing out manuscripts was not surprising.

The dam burst in 1926. New artists were used in issue after issue and by the end of the year, Brosnatch was gone from the interiors (and soon from the covers).

Farnsworth Wright allowed his interior artists a great deal of leeway in their work. He rarely gave any instructions other than to caution the artists who illustrated the lead story not to do the same scene as was being done as a cover. As the cover paintings were done first, this rarely was a problem. From time to time, Wright would request "an action scene" or "a particularly weird scene" but beyond this, his illustrators had a free hand. Thus, from time to time, artist would choose the most exciting scene of the story to illustrate. More than one surprise ending was ruined by a less than astute artist. To B. Goldschager went the honor of revealing the surprise ending of "The Outsider" with his illustration at the beginning of the tale.

Just as bad were those artists who did not read the manuscript. Instead, they would just open to a page at random and read a few paragraphs until coming upon something they could illustrate. Some of the worst examples of this type of blunder which often resulted in art which had nothing to do with the story occurred in the 1930's.

July 1926 featured Ed Whitham illustrating most of the stories in the issue. Whitham was a fairly competent artist who was not afraid to draw monsters, a common failing among most *Weird Tales* artist. However, while he was not bad on monsters, his people were terrible. R.E. Banta did a very fine illustration for the Jules de Grandin story, "The House of Horror," but for some reason did nothing else for "The Unique Magazine."

Used more often but suffering from the same faults as Whitham was G.O. Olinick. Monsters were usually well drawn, often with satanic, leering smiles. People, though, were wooden and lacking any semblance to humanity. Olinick did some reasonably good work including his group of devils for Lovecraft's "He." Also quite good was his illustration for Quinn's "The Great God Pan." But Olinick's bad points far outweighed his good ones and he passed swiftly from the *Weird Tales* scene.

The first major artist to work for *Weird Tales* was Hugh Rankin. He joined the art staff in the middle twenties and did work for the magazine for nearly ten years. A majority of Rankin's work was done on textured board by a grease pencil. Rankin used soft pencil shading which gave his pictures a strange, misty look that created a fine weird effect. Rankin later did some bold stroked linework, signing these illustrations DOAK to keep them separate from his grease pencil pictures.

Rankin was everything a fantasy fan could want in an artist. He was capable of drawing weird monsters with skill and he did not shirk from portraying the most gruesome of such creatures. He usually took a dramatic

SALADIN'S THRONE-RUG

By E. HOFFMANN PRICE

Fig. 3

scene to illustrate. His people were reasonably believable and his women, attractive. Rankin enjoyed drawing nudes and he did them well.

One of Rankin's earliest and best pieces of art was his illustration for E. Hoffmann Price's oriental story, "Saladin's Throne Rug" (Fig. 3). Rankin and Price became good friends during the period that the two men both lived in Chicago and worked for *Weird Tales*. Many years later Price renewed his friendship with Rankin in California. When visiting the artist, Price asked him why the art in the early *Weird Tales* before he began to work was so mediocre?

"That was Bill Sprenger's doing. One of his ways of cutting costs. Farnsworth could get good fiction at low rates but unless an illustrator was really stinking, he could get work elsewhere."

However, Wright began to realize the importance of good interior artwork as the magazine prospered in the middle twenties. Sprenger's wishes were made secondary. Rankin was the mainstay of the art department for several years, turning out numerous quality illustrations. He often illustrated entire issues, such as the January 1928 number. While several of his grease pencil illustrations in the issue reproduced so poorly that they were just masses of gray, others were quite effective. A drawing for the first installment of "The Giant World," featuring a malevolent giant, was especially effective.

December 1928 featured an even better Rankin picture. His illustration for "The Chapel of Mystic Horror" was an exceptional picture that captured the spirit of the story, with the young heroine sleepwalking through a horde of

"Hobgoblin shades marched along beside her like an escort of unclean genii."

Fig. 4

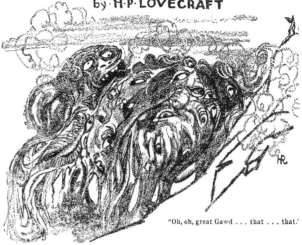

"Oh, oh, great Gawd . . . that . . . that.'

Fig. 5

tenuous hobgoblins. The monsters were perfect examples of grease pencil use (Fig. 4).

Rankin illustrated a number of Lovecraft's stories. His picture for "The Call of Cthulhu" showed the dance of Cthulhu Cult members in New Orleans as they cavorted around the monolith in the swamps. His drawing for "The Silver Key" was done in clear black lines and showed a sea creature with a background of a turreted tower. The best picture done by Rankin for a Lovecraft story was for "The Dunwich Horror" in April 1929. Rankin drew a powerful picture of the revelation of Wilbur Whatley's brother at the end of the story. It was not an illustration that many other artists would have attempted but Rankin did, and did it well. The crawling monstrosity was one of the best pieces of art ever to appear in "The Unique Magazine" (Fig. 5).

Issue after issue featured Rankin's best artwork. Farnsworth Wright evidently took a fancy to the mermaid done for the Weird Tales Reprint department and used it from 1928 through 1937 (Fig. 6). Rankin continued to illustrate stories by his friend, E. Hoffmann Price, and one of his most effective nudes highlighted "The Return of Balkis" (Fig. 7). His illustration for "Charon" by Laurence Cahill in

1935 succeeded in capturing the somber mood of the story (Fig. 8).

Rankin left *Weird Tales* in 1935. By that time, a number of other artists were being used by Farnsworth Wright. It was much harder now for any one artist to dominate the magazine for any period of time the way Brosnatch and then Rankin did. *Weird Tales* art rates had now risen to $8 an interior illustration, a high rate for the pulps. There were many artists interested in working for this price. Chicago was a center of publishing and with the famous Art Institute located in the city, there were many aspiring artists.

Not that they didn't have to work for their money. Wright often would give his artists stories that had to be illustrated in only a few days. Any young artist had to sacrifice dreams of great art if he wanted to work in the pulps. Artwork did not reproduce well on pulp paper, with most of the detail being lost because of the poor stock. Also, the magazines were printed on a rotary press which destroyed any delicate effects that the artist might use. In retrospect, it was astonishing that the fine work done by Rankin, Finlay, Bok, Coye and other *Weird Tales* artists reproduced as well as it did.

Fig. 6

Hugh
Rankin

"She was one flight below and
centuries away."

Fig. 7

Hugh Rankin

"From among the tombstones he lifted in his arms a limp, lifeless thing which he threw in the boat before him."

Fig. 8

The late 1920's and the early 1930's saw a succession of interior artists working for "The Unique Magazine." Probably the worst was Curtis C. Senf. He could draw people reasonably well and his wild animals were usually quite well done. However, Senf had little imagination. He also did not seem to realize that he was illustrating stories of fantastic adventure and weird horror. If anything, Senf's pictures suffered from a lack of any inventive spark. "The Master Assassin," as he was called by several *Weird Tales* authors, was the man responsible for some of the most spectacular goofs in the art history of the magazine.

In 1931, Senf was given the task of illustrating "The Horror from the Hills" by Frank Belknap Long. Senf was one of those artists who did not read the whole story he illustrated. In one passage of the story, Long mentioned that his hideous monster god had a trunk "like an elephant." Senf blithely proceeded *to draw a picture of an elephant* for the Cthuloid monster!

Equally as bad was his work for "The Whisperer in Darkness" by H.P. Lovecraft. Though the surprise ending of the story was never much in doubt, Senf made sure that no one would be caught unawares. The accompanying illustration for the story, on the first page of the tale, showed the narrator finding the chair containing the masks used for the hands and face of Henry Akeley!

Fortunately, Senf stopped working for *Weird Tales* in 1933 and other artists took over. Typical of his better work

for the pulp was his picture of "The Footprint" (Fig. 9).

Illustrations changed somewhat during this period. Instead of having the artist do the lettering, standard lettering was used for the story title and the author's name. This left Wright free to use the illustration above or below the title, or even on the page facing the title. This structure provided a nice change and also allowed the artist to concentrate more on the illustration, without worrying about trying to squeeze in the title. Oftentime, the line of the story used by the artist for inspiration was printed with the picture.

Joseph Doolin returned after a long absence to the magazine. Doolin was capable of some very fine work and used various shades of black and gray to achieve some good results. His people were very well done and his monsters were believable. Doolin was capable of capturing the expressions of his characters. He did a number of fine illustrations for the serial, "The Devil's Bride" (Fig. 10). The evil ghost in his picture for "From the Dark Halls of Hell" matched the evil spirit in the story (Fig. 11). His dragon for "The Dragon Girl" was masterfully executed (Fig. 12). One could only wish that Doolin was used more often on stories with scenes of sheer terror as in "Those Who Seek" (Fig. 13). Doolin had the one bad habit of often drawing a very prosaic scene for a particularly gruesome story, but in general his work maintained a very high level of quality.

Frank Utpatel only did a few illustrations for *Weird Tales* but they were all of high quality. Two of his best were for stories by August Derleth, "The Sheraton Mirror"

The FOOTPRINT
by G. G. Pendarves

"He ran as though pursued by all the fiends of hell."

Fig. 9

and "The Lair of the Star-Swarm" (Figs. 14 and 15).

Clark Ashton Smith often did the illustrating of his own stories. Smith's art was highly unusual and he knew exactly what he wanted to portray. However, his figures were little more than stick figures and his monsters were laughable creations. Smith was best at weird and grotesque faces but he never had a chance to draw such things for *Weird Tales*. His work for "The Death of Malygris" was extremely detailed and probably his best work for the pulp (Fig. 16).

Not remembered at all as an artist, Catherine Moore illustrated several of her early Northwest of Earth stories. The pictures were very good and fairly weird in nature.

Jayem Wilcox did a number of illustrations for *Weird Tales* in the early 1930's. Wilcox was a veteran pulp illustrator who did a great deal of work for detective pulps. He was much better at human figures than monsters or weird creatures. Wilcox did a very creditable job for his illustration for Murray Leinster's "The Monsters," with several

"A pair of little hands, crudely severed at the wrists, lay on the table's porcelain top."

Fig. 10

"It's her . . . she's here . . . she . . . how devilish!"

Fig. 11

giant bugs attacking people on a city street (Fig. 17). Also well done was his picture for the Jules de Grandin adventure "The Thing in the Fog" (Fig. 18).

Best known for his illustrations of Edgar Rice Burroughs' novels, J. Allen St. John did a number of interiors for *Weird Tales*. These black and whites were usually done to accompany stories for which St. John also painted a cover. In 1932, he did four covers for "Buccaneers of Venus" and he drew a number of interiors for the serial as well. All were quality pieces of art in his best style (Figs. 19 and 20). In 1936, St. John did the cover for "The Isle of the Undead" and he did the interior illustration for that story as well (Fig. 21).

The three Binder brothers all did work for *Weird Tales* in the 1930's. Earl and Otto combined to write stories under the pseudonym, Eando Binder. Jack Binder was an artist who illustrated some of his brothers' work as well as a number of other stories. His illustrations for Arlton Eadie's serial, "The Carnival of Death," were typical of his delicate linework (Figs. 22 and 23).

H.R. Hammond did a great deal of artwork for *Weird*

Tales in the middle 1930's. Hammond had a distinctive style that set him apart from most of the other artists who worked for "The Unique Magazine." The only problem was that Hammond's style was terrible. He was capable of very detailed line drawings, making good use of black and white, but he was incapable of drawing human beings or weird creatures. Even his machinery looked bad. Perhaps Hammond's best picture was for Edmond Hamilton's "Corsairs of the Cosmos" (Fig. 24). More typical of his work were his drawings for "Vine Terror" (Fig. 25) and "The Trail of the Cloven Hoof" (Fig. 26). The latter story had the distinction of being one of the worst stories ever published in *Weird Tales*, accompanied by some of the worst illustrations!

One of the best artists to work for *Weird Tales* in the 1930's was James Vincent Napoli (James later being dropped by the artist). Napoli first began working for the pulp in 1932. He lived in Ohio and Wright mailed him several stories to illustrate. Napoli saved his letters from Farns-

"She cowered against the tree-trunk."

Fig. 12

worth Wright and one such missive pointed out a strange occurrence.

In a letter mentioning several illustrations as being received, Wright mentioned that while he thought all the art was good, he did not care for the one illustrating "Mrs. Lorriquer" by Henry Whitehead (Fig. 27). Not much later, Napoli received a letter about the same illo, this time from Henry Whitehead. The author highly praised the picture, calling it one the of the best illustrations ever done for one of his stories. Whitehead continued that he had requested Wright to have all of his future stories illustrated by the same artist!

Wright's letters to Napoli also revealed that the artist was often given only two or three weeks to illustrate all of the tales sent to him, sometimes as many as six or seven different pictures.

Napoli was unique in that he did work for *Weird Tales* during two periods of the magazines's history. He worked during the 1930's for several years, illustrating dozens of

"There were figures of men running wildly from something that slobbered and gibbered."

Fig. 13

"Look! The shadow in the glass!"

Fig. 14

"I am Doctor Fo-Lan!" he said.

Fig. 15

"The viper had turned to a vast python."

Fig. 16

major stories. Then he disappeared from that magazine, moving over to the science fiction magazines. In the late 1940's, Napoli was doing work for *Short Stories* and thus found it easy to move back over to *Weird Tales*. Typical of his work for the early years was an illustration for the Dr. Satan series (Fig. 28).

Another fine artist who only did a few illustrations for *Weird Tales* was Harold DeLay. A fine cover artist who did work for several pulps, DeLay did a number of fine illustrations for "The Unique Magazine" in the thirties and forties.

Fig. 17

A plague of gigantic insects, as tall as skyscrapers, descends upon New York, ravaging, destroying, devouring.

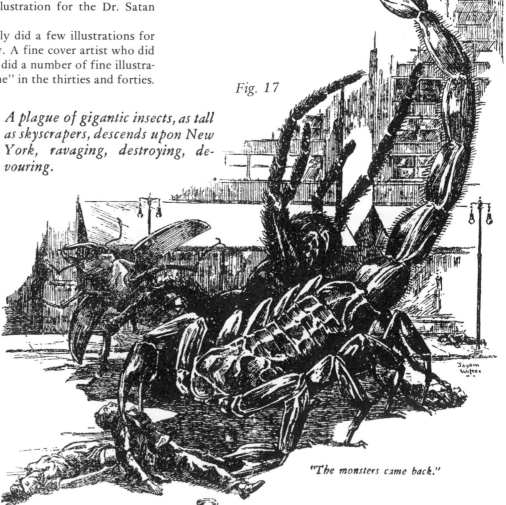

"The monsters came back."

The Thing in the Fog

By SEABURY QUINN

"It shook its teeth loose from my coat-sleeve and clawed at my face and throat with its fore-paws."

Fig. 18

Fig. 19

"He was slung across the saddle-bow, and the cavalcade rode away."

"The Earth-man attacked with the brilliant display of swordsmanship which had made him famous throughout all Zorovia."

Fig. 20

Fig. 21

"One hand closed on his thin neck, and the other, a rock-like fist, made a bloody ruin of his mouth."

"You can't kill the dead," she shrieked hysterically.

Fig. 22

Fig. 23

"From her breast protruded the hilt of the sacrificial dagger that had been found in the coffin of the Golden Mummy."

Jack Binder

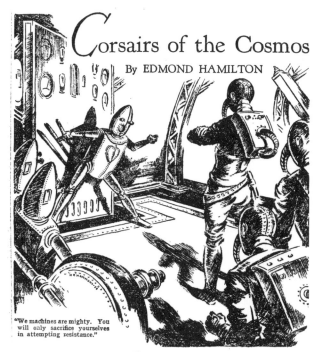

Corsairs of the Cosmos

By EDMOND HAMILTON

"We machines are mighty. You will only sacrifice yourselves in attempting resistance."

Fig. 24

His dragon for the Conan story, "Red Nails," was one of the best interiors published in the magazine during 1936 (Fig. 29). This was high praise, for DeLay was competing against the one artist whose name has become linked eternally with *Weird Tales*. The greatest of all black-and-white fantasy artists began a reign of artwork that would totally dominate "The Unique Magazine" through 1940. Virgil Finlay was the man and within a short time after his first appearance, he was in complete control of the interior artwork of *Weird Tales*.

Virgil Finlay (1914-1971) was born in Rochester, New York. He was always fascinated by art and took courses in it in high school and later in night school. In the fall of 1935, Finlay submitted several unsolicited drawings to *Weird Tales*. The 21-year-old artist had been a regular reader of the pulp for years and felt that he could draw better than most of the artists working for the magazine. He was right. The first Finlay picture published in *Weird Tales* was a medusa on a couch, one of the first group of pictures he sent Wright (Fig. 30).

Farnsworth Wright knew quality when he saw it and he quickly had Finlay doing all the art he could handle. Finlay illustrated three stories in the December 1935 *Weird Tales*, including the illustration for "Dancing Feet" (Fig. 31). His next work appeared in the March 1936 issue. He continued with two or three illustrations for each issue for the rest of the year. Reader enthusiasm was unbounded. Even H.P. Lovecraft was an enthusiastic Finlay fan. The two men corresponded for a short time and Lovecraft even wrote a sonnet, "To Mr. Finlay Upon His Drawing For Mr. Bloch's Tale, 'The Faceless God'." The illustration in question was published in May 1936 and was just one of a series of superb Finlay black-and-white illustrations that helped establish the artist as the top interior artist in the fantasy field.

By 1937, Finlay was illustrating most, if not all of the

stories in every issue of *Weird Tales*. Some issues would feature as many as eight different Finlay pictures. Finlay would spend days on his drawings. The art was done in a very detailed stipple, with Finlay putting in every dot and line. This technique was time consuming and tiring but it made each Finlay illustration a work of art. Trying to single out particular pieces of art as Finlay's best is nearly impossible. He did some exceptional work for both Robert Bloch and H.P. Lovecraft's work. For Bloch, Finlay did great illustrations for "The Faceless God," "The Opener of the Way" and "The Mannikin." Even better was his work for "Psychopompos," an unusual illustration inspired by a line from the poem. Also for Lovecraft, Finlay did a superb picture that had little to do with the actual story in "The Thing on the Doorstep." Perhaps his best illustration for *Weird Tales* was his masterpiece for "The Shunned House" (Fig. 32). Well-known H.P. Lovecraft collector, John Vetter, called the last illustration "the finest Lovecraft illustration ever done."

In 1938, Farnsworth Wright began a poetry page to answer the call for still more Finlay art. Finlay would take a few lines of a famous poem and draw a full-page illustration for the couplet. Some of the artist's best work was done for this series. Finlay was paid $11 each for these pictures, just $3 more than his regular fee for story illustrations. Two of his best pieces for the series were "The Horns of Elfland" (Fig. 33) and "The Ancient Mariner" (Fig. 34).

In 1938, *Weird Tales* was sold to a corporation based in New York. For the first time in many years, profit became a serious goal of the publisher. Rates immediately went down for artwork. The price paid for an interior drawing dropped from $8 a picture to $5 a piece. Finlay continued to do work for the magazine but the quality of his work dropped off as he tried to make up in quantity the loss of money suffered from the rate change. Typical of this later

"There was a violent explosion of radiant energy that shocked him into temporary blindness."

Vine Terror

By HOWARD WANDREI

Fig. 25

92

work was his picture for "Cross of Fire" (Fig. 35), in no way comparable to his earlier work for the magazine.

Finlay had obtained a full-time job working for *The American Weekly* and with the science fiction boom of 1939-40, was doing a great deal of freelance work for the new magazines. When Farnsworth Wright was replaced as editor of *Weird Tales* in 1940, the association between Finlay and the magazine ended. He was not to return for more than a decade.

Strangely enough, as one great artist left *Weird Tales*, another joined the art staff. Ray Bradbury, in New York for the first World Science Fiction convention, stopped in to see Wright. The young Bradbury showed Wright some work by a Seattle artist named Hannes Bok. Wright liked what he saw and Bok moved to New York to join the *Weird Tales* art staff. The new artist's outre style and unusual pictures soon filled the pages of "The Unique Magazine." Bok left *Weird Tales* within a few years in protest of the poor pay but in the interim did some exceptional work.

Bok was another artist who spent several days on an illustration getting it just right. Unlike Finlay, Bok strived not for realism but for a fairy-like beauty and strangeness. While he was never formally trained in art, his work was greatly influenced by Maxfield Parrish but with a flair uniquely his own. One of Bok's most unusual pictures was the illustration done for Henry Kuttner's "Dragon Moon" (Fig. 36). While Bok's use of stipple was not as good as Finlay's, he could use it just as effectively as demonstrated in his work for "Compliments of Spectro" (Fig. 37). Best of all his specialties were Bok's females. They were not as voluptuous or as breathtakingly beautiful as Finlay's but they possessed an unearthly beauty and daintiness that no other artist in the field could capture. A typical Bok female was featured in the very Parrish-like illustration for "Haunted Hour" (Fig. 38).

Several other artists did good work for *Weird Tales* during the early 1940's. When Bok left, they handled most of the interior art for the magazine. Chief among them were Harry Ferman and Boris Dolgov.

Ferman began working for *Weird Tales* in the late 1930's and continued to work throughout the early 1940's. He usually did dark, brooding illustrations, making good use of dark heavy lines and a great deal of shading. His pictures rarely illustrated an actual scene from the story but instead were symbolic of some idea generated by a scene or of the tale in general. He was to set the style for a majority of artists to follow. Gone were the detailed drawings that were actual illustrations of events in the tale. The type of art used in the early twenties was back.

The best of Ferman's work appeared in 1941-42. Typical of his artwork was an illustration for "The Case of Charles Dexter Ward" (Fig. 39) and his heading for "Drifting Atoms" (Fig. 40).

Boris Dolgov was a young artist who met Hannes Bok in Greenwich Village. Dolgov was impressed by Bok and his work often closely followed that of the older artist. Sometimes the two would even collaborate on a picture, signing it "Dolbokgov." However, Dolgov was by no means just an imitator. His work had a unique style all its own and he contributed a great deal of fine art to *Weird Tales* from the

The Trail of the Cloven Hoof

By ARLTON EADIE

"At any moment the ball might shatter and bring death to both."

Fig. 26

early 1940's on. His early work was much cruder than his later illustrations but all of his work was quality material. One of Dolgov's most successful drawings was his splendid evocation of "Yours Truly, Jack the Ripper" (Fig. 41).

A number of other artists did work for *Weird Tales* in the 1940's. With the low rates, the magazine did not attract many of the top artists in the field. With all of the other science fiction and fantasy magazines being published, most artists could find better paying markets. Also, *Weird Tales* was printed on the cheapest of pulp paper and artists could get much better results doing work for the bigger, better-produced pulps. While Ziff-Davis was not noted for the contents of their magazines, their pulps were printed on a better grade of paper. Illustrations reproduced much better than on the low-grade pulp used by *Weird Tales*.

Because of these problems, *Weird Tales* primarily used artists just starting out in the field or men whose work was so unusual or outre that "The Unique Magazine" was the only market for their material.

By the middle of the 1940's, artists such as Bennett, Damon Knight, A.R. Tilburne, Matt Fox and Harold Rayner were relegated to a minor role illustrating for the magazine. Lamont Buchanan, the associate editor of *Weird Tales*, also doubled as the art editor. He primarily used a stable of five artists throughout the last half of the decade and into the early 1950's.

John Guinta was capable of both good and bad art. Many of his pictures suffered from the fact that they were little more than detailed sketches. When Guinta tried, he was capable of doing some very fine work, as shown by his picture for "Speed the Parting Ghost."

An artist who did a great deal of work for *Weird Tales* was Fred Humiston. Unfortunately, Humiston's art ranged

REGISTERED IN U.S. PATENT OFFICE

A MAGAZINE of the   BIZARRE and UNUSUAL

840 N. Michigan Ave.   Chicago, Ill.

EDITORIAL ROOMS

January 18, 1932.

Mr. James Napoli
1259 E. 102nd Street
Cleveland, Ohio

Dear Mr. Napoli

    Your pictures arrived in good condition.
They were very good, and all three were well
drawn, though I do not particularly care for
the one that illustrates MRS. LONNIQUER.

    We are trying out several artists at
present, but I hope soon to give you an issue
of ORIENTAL STORIES or WEIRD TALES to illustrate.

    Your check for the three drawings already
done will be mailed out to you in a few days.

                    Sincerely yours,

                    Farnsworth Wright,
                    Editor

F.W.:MM.

"You are mine, Beatrice Dale,"
Doctor Satan said softly.

Fig. 28

Fig. 29

95

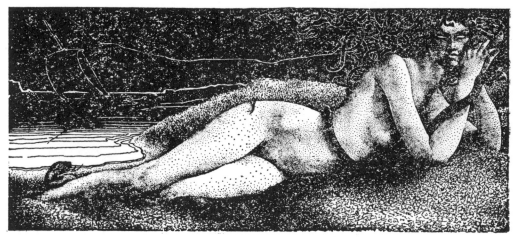

Fig. 30

from bad to terrible. He only did linework with little or no shading. His *best* work resembled cartoons. His people were unbelievable and he was rarely able to draw a weird scene. His devils and demons were laughable. For some unknown reason (probably cost), Buchanan used Humiston continually. He was the Hammond of the 40's.

Boris Dolgov was already mentioned as one of the better illustrators who worked for *Weird Tales* in its years after Farnsworth Wright's death. In the late 1940's, Dolgov's style matured to the point where every one of his illustraitons was an accomplished piece of art. Dolgov was forgotten as soon as he died in the early 50's, but he was one of the best artists ever to work for *Weird Tales*. Typical of his work were his pictures for "The Last Adam and Eve" (Fig. 42) and "Three in Chains" (Fig. 43).

The fourth artist used regularly by Lamont Buchanan

Fig. 31

Fig. 32

O sweet and far, from cliff and scar,
The horns of Elfland faintly blowing.
—*Tennyson.*

Fig. 33

Like one, that on a lonesome road
Doth walk in fear and dread,
And having once turn'd round, walks on,
And turns no more his head;
Because he knows a frightful fiend
Doth close behind him tread.
—Coleridge: *The Ancient Mariner*.

Fig. 34

Fig. 35

Fig. 36

100

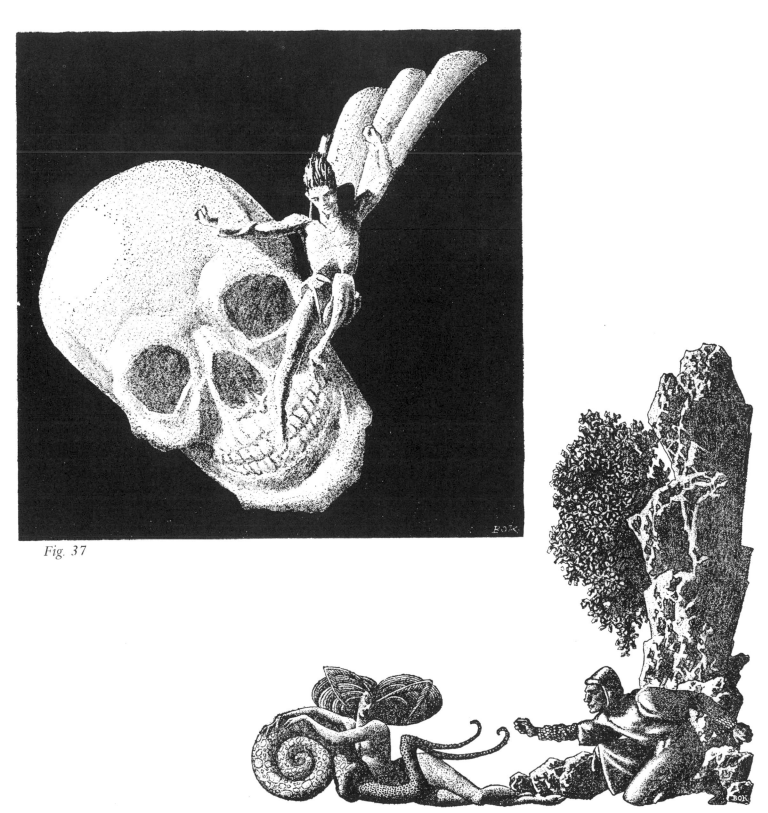

Fig. 37

Fig. 38

Fig. 39

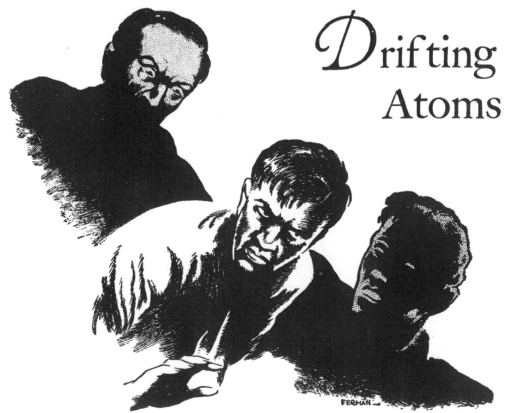

Drifting Atoms

102

Fig. 40

Yours Truly—
Jack the Ripper

By ROBERT BLOCH

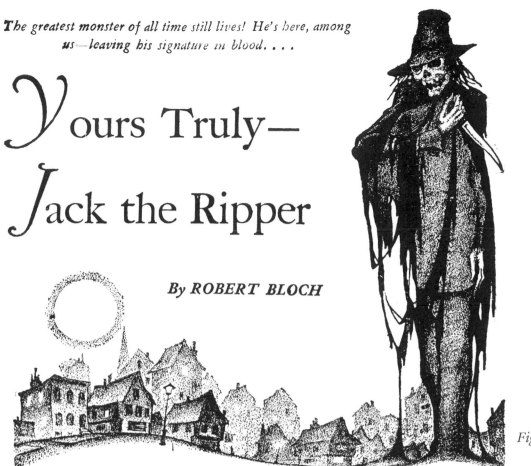

Fig. 41

was an old favorite. Vincent Napoli returned to the pages of "The Unique Magazine" in 1948. Napoli's best work resembled that of Austin Briggs but was unique in its own right. His ink work was detailed and involved. He was capable of drawing realistic humans and did not shy away from gruesome monsters. Napoli liked symbolic illustrations and often used montage effects in his art. Among his best work during the period were his studies for "The Haunted" (Fig. 44) and "Thinker" (Fig. 45).

Lee Brown Coye was the fifth of Buchanan's regulars. Coye was the master of the weird and grotesque illustration. There was never an artist who came close to capturing horror and dread like Lee Brown Coye. Of Coye, John

Vetter stated, "Coye has a fascination for the grotesque, the horrible and the abnormal that would be worthy of Richard Upton Pickman." The late August Derleth declared, "Old houses, haunted rooms and people, distortions in time and space all come to strange life under his pen . . . What such writers as J. Sheridan LeFanu and Montague Rhodes James were to the macabre story, Lee Brown Coye is to macabre art." To pick out any of Coye's art above any other is almost impossible, as all of it was first class. Coye's own favorite for *Weird Tales* was "The Wizard" (Fig. 46), one of a series of full-page pictures he did entitled, "Weirdisms." Another Coye favorite for the magazine was "The Whippoorwills in the Hills" (Fig. 47). Typical of Coye's unusual

Vincent Napoli

Lee Brown Coye

103

Fig. 42

"—as if that dreadful geyser of sound were being sucked down into some hellish drain-pipe."

Fig. 43

Fig. 44

Fig. 45

houses was his picture for "The Inn by Doomsday Falls" (Fig. 48). Coye's people could have walked the streets of Lovecraft's Dunwich without causing undue attention. Typical of such misshapen people were his inhabitants of "Serpent Princess" (Fig. 49).

The fifties was a time of slow dying for *Weird Tales*. With rates the lowest ever, a number of new artists again began to make their presence felt. Most of these newcomers were poor artists whose only work appeared in *Weird Tales*, and only there for a few issues. One old-timer, though, did return. With markets drying up as magazines died and rates went down, Virgil Finlay returned, working for a rate much lower than what he had been receiving the past few years. Finlay was still an exceptional artist but he was forced to turn out art as quickly as possible in an effort to keep up with the cost of living. Typical of Finlay's work during this period was his picture for "The Night Road" (Fig. 50).

To accomplish the evil designs of their master, the Devil, it was essential that wizards mingle with people. Thus we find them in the role of medicine men. They journeyed over the countryside laden with the traps of their trade - a knapsack hung on their back & a pouch at their side. Herein they carried charms, hex-signs & herbs & not infrequently, needles, thread, prettys & sundry other notions to tempt the public. In spite of their debased character wizards held a certain charm about their personality which let them into the confidence of the people they set out to bewitch.

Fig. 46

The Whippoorwills in the Hills

Fig. 47

Heading by LEE BROWN COYE

Fig. 48

Heading by LEE BROWN COYE

Fig. 49

Fig. 50

Joseph Eberle was the last artist of note to work for *Weird Tales*. Eberle was a fine craftsman who could turn out fine pieces of artwork. His one problem was that while he could handle the main character of the picture, his backgrounds were often hurried and not well defined. Typical of his style was "Once There Was A Little Girl" (Fig. 51).

Weird Tales folded in 1954. In its more than thirty-year history, the magazine established itself as the foremost showcase of fantasy artists and their art ever published. It was *Weird Tales* that set the standard of high-quality art that other magazines in the science fiction and fantasy field followed. In its pages developed the most popular artists ever to work in the pulps. The magazine has been gone for more than twenty years, but like "The Unique Magazine" itself, the artists who gained fame in it will never be forgotten.

Fig. 51

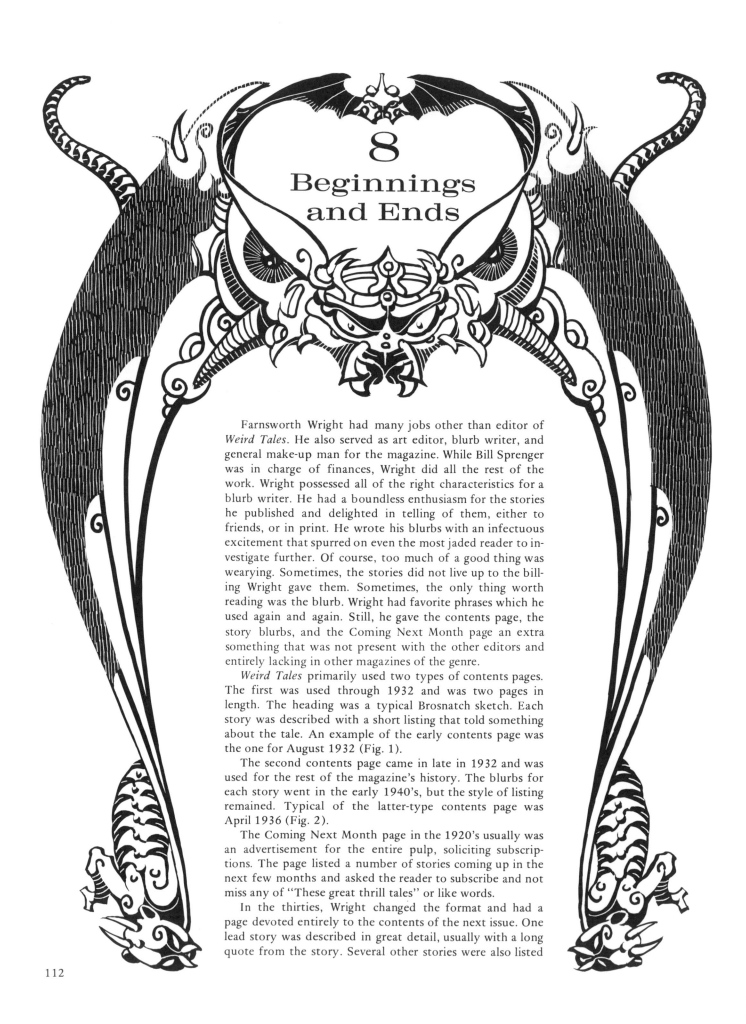

8
Beginnings and Ends

Farnsworth Wright had many jobs other than editor of *Weird Tales*. He also served as art editor, blurb writer, and general make-up man for the magazine. While Bill Sprenger was in charge of finances, Wright did all the rest of the work. Wright possessed all of the right characteristics for a blurb writer. He had a boundless enthusiasm for the stories he published and delighted in telling of them, either to friends, or in print. He wrote his blurbs with an infectuous excitement that spurred on even the most jaded reader to investigate further. Of course, too much of a good thing was wearying. Sometimes, the stories did not live up to the billing Wright gave them. Sometimes, the only thing worth reading was the blurb. Wright had favorite phrases which he used again and again. Still, he gave the contents page, the story blurbs, and the Coming Next Month page an extra something that was not present with the other editors and entirely lacking in other magazines of the genre.

Weird Tales primarily used two types of contents pages. The first was used through 1932 and was two pages in length. The heading was a typical Brosnatch sketch. Each story was described with a short listing that told something about the tale. An example of the early contents page was the one for August 1932 (Fig. 1).

The second contents page came in late in 1932 and was used for the rest of the magazine's history. The blurbs for each story went in the early 1940's, but the style of listing remained. Typical of the latter-type contents page was April 1936 (Fig. 2).

The Coming Next Month page in the 1920's usually was an advertisement for the entire pulp, soliciting subscriptions. The page listed a number of stories coming up in the next few months and asked the reader to subscribe and not miss any of "These great thrill tales" or like words.

In the thirties, Wright changed the format and had a page devoted entirely to the contents of the next issue. One lead story was described in great detail, usually with a long quote from the story. Several other stories were also listed

A MAGAZINE OF THE BIZARRE AND UNUSUAL

Weird Tales

REGISTERED IN U.S. PATENT OFFICE

| Volume 27 | CONTENTS FOR APRIL, 1936 | Number 4 |

Published monthly by the Popular Fiction Publishing Company, 2457 East Washington Street, Indianapolis, Ind. Entered as second-class matter March 20, 1923, at the post office at Indianapolis, Ind., under the act of March 3, 1879. Single copies, 25 cents. *Subscription rates:* One year in the United States and possessions, Cuba, Mexico, South America, Spain, $2.50; Canada, $2.75; elsewhere, $3.00. English office: Otis A. Kline, c/o John Paradise, 86 Strand, W. C. 2, London. The publishers are not responsible for the loss of unsolicited manuscripts, although every care will be taken of such material while in their possession. The contents of this magazine are fully protected by copyright and must not be reproduced either wholly or in part without permission from the publishers.

NOTE—All manuscripts and communications should be addressed to the publishers' Chicago office at 840 North Michigan Avenue, Chicago, Ill. FARNSWORTH WRIGHT, Editor.

WEIRD TALES ISSUED 1st OF EACH MONTH

W. T.—1   *Fig. 2*   385

VOLUME 20   NUMBER 2

Published monthly by the Popular Fiction Publishing Company, 2457 E. Washington Street, Indianapolis, Ind. Entered as second-class matter March 20, 1923, at the post office at Indianapolis, Ind., under the act of March 3, 1879. Single copies, 25 cents. Subscription, $2.50 a year in the United States, $4.00 a year in Canada. English office: Charles Lavell, 13, Serjeant's Inn, Fleet Street, E. C. 4 London. The publishers are not responsible for the loss of unsolicited manuscripts, although every care will be taken of such material while in their possession. The contents of this magazine are fully protected by copyright and must not be reproduced either wholly or in part without permission from the publishers.

NOTE—All manuscripts and communications should be addressed to the publishers' Chicago office at 840 North Michigan Avenue, Chicago, Ill.

FARNSWORTH WRIGHT, Editor.

Copyright 1932, by the Popular Fiction Publishing Company.

Contents for August, 1932

[CONTINUED ON NEXT PAGE]

146   COPYRIGHTED IN GREAT BRITAIN
                              Fig. 1

For Advertising Rates in WEIRD TALES Apply Direct to

WEIRD TALES

Western Advertising Office: Central Advertising Office: Eastern Advertising Office:
NORMAN C. NOURSE   HARLEY L. WARD, INC.   D. P. RIKER, Mgr.
1031 S. Broadway   360 N. Michigan Ave.   303 Fourth Ave.
Los Angeles, Calif.   Chicago, Ill.   New York, N. Y.
Phone, Central 6269   Phone, Gramercy 5380

Coming Next Month

"YOU mean that I am to allow myself to be sent as a life prisoner to Rose Crater?"

"Precisely!"

I rose from the chair and took my hat in my hand. But the man took me by the shoulder.

"Don't go," he urged. "I am in earnest."

"So am I," I replied, rather angrily. "You must think that just because I am a college professor and out of work I am nothing but a fool! If you want to know about Rose Crater, why not ask the Government? I understand that it is a penitentiary for Federal prisoners convicted under the Interstate Criminal Act. Suppose you did want to make a private investigation? Why not hire a detective agency to do your work for you? Certainly not a college professor who is more interested in ants than in criminals and in butterflies than prisons. And to go there as a criminal! As a murderer! I may be poor, but I still have my good name."

The man took me by both shoulders and jammed me into an overstuffed armchair. I was surprized to see the tremendous strength he had.

"You have to listen to me, Professor. I am supposed to be a gangster; in fact, I am supposed to be their leader, their brains in America. Guess I have some intelligence to be a free man today. If power or wealth or brute force could have been employed so that I could find out what I want to about Rose Crater, I should have enough of all three. But it takes more than that. Someone has to go in there and come out, and so far the road to that prison is a one-way road. The prisoners go in, *but they never come out. Not even after they die.* I am looking for a man brave enough to go in, intelligent enough to find out what is going on in there and clever enough to escape."...

This powerful weird novel of the blood-freezing horror that awaited the doomed men who were sent to a living death inside the crater of an extinct volcano will begin in the January WEIRD TALES.

THE SOLITARY HUNTERS
By DAVID H. KELLER
—ALSO—

ROGUES IN THE HOUSE
By ROBERT E. HOWARD

A tale to make the blood tingle—the story of a barbarian soldier of fortune and a squatting monstrosity that sat in the chambers of death in the house of the wizard Nabonidus.

THE RED KNIFE OF HASSAN
By SEABURY QUINN

A vivid thrill-tale of a weird murder-mystery, and the exploits of the fascinating little French detective, Jules de Grandin—a tale of the Assassins of Syria.

INVADERS OF THE ICE WORLD
By JACK WILLIAMSON

An astounding weird-scientific tale of the far-distant future, when the sun grows wan, and sentient creatures spawned by the frost make war upon the survivors of the human race.

THE WEAVER IN THE VAULT
By CLARK ASHTON SMITH

A story of the weird and ghastly-beautiful horror that came upon the searchers in the eery tombs of Chaon Gacca.

A PHANTOM IN THE SKY
By DALE CLARK

A strange tale of an aviator's weird experience in a doomed airplane that fell from the sky—a fascinating story.

January WEIRD TALES Out January 1

Fig. 3

777

COMING NEXT MONTH

JIREL stiffened, one hand halting in a futile reach after the knife that no longer swung at her side; for among the trees a figure was approaching.

It was a woman—or could it be? White as leprosy against the blackness of the trees, with a whiteness that no shadows touched, so that she seemed like some creature out of another world reflected in dazzling pallor upon the background of the dark, she paced slowly forward. She was thin—deathly thin, and wrapped in a white robe like a winding-sheet. The black hair lay upon her shoulders as snakes might lie.

But it was her face that caught Jirel's eyes and sent a chill of sheer terror down her back. It was the face of Death itself, a skull across which the white, white flesh was tightly drawn. And yet it was not without a certain stark beauty of its own, the beauty of bone so finely formed that even in its death's-head nakedness it was lovely.

There was no color upon that face anywhere. White-lipped, eyes shadowed, the creature approached with a leisured swaying of the long robe, a leisured swinging of the long black hair lying in snake-strands across the thin white shoulders. And the nearer the—the woman?—came the more queerly apart from the land about her she seemed. Bone-white, untouched by any shadow save in the sockets of her eyes, she was shockingly detached from even the darkness of the air. Not all of the dark land's dim, color-veiling atmosphere could mask the staring whiteness of her, almost blinding in its unshadowed purity. . . .

Who was that eldritch white woman, that menaced not only Jirel's life but her very soul?—a creature so gruesome, so ghastly and so deadly that only the pen of C. L. Moore can adequately describe her? You cannot afford to miss this utterly strange and different story. It will be printed complete in WEIRD TALES for January:

THE DARK LAND
By C. L. Moore

——Also——

A RIVAL FROM THE GRAVE
By SEABURY QUINN

A tale of creeping horror that rises to a climax of sheer terror—a story of Jules de Grandin.

THE SATIN MASK
By AUGUST W. DERLETH

What weird doom made the wearing of that old mask so deadly? A strange and eery story.

HORROR INSURED
By PAUL ERNST

Another amazing story about the exploits of the sinister figure who calls himself Doctor Satan, the world's weirdest criminal—a tale of breath-taking incidents and eery power.

January Weird Tales . . . . . Out January 1

Fig. 4

773

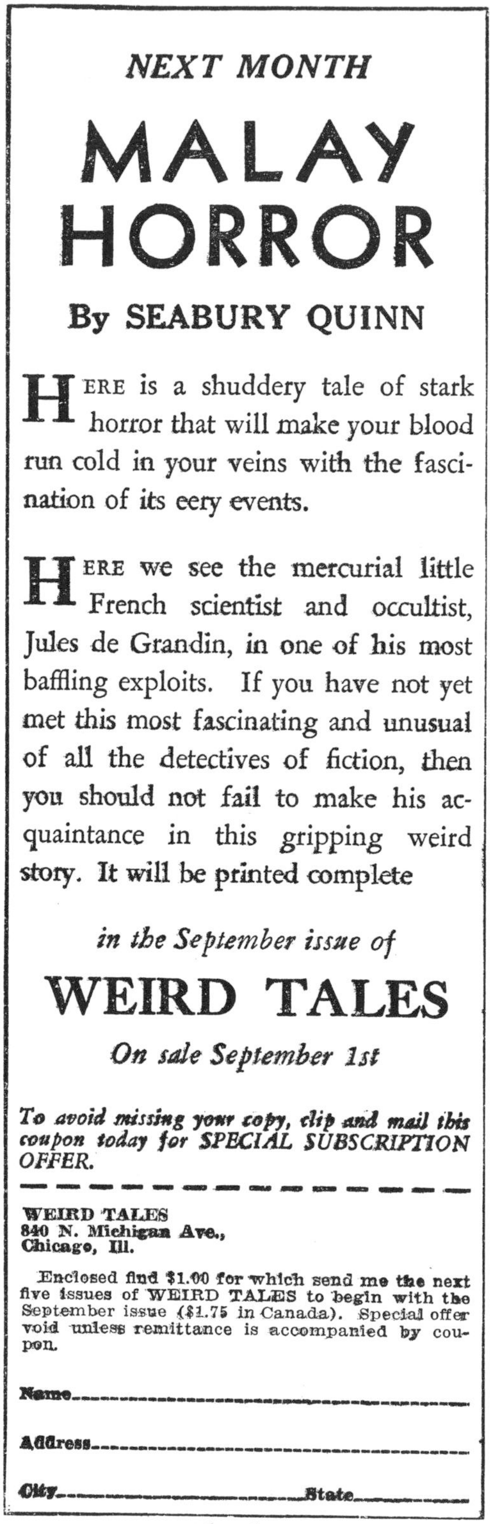

NEXT MONTH

MALAY HORROR

By SEABURY QUINN

HERE is a shuddery tale of stark horror that will make your blood run cold in your veins with the fascination of its eery events.

HERE we see the mercurial little French scientist and occultist, Jules de Grandin, in one of his most baffling exploits. If you have not yet met this most fascinating and unusual of all the detectives of fiction, then you should not fail to make his acquaintance in this gripping weird story. It will be printed complete

in the September issue of

WEIRD TALES

On sale September 1st

To avoid missing your copy, clip and mail this coupon today for SPECIAL SUBSCRIPTION OFFER.

WEIRD TALES
840 N. Michigan Ave.,
Chicago, Ill.

Enclosed find $1.00 for which send me the next five issues of WEIRD TALES to begin with the September issue ($1.75 in Canada). Special offer void unless remittance is accompanied by coupon.

Name

Address

City State

Fig. 5

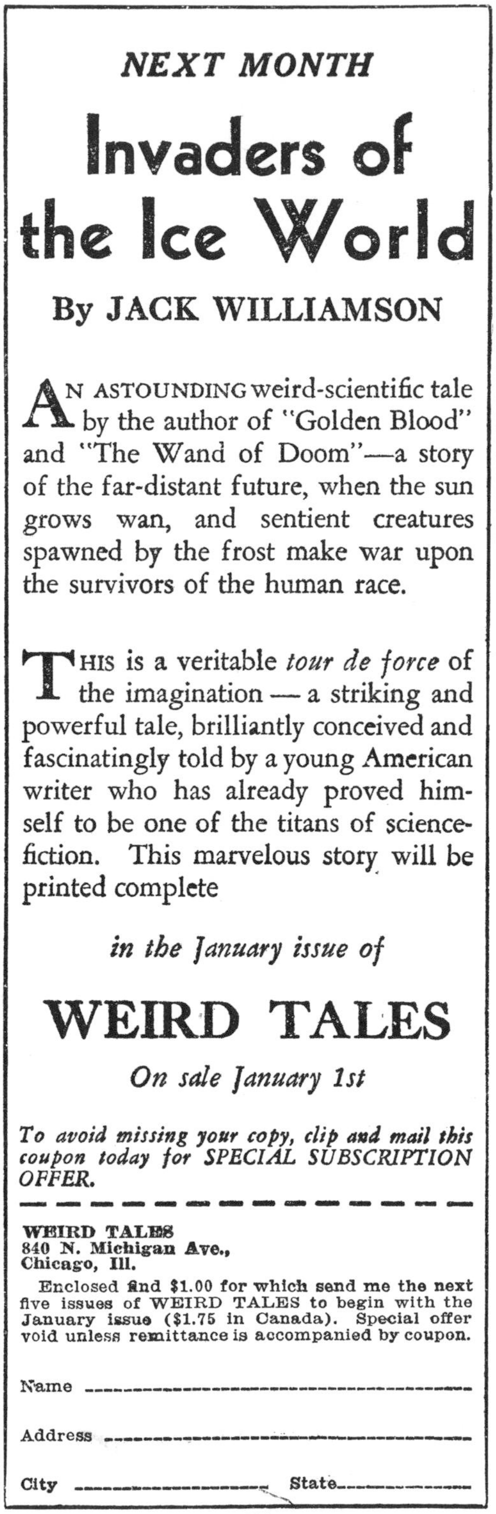

NEXT MONTH

Invaders of the Ice World

By JACK WILLIAMSON

AN ASTOUNDING weird-scientific tale by the author of "Golden Blood" and "The Wand of Doom"—a story of the far-distant future, when the sun grows wan, and sentient creatures spawned by the frost make war upon the survivors of the human race.

THIS is a veritable *tour de force* of the imagination — a striking and powerful tale, brilliantly conceived and fascinatingly told by a young American writer who has already proved himself to be one of the titans of science-fiction. This marvelous story will be printed complete

in the January issue of

WEIRD TALES

On sale January 1st

To avoid missing your copy, clip and mail this coupon today for SPECIAL SUBSCRIPTION OFFER.

WEIRD TALES
840 N. Michigan Ave.,
Chicago, Ill.

Enclosed find $1.00 for which send me the next five issues of WEIRD TALES to begin with the January issue ($1.75 in Canada). Special offer void unless remittance is accompanied by coupon.

Name

Address

City State

Fig. 6

with a short paragraph description of each story given. Wright knew how to pick his facts well and the most uninteresting story could sound like a classic with the right handling (Figs. 3 and 4).

In addition to the Coming Next Month page, the last page of each issue featured a short half page ad for the next issue describing another story in the next issue. This ad was used as a subscription come-on for *Weird Tales*. Again, Wright pulled out all stops in describing the stories in the brief space he had (Figs. 5 and 6).

More than likely, Wright also wrote the ads for various other publications such as *Magic Carpet* and *Oriental Stories* that were published by Popular Fiction Publishing Co. And, he was probably stuck with the dreadful job of thinking up new ads for THE MOON TERROR, the book published in 1927 that didn't sell out until the late 1940's. The 1930's featured dozens of different ads for the book and Wright must have racked his brain in trying to make it sound better than it was. An editor's job was never an easy one. Wright's job was near impossible!

9 Out of the Eyrie

As was the case with many of the pulps of the twenties and thirties, *Weird Tales* did not have an editorial page. In the whole life of the magazine, there were only two actual editorials—the first appearing the the First Anniversary Issue in 1924, the second in the Twenty-Fifth Anniversary Issue in 1948. Strangely enough, neither of these pieces were written by the usual editors. The first editorial, reprinted in this book, was titled "Why *Weird Tales*?" It was written by Otis Adelbert Kline who also edited that one issue of "The Unique Magazine." In 1948, several popular authors wrote about the long history of the pulp and its important place in the annals of weird fiction in America.

However, there was no actual need for an editorial column where the views of the editor were set forth. As most pulp editorials were basically nothing more than expositions extolling the virtues of the stories in the magazine, this purpose was extremely well served by short editorial notes on the contents page, the blurbs for each story, and in the letter column of *Weird Tales*, The Eyrie.

The Eyrie, as a department, was announced in the first issue of the magazine and appeared in every issue after that till the end in 1954. The format, though, of the column changed radically over the years. The two major editors of the magazine, Farnsworth Wright and Dorothy McIlwraith, had different ideas on what a letter column should be and each used The Eyrie in the manner they thought best for the magazine.

In early issues of *Weird Tales*, The Eyrie was set in one long column of type across the page instead of the usual two column spread used throughout the rest of the pulp. Letters were not printed in full but quoted, with usually one person's view per paragraph. However, there was no actual setting apart separate comments so when reading through the column, it was like examining one long piece of criticism on the magazine and its contents as expressed by the readers. Editor Wright was not adverse to stringing several letters together to illustrate a certain viewpoint or thought. Nor was Wright hesitant about answering questions or criticisms raised by his buyers. The Eyrie served more as a discussion ground for the contents than an actual letter page.

At times in the early years, Wright would dominate the column with very long and detailed reports on the magazine and efforts made to keep it what the readers wanted. A sample from the column for the August 1925 issue had Wright at his florid best:

> Now that *Weird Tales* has firmly established itself, it is possible (with the help of the readers) to lay out a definite program of even more wonderful stories for the future. The first issue of *Weird Tales* appeared in March 1923, and the magazine has in its more than two years of existence made many very valuable contributions to literature . . .

> Certain stories have been so outstanding that they have called forth scores of enthusiastic letters from our readers; and it is from these outstanding stories and the readers' comments on them that we are enabled to find out what manner of stories you want . . . *Weird Tales* has firmly established itself and we feel, therefore, that we are filling a very important place in the magazine world; but we want to give you better and better stories with each issue.

No matter how pompous or proud Wright might have appeared with such statements, he could never match the praise of his readers. From time to time, there was criticism of a story—or a debate might rage on a particular issue or policy, but, in general, the letters published in The Eyrie were enough to make even the proudest editor blush. From that same issue:

> My friends who have read *Weird Tales* all agree with me that "Invaders from the Dark" is the best story that has yet been published between the covers of the finest fictional magazine on the market.

While another reader proclaimed:

> Your page of contents is a veritable Hall of Fame. I have read nearly every magazine on the market but none is half as high in my esteem as *Weird Tales* . . .

Many of the authors whose names you are displaying will go down the pages of literary history on a par with Poe.

Not only regular readers praised the magazine. The Eyrie was a gathering place for authors as well as fans. And, at times, the comments were not only on the stories:

> Junius B. Smith, author of "An Arc of Direction" in the June issue, writes: "I wish to congratulate you on the perfect typesetting of this story. It so frequently happens in all-fiction magazines that errors creep in which mutilate the story, that it is a pleasure to find a story set so well that not even a minor defect greets the eye as it is read."

Another, younger, author commented:

> Frank Belknap Long Jr. writes from New York City: "The June cover grows on me! Ye gods!—I cannot imagine a more gigantic, reddish, loathsome or delicious—but I sputter and go out! Andrew Brosnatch is to be congratulated."

The first real signs of life of another sort came into The Eyrie in 1926, soon after the publication of "The Wicked Flea" in the October 1925 issue. A humorous story (supposedly) of a flea that grew to enormous size and went around chasing dogs, the story was heartily condemned by readers in The Eyrie. Numerous letters were printed complaining of the continual use of slapstick humor in "The Unique Magazine." While the complaints were not very loud or detailed, editor Wright was quick to respond. After "The Wicked Flea," slapstick was rarely featured during Farnsworth Wright's tenure as editor.

Wright, like any good editor, knew that the letter writers represented only a small minority of his readership. Like all editors, he respected that voice because it usually spoke what most of the other magazine readers thought. Wright was always urging his readership to write in and state what their favorite story was in each issue. A coupon was even provided in The Eyrie for the votes. The editor always gave prominent note of what story was the most popular in previous issues and there can be little doubt that Wright determined much of his future contents by reviewing what stories were earlier hits with the readership. As he stated in October 1926, "It is only by hearing from you that we are able to keep *Weird Tales* up to the standard that you desire."

"Lochinvar Lodge" by Clyde Casson, in the March 1926 issue, was another story that brought forth a flurry of letters. A very minor tale, it suffered from an inconclusive ending. Some years later, Wright stated that the story generated more mail than any other tale in the magazine's history. Approximately half of the mail praised the story as being the best ever published up to that time. However, the other half of the mail condemned "Lochinvar Lodge" as the worst story in the magazine's history! What Wright made of this situation we can't even guess—except perhaps to keep away from stories with inconclusive endings.

April 1926 saw an event that was to make an important change in both *Weird Tales* and in The Eyrie. In that month, the first widely-circulated science fiction magazine, *Amazing Stories*, make its debut. *Amazing* featured all science fiction stories and within a short time it was pub-

lishing stories by *Weird Tales* regulars including J. Schlossel and Otis Adelbert Kline.

Before the newcomer, *Weird Tales* had been the only magazine devoted entirely to fantastic fiction on the market. *Argosy All-Story Weekly* also featured fantastic stories but it was primarily an adventure magazine and its science fiction was more in the Edgar Rice Burroughs tradition than the more scientific and bizarre nature of the "weird-scientific" stories published in *Weird Tales*.

In the early years, reader reaction to these "weird-scientifics" was overwhelmingly in favor of them. "The Moon Terror" by A.G. Birch, a two-part serial about a group of Chinese wizards who first attempt to conquer the world, then after that fails, try to destroy it, was so popular with the readership that Popular Fiction Publishing Co. brought it out in a hardcover edition—much to their later regret. "When the Green Star Waned" by Nictzin Dyalhis, a combination of weird fantasy and science fiction was another of the more popular "weird-scientific" stories in the 1920's. However, all of this happened before *Amazing Stories*. Once that magazine made its appearance, the market changed. Readers began to question the use of science fiction in *Weird Tales*. This debate continued right through the 1930's, when there were numerous science fiction magazines on the market.

On one side were those who were against all science fiction stories. Their comments ranged from "I vote no on weird-scientific stories" to the more common "Keep *Weird Tales* weird."

A second point of view was expressed by a bemused reader writing to the December 1928 Eyrie:

> I have been reading *Weird Tales* for three years and am wild about it in every particular save one. That is, I wish you would not publish such stories as "Crashing Suns," or in fact, any scientific story. They are far too imaginative for me to enjoy . . . My idea is that the scientific nature of these stories takes away all of the pleasure of reading them.

The third group in the debate was the one which won out. The vast majority of readers wanted science fiction and this included Farnsworth Wright:

> This magazine has received a vast number of letters from enthusiastic readers who want more weird-scientific stories of the type that Edmond Hamilton writes. We pride ourselves on having printed in *Weird Tales* some of the best weird-scientific stories ever written, and will continue to print the cream of the world's contemporary weird-scientific fiction . . . The pseudo-science of today is the real science of tomorrow.

Wright was not loath to praise a story highly in The Eyrie—especially after a strong reader reaction to the tale. He always wrote highly of the Jules de Grandin stories, referring to "that lovable little Frenchman" or "the little ghost breaker, de Grandin" in many of the letter columns. From time to time, other authors received the editor's acclaim. H.P. Lovecraft was prime among this list. Of one of Lovecraft's most famous stories, Wright wrote:

> You have long ago passed the stage where you hang

with breathless interest on a ghost tale which merely describes how a ghost appeared and its appearance threw the spectators into a panic. This happened in Lovecraft's tale, "The Outsider," but was a mere incident in the story; the author with consummate literary artistry made of the ululating ghoul who crept out of the tomb a character that will live in the memory when most other stories have faded into oblivion.

In June 1929 Wright made the following remarks:

A friend of *Weird Tales* recently remarked that not only does this magazine publish a multitude of fascinating stories but that it also prints more *great* stories than any other magazine in the world in his opinion . . . One of these masterworks of fiction, to judge by the acclaim of the many readers who have written in to express their opinion, is "The Dunwich Horror" by H.P. Lovecraft, in our April issue.

Reader acclaim was as Wright had stated. From that same issue came:

I have just finished "The Dunwich Horror" by the great H.P. Lovecraft. I am a graduate of Indiana University and have taught physics for six years. During this time I have read stories by some "real authors"; for instances I have read all of Shakespeare's plays and many of Poe's works. I say that Lovecraft has an uncanny, nearly superhuman power of transporting one bodily to scenes of his unparalleled "horrors" and forcing upon us the exquisite pleasure of living the story. . . . Again I say that surely he is as great a writer as ever lived.

Another reader wrote:

I have just finished reading about the best story I have read in the three and half years I have been reading your extraordinary magazine. To me, H.P. Lovecraft has outdone himself in "The Dunwich Horror." Since I can not find words to express my appreciation of this story, let it suffice that I find it utterly enthralling.

While Lovecraft received this tremendous acclaim for this and every other story, it was not his name that dominated The Eyrie. Seabury Quinn and his creation, Jules de Grandin, were the favorites of the letter writers. In late 1928 and early 1929, many readers wrote in and asked for a hardcover collection of the best of the de Grandin stories. Strangely enough, one of the titles proposed by the readers was THE PHANTOM FIGHTER, the title used on the one de Grandin collection published many years later by Arkham House. Some random comments on the Quinn narratives include:

The last ten lines of Seabury Quinn's "The House Without a Mirror" are worth the cost of the magazine ten times over.

The best writer since Poe.

I never get tired of reading Seabury Quinn's fine stories.

How I did miss Jules de Grandin when I failed to find a story about him in the September issue.

My favorite author is Seabury Quinn . . . Out of all others, I like his stories the best. His "The Man Who Cast No Shadow" and "The House of Golden Masks" were superb . . . I doubt if any one can secure better stories than Quinn's!

The de Grandin stories were immensely popular and even in the late thirties when they appeared less and less frequently, whenever they did, reader response was astonishing.

One reader, however, pointed out one of the series' faults:

By now, Harrisonville (where Mr. Quinn's characters work out his plots) must be simply deserted, because the little Frenchman, de Grandin, has been killing the terrible fiends there, who seem to get the biggest kick in coming from very distant lands to settle in that little New Jersey city. And just think of all the respectable people these fiends have also wantonly murdered; sometimes coming back even from the very dead to do their dastardly deeds!

From time to time, Farnsworth Wright would reprint a short article or mention some piece in a magazine or book praising *Weird Tales*. Such an example appeared in The Eyrie for May 1930:

Where do you think Poe and E.T.A. Hoffmann would take their stuff if they were alive today? asks William Bolitho, in his article on "Pulp Magazines" in the *New York World*. And he supplies by inference, the answer. In *Weird Tales*, of course.

The pulp magazines have had few defenders, for it is the custom of snobbery to look down on them, as something inferior of literary merit. It is refreshing, therefore, to see a recognized authority on contemporary literature rise to their defense.

". . . the range is, roughly, to use names; from *Astounding Stories of Superscience*, as the French would say, on the right, through *Amazing Stories* in the center, to the extremely admirable—that is my personal taste—*Weird Tales* on the extreme left of imagination, which adds proudly to its title, The Unique Magazine.

. . . Here and not in the artificial heat of tender little highbrow reviews is where one should look for the real new talent. In this world there are chiefs, evidently. I am inclined to think they must be pretty good. They are Otis Adelbert Kline and H.P. Lovecraft, whom I am sure, I would rather read than many fashionable lady novelists they give teas to; and poets too. Meditate on that, you who are tired of strained prettiness of the verse in the great periodicals that there are still poets here of the pure Poe school who sell and are printed for a vast public.

Heady praise for a pulp magazine, but nonetheless deserving. Editor Wright, always one to tout the literary excellence of his magazine, was sure to insure that his readers read any line of praise that might be published in other places. Wright knew the quality of his magazine. He just wanted to make sure that others did also.

The 1930's were the golden age of *Weird Tales* as far as material. It was also a golden age for The Eyrie. The letter column, while never a source of great criticism or debate, was at its best during this period. This was due to two facts.

One was that in 1934 Wright changed the format of The Eyrie. Instead of one column of type with one letter after another with little separation, each contribution was published as a distinct piece with the main topic of the letter noted in bold letters at the top. While the letters were still abridged, they were usually longer selections. They now were published in two columns of type and The Eyrie was expanded from the usual three or four pages to sometimes as much as seven or eight pages, thus doubling or tripling the number of comments in each issue. Wright always published a section of "Pithy Remarks" or "Concise Comments" of excerpts from a half-dozen other letters as well.

The second reason for the increased entertainment in the letter column was a happening completely divorced from The Eyrie itself. It was the change in cover artists. Margaret Brundage, with her delicate, erotic pastel nudes made her debut on Weird Tales covers in September 1932. Nude women had been featured on many earlier covers and had produced some comments. However, artwork had rarely been a major subject in The Eyrie. Not so after Mrs. Brundage's nudes began. A debate raged for years as to whether nude women should appear on the covers of "The Unique Magazine." Reader reaction was strong, both pro and con.

A female reader was the first ever to register a comment on the September 1932 cover, and it was a mild reaction compared to what was to follow. "Before making comments on the contents of the September issue, I wish to say that the cover is very unusual and beautiful, one which I intend to preserve carefully."

Brundage did both the September and October 1932 covers and neither raised much fuss. St. John was featured on the next four covers with illustrations for the Otis Adelbert Kline serial, "Buccaneers of Venus." Brundage returned in March with a totally nude woman and pack of wolves. St. John was back for the next two issues but after that, it was all Brundage. And, the letter-column battle began.

However, even before that war, another began. Wright innocently asked in an earlier issue what readers' thoughts were on interplanetary novels, especially Otis Kline's Venus novel (which had originally been written for *Argosy*). Reaction was obviously well beyond what Wright had expected:

> We started a raging controversy among you, the readers, when we asked your advice as to whether we should keep on publishing interplanetary stories. Tales of distant worlds seem to be like fine wine to many of you, but to others they are rank poison.

Wright went on to state that more people were in favor of the interplanetary stories than against them. (This was supported by the billing Kline received, as well as the four covers for his serial; not to mention that science fiction serials were used throughout the thirties.) However, Wright did publish some of the complaints:

> Your magazine is going to the rocks; that is, if you keep printing this interplanetary rot and attempting to fool your readers into believing it is weird. If Otis

ADDLEBRAIN Kline thinks he can make a reader feel weirdly horrified at the attempt of a man to rescue his bride from kidnappers, he is hopelessly doped. *Weird Tales* at this rate will be just another of those crazy "go to the moon" magazines in a very short while.

Another reader declared:

> It is my urgent plea to you not to publish any more so-called weird-scientific stories. Truly, they are not weird and consequently they have no place in your magazine.

The controversy continued for a number of issues, though most of the letters were less passionate than the two quoted. Wright finally settled the issue with the remark that "the preponderance of letters on this subject is in favor of a small percentage of scientific tales, requesting only that such tales be truly weird. It seems to be a reasonable request and we shall heed it"

The interplanetary debate was over but the Brundage controversy was soon to begin. The storm was brewing but did not yet come into being. In August 1933, Wright was able to state:

> The cover designs of M. Brundage seem to have caught the fancy of our readers. Enthusiastic letters from all parts of the United States have been received praising this artist's covers since we first began using them a year ago.

Wright continued to declare that there was a flood of approval for the June 1933 cover, which featured a nude girl before a giant statue, a scene from "Black Colossus." He then commented:

> This artist's color work is done with pastel crayons and the originals are so delicate that we are afraid even to sneeze when we have a cover design in our possession, for fear the picture will disappear in a cloud of dust.

A number of comments published in The Eyrie supported the claim of widespread popularity:

"May I extend congratulations upon the June cover design? It is the most artistic, I consider, in years."

"The cover on the last (issue) was a knockout."

Henry Kuttner, a writer to The Eyrie long before he ever sold a story to *Weird Tales*, proclaimed:

> Compliments on your June "Black Colossus" cover! It embodies the spirit of the magazine excellently; and the conventional jade background of the statue against the vibrant nude, together with the black backing, is mighty effective.

In the same issue, another writer made an amusing observation:

> I am delighted with your attractive blue *Weird Tales* cover for July. Or should I say amused?—for it is of great interest to watch how your artist monthly contrives to keep the charms of unclad girls *just* concealed by a wisp of smoke or some tenuous bit of material. It's lucky the villains usually make it hot for them.

However, not all readers were so amused. Letters of criticism began pouring into The Eyrie:

> I do not agree with many of your readers as to the attractiveness of your covers at present. The appearance of nude females gives the impression that *Weird Tales* is sexy and trashy.

Another reader wrote:

> Whatever you do, do not continue to disgrace the magazine with naked women as you did in the June and July issues.

Wright stated that there was not enough room to print all the letters protesting or upholding the artistic use of nudes but did print the following as examples of those received:

> May I register my protest among others, against the pictures of nude women on the magazine. In no way do they carry out the real purpose of the magazine or its ideals.

On the other hand:

> Your September issue cover was a masterpiece. Who could resist buying a copy after seeing that?

Henry Kuttner switched from his earlier praise after a Brundage cover featured a whipping scene:

> Allow me to pan you for your charmingly sadistic cover illustrating "The Slithering Shadow." I haven't the slightest objection to the female nude in art, but it seems rather a pity that it is possible to find such pictures in any sex magazine, while *Weird Tales* is about the only type of magazine which can run fantastic and weird cover illustrations and doesn't.

One woman wrote: "Please, please dispose of the unclad ladies on your cover for good. They cheapen and degrade your otherwise splendid magazine."

Another reader made the oft-used point, "No one can say there is anything supernatural or uncanny about a naked woman."

A very practical letter presented the argument which was probably the most important factor in Wright's using the Brundage covers, one which was never touched on by any other reader:

> My opinion on that subject would be that as long as this type of cover illustration increases circulation, which I am sure it must do, by all means, let it remain.

And backing up that statement, in the same issue—"I looked around for a good magazine to read and found the September issue standing out over all the rest, and I immediately bought it."

Most readers seemed more worried about the reputation of *Weird Tales* from the use of nude covers than the financial health and well-being of the magazine.

The debate raged on for years to come. The main argument used by those who were against the nudes on the covers was that they degraded the magazine and did not mirror accurately the contents of *Weird Tales*. One point raised almost always by those opposed to the nudes was, "I am no prude, but . . ." or "I have nothing against the nude female figure, but . . .". Nearly all of the readers against the nudes seemed ashamed to admit that they might not like the nudes because of the strong sexual slant they gave the covers. Objections were always because the covers were *not* weird, *not* fantastic, and not that they *were* erotic.

Some readers more than liked the nudes—they demanded them back if they were gone for even an issue:

> Clothing is a disgrace for the former nudes of the rare artistry of M. Brundage . . . How can people be so vulgar as to always see evil and wantonness in such sublime masterpieces of an artist as M. Brundage gives her nudes.

Even master fantasy writer, A. Merritt, commented in The Eyrie on the Brundage covers. "Glad to see a naked lady again on the cover. I've been following that controversy with interest."

It wasn't until October 1934 that Wright revealed, in the heading of a letter, that M. Brundage was a woman, the *M* standing for Margaret. In later issues, he would reveal that Mrs. Brundage was married and had a young son. Mrs. Brundage always felt that revealing her sex was a mistake by Wright and that much of the controversy about the nudes occurred because the artist was a woman.

One reader had what had to be the final word in solutions for those readers who did not like the Brundage covers:

> Personally, I am for beautiful girls, even though they're not weird. But let's devise a scheme to satisfy all. I suggest the usual girl cover, with perforations on the side of the cover. Those who are shocked simply tear off the cover. And there, lo and behold, will be another cover, sedate and serene.

While the majority of letters during this period were concerned with the Brundage nudes, other topics did come up. One of the most unusual letters ever to appear in The Eyrie had to be one published in the November 1933 issue:

> I don't like the aggravatingly inane habit of referring to your various authors as "a second Poe" or a second "Haggard"; or "worthy of Blackwood" except for the fact that they exceed for beauty, ability and sheer weirdness Poe, Haggard, Blackwood and whom-have-you. Poe is boring with his endless italics, continuous interpolations of paragraphs . . . and his attempts to impress the reader with the horror of a situation where little or no horror exists. Haggard is impossibly verbose, giving minute descriptions of absolutely meaningless incidents. But, most people are so convinced that these men are great masters that their one expression of praise consists of referring to some author as a "second" something-or-other, or having produced something "worthy" of somebody long dead.

As stated earlier, not only did fans of the magazine write to The Eyrie, but professional writers as well. Also, many of those who were originally fans later became professionals, as was the case of Henry Kuttner and Robert Bloch. Some of the many readers who were both authors and Eyrie contributors were Edmond Hamilton, Seabury Quinn, Manly Wade Wellman, H.P. Lovecraft, August Derleth, Clark Ashton Smith, Robert E. Howard, E. Hoffmann Price and Donald Wandrei. In later years, Ray Bradbury was also a contributor to The Eyrie, before and after his professional sales.

Most of the time, the authors wrote in praising one story or another. Comments would range from just barely interesting notes to extremely fascinating letters. Few of the authors, however, criticized the work of another. Typical was this letter from Clark Ashton Smith:

> So far I haven't found time to read many of the stories in the current WT. The one by John Flanders struck me as being quite well-written . . . I look forward to Howard's new serial with great anticipation.

Lovecraft, while not a frequent contributor to The Eyrie, was usually quite enthusiastic with his praise when he did write:

> "Shambleau" is great stuff. It begins *magnificently* on just the right note of terror and with black intimations of the unknown . . . It has real atmosphere and tension—rare things amidst the pulp traditions of brisk, cheerful, staccato prose and lifeless stock characters and images.

or from a later letter:

> "The Way Home" is one of the most atmospherically satisfying things I have seen lately, and I was interested to note that the author is Paul Ernst under an anagrammatic alias (Paul Stern).

Even less frequent a contributor to The Eyrie was Robert E. Howard, but in 1936 the Texas author wrote:

> Enthusiasm impels me to pause from burning spines off cactus for my drouth-bedeviled goats long enough to give three slightly dust-choked cheers for the April cover illustration. The color combination is vivid and attractive, the lady is luscious, and altogether, I think it is the best thing Mrs. Brundage has done since she illustrated my "Black Colossus" . . . I hope readers have liked my yarn as well as I liked writing it.

Henry Kuttner was not so easygoing and praiseworthy as his fellow authors. He wrote concerning Gaston Leroux's "The Mystery of the Four Husbands:"

> It seems to me that M. Leroux has produced a rather wild tale, appealing to the sadistic element in a certain proportion of readers—the kind who would ignore the practiced skill of the matador, the courage of the cuadrilla as a whole and the agility of the banderilleros, and ENJOY the gut-ripping of the sorry nags who bore the picadores. I think . . . "The Mystery of the Four Husbands" detracts sadly from the December issue.

April 1934 contained a letter designed to raise the eyebrows of the faithful and the wrath of many. It was from a fan destined to become one of *Weird Tales'* most popular writers, Robert Bloch:

> Howard, by the way, is wonderful in this issue; if he sticks to atavism, the ancient Britons, and Solomon Kane, and drops Conan the Cimmerian Chipmunk, he will maintain his present supremacy in your pages.

Bloch, in the same letter, suggested a 25¢ reprint volume of some of the best of *Weird Tales*. Wright replied that "for some time we have been toying with the notion of publishing such a volume. We expect to put out several such volumes in the future." Unfortunately, such a project never materialized.

Robert Bloch was not the only one who did not care for Conan. In the same issue, another future professional named Donald Wollheim stated, "This Conan is the most cold-blooded cutthroat ever in print . . ."

A few months later saw another Bloch letter on Conan:

> I am awfully tired of poor old Conan the Cluck . . . I cry, "Enough of this brute and his iron-thewed sword thrusts—may he be sent to Valhalla to cut out paper dolls."

Wright responded by putting Bloch on the spot with the notice, "Sharpen your axes, you loyal supporters of the Conan tales for we shall publish a short story by Mr. Bloch, the author of the above letter."

Surprisingly, Bloch did not receive very much criticism for his complaints about Conan. And, he soon developed into a very popular author, whose own stories received a good deal of attention in the reader's column.

Another soon-to-be author, Henry Kuttner, was one of the few people ever to criticize any of H.P. Lovecraft's works in late 1934 with the following complaint:

> It seems to me that mystery is essential to the weird and when in such a story as Mr. Lovecraft's ("Through the Gates of the Silver Key") the author tries to cover Heaven and Hell, humans and non-humans, explaining everything in one colossal sweep, the story falls flat and becomes more preachy than interesting or weird. Little need be said about the surprise ending of the yarn. Lovecraft, at one time, could supply a good ending but now he is getting trite as hell.

Whether lively or dull, entertaining or not, it was this extra touch, of the writers writing to *their* magazine, their special sort of club, that made The Eyrie interesting and *Weird Tales* the unique magazine.

May 1934 was the first issue to feature letters published separately, each under a special heading. The titles were usually something like "A Weird Suggestion," "He Doesn't Like Vampires," and other remarks giving the general gist of the letter. What was more interesting was that now, with the separation of letters, one began to notice that there were many regular writers to the column. Chicago fans were the most dominant. Jack Darrow wrote so often that after some time Wright would head his letters with the remark, "Here's Jack," or "Good Old Jack Darrow Writes."

Another regular was Gertrude Hemken, whose letters were disjointed patches of baby talk nonsense:

> "The Door Into Infinity" was rather a chiller, one of those oogy-woogy tales that keeps one wondering what the deuce is going on behind that door that can be opened only by incantations . . . Guess I didn't like those woims and I'm glad the hero saved his li'l wifie and nassy nassy Chandra Sass a a gone. Goody, goody! Yessir, it was exciting, ever' bit of it.

Strangely enough, Gertrude Hemken had a number of followers in the column who wrote in praising her letters and complaining when Wright did not feature one. He usually did, as she was one of the most prolific writers ever to The Eyrie.

With the new style Eyrie, Wright did not comment as often on a particular letter but he did use the beginning of each letter column to editorialize somewhat more than before. His love for the magazine and the fiction it published never shone more strongly than in the statement of policy that opened the October 1934 Eyrie:

> Your editor has just returned from a three-week vacation and is appalled at the number of manuscripts awaiting him to be read. Stacked neatly in two piles on the desk in front of him, they completely shut off his view of the outer office . . .

> The bulk of the manuscripts are from unknown authors and the editor is hoping that he may discover a new C.L. Moore, a new Robert E. Howard, a new Edmond Hamilton, a new August Derleth, a new Arthur J. Burks, just to mention a few of the literary discoveries that have been made by *Weird Tales*.

Sometimes even the editor could wax a little too lyrically about his magazine as was the case in:

> This magazine is the pioneer periodical devoted entirely to stories of the weird and supernatural. It has had many imitators, some of which have fallen among thorns and perished. But for more than twelve years, *Weird Tales*, like Old Man River, has kept rolling along.

Not only did Wright know and love his magazine, but he also knew his authors quite well, as revealed in the answer to a question if Seabury Quinn was a real name or a pseudonym:

> Yes, Seabury Quinn is a real name of a real person. When Mr. Quinn first wrote stories, he used his full name Seabury Grandin Quinn. It was his middle name that suggested the character of Jules de Grandin to him. Mr. Quinn is a descendant of the first Anglican bishop in the colonies, Bishop Seabury, for whom he is named.

May 1935 saw Wright begin publication of weird detective stories in an effort to lure away some of the readers of the many detective magazines and the new horror pulps (such as *Dime Mystery* and *Terror Tales*). This policy did not last long and probably one of the major reasons was the reader reaction to this move.

Of the stories, the Doctor Satan series by Paul Ernst was Wright's ambitious attempt to capture this new readership while at the same time retaining his loyal fans:

> We await with eager interest your verdict on the stories about Dr. Satan, the first of which is published in this issue; for it is you, the readers, who determine the editorial policy of this magazine. To those of you who are afraid that *Weird Tales* will degenerate into just another detective magazine, we definitely promise that it will not do so . . . If the stories about Dr. Satan and Ascott Keane—the world's strangest criminal and strangest criminologist—are ordinary detective stories, then we do not know a weird story when we see one.

Wright was correct in stating that the Dr. Satan stories were weird. They featured plenty of magic and super science. At first, it seemed like they would catch on with the readership, as one reader proclaimed:

> Ascott Keane is so far above all other detectives in fiction including Sherlock Holmes and Monsieur Lecoq in his mastery of weird powers and his knowledge of occult forces that he should not even be called a "detective" but a "criminologist."

However, within a short time, the protests began:

> Probably by now you are receiving many a protest about Dr. Satan and I hereby add mine. Now I'm not objecting because it is a detective story, although many will, but because it is *punk*. Any series of stories in which a master crook and master detective match wits is bound to be poor.

Another reader was more concise but the thought was the same:

> "Hollywood Horror" is a formula story.

Still another presented a strong case against the series:

> Paul Ernst's Dr. Satan stories are perfectly ridiculous; the old-school type of weird thriller—with arch-fiend and super-super detective trying to triumph over each other; beautiful secretary in the background being on hand in case archfiend would like to kidnap her so that super-super detective will go berserk at thoughts of the girl—he suddenly realizes he loves—in the clutches of the fiend and rushes to her rescue.

While not as analytic as the above, the main point against the Dr. Satan stories was made clear by:

> The point is when I want to read weird detective stories I'll buy them but when I sit down to read your magazine, I don't expect to find weird detective stories included therein.

> Glad you left out Dr. Satan. We readers can struggle along very nicely without him. A super detective against a super crook has no place in a magazine devoted to Weird Tales.

The purpose of running the Dr. Satan stories was a financial one, to lure new readers to the magazine. When Wright saw that it was doing the exact opposite, he changed his editorial mind:

> One year ago we broadened the scope of this magazine to include a weird detective story in each issue of *Weird Tales* and asked you, the readers, whether you approved. Quite decidedly you did NOT approve . . . You who object to detective stories in *Weird Tales* have won your fight.

The readers had won. Another demonstration of the respect the editor had for his readership and their views.

Along with all of its other purposes, The Eyrie served one other function—it was an obituary column for the greats of *Weird Tales*.

The list began in 1933 with the death of Henry Whitehead. A full-page obituary, unsigned but written by H.P. Lovecraft, reported Whitehead's death and told a good deal about the man. However, reader response was almost totally missing in The Eyrie.

In the June 1935 issue, Wright sadly reported the death of the popular English author, Arlton Eadie, on March 20,

1935. Only a few months later, in November 1935, a fan and poet died:

> Once again it becomes our sad duty to record the death of a valuable contributor. Robert Nelson died at his home in St. Charles, Illinois, after a two weeks' illness. Though he was a young man in his early twenties, he had developed a deep poetic feeling and a keen sensitivity to the overtones and undertones of words. He received his first encouragement from no less a poet than Clark Ashton Smith himself. His work gave clear promise that he would some day occupy an important place among the great poets; a promise, that now, alas!—can never be fulfilled.

But the telling stroke of doom was sounded a little more than a year later when Wright told *Weird Tales* readers in The Eyrie:

> As this issue goes to press, we are saddened by the news of the sudden death of Robert E. Howard of Cross Plains, Texas. Mr. Howard for years has been one of the most popular magazine authors in the country... It was in *Weird Tales* that the cream of his writing appeared. Mr. Howard was one of our literary discoveries... Prolific though he was, his genius shone through everything he wrote and he did not lower his high literary standards for the sake of mere volume ... His loss will be keenly felt.

Response from both readers and authors was immediate. In the next issue, October 1936, tributes began to appear. Wright noted:

> H.P. Lovecraft, one of the acknowledged masters of weird fiction... makes the following comment on Howard's work: "Howard's death forms weird fiction's worst blow since the passing of good old Canevin (Henry Whitehead) in 1932. Scarcely anybody else in the pulp field had quite the driving zest and spontaneity of Robert E. Howard ... How he could surround primal megalithic cities with an aura of aeon-old fear and necromancy ... Weird fiction certainly has occasion to mourn.

To which E. Hoffmann Price, the only author who wrote for *Weird Tales* who knew Howard, added:

> There is going to be much wailing among the fantasy fans and just as much among those who read only Howard's vivid action stories in other books—but the heaviest of all of it is coming from those who met him in his native territory.

Robert Bloch, who had been one of Howard's few critics; wrote:

> Robert E. Howard's death is quite a shock—and a severe blow to WT. Despite my standing opinion of Conan, the fact always remains that Howard was one of WT's finest contributors, and his King Kull series were among the most outstanding works you ever printed.

Seabury Quinn wrote to The Eyrie:

> The field of fantastic fiction has lost one of its out-

standing and recognized masters in Robert E. Howard. His Solomon Kane stories, his tales of Kull; and latterly his Conan sagas, all of them were superb in their own way. He was a quantity producer, but always managed to keep his stuff fresh and vigorous. There are few who can do this.

By the next month, reader reaction began pouring in:

> The news of Robert E. Howard's death is indeed tragic. His outstanding character and exceptional writing talents were revealed in every one of his works.

> Robert E. Howard's death is truly a great loss to our magazine for he was one of the real masters of weird fiction. In view of his untimely departure, I suggest that you print a collection of his best works, selections to be made by the readers of WT. I also think that you might print a picture or sketch of Mr. Howard with a brief biography. Why do I think you should do this? Just because Robert E. Howard was one of the most popular writers *Weird Tales* ever had and probably ever will have.

> It was with deep regret that I learned of Robert E. Howard's sudden and untimely death. A great favorite with all of us, I know that he and his work will always be remembered.

> His work had the subtle touch of genius and a fascinating style. His stories, in your own words "fired the imagination by the compelling sweep of its fantasy and the strange power of its style." Howard is *irreplaceable*. I doubt if you ever will get another author like him.

Tributes continued to come in and for the next few years *Weird Tales* published letters about Howard and his works. A number of readers suggested that another author should continue the Conan stories. Wright had a perfect answer for that suggestion, one which should be noted even today:

> Sorry to deny your request for some other author to carry on the Conan stories of the late Robert E. Howard. His work was touched with genius, and he had a distinctive style of writing that put the stamp of his personality on every story we wrote. It would hardly be fair to his memory if we allowed Conan to be recreated by another hand, no matter how skillful.

Bad as the news was of Howard's death, it was compounded in less than a year by the passing of H.P. Lovecraft, as reported in the June 1937 Eyrie:

> Sad indeed is the news that tells us of H.P. Lovecraft's death on March 15 in the Jane Brown Memorial Hospital in Providence, Rhode Island. He was a titan of weird and fantastic literature whose literary achievements and impeccable craftsmanship were acclaimed throughout the English-speaking world ... His death is a serious loss to weird and fantastic fiction; but to the editors of *Weird Tales*, the personal loss takes precedence. We admired him for his great literary achievements, but we loved him for himself; for he was a courtly and noble gentleman, and a dear friend. Peace be to his shade!

Since Lovecraft's death was picked up by the wire services due to an erroneous story on his last days, it was known to *Weird Tales* fans and authors the same time as it

In Memoriam

HENRY ST. CLAIR WHITEHEAD

READERS of WEIRD TALES will be grieved to hear of the death of that distinguished author, the Reverend Henry S. Whitehead, Ph. D., who was a regular contributor to this magazine. His death was caused by a painful gastric illness of more than two years' duration.

Doctor Whitehead, descended paternally from an old Virginian family and maternally from a noted line of Scottish West Indian planters, was born in 1882 in Elizabeth, New Jersey. As a boy he attended the Berkeley School in New York City, and in 1904 was graduated from Harvard University, a classmate of President-elect Franklin D. Roosevelt. Studying under men like Santayana and Münsterberg, he later took his degree as Doctor of Philosophy. His first literary work was published in 1905, and from that time forward he was an increasingly well-known writer in many fields.

In 1912, having graduated from the Berkeley Divinity School, Doctor Whitehead was ordained a deacon of the Episcopal Church; and was advanced to the priesthood in 1913. From 1913 to 1917 he was rector of Christ Church in Middletown, Connecticut, and was later children's pastor at St. Mary the Virgin's in New York City. During 1919-23 he was senior assistant at the Church of the Advent in Boston, and in 1923-5 was rector of Trinity Church at Bridgeport, Connecticut. Subsequently Doctor Whitehead served as acting archdeacon in the Virgin Islands, where he had previously served several winters in a similar capacity.

As an author Doctor Whitehead specialized in fiction, though writing much on ecclesiastical and other subjects. Beginning in 1923, when his story, *The Intarsia Box* (in *Adventure*), received a first-class rating as a story of distinction from the O. Henry Memorial Committee, many similar honors were accorded his work. In 1927 he contributed to the *Free Lance Writers' Handbook* an article on the technique of weird fiction which is still a standard text on the subject.

It is for weird fiction of a subtle, realistic and quietly potent sort that he will be best remembered by readers of this magazine, in which twenty-five of his greatest tales have been published. Deeply versed in the somber folklore of the West Indies, and of the Virgin Islands in particular, he caught the inmost spirit of the native superstitions and wrote them into tales whose accurate local background created an astonishing illusion of genuineness. His "jumbee" stories—popularly so-called because of their frequent inclusion of a typical Virgin Island belief—form a permanent contribution to spectral literature, while his recurrent central character and narrator, "Gerald Canevin" (embodying much of his own personality), will always be recalled as a life-like and lovable figure.

Prominent among Doctor Whitehead's tales are *Sea Change, Jumbee, The Tree Man, Black Tancrede, Hill Drums,* and *Passing of a God*—the latter perhaps representing the peak of his creative genius.

was reported in the magazine. So, in the same issue, tributes appeared which would continue to pour in till the end of the decade.

Manly Wade Wellman wrote:

> The death of H.P. Lovecraft is a staggering blow, I am sure, to your magazine and to fantasy fiction in general. I had hoped to meet Mr. Lovecraft and mourn my ill luck in not doing so; I can say, at least, that he was my early inspiration and constant study in this field, as he must have been for many younger writers.

Hazel Heald, who had several of her stories revised and rewritten by Lovecraft for publication in *Weird Tales* declared:

> I want to express my sorrow in the passing of H.P. Lovecraft. He was a friend indeed to the struggling author and many have started to climb the ladder of success with his kind assistance. To us who really knew him, it is a sorrow that mere words cannot express.

Robert Bloch's letter on Lovecraft's passing was probably the most remembered of all missives commenting on the master's death:

> He was a great writer but even a greater friend; a real New England gentleman of the old school. I think we ought to count ourselves proud to have known him. Of course there ought to be a memorial volume with stories chosen by the readers. That's the smallest tribute one can pay. But there's an end of the world—the world of Arkham, Innsmouth, Kingsport; the world of Cthulhu, Yog-Sothoth, Nyarlathotep, and Abdul Alhazred; the finest world of fantasy I know.

Seabury Quinn, while not a close friend of Lovecraft, still wrote this moving letter:

> Lovecraft, whom I had the pleasure of knowing personally, was both a scholar and gentleman and his writings disclosed both his scholarship and his gentility, as well as a genius which has not been observable since the death of Poe and Hawthorne. We who knew him personally shall miss his quiet humor and his always-interesting conversation; thousands of those who had never met the man will join us in deploring the loss of his contributions to a field of literature which he made peculiarly his own. God rest his soul.

The tributes filled the letter column from writers from all over the country. Clark Ashton Smith wrote a long letter about his friendship with Lovecraft:

> I am profoundly saddened by the news of H.P. Lovecraft's death after a month of painful illness . . . I—alas!—never met him but we had corresponded for about seventeen years, and I felt that I knew him better than most people with whom I was thrown in daily intimacy. The first manuscript of his that I read (probably 1920) confirmed me in the opinion of his genius from which I never swerved at any time . . . Others will venture into the realms that the Silver Key of his mastery has unlocked; but none will read them with the same wizard surety, or bring them back for our delectation essences of equal dread and beauty and horror.

Edmond Hamilton wrote from Pennsylvania:

> I just heard the news of H.P. Lovecraft's recent death. This is quite a shock, coming so soon after the death of Howard. While I never met either of them, I have been appearing with them in *Weird Tales* for so long that I had a dim feeling of acquaintance. I think I read every one of Lovecraft's stories from "Dagon" years ago. It is too bad that he is gone—there will never be another like him.

Henry Kuttner, another of Lovecraft's correspondents, wrote:

> I've been feeling extremely depressed about Lovecraft's death. Even now I can't realize it . . . The loss to literature is a very great one, but the loss to HPL's friends is greater.

September 1937 contained first notice of a venture that was to become Arkham House when Wright announced:

> Since the death of H.P. Lovecraft last March, there has been a growing demand for a book collection of his marvelous stories. Now it seems that Mr. Lovecraft's admirers will have their wish; for Donald Wandrei and August Derleth are preparing a collection of his tales, prose, miscellany poems, and letters, which will run to at least four volumes.

Still the obituaries continued. In December 1938, Wright again used the opening of The Eyrie to report:

> As this issue goes to press, we are saddened by the news of the death of Gladys Gordon Trenery in England. Under her pen name, G.G. Pendarves, Miss Trenery was well known to the readers of *Weird Tales*, her stories being eagerly read by many thousand of you . . . Peace to her shade.

There were more deaths to be reported but it was not Wright's fate to be the teller. In poor health, he left *Weird Tales* in May 1940. Only a few months later, he died. His death was reported by Seabury Quinn in the November 1940 Eyrie:

> Like everyone who has long been a reader of or contributor to *Weird Tales*, I was greatly shocked and grieved at the news of Farnsworth Wright's passing. Anyone who has read *Weird Tales* must have been impressed by his thorough knowledge of weird literature, his complete understanding of the great background of folk lore, superstition and comparative religion from which such literature is drawn, and his nice sense of discrimination in selecting the cream of such stories by modern authors to carry on the tradition of the Georgian and early Victorian masters of Gothic tales. Helped and encouraged by his expert criticism and kindly advice a whole generation of writers was developed, and though many of these have "graduated" to other media of expression, none, I am sure, will ever forget the debt he owes to Farnsworth Wright. There is today hardly a writer of fantasy whose success does not date from the encouragement he received from Mr. Wright, and there is certainly no one engaged in creative work who ever dealt with Farnsworth Wright who does not think kindly of him.
>
> To those of us who were privileged to know him per-

sonally the loss is ever greater. We knew him as a cultured gentleman, a charming host, an incomparably congenial companion, and a true and loyal friend. His steadily failing health caused us all concern, but his courage and resolution were so great that none of us realized how near the great beyond he was. His cheerful letters lulled us into a sense of false optimism and when news of his death came out surprise was almost equal to our grief.

As to his abilities, his work provides the finest monument possible. In the old files of *Weird Tales* can be read the biography of a man whose genius made possible a magazine which was and is truly unique.

With Wright's death, The Eyrie was to change as did all of *Weird Tales*. Dorothy McIlwraith had a different notion of what the department should be and a letter column was not included.

The first changes were quick in coming. The reader coupon to vote and comment on each issue was reduced to a tiny little square for votes. The results were never announced. Soon, The Eyrie was dropped to only a few pages of letters at the end of the magazine. A Weird Tales club was started. The Club was hardly that. One wrote in and received a free membership card as well as having his name and address listed in one issue of the magazine. It was supposed to serve as a place where fans of the weird and fantastic could meet one another but it is doubtful that it provided anything more than a mailing list for used book dealers.

The one interesting thing about the *Weird Tales* club was to look over the roster and note the number of well-known authors and fans who were members of the club. In the January 1943 issue, for example, was the name of a Chicagoan, Hugh Hefner, who was to go on to bigger and better things.

Readers' letters were soon dropped and instead The Eyrie became a place for the editor to discuss the stories featured in the issue as well as a spot for short letters from the authors of the main stories to give backgrounds for the tales.

When *Weird Tales* serialized "The Case of Charles Dexter Ward," Donald Wandrei related how he first encountered the story:

When I first visited Lovecraft in Providence in the summer of 1927, he showed me among other things the MS. of a long story he had just written. This was "Ward." He had spent months writing it, but he simply hated to typewrite anything, even a letter . . . At the time I was just learning how to operate a typewriter; I therefore proposed to gain experience in practicing on his story. He agreed with alacrity and I brought the MS. back to St. Paul with me.

Then I discovered the full magnitude of what I had let myself in for. The story was written in longhand on the reverse side of letters he had received, some 130 or 140 sheets of all sizes and colors. He didn't believe in margins or "white space." Every sheet was crowded from top to bottom, from left edge to right, with his small cramped handwriting. That was his original draft; you can imagine what happened when he got through revising, words and sentences crossed out or written in, whole paragraphs added, inserts put on

the back of the sheet where they got tangled up with the letters from his correspondents, and the inserts themselves rewritten with additional paragraphs to be put in the insert which was to be put in its proper place in the story.

After reading this account, which also told how the manuscript was later lost and then found, it was astonishing that *Weird Tales* finally did publish the story, even fourteen years after it was first written!

When a reader complained that Robert Bloch's oriental philosophy in one of his stories was mixed-up, Bloch returned:

I choose to resent that. My Hindu philosophy was not a trifle mixed but *completely* mixed. As an author, I took the liberty to construct my own supernatural background to serve the plot . . . In that spirit, "A Sorceror Runs for Sheriff" is offered. If any reader disbelieves the tenets therein, I ask him merely to go out, buy himself a pound of wax, and start modeling. If his enemy doesn't die in three days, he might just as well demand his money back. Me, I've killed hundreds that way. Literally hundreds. I intend to kill hundreds more if my typewriter paper holds out. And the patience of the readers.

The readers definitely had plenty of patience with Bloch as he was to remain one of the magazine's most popular authors right until the end of its existence.

The letters from the authors were mainly of two categories. One, the more usual, gave the background for the story in the issue. Seabury Quinn told of his inspiration for "Stoneman's Memorial":

I should make a deeper bow to Lord Dunsany for his walking idol in "A Night at an Inn" or to Wolfgang Mozart for the walking statue of the Commandant in his opera "Don Giovanni." In any event, this moving statue business ain't entirely new—but the way I've presented it is brand new, I'll be bound.

And Greye La Spina stated:

"The Deadly Theory" is a story done in Frank Stockton's "The Lady or the Tiger" style. It is based on the recital by Paracelus of revivifying a living thing from its ashes a la the well-known Phoenix.

Manly Wade Wellman, who was one of the most popular contributors to the 1940's *Weird Tales* often gave the background to his stories, showing why they rang so true:

Behind and beyond the simple story-mechanics of "Coven" is my constantly growing conviction that American witchcraft—as a cult, a folklore belief, and perhaps as a real power—can't be passed off with a laugh.

The basis of this story, like many more I have written for *Weird Tales*, is truth. A real scholar like Lovecraft would have been deeply rewarded by prying and probing into customs and actions of certain Ozark natives I've met. As usual, my spells, book references and so on are taken from rare but real sources.

In the same vein, there were letters which had very little to do with an actual story in the issue but more about the questions such a story raised. A prime example was Seabury Quinn's letter discussing what exactly makes a story weird, which was published in the September 1942 Eyrie:

Frankly, despite the help of several dictionaries, I can't arrive at a satisfactory--to me--definition of "weird" as applied to literature. Like a lot of other things, "weird" is one of those which I can define perfectly as long as you don't ask me. Nearly everyone can spot a weird story instantly, but can he say what makes it weird? I can't, nor do I think that anyone can draw a hard and fast definition within whose terms a story must fall in order to qualify. Must it have a ghost in it? Then such stories as Ambrose Bierce's "The Man and the Snake," Tod Robbins' "Silent, White and Beautiful" and Poe's "Black Cat" and "Tell-Tale Heart" are automatically excluded. Yet who would have the effrontery to label any one of those as "Un-weird?" . . . Must it be so fantastic as to be not even remotely possible? What is, and what is not nearly or remotely possible? Few authors would be bold enough to risk an editorial "unconvincing" by bringing such characters as John Brown, Robert E. Lee, Jeb Stuart, and John Wilkes Booth together, yet history shows us that is just what took place in the fall of 1859 at Harper's Ferry, West Virginia. Unconvincing? Certainly. But true, nevertheless.

The other type of letter-article published in *Weird Tales* was a brief biographical note from a new author or an old favorite. However, while most were written by authors, a few were written, by necessity, by others, as was this note from Willis Conover:

The Green Star has waned a little more; on May 18th, at 10:20 A.M., death by heart failure came to Nictzin Dyalhis, author of "The Sapphire Goddess," "The Sea Witch," "When the Green Star Waned" and many other famous *Weird Tales*. It is my duty to write of him, because it was my privilege to know him as no other member of the fantasy circle was able to know him. I should not like to number the unforgettable week-ends I spent at his home in Salisbury, Maryland —foregoing sleep for days and nights, talking or more often, listening, fascinated, to the endless story of his life . . .
He had known wealth and poverty. He had lived much in the Orient, and had known intimately its splendor and squalor. A tiny blue dragon, tattooed on a vein on his wrist proclaimed him as a member of a Chinese occult society. He was one of the few white men to enter Tibet and leave with its secrets. Once he had stained his body and bluffed his way into a genuine voodoo ceremony in Haiti. For many years, Rudyard Kipling was a close friend . . . I don't know to which world the gods have delivered him this time. But I'm sure of this—he's no stranger there.

Robert Bloch gave readers a brief insight into his real character with a biographical sketch published when his first humorous weird story was published in "The Unique Magazine:"

If the typing of the manuscript of "Nuresemaid to Nightmares" was a little shaky, blame it on the fact that my hands trembled when I thought of doing a *Weird Tales* yarn with a humorous background. Ever since January 1935, I've put my name on gory allegories—and I almost felt guilty of cheating my readers (both of them) by fanning out a fantasy where

scarcely a dozen people get killed.
Frankly, though, "Nursemaid to Nightmares" is the kind of thing I've always wanted to do—much in the manner of the late esteemed Thorne Smith . . .
So I gritted my teeth at last and wrote it up. It may help to clear up some of those malicious rumors about me. This vicious gossip that I am a fiend in more or less human form is utterly incorrect. I have *never* strangled anyone with my bare hands. Always use gloves, because of fingerprints. The only time I ever tasted human flesh was during a wrestling match when I accidentally chewed off a man's arm. As a matter of fact, I am a very lovable person, as my friends tell me—or they would, if I had any friends. Deep down underneath it all I have the heart of a small boy. I keep it in a jar on my desk.

Not all of the biographies were so entertaining. Most were like Harold Lawlor's, one of the many autobiographical articles by new authors in *Weird Tales* of the forties:

I wrote my first story at the age of nine—a thriller called "The Taxicab Boys." Unhappily, this valuable first is no longer in existence. It would probably bring a fortune today . . .
It was during the Depression that I once again felt the desire to write. Escape, probably—increasing deafness made jobs hard to get. And, then, too, writing seemed such an easy way to make some money.

Other autobiographies were usually as proasic as this, even when the writer was someone like Ray Bradbury or Hannes Bok, both of whom had autobiographical sketches in The Eyrie. From time to time, though, an old-timer appeared in the department and revealed some information of interest. Such was the case when Frank Owen told of himself in the May 1943 issue:

The manner in which I began to write Chinese stories had nothing whatever to do with China. I wanted to write a story in yellow with no other color mentioned, therein. I called it "The Yellow Pool" It took place in the Canal Zone during the time they were building the Panama Canal. I wanted a yellow girl to be the heroine. The story was published in *Brief Stories*. The magazine received a number of letters praising it. A few of the letters were published. Later, *Weird Tales* used it as a reprint. Still later, it was reprinted again in *Tales of Magic and Mystery*.
My next Chinese story was "The Wind That Tramps the World" published in *Weird Tales* in 1924 and reprinted in 1929. In 1929 it was used as the title of a collection of Chinese stories published in book form. After that, I began studying the lore of China in all its amazing aspects. So far, I have only scratched the surface but nevertheless, I have read many hundreds of volumes. The main reason I write Chinese stories is that the Chinese is the oldest existing civilization in the world. They gave us an idea for almost everything we treasure today.

Another writer referred to editor McIlwraith as a long timer contributed the following to a later Eyrie:

Frank Belknap Long writes: Several months ago Mr. Seabury Quinn brought forcibly to my attention something I've been trying to forget—the realization that my first story was published nearly a quarter of a century ago. Mr. Quinn achieved this feat of gruesome exhumation simply by mentioning the date of *his* first *Weird Tales* story in an Eyrie letter.

My mind instantly went back across wide wastes of time and recalled that I'd also had a story in one of those early issues. Now the fact that my first published tale appeared in WT and was adorned with a cover illustration by Brosnatch caused me no grief. Indeed, I've always harked back to it as a glowing milestone in my writing career, for I was younger than you'd suspect when I wrote it, and the editorial policy of *Weird Tales* was as mature and discriminating in those days as it is now . . .

As for ancestry—old New England stock, including a notorious tinsmith and counterfeiter and the first man to fight a duel on the American continent. My paternal grandfather, a building contractor, erected the pedestal of the Statue of Liberty in 1883 and was the statue's superintendent until it was taken over by the government several years later. I still have the flag which was draped around Miss Liberty's arm at the time of the unveiling.

From time to time, Robert Bloch would return to The Eyrie. His letters were always sure to entertain:

It occurs to me that I have never been represented in *Weird Tales* with a vampire story . . . and the error of omission I hasten to rectify with "The Bat is My Brother."
I recently asked myself, "What would *you* do if you were a vampire?" The only answer I could think of was "Go out and get a bite to eat." . . .

I hope the readers (including the vampires amongst them of course) will get a few ideas. I am always glad to give a vampire something he can get his teeth into. Hoping you are the same.

However, The Eyrie was fast vanishing from the magazine. Each issue had it cut a little more. It soon was nestled between the classified ads in the back of the magazine, usually with just one letter or two and the Weird Tales Club listing. However, every once in a while something extraordinary would appear:

Jack Snow writes: The Bible of all alert book dealers in the United States, Great Britain and many other lands, *Publishers' Weekly*, features a section wherein book dealers may advertise for rare and out-of-print books . . . The above is a preamble to an incident which will delight H.P. Lovecraft's readers and admirers. For in the July 7, 1945 issue of *Publishers' Weekly*, a New York book dealer listed among books he is searching for THE NECRONOMICON and Ludvig Prinn's MYSTERIES OF THE WORM.

By the late 1940's, The Eyrie rarely printed more than a page of remarks about one story in the issue. A rare departure from this policy was the March 1948 issue when The Eyrie appeared at the front of the magazine and contained two letters of congratulations and remarks by August Derleth and Seabury Quinn on the 25th Anniversary of the magazine. It was the last breath of a letter column dying slightly ahead of the magazine housing it.

By 1949, The Eyrie was no longer appearing in the magazine, with only an infrequent listing of the Weird Tales Club. The department returned in 1950, now featuring readers' letters. However, there was little life left in The Eyrie. Most of the letters were short comments on the stories and most revealed an ignorance of the magazine's greater days. Several readers when after reading a reprint of Lovecraft's "The Horror at Red Hook" casually asked if Mr. Lovecraft would be contributing more stories to the magazine. Another asked if Lovecraft was a new author as he had not appeared on the contents page in earlier issues. The Eyrie was rarely more than a few pages in length. In its last days, it also served as a book review column. The glory of *Weird Tales* was gone. So was that of The Eyrie. It began in the first issue of "The Unique Magazine" and it ended in the last issue, in September 1954. From beginning to end it was an integral part of *Weird Tales* and added much of the uniqueness of "The Unique Magazine."

10
Competition

As *Weird Tales* grew successful, it was natural for other magazines to copy its formula in an attempt to duplicate its success. This was the standard pattern followed by all publishers during the pulp years. The surest sign of success was the number of imitators that copied your policies. As *Weird Tales* was never very successful, there were not very many competitors.

The first magazine to use "The Unique Magazine" as a model was *Tales of Magic and Mystery*. The magazine began in late 1927 and was published for five monthly issues before folding. It was an undistinguished pulp, devoted more to magic and the supernatural than to weird fiction. Its one claim to fame was publication of Lovecraft's story, "Cool Air." The magazine never offered any serious threat to *Weird Tales*.

A much more serious rival was *Strange Tales*. Published by the Clayton chain of magazines, the first issue came out in 1931. The pulp was edited by Harry Bates, a veteran pulp editor. The Clayton chain had money behind it and could afford to pay well for its stories. The magazine had attractive covers by H.W. Wesso. It had a policy of running a complete short novel in each issue. Authors who contributed included most the the regulars from *Weird Tales*. Robert E. Howard, Clark Ashton Smith, Paul Ernst, and Henry Whitehead were among the contributors. The magazine began as a bimonthly. Bates had strong opinions on what sold and strictly enforced his ideas. Stories were more action-oriented with less atmosphere. Contents of *Strange Tales* were not as varied as that of *Weird Tales*. The new magazine was much more pulp-reader oriented. However, it did not have a chance. The Depression and Clayton's mismanagement of his magazine chain were factors that were beyond Bates' control. In the middle of 1932, *Strange Tales* went quarterly. The entire empire collapsed. Several titles were bought by other pulp publishers. *Strange Tales* was not one of the magazines kept alive. It lasted only seven issues.

The middle 1930's saw a different type of competition arise. Popular Publications started a series of horror pulps which included *Dime Mystery*, *Horror Stories* and *Terror Tales*. These pulps were formula-oriented magazines which dealt with sex-and-sadism type adventures, seemingly supernatural, but usually with logical explanations. A number of other magazines soon followed this pattern. While these magazines were not in direct competition with *Weird Tales* they evidently presented some threat. Wright tried to combat their menace with the Dr. Satan series and other stories of like nature. This effort didn't last long and is dealt with in more detail in earlier chapters of this book.

In 1939, Better Publications brought out what probably was the most serious threat ever to *Weird Tales*. *Strange Stories* was an attractive pulp, with thirteen short stories per issue. It had well-done covers, though somewhat garish, and featured most of the best weird fiction writers of the time. Contributors included Henry Kuttner, Robert Bloch, Manly Wade Wellman, August Derleth, Carl Jacobi, David Keller, Frank Belknap Long and many other authors who were regulars for *Weird Tales*. Interiors were well done, with Virgil Finlay a regular contributor. The magazine was much more pulp-oriented and cost only 15¢. Significantly, this was when *Weird Tales* first raised its page count to 160 pages, then soon afterwards, dropped its price also to 15¢. *Strange Stories* then dropped its price to 10¢. It was serious competition during a period when *Weird Tales* was experiencing a huge drop in sales.

Ziff-Davis started *Fantastic Adventures* in early 1939, but despite its title and a time-to-time fantasy, the magazine was really science fiction oriented and presented little competition. Not so with Street and Smith's entry in the fantasy field. *Unknown* (later *Unknown Worlds*) offered a new type of story in direct contrast with *Weird Tales*.

Under the editorial direction of John W. Campbell, Jr., *Unknown* printed adult fantasy fiction. Horror stories were rare. Instead, Campbell had his writers concentrate on the logical aspects of magic and fantasy. Tales had a strong logical background and very-down-to-earth heroes. The usual monsters, werewolves, and vampires of folklore were rare, and if present, in strangely altered forms. The authors for *Unknown* were mainly recruited from Street and Smith's science fiction magazine, *Astounding Stories*, or right from the pulp market. Few *Weird Tales* writers did much work for the magazine. Within a short time, its effect on *Weird Tales* was clear. Humor, a rare item in "The Unique Magazine," began appearing. The stories were not very good and often read like rejects from *Unknown*. Fortunately, this attempt to cash in on the Street and Smith magazine did not last long.

Neither *Unknown* or *Strange Stories* sold very well. Both magazines were victims of the war-time paper shortage. Only *Weird Tales* continued as a fantasy magazine. Several other pulps, such as the previously mentioned *Fantastic Adventures* and *Famous Fantastic Mysteries*, a reprint magazine, featured occasional fantasy but *Weird Tales* was the only magazine regularly publishing weird fiction.

After the war, Street and Smith published a one-shot issue of reprints from *Unknown* to test the market for re-turning the magazine to the stands. Sales were poor and the pulp was gone. Returns had always been high from newsstands. Fantasy just did not sell. Only *Weird Tales* struggled on.

In 1949, *The Magazine of Fantasy* (soon changed in name to *Fantasy and Science Fiction*) began publication. An attractive digest-sized magazine, it featured literate fantasy, both new and reprint. In most cases, it shied away from the material used by *Weird Tales*, instead keeping in the *Unknown* tradition. The magazine was reasonably successful. However, by that time, *Weird Tales* was on a downward slide and competition meant little. Several other magazines printing only fantasy appeared in the early 1950's but it is doubeful that they hastened the end of "The Unique Magazine." *Weird Tales* died from internal injuries, not from external wounds.

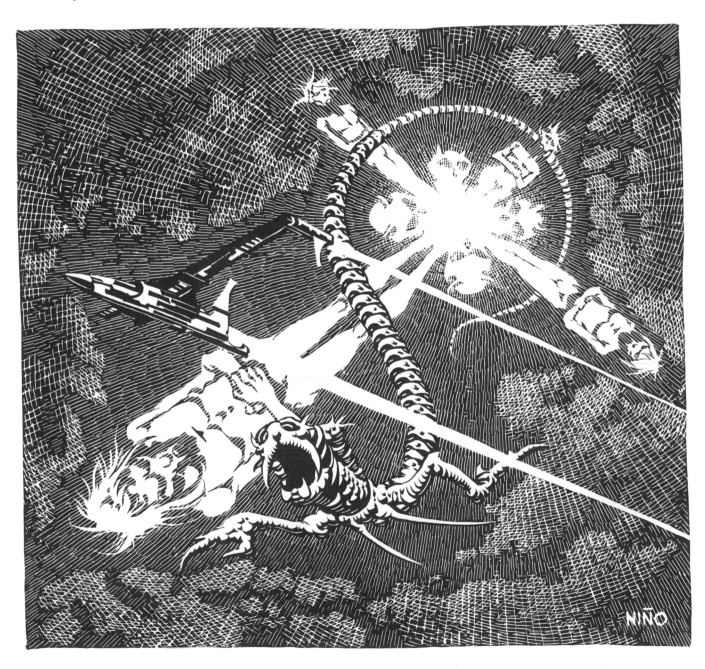

11
A Brief Resurrection

In 1973, fifty years after its first issue was published, *Weird Tales* again hit the newstand. Long-time pulp publisher, Leo Margulies, had bought the rights and title of the magazine some time after it went out of business. In 1973, he brought out a new edition of the pulp. It was approximately the same size as the 6″ x 9″ magazine and was edited by long-time science fiction fan, historian and expert, Sam Moskowitz. Contents consisted mainly of reprints, with some new material.

The resurrected pulp lasted four issues. Much of the material was fiction rescued from oblivion by Moskowitz from sources other than the original pulp. Too much was rare but uninteresting. Distribution was spotty and sales were not good. The awkward size of the magazine relegated it to the shelves behind *Time* and *Newsweek*. It was a good try but it had little chance of success. There never has been a big market for literate weird fiction. The latest attempt further helps point out the determination of J.C. Henneberger and those who helped him make *Weird Tales* work. It was a unique magazine, the type of which will never be seen again.